Sinclair Lewis (1885–1951) was born in Sauk Centre, Minnesota, studied at Yale University, and began writing after taking a publishing job in New York City in 1910. His celebrated novels include *Main Street*, *Babbitt*, *Arrowsmith*, *Elmer Gantry*, and *Dodsworth*; in 1930 he became the first American writer to be awarded the Nobel Prize for literature.

SELECTED SHORT STORIES
OF
SINCLAIR LEWIS

SELECTED
SHORT STORIES
OF
SINCLAIR
LEWIS

With an Introduction by
James W. Tuttleton

ELEPHANT PAPERBACKS
Ivan R. Dee, Publisher, Chicago

First ELEPHANT PAPERBACK edition published 1990 by Ivan
R. Dee, Inc., 1332 North Halsted Street, Chicago 60622.
Manufactured in the United States of America.

Library of Congress Cataloging-in-Publication Data
Lewis, Sinclair, 1885–1951.
    [Short stories. Selections]
    Selected short stories of Sinclair Lewis / with an introduction by
James W. Tuttleton.
    ISBN 0-929587-22-7
    I. Title.
PS3523.E94A6   1990
813'.52—dc20   89-23613

CONTENTS

INTRODUCTION

ALTHOUGH Sinclair Lewis's reputation as an author has declined since his death, it was his distinction to be the first American writer to win the Nobel Prize for literature. This award, conferred on him in Stockholm in 1930, honored a career highlighted by such fictional successes as *Main Street, Babbitt, Arrowsmith, Elmer Gantry,* and *Dodsworth*. Few American writers had ever produced so many remarkable novels, and novels provocative of so many extreme critical reactions, and all in a single decade, the 1920s.

Main Street (1920), Lewis's first triumph and a remarkable best-seller, was a hilarious satire of American small-town bourgeois philistinism and anti-intellectualism. Debunking the myth that although "cities were evil and even in the farmland there were occasional men of wrath, our villages were approximately paradise," *Main Street* was an overnight sensation. The novel dealt with the quality of village life in America just at the time when it was drying up, as economic and cultural energies, as well as young people, were gravitating toward the cities. The heroine, Carol Kennicott, is a young woman brought into the village of Gopher Prairie through marriage. Although she tries valiantly to elevate the town's social tone, refine its artistic style, raise its educational level, and invest it with life and vitality, she is a total failure. In indicting village life, Lewis complained of its

> unimaginatively standardized background, a sluggishness of speech and manners, a rigid ruling of the spirit by the desire to appear respectable. It is ... the contentment of the quiet dead, who are scornful of the living for their restless walking. It is negation canonized as the one positive virtue. It is the prohibition of happiness. It is slavery self-sought and self-defended. It is dullness made God.

The reaction to *Main Street* was a critical firestorm. A thinly veiled picture of life in Sauk Centre, Minnesota, where Lewis had been born, the novel outraged his own family and the townsfolk, who ostracized him. Carping small-town Jaycees and village boosters praised their wholesome lives and cited statistics on how many player pianos had been sold in small towns across America. Yet scores of women readers wrote Lewis to thank him for having portrayed in Carol their desperate lives. Sales of the novel soared. *Main Street* was parodied or answered in *Jane Street*, *Ptomaine Street*, and Meredith Nicholson's *The Man in the Street*. Lewis kept the furor going by contributing an introduction to Frazier Hunt's *Sycamore Bend*, a defense of the small town by one of his friends. In that introduction he reversed his satire and turned it on urban readers who pitied the villagers for "not knowing gunmen, burlesque girls, bootleggers, and gum-chewing stenographers of the cities." *Main Street* was such a remarkable literary phenomenon that it was nominated by the committee of judges for the 1920 Pulitzer Prize, but the Trustees of Columbia, who give the prize, overruled the jury and awarded it instead to Edith Wharton for *The Age of Innocence*. Their reason: *Main Street* did not fulfill the terms of the award—namely, to "present the wholesome atmosphere of American life, and the highest standard of American manners and manhood."

Lewis's next novel, *Babbitt* (1922), though offending tired businessmen everywhere, was likewise a popular success for its free-swinging attack on the commercial "religion of business" then so commonly acclaimed in the popular media. The protagonist George Babbitt, a middle-aged, middle-class, paunchy real estate man, is a satiric composite of all the Regular Guys in the Chamber of Commerce, Lions, Rotary, Elks, Kiwanis, and other social clubs. And Zenith, a symbol of mid-sized cities everywhere in America, is burlesqued for its class-conscious, status-oriented, upwardly mobile, racially prejudiced, and materialistic conformists who engage in "orgies of commercial righteousness" as they hustle for profits.

Less satirical was *Arrowsmith* (1925), his next novel, a celebration of the scientist-physician who devotes himself to the noble end of saving human lives. In the portrait of Martin Arrowsmith, Lewis may have indeed intended to depict the highest standards in American manhood. At least the Columbia Trustees apparently thought so, for the novel won the Pulitzer Prize in 1926. But in hurt vanity and protesting that the first prize had been "stolen" from him, Lewis created another public uproar that year by declining the award. *Elmer Gantry* (1927) also created a tumult, this time with ministers and pious churchgoers, by presenting a charismatic preacher as a fraud, a hypocrite, and a lecher. By the time of *Dodsworth* (1929), which explored the battle of the sexes through an international theme—in which the contrast between Europe and America is usually to Europe's advantage—Lewis had managed to stir up about as much controversy over his themes and techniques as any American novelist ever has.

By 1930, then, Lewis was internationally known for burlesques and satires on nearly every phase of American life—

provincial hicks, bogus artistic types, lazy expatriates, bohemian frauds, mendacious admen, back-slapping and devious salesmen, crass movie producers, ignoramus college professors, psychiatrists, spiritualists and New Thought devotees, castrating females, corrupt evangelists, Prohibitionists, snobs, fools, and pretentious intellectuals and artists. It is no wonder that a common American view was that the Nobel Prize committee had given him the award because of Lewis's scathing satires on America's people, her values, and her institutions. As Lewis Mumford wryly remarked, Sinclair Lewis had

> created a picture of America that corresponds in a remarkable degree with the naive caricature of America that all but the most enlightened and perceptive Europeans carry in their heads. In crowning Mr. Lewis's work the Swedish Academy has, in the form of a compliment, conveyed a subtle disparagement of the country they honored.

Sherwood Anderson put it more jingoistically: Lewis got the prize "because his sharp criticism of American life catered to the dislike, distrust, and envy which most Europeans feel toward the United States."

In fact, however, the America that emerges out of Sinclair Lewis's fiction is largely a country of his own invention. Born in 1885 in Sauk Centre, Minnesota, Harry Sinclair Lewis was the third son of Dr. Edwin J. and Emma Kermott Lewis. A small village with little claim to culture, Sauk Centre was nevertheless a complete world of social types for the future fiction writer. Lewis grew up to be a tall, shy, skinny, awkward boy, doomed with an impossibly bad facial complexion. (Budd Schulberg called it "one of the ugliest faces I had ever seen," and Frederick Manfred described it as "a face to haunt one in dreams.") Lewis compensated for his loneliness by nothing else than continuous boyhood reading—largely romances of fantasy and escape. After a teenage job at the *Sauk Centre Herald* and the *Avalanche*, in 1903 Lewis went off to Yale, where he apprenticed himself to the *Yale Literary Magazine* and the New Haven papers.

Yale was a traumatic experience for the lonely provincial boy. In New Haven he found a great deal of genuine learning, but he was estranged by Yale's pedantry and by its social and intellectual pretensions. As a provincial Midwesterner without intellectual distinction or any of the social graces, Lewis felt himself to be always an outsider. His professor William Lyon Phelps noted in his autobiography that Lewis "was not disliked in college, but was regarded with amiable tolerance as a freak." And another teacher, Chauncey Brewster Tinker, later remarked that "The conventions and restrictions of good society—especially of collegiate society—were offensive to him. His abiding temptation was to undermine them and blow them at the moon."

Something of Lewis's disappointment with Yale is poignantly mirrored in one of the stories in this book, "Young Man Axelbrod," first published in June 1917 in the *Century* magazine. There the Midwestern dreamer who seeks after truth and beauty is ridiculed by his townsfolk as a crank and a crackpot. Knute Axelbrod, as a young Scandinavian, came to the New World to fulfill a dream, to find in America "the world's nursery for justice, for broad, fair towns, and eager talk." Yet after a lifetime of hard farm labor, Axelbrod is left unsatisfied, and he is overcome by the dream of making "a great pilgrimage to the Mount of Muses; for he really supposed college to be that sort of place." In spite of the town view that he is a crazy old man, he strikes off for Yale in the East, only to discover there that the callow undergraduates and pedantic professors likewise consider him cracked. It cannot be imagined that Axelbrod is equal to the Ivy League; but his dream reflects a noble idealism and marks his spirit as that of perennial youth. Lewis's sense of not belonging at Yale, of being regarded as a freak, is very strong in this tale. Only in Young Axelbrod's night out with Washburn, when they go to Hartford to hear Ysafe play, visit

the exotic Jewish ghetto in search of rich food, and talk till
dawn about art and life in Washburn's rooms, only then does
Axelbrod finally experience what he had hoped to find in the
East: "This is what I come to college for—this one night. I will
go away before I spoil it." And he returns to the town of
Joralemon with a single memento, Washburn's volume of
Musset's poetry.

This volume of French poetry, which Axelbrod cannot read
together with Washburn's, crystal, silver plate, Persian rugs,
and handsomely bound volumes are, it must be said, inadequate
indices of genuine high culture and learning. For Lewis never
knew how to represent the real thing and always sentimentally
fixed upon material objects to imply elegance and culture. What
Axelbrod essentially gains from his moment of initiation is not
learning and high culture but rather an experience of accep-
tance, of friendship, of fellow feeling, from a young man for
whom this style of life—a European style, incidentally, rather
than an American one—is natural and unforced. It is a shared
moment of reverence for the elements of a culture higher than
the author, or Axelbrod, or the Midwestern town could claim.
In any case, the theme in "Young Man Axelbrod" is the same as
that in *Main Street, Babbitt,* and many other Lewis works: the
fate of the protagonist who, as Mark Schorer has said, finds
himself "in a stultifying environment, tries to reform and then
break out of that environment, succeeds for a time, and then
makes a necessary compromise with it."

After graduation in 1908, Lewis traveled about the country,
holding down odd jobs, until he settled in New York in 1910
and took work in the publishing business. During the next
decade he published six unsuccessful novels which are worth
mentioning only as apprentice work. *Hike and the Aeroplane*
(1912), *Our Mr. Wrenn* (1914), *The Trail of the Hawk*
(1915), *The Job* (1917), *The Innocents* (1917), and *Free
Air* (1917) did not satisfy Lewis, nor did they impress his

family, for they always thought he ought to have been a professional man like his father. In fact, Lewis later confessed that "I never quite get over the feeling that writing isn't much of a profession, compared with being a doctor, that it's not quite manly to be sitting on the seat of your pants all the time." Still, he persisted in his chosen vocation: editing, writing short stories, working on novels, hoping for a big breakthrough.

In 1914 this socially awkward young man who aspired to the high culture of the East achieved the remarkable feat of marrying one of the most elegant young women he had ever met, Grace Hegger. This "lady from the Upper West Side," who had escaped "the trap of shabby gentility" by taking up a career at *Vogue*, had stylish clothes, an English accent, and aristocratic ways—including a French maid, because, as she later confessed in *With Love from Gracie: Sinclair Lewis: 1912–1925* (1951)—it pleased her to "give orders in French before guests." Their whole high style of life was rather "furrin" to Lewis, but there was no doubt that Gracie had class. But consorting with the Eastern "quality" naturally enough produced a reaction. The biographical record is full of anecdotes about Lewis's talent for violating the dictates of decorum. He often failed to show up at dinner parties (including his own), or, when he did, he would scandalize the hostess by singing dirty songs or daring guests to take off their shoes. Once he got out on a window ledge two stories above ground and crawled about like a human fly. That he was drunk most of the time suggests that Lewis's impossible shyness and social discomfort led him to act out in the most self-destructive ways. As he later admitted, he "detested polite dinner parties," couldn't stand the "amiable purring of nice matrons," and was "a barbarian in the arts of the table."

Needless to say, his first marriage was full of irremediable conflicts. By 1928 he and Gracie had divorced, whereupon he immediately married Dorothy Thompson, a journalist playmate with fewer social pretensions. Throughout the 1920s, the decade of his great success, Lewis traveled widely, collecting material for *Babbitt, Arrowsmith,* and the other novels. But city life and continual traveling produced in him a longing for the country, and he and Dorothy bought a farm in Vermont. There Lewis fulfilled a dream, temporarily, that Sidney Dow in the story "Land" (*Saturday Evening Post,* 1931) is never able to realize. Always moody, bibulous, and egotistical, Lewis was divorced from Dorothy Thompson in 1942.

Lewis's reputation declined sharply after 1930, but he continued to write, producing a series of novels which include *Ann Vickers* (1933), *Work of Art* (1934), *It Can't Happen Here* (1935), *The Prodigal Parents* (1938), *Bethel Merriday* (1940), *Gideon Planish* (1943), *Cass Timberlane* (1945), *Kingsblood Royal* (1947), and *The God-Seeker* (1949). During these years Lewis also cultivated his interest in the theater as an actor, producer, and director of a good many plays, and he taught creative writing classes at Wisconsin and Minnesota. Aside from the Pulitzer and Nobel prizes, he was also elected to the National Institute of Arts and Letters and was given an honorary degree by Yale in 1936. He died in 1951 in Rome of a heart ailment and was buried in Sauk Centre, which has now embraced him as the man who put the town on the map. His last novel, *World So Wide,* was posthumously published in 1951.

While Lewis is unquestionably best known as a novelist, between 1904 and 1947 he published approximately 117 short stories. The present volume contains those selected by Lewis himself for the 1935 *Selected Short Stories of Sinclair Lewis.* During this forty-four-year span as a story writer, Lewis had the good fortune to write at a time when the magazine business was at its peak. The large number of weekly and monthly periodicals publishing short stories made it possible for him to travel abroad and live very well at home while at the same time he worked on the novels.

By Lewis's time the short story had attained the brilliance we associate with the names of Irving, Hawthorne, Poe, James, Crane, Anderson, Hemingway, and Faulkner, and to these American masters we must of course add the names of Chekhov, Joyce, and other European writers of distinction. Yet Lewis learned little from these masters of the art of the short story, and he had no interest in little magazines, like the *transatlantic review* or *The Little Review*, where some of the most interesting and experimental short fiction was often published. In fact, Lewis told Gracie that "he hated these sophomoric little magazines" and did not intend to publish in them. As Wiliam Peden has noted in *The American Short Story*, "In one major line of its early development, the short story became a piece of literary merchandise written to conform to the unsophisticated tastes of a rapidly expanding middle-class audience." To this line of development Lewis's stories belong, for he preferred to adapt his work to the editorial demands of the large, mass-market slick magazines that paid and paid well. Lewis's tales thus form a part of the popular tradition of commercial short fiction associated with the names of writers like O. Henry, Jack London, and Richard Harding Davis—writers for whom the *Saturday Evening Post, Redbook, Cosmopolitan,* and the *Pictorial Review* were favorite outlets. Lewis, as D. J. Dooley has remarked in *The Art of Sinclair Lewis*, "never practiced the short story as an art form—it was a frankly commercial product."

Lewis's short stories fall into several recognizable categories: tales of romantic fantasy or escape, melodramas of heroic or mock-heroic adventure, boy-meets-girl stories, satires of pretension and folly, and tales of isolation and loneliness. Often played are variations on a theme more fully developed in the novels. In style and form the tales change very little between the earliest stories and the last. Even so, Lewis was an excellent storyteller with an enviable command of narrative development. His tales have a remarkable vividness produced by colorful and concrete detail, rapidly paced action, and a gallery of characters and a medley of dialects that are *sui generis*. What other writer has come up with character names like Rippleton Holabird, Myron and Ora Weagle, Omar Gribble, Sara Hetwiggin Butts, Jared Sassburger, Grover Butterbaugh, and Opal Emerson Mudge? And these characters do not merely talk, as has been frequently noted, but rather whinny, boom, chirp, bumble, warble, carol, gurgle, and yammer in Lewis's inimitable slang.

The elements of style so famously evident in the novels are apparent in his stories as well: the bizarre blend of realism and bald romanticism; the stylized diction that sounds so much like, but was not, vernacular American speech; the exaggeration of that speech through mimicry and slang; the flat characters; the improbable plots somehow sustained despite the dizzying divagation into farce and burlesque; the O'Henrylike trick endings; the wild exaggeration and hyperbole; the staccato effect produced by Lewis's gusto and nervous energy; and the sacrifice of any plot or character or consistency of theme for the sake of a bellylaugh. In this last respect, though Lewis has often been called the American Dickens, he is really the child of Mark Twain—as "Let's Play King," with its uproarious amalgam of *Huck Finn* and *The Prince and the Pauper*, makes clear. When he read over these stories in 1935, Lewis remarked that "One of the things interesting to the author, though perhaps to no one else, in rereading these stories, is the discovery that he, who has been labeled a 'satirist' and a 'realist,' is actually a romantic medievalist of the most incurable sort."

We can see the romantic medievalism clearly enough in the "boy-meets-girl, boy-rescues-girl" theme in "Speed," originally published in *Redbook* in 1919, where the Knight who rescues the lady is a cross-country automobile racer; or in "Moths in the Arc Light" (*Saturday Evening Post*, 1919), where a couple's romantic fantasies sustain their long-distance relationship. In "The Ghost Patrol," which appeared in *Redbook* in 1917, the rescuer is a cop on the beat who is not content to stay in retirement. Lewis had an ardent longing to believe in acts of nobility and heroism, as we see in "The Kidnaped Memorial" (*Pictorial Review,* 1919), where the decent and generous Mr. Gale, a Confederate veteran, shames a Northern community into honoring its G.A.R. dead.

More realistic in tone is "The Willow Walk," a 1918 *Saturday Evening Post* tale. This story is a marvel of suspense as we watch the bank teller Jasper Holt—in a doppelgänger transformation worthy of a Poe or a Dostoevsky—become his invented alter ego. In the most comprehensive study ever made of Lewis's tales, Tobin Simon has argued in his doctoral dissertation, "The Short Stories of Sinclair Lewis" (New York University, 1972), that "The Willow Walk" is "probably Lewis's finest executed story": "Carefully and poignantly Lewis has probed the theme of identity, and in Jasper Holt one reads the inevitable fate of men who in putting on faces to meet faces cannot find the face they once claimed as theirs."

In "The Cat of the Stars," first published in the *Saturday Evening Post* in 1919, Lewis offers the *reductio ad absurdum* of astrological determinism, in showing how little Willis Stodeport brings down a kingdom merely by petting a cat. Lewis's satiric vein also surfaces in "Things" (published in 1919 in the *Saturday Evening Post*) and "The Hack Driver" (*Nation*, 1923), where the ordeal of polite society and the evil effects of material possessions are ridiculed. If we can locate Lewis's deepest social values anywhere in his wide-ranging, self-contradictory satire, it is in the Thoreauvian desire for freedom from polite society and from the aspiration for material possessions that leads him improbably to observe in "The Hack Driver" that

we retain a decent simplicity, no matter how much we are tied to Things, to houses and motors and expensive wives. . . . [The] apparently civilized man is at heart nothing but a hobo who prefers flannel shirts and bristly cheeks and cussing and dirty tin plates to all the trim, hygienic, forward-looking life our women-folks make us put on for them.

In "Letter from the Queen," published in *Cosmopolitan* in 1929, we have a splendid instance of Lewis's satire on ignoramus college professors; and the 1930 tale, "Go East, Young Man" (*Cosmopolitan*), should be read alongside *Main Street* and *Babbitt* as an instance of how Lewis could switch sides, idealize the Midwestern small-town life and a business career, and satirize the phony pretensions of artistic life in the East and in Paris.

Despite the stylistic zest that carries his stories along, they embarrassed Lewis into virtual silence. Gracie said that Lewis "was the first to declare that he was not a great story writer." At times Lewis regarded his stories as merely a means to pay the bills. Although he had been writing them for more than a decade, he confessed to Joseph Hergesheimer in 1916 that "I am not a short story writer, but a novelist . . . and I turn to short stories with difficulty—as yet." What bothered him about "this short story game" was its "formula, pat philosophy, rot! Man, if you and I don't make it good among these stubfooted plaster gods, go farther than any of them," he told Hergesheimer, "then may God take us and boil us in olive oil taken from the claret-spotted table of a Hobohemian restaurant in Greenwich Village." As the formulaic construction, the pat philosophy, the obligatory love angle, and the optimistic ending turned stale, Lewis came to regard story writing as involving "slick, nimble tricks," a kind of "fictional vaudeville" that, as he warned his Minnesota students, "will ruin you." He advised Charles Breasted not "to waste your energies on short stories and stuff for ephemeral publications. Write *books*!" During the public furor over *Main Street*, Lewis even conveyed a fear to his publisher Alfred Harcourt that a volume of short stories might kill interest in the novel:

I am, frankly, having a hell of a time in trying at once to
turn myself back into the successful S.E.P. [*Saturday
Evening Post*] writer I was a year ago—and yet to do for
them nothing but stories so honest that they will in no way
get me back into magazine trickiness nor injure the M. St.
furore [sic]. . . . I don't believe I shall ever again be the
facile *Post* trickster I by God was—for which, doubtless,
we shall in the long run be glad.

This kind of candor led George Jean Nathan to observe in his
Intimate Notebooks that, "always forthright and completely honest with himself," Lewis "made no bones of what he was doing,
but frankly announced to anyone who would listen that he was,
to use his own locution, turning out a swell piece of cheese to
grab off some easy gravy."

Lewis's deepest theorizing about the craft of fiction was no
more profound than that "the art of writing is the art of
applying the seat of your pants to the seat of your chair." And he
loved to repeat the maxim that "a mighty important thing for all
authors to cultivate is this thing [H. L.] Mencken refers to as
'Sitzfleisch.'" Lewis felt that "almost all rules about 'how to
write' are nonsense" because they are based "upon what some
writer did in the past, upon something which may have been
very useful for him but may not suit anybody else." He despised
the self-consciousness of some of his contemporaries and insisted
on the utter naturalness of the creative process. The writer
writes "as Tilden plays tennis or as Dempsey fights, which is to
say, he throws himself into it with never a moment of the
diletante's [sic] sitting back and watching himself perform."
"Brother Lewis," he said of himself on another occasion, is
"essentially a story teller—just as naive, excited, unself-conscious
as the Arab story-tellers beside the caravan fires seven hundred
years ago, or as O. Henry in a hotel room on Twenty-third
Street furiously turning out tales for dinner and red-ink money."
Even so, Lewis had to live with himself as a short story

writer, and that meant coping with the conventions dictated by popular magazine editors. To write the kind of stories he wanted to write and still to satisfy editors like George Horace Lorimer at the *Saturday Evening Post*, Lewis played variations on the themes they liked and recombined and altered, ever so slightly, the old familiar formulas. Gracie defended his stories in saying that "swiftly though he wrote there was no 'dashing off a story': his revisions were always painstaking." And when the critic Carl Van Doren described his tales as "brisk and amusing chatter," Lewis vigorously defended himself by saying that

> even in my magazine stories...I have steadily sought to work out a means of doing as honest work as the powerful negations of the magazine editors would permit. Out of perhaps fifty stories in Saturday Evening Post, Century, Harper's and so on, I doubt if more than ten could with the slightest justice be classified as "brisk and amusing chatter."

In this respect Lewis was quite right, but his academic critics have rarely agreed. In fact, tested against the great masters of the form, Lewis has even been denied the status of an artist. Mark Schorer, whose *Sinclair Lewis: An American Life* (1961) is the definitive biography, has remarked that "perhaps it is futile to approach any Lewis novel as a work of art." And Sheldon Grebstein has remarked in *Sinclair Lewis* that, of the thirteen stories collected here,

> all but a few range from the canned, slick, or unforgivably sentimental to the merely contrived. Such a collection forces conclusions hostile to Lewis. If we presume that these stories are Lewis's best or representative of his best short fiction, then his best was inferior. It is also impossible to trace any consistent values or standards in the stories; rather, they contain some direct contradictions.

Certainly they are not stories of the greatest aesthetic distinction, worthy to be classed with the best of Chekhov, Joyce, Faulkner,

Hemingway, and Henry James. Lewis himself, in 1935, also had some doubts about them because they were "so optimistic, so laudatory"; somehow they seemed tonally off-key during the Depression. But he speculated whether "this American optimism, this hope and courage" were not "authentic parts of American life"—as indeed they are. But most literary critics in our century have preferred stories of "the power of blackness," tales that convey a bleak existential condition, that—in Melville's phrase, say "NO, in Thunder!" In this respect, American critics have been largely at odds with a fundamental aspect of the American spirit.

Of Lewis's critics, only Stuart P. Sherman appears fully to have appreciated Lewis's grasp of American life, for, in *The Significance of Sinclair Lewis* (1922), he was led to call him "one of the foremost short story writers of this century." The century was still young in 1922, and Sherman's judgment was made before Lewis had gone on to write scores of not very remarkable commercial tales. But at his best Lewis's short stories, like his novels, accomplish the remarkable feat described by E. M. Forster: "What Mr. Lewis has done for myself and thousands of others is to lodge a piece of a continent in our *imagination*." However we may respond to his stories, there can be no doubt that Lewis created a distinct fictional style, an authentic signature, a genuine idiom. And Dorothy Thompson was quite right in observing that Lewis is "an ineradicable part of American cultural history" and that "no one seeking to recapture and record the habits, frames of mind, social movements, speech, aspirations, admirations, radicalisms, reactions, crusades, and Gargantuan absurdities of the American *demos* . . . will be able to do without him."

JAMES W. TUTTLETON

New York University
October 1989

LET'S PLAY KING

LET'S PLAY KING

In FRONT of the Y Wurry Gas & Fixit Station, at Mechanicville, New York, the proprietor, Mr. Rabbit Tait, sat elegantly upon a kitchen chair. He was a figure, that Rabbit Tait—christened Thomas. His trousers might be spotty, and their hem resembled the jagged edges of magnified razor blades shown in the advertisements, but his shirt was purple, with narrow red stripes, his sleeve garters were of silvered metal, and on one sausage-like forefinger was a ring with a ruby which would have been worth two hundred thousand dollars had it not been made of glass.

Mr. Tait was not tall, but he was comfortably round; his face was flushed; his red mustache was so beautifully curled that he resembled a detective; and his sandy hair was roached down over his forehead in one of the most elegant locks ever seen on the wrong side of a mahogany bar.

Out from the neat white cottage behind the filling station, a residence with all modern conveniences except bathrooms, gas and electricity, charged his spouse, Mrs. Bessie Tait, herding their son Terry.

3

Now Bessie was not beautiful. She had a hard-boiled-egg forehead and a flatiron jaw, which harmonized with her milk-can voice to compose a domestic symphony. Nor was Rabbit Tait, for all his dashing air, an Apollo. But Terry, aged six, was a freak of beauty.

He was too good to be true. He had, surely, come off a magazine cover. He had golden hair, like blown thistle-down in a sunset, his skin was white silk, his big eyes violet, his nose straight, and his mouth had twisting little smiles which caused the most loyal drunkards to go home and reform.

How he had ever happened to Rabbit and Bessie Tait, how the angels (or the stork, or Doc McQueech) had ever happened to leave Terry in the cottage behind the Y Wurry Filling Station instead of in the baronial clapboard castle of the Mechanicville banker, is a mystery which is left to the eugenists.

Bessie was speaking in a manner not befitting the mother of a Christmas-card cherub:

"For the love of Mike, Rabbit, are you going to sit there on your chair all afternoon? Why don't you get busy?"

"Yeah?" contributed the cherub's father. "Sure! Whajjuh wamme do? Go out and grab some bozo's bus by the radiator cap and make him come in and buy some gas?"

"Well, you kin fix the screen door, can't you?"

"The screen door?"

"Yes, the screen door, you poor glue!"

"The screen door? Is it busted?"

"Oh, heck, no; it ain't busted! I just want you to come and scratch its back where the mosquitoes been biting it, you poor sap! And then you can take care of this brat. Under my feet the whole dog-gone day!"

She slapped Terry, generously and skilfully, and as Terry howled, Rabbit rose uneasily, pale behind the bronze splendor of his curled mustache. Bessie was obviously in one of her more powerful moods, and it is to be feared that we should have had the distressing spectacle of Mr. Tait going to work, driven by his good lady's iron jaw and granite will, had not, that second, a limousine stopped at the filling station.

In the limousine was a lady so rich, so rich and old, that she had to be virtuous. She had white hair and a complexion like an old china cup. Glancing out while Rabbit Tait cheerily turned the handle of the gas pump, she saw Terry.

"Oh!" she squealed. "What an angelic child! Is it yours?"

"Yes, ma'am," chuckled Rabbit, while Bessie ranged forward, beaming on the treasure she had so recently slapped.

"He ought to be a choir boy," said the refined old lady. "He would be simply darling, at St. Juke's, in Albany. You must take him there, and introduce him to Doctor Wimple, the curate—he's so fond of the little ones! I'm sure your dear little boy could be sent to some church school free, and *think*—these dreadful modern days—otherwise, with his beauty, he might get drawn into the movies as a child star, or some frightful thing like that, and be ruined! Good morning!"

"Jiminy, that's a swell old dame!" observed the dear little boy as the limousine swam away.

Bessie absently slapped him, and mused, "Say, Rabbit, the old lettuce gimme a good idea. The kid might do good in the movies."

"Say, he might, at that. Gee, maybe he could make a hundred bucks a week. I've heard some of these kids do.

Golly, I'd like to have a cane with a silver dog's-head top!"

"Tom Tait, you get on your coat, and as soon as I scrub the kid's mug and change his clothes, you take him right straight down to the Main Street Foto Shoppe—I'll mind the pump—and you get some pictures of him and we'll shoot 'em out to Hollywood."

"Oh, you gimme a big fat pain—hot day like this," sighed Mr. Tait and, gloomily, "Besides, I might miss a job changing an inner tube. Just like you—throw away fifty cents on a fool chance that we might be able to farm the brat out at maybe fifty bucks a week some day, *maybe!*"

"I don't play no maybes, never," said Bessie Tait.

Mr. Abraham Hamilton Granville, president and G. M. of the Jupiter-Triumph-Tait Film Corporation, had adorned his Spanish mansion at Poppy Peaks, California, with the largest private fish bowl in the known world. Other movie satraps might have Pompeian swimming pools, cathedral organs and ballrooms floored with platinum, but it was Mr. Granville's genius—so had it been, indeed, ever since he had introduced the Holdfast Patent Button, which had put over the renowned Abe Grossburg Little Gents' Pants Co., back in 1903—I say it was Mr. Granville's peculiar genius that he always thought up something a little different.

He had caused cunning craftsmen to erect a fish bowl —no vulgar aquarium but a real, classy, round, glass, parlor fish bowl—twenty feet high and sixty in circumference, on the red-and-green marble terrace of his mansion, Casa Scarlatta.

Poppy Peaks is an addition to Hollywood, built by the more refined and sensitive and otherwise rich members of the movie colony when Hollywood itself became too common for their aristocratic tradition. And of all the county families and nobility of Poppy Peaks, none were more select than the intellectual powers gathered about Mr. Granville this hazy California August afternoon.

Besides Mr. Granville and the production manager, Mr. Eisbein, there was Wiggins, the press agent—formerly the most celebrated red-dog player and mint-julep specialist on the coast, a man who was questionable only in his belief that mange cure will cause thinning mouse-colored hair to turn into raven richness. Was also Miss Lilac Lavery Lugg, writer of the scenarios for such masterpieces of cinematographic passion as "Mad Maids," "Midnight Madness," and "Maids o' the Midnight." She was thirty-eight and had never been kissed.

But even more important than these mad magnates o' midnight was a quiet and genteel family sitting together in scarlet-painted basket chairs.

The father of the family was a gentleman named Mr. T. Benescoten Tait. He had a handsome ruddy mustache, curled, and a gold cigarette case; he wore a lavender suit, white spats, patent-leather shoes, eyeglasses with a broad silk ribbon, and a walking stick whose top was a dog's-head of gold with ruby eyes.

His lady was less cheering in appearance, but more notable; she wore a white-striped black suit with python-skin slippers. She sat rigid, with eyes like headlights.

And the third of the family was Terry Tait, billed throughout the entire world as "The King of Boy Comedians."

He was in English shorts, with a Byronesque silk shirt open at the throat. But on the back of one manicured hand was a grievous smear of dirt, which more suggested raising Cain in Mechanicville, New York, than being

sweet in Poppy Peaks; and crouched behind him was a
disreputable specimen of that celebrated breed of canines,
a Boy's Dog, who would never be exhibited in any dog
show except a strictly private one behind an ill-favored
barn.

Terry was ten, this summer of 1930.

"Well, Miss Lugg," Granville said briskly, "what's
your idea for the new Terrytait?"

"Oh, I've got a perfectly priceless idea this time. Terry
plays a poor little Ytalian bootblack—he's really the son
of a count, but he got kidnaped——"

Terry crossed over center stage and yammered, "I
won't do it! I've been the newsboy that squealed on the
gang, and I've been the son of the truck driver that got
adopted by the banker, and I've been Oliver Twist and—
I hate these dog-gone poor-city-boy rôles! I want to be a
boy cowboy, or an Apache!"

Miss Lugg squealed, "I've got it! How about his playing
the drummer boy of the regiment—Civil War stuff—
saves the General when he's wounded, and Lincoln invites
him to the White House?"

Miss Lugg was soaring into genius before their awed
eyes. But she was interrupted by the circular-saw voice
of Mrs. T. Benescoten Tait:

"Not on your life! Not a chance! Terry in them awful
battle scenes with all them tough mob extras falling over
him? That's always the trouble with wars—they make
good scenes but somebody is likely to get hurt. No,
sir!"

"*Was ist das denn fur ein Hutzpah!*" growled Mr.
Abraham Hamilton Granville. "Der Terry should take
a chance, what we pay him!"

Mrs. Tait sprang up, a fury on ice. "Yeah! A miserable
two thousand a week! Believe me, on the next contract it's

going to be four thousand, and if it don't come from Jupiter, there's others that'll pay it. Why, we don't hardly make expenses on two grand, having to keep up a swell social position so none of these bozos like Franchot can high-hat us, and Terry's French tutor and his dancing teacher and his trainer and his chauffeur and—and—— And thank heaven I'm not ambitious like a lot of these bums that want to show off how swell they are.

"Hones' sometimes I wish we'd stayed back in Mechanicville! Mr. Tait had a large garage there—we saved more money than what we can here, the way you hogs want to grab off all the coin and don't never think about the Artist and his folks and how they got to live."

"Yes, yes, yes, maybe that's so. Well, what's your idea of his next rôle, Bessie?" soothed Mr. Granville.

Mr. Tait suggested, "I got an idea that——"

"You have not! You never did have!" said Bessie. "Now, I think it would be nice if—I'd just love to see my Terrykins as this here Lost Dophing—this son of Napoleon or Looey or whoever he was—you know, Leglong. Miss Lugg can look up all the historical dope on him. I think Terry'd look lovely in satin tights with a ruff!"

"Oh, gee!" wailed Terry.

"I don't," continued Mrs. Tait, with severe virtue, "like to see my little boy playing these newsboy and hard-up rôles all the time. I don't think it's a good influence on all his Following. It ain't progress. And him with his wardrobe!"

While Mrs. Tait sermonized, the butler had brought out the four-o'clock cocktail tray and the afternoon papers, and Wiggins, the rusty press agent, had escaped from the sound of Bessie's voice into a nice wholesome Chicago murder story.

He piped, now:

"Say, talking about your Lost Dauphin dope, Bess, here's one in real life. Seems in the paper, King Udo of Slovaria died last night of heart failure and his heir is his son, Maximilian—King Maximilian III, he'll be—and the poor kid is only ten. Youngest king in the world. But where the heck is Slovaria?"

"You tellum, Terry," said Bessie Tait. "Terry is a wonder at jography, same as I always was."

"I don't want to!" protested the wonder.

"You do what I tell you to, or I won't let you play baseball with the butler's kids! I'll—I'll make you go to tea at Princess Marachecella's!"

"Oh, darn!" sighed Terry.

Then he recited, with the greatest speed and lack of expression, "Slovaria is a Balkan kingdom bounded on the north by Roumania, on the east by Zenda, on the south by Bulgaria, and on the west by Graustark. The capital is Tzetokoskavar. The principal rivers are the Rjekl and the Zgosca. The exports are cattle, hides, cheese and wool. The reigning monarch is Udo VII, who is descended from the renowned warrior King Hieronymus, and who is united in wedlock to the famous beauty Sidonie, a cousin of the former German Kaiser . . . Say, Mamma, what's a Balkan kingdom? Is it in China?"

"Now listen to him, will you? I bet there ain't a kid in Hollywood that's got as swell a tutor or 's educated as good as he is!" purred Mrs. Tait. "I was always like that, too—just crazy about books and education."

"Wait! Wait! I've got it!" shrieked Miss Lilac Lavery Lugg. "Here's our scenario, and the publicity about this new kid king will help to put it over. Listen! Terry is the boy king of a——"

"I don't want to be a king! I want to be an Apache!" wailed Terry, but no one heeded.

Everyone (excepting Terry, Terry's mongrel pup and the butler) listened with hot eyes, as they were caught up by the whirlwind of Lilac's genius:

"Terry is the boy king of a Near-Eastern country. Scenes in the palace—poor kid, awful' lonely, sitting on throne, end of a big throne room—the Diplomatic Hotel might let us shoot their lobby again, like we did in 'Long Live the Czar!' Big gang of guards in these fur hats. Saluting. Show how he's a grand kid—scene of him being nice to a poor little orphan in the yard at the castle and his kitty had busted her leg, but he's so sick and tired of all this royal grandeur that he turns democratic on his guard and the court and all them, and he's meaner than a tooth-ache to his guards and the prime minister—the prime minister'll be a grand comedy character, with long whiskers. And the sub-plot is an American reporter, a tall, handsome bird that's doing the Balkans, and say, he's the spitting image of the king's uncle—the uncle is the heavy; he's trying to grab the throne off the poor li'l' tike. Well, one day the king—the kid—is out in the castle grounds taking his exercise, riding horseback. He's followed by a coupla hundred cavalry troops, and he treats 'em something fierce, hits 'em and so on.

"Well, this American reporter, he's there in the grounds, and the king sees him and thinks it's his uncle, and he says to his troops, 'Go on, beat it; there's my uncle,' he says; 'he wants to grab the throne, but I'm not scared of him; I'll meet him alone.' And so he rides up to this fellow and draws his sword."

"Would he have a sword, li'l' kid like that?" hinted T. Benescoten.

"Of course he would, you fathead!" snapped Bessie. "Haven't you seen any pictures of the Prince of Wales? Kings and all like that always wear uniforms and swords

—except maybe when they're playing golf. Or swimming."

"Certainly!" Lilac looked icily at T. Benescoten.

Everybody, save his son Terry, usually looked icily at T. Benescoten.

"Ziz saying," Lilac continued, "he draws his sword and rushes at what he thinks is his uncle, but the fellow speaks and he realizes it ain't his uncle. Then they get to talking. I think there ought to be a flashback showing the reporter's—the hero's—happy life in Oklahoma as a boy; how he played baseball and all that. And then the reporter—he's seen how mean the boy king is to his men, and he gives the poor li'l' kid his first lesson in acting nice and democratic, like all American kids do, and the king is awful' sorry he was so mean, and he thinks this reporter is the nicest bird he ever met, and they're walking through the grounds and they meet the king's sister—she's the female lead—I can see Katinka Kettleson playing the rôle—and the reporter and the princess fall in love at first sight—of course later the reporter rescues the princess and the king from the uncle—big ball at the palace, with a ballet, and the uncle plans to kidnap the king, and the reporter, he's learned all about the extensive secret passages, or maybe they might even be catacombs, under the palace, and he leads them away and there's a slick fight in the woods, the reporter used to be a fencing champion and he engages the uncle in battle—swords, you know—while the poor little king and the unfortunate princess crouch timorously amid the leaves on the ground and the reporter croaks the uncle and—say, *say*, I got it, this'll be something ab-so-tively new in these royal plot pictures, they make their getaway, after the fight, by airplane—probably they might cross the ocean to America, and the pilot drops dead, and the reporter has a secret wound that he has gallantly been concealing from the princess and he faints but the pilot has taught the king how to fly and he grabs the controls——"

"Can I fly, really?" gloated Terry.

"You can not!" snapped his mother. "That part's doubled. Go on, Lilac!"

And Terry listened gloomily while Lilac led the boy king on to a climax in which he was kidnaped by New York gun men and finally rescued by the reporter and the prime minister—whiskered, comic, but heroic.

"It's swell!" said Abraham Hamilton Granville.

"It'll be all right, I guess," said Mrs. T. Benescoten Tait.

"Oh, Lord!" said Wiggins the press agent.

And as for Terry Tait and the Tait mongrel, they said nothing at all, and said it vigorously.

While Castello Marino, the residence of the Benescoten Taits, was not so extensive as the mansion of Mr. Abraham Granville, it was a very tasty residence, with a campanile that was an exact copy of the celebrated Mangia tower at Siena, except that it was only one fifth as tall, and composed of yellow tiles instead of rusty old-fashioned brick.

In this select abode, the loving but unfortunate parents, trying so hard to give their little boy a chance to get on in the world, were having a good deal of trouble.

This morning Terry simply would not let his nice valet dress him. He said he did not like his nice valet. He said he wanted to be let alone.

"I think, Polacci," Mrs. Tait remarked to the valet, "that Master Tait ought to wear his polo suit to Mr. Granville's office."

"Oh, no, please, Mother!" Terry begged. "It looks so foolish! No other boy wears polo costume."

"Of course not! That's why I got it for you!"

"I won't wear it! Not outside the house. Everybody laughs at me. If I wear it, I won't act."

"Oh, dear me, why I should be cursed by a son that——"

"Now put on your polo rags and mind your mother," said T. Benescoten Tait.

"Rabbit!"

"Yes, my dear?"

"Shut up!... Now, Terry, I'll let you wear your sailor suit. The English one. Imported. But I want you to realize that your disobedience just almost breaks your mother's heart! Now hurry and let Polacci dress you. The limousine is waiting."

"Oh, Mother, please, have I got to go in the limousine? It isn't any fun to ride in a limousine. You can't see anything. I want to go on the trolley. You can see all kinds of different people on the trolley."

"Why, Terence McGee Tait! I never *heard* of such a thing! Who in the world has been talking to you about trolleys? They're common! There's just common vulgar folks, on trolleys! Besides! Give people a chance to look at you without paying for it? What an idea! Oh, dear, that's what comes from mixing with these extra people on the lot, picking up these common ideas! If you don't come with me in the limousine, I won't give you one bit of caviar for dinner!"

"I hate caviar!"

"Oh, I just don't know what I've done to deserve this!"

T. Benescoten spoke tentatively: "How about me and Terry going on the trolley and meeting you at Abe's? I'd kind of like to ride on the street car myself, for a change."

"And pick up one of those Hollywood cuties? Not a chance!"

They took the limousine.

In Mr. Granville's office were gathered the higher nobility of the Jupiter-Triumph-Tait organization, to listen to the completed scenario of "His Majesty, Junior," the film suggested three weeks ago by Lilac Lavery Lugg. But before Miss Lugg had a chance to read it, Wiggins, the press agent, prowling up and down in the ecstasy of an idea as he talked, announced that the evening newspapers said young Maximilian III of Slovaria, with his mother, Queen Sidonie, was about to visit London.

It was hinted in the papers that the astute Sidonie wanted to secure the sympathy and alliance of the British people by exhibiting the boy king.

"And here," squealed Wiggins, "is the grandest piece of publicity that's ever been pulled. Bessie, you and Tom and Terry go to London. I'll stay out of it, so they won't smell a mice. Clapham, our London agent, is a smart publicity grabber, anyway. You fix it, somehow, so Terry and this King Maximilian get acquainted. The two boy kings, see? They get photographed together, see? Besides, Terry's public know him as a common newsboy, and they won't hardly be loyal to him as a king unless they see him really mixing up with the élite, see?"

Mrs. Tait looked doubtful. Poppy Peaks she knew, and Hollywood was her oyster, but neither she nor T. Benescoten nor Terry had ever tackled the dread unknown lands beyond the Atlantic. But she brightened and looked resolute as Wiggins cunningly added:

"And this will give you a chance, if you rig it right and the two kids hit it off together, to get chummy with Queen Sidonie, Bessie, and maybe you can get her to come to the Peaks as your guest, and then, believe me, you'll make Garbo and Kate Hepburn look like deuces wild, very wild!"

"That's not a *bad* idea," mused Mrs. Tait.

In the sacred recesses of the Benescoten Tait home, in the Etruscan breakfast room, where love birds and Himalayan canaries billed and cooed and caroled in red enameled cages, and the solid-marble dining table glowed prettily with nineteen dollars' worth of orchids, the Tait family discussed the invasion of Europe. They had just returned from Mr. Granville's office, where they had accepted Lilac's scenario of "His Majesty, Junior."

"I think," said T. Benescoten, "that if we get held up in London very long, I'll run over to Paris, if you don't mind, Bessie."

"What do you want to do in Paris?"

"Huh? Why, I just want to see the city. You know, get acquainted with French customs. Nothing so broadening as travel."

"Then I guess you're going to stay narrow. Fat chance, you going to Paris by yourself and drinking a lot of hootch and chasing around after a lot of wild women. In fact, come to think of it, Rabbit, I guess Terry and I can pull this off better if we leave you home."

"Mother!" Terry was imploring. "Please! I want Father to go along!"

Bessie faced her two men with her hands on her hips, her jaw out, and when she stood thus, no one who knew her opposed her, unless he was looking for death.

T. Benescoten grumbled, Terry wailed, but Bessie glared them down. Then she stalked to the telephone and ordered the immediate attendance of a dressmaker, a women's tailor, a shoemaker, a milliner, a hairdresser, a masseuse, an osteopath, a French tutor and a Higher Thought lecturer.

"I'm going to Europe and I'm going right," she said.

When, two weeks later, she took the train, she had fourteen new evening frocks, eight new ensembles, thirty-seven new hats, eight new pairs of snake-skin shoes, a thumb ring of opals, a gold-mounted dressing bag, and a lovely new calm manner purchased from the Higher Thought lecturer.

All the way from Poppy Peaks to New York, Terry and his smiling, his tender mother were hailed by the millions to whom Terry had become the symbol of joyous yet wistful boyhood.

Wiggins had generously let the press of each city and town through which they would pass know just when the King of Boy Comedians would arrive, and at every stop Terry was dragged, wailing, to bow and smile his famous Little Lord Fauntleroy smile at the cheering gangs.

The horror of facing the staring eyes, the horror of trying to look superhuman for the benefit of these gloating worshipers, while he felt within like a lonely and scared little boy, so grew on Terry that it was only his mother's raging, only the fury of Mr. Abraham Hamilton Granville and the coaxing of Wiggins, that would draw Terry out of his safe drawing room to the platform.

Despite a certain apprehension about the perils of the deep, despite a slight worry as to how he would talk to King Maximilian—who was, said the papers, to arrive in London one day before the Taits were due—Terry was delighted when Wiggins and Granville had left them, when the steamer had snarled its way out to sea, and he could hide in a corner of the S. S. *Megalomaniac's* royal suite.

He slept for sixteen hours, then, and even the indomitable Bessie Tait slept, while the S. S. *Megalomaniac* thrust out to sea, and expectant Europe awaited them as it awaited the other royal family from Slovaria.

Aside from gently persuading Terry to be the star in the ship's concert, at which he recited "The Shooting of Dan

McGrew" and "Gunga Din," and gave imitations of
Napoleon and a sitting hen; aside from permitting him to
be photographed by every passenger aboard, and lovingly
insisting that he wear a new costume every afternoon—
including the polo costume, the baseball suit, the Eton suit
with top hat, and the Fauntleroy black velvet with lace
collar—aside from these lighter diversions, Bessie gave
Terry a rest on the crossing. He must be saved to over-
whelm London, Britain, and Queen Sidonie.

Bessie was disappointed in landing at Southampton
when she saw no crowd hysterical with desire to worship
the King of Boy Comedians.

In fact, no one was awaiting them save Mr. Percival
S. F. Clapham, press agent and secretary to the chairman
of the Anglo-Jupiter Film Distributing Corporation, which
acted as missionary in introducing the Terrytaits to
Britain.

Mr. Clapham greeted Bessie and Terry in what he considered American: "Pleased to meet you! At your service,
folks, as long as you're here."

"Where's the crowd?" demanded Bessie.

"They, uh—Southampton is a bit indifferent to Americans, you might say."

Bessie and Clapham looked at each other with no great
affection. The international brotherhood was not working
out; the hands across the sea were growing cold; and
when the three of them were settled in a railway com-
partment, Bessie demanded crisply:

"Terry and I can't waste a lot of time. I don't want to
hustle you, but have you fixed it up yet for Terry to meet
this kid king and the quince?"

"The *quince?*"

"Good heavens! The queen! Sidonie!"

"But—the *quince!* Really! Oh, I see! The queen! Of course. I see. No, I'm sorry; not quite arranged yet."

"They've arrived?"

"Oh, yes, quite. Splendid reception. The young king the darling of London."

"Well, all right; then Terry and I can go right up and call on 'em. I expect they've seen a lot of his pictures. If you haven't made a date for us, I guess we'd better just send in our cards. Or had we better phone? Where they staying?"

"They're at the Picardie Hotel, because of being in mourning. This is an unofficial visit. And really, my dear lady, it would be quite impossible for you even to try to call on His Young Majesty and Queen Sidonie! It simply isn't done, d'you see? It isn't *done!* You must make application to your ambassador, who will present the request to the British foreign office, who will communicate with the Slovarian foreign office, who will determine whether or not they care to submit the request to Queen Sidonie's secretary, who may care to bring the matter to Her Majesty's attention, at which time——"

"At which time," remarked Mrs. T. Benescoten Tait, "hell will have frozen over a second time. Now listen! I'm not much up on meeting queens, but I guess I'm about as chummy with the royalty as you are! Now listen——"

Mr. Clapham's native ruddiness paled as he heard the subversive, the almost sacrilegious plans of Bessie Tait.

"My dear madame, we are all of us eager to help you," he implored, "but really, you know, a king is a king!"

She looked at Terry. "You bet," she observed. "And a king's mother is a queen. You bet!"

Which profound and mysterious statement puzzled Mr. Clapham until the train drew in at Waterloo.

There were five reporters and a group of thirty or forty admirers, very juvenile, to greet them. The most respectable Mr. Turner, chairman of the Anglo-Jupiter Corporation and boss of Mr. Clapham, met them with his car.

"Shall we go right to the Picardie, or kind of parade through London first?" demanded Bessie.

"Oh! The Picardie!"

"Why, sure! That's where King Maximilian and his ma are staying, isn't it? It's the swellest hotel in town, isn't it?"

"Oh, yes, quite!" Mr. Turner looked agitated, as he fretted: "But I say! A lady traveling alone, with a boy, couldn't go to the Picardie! People might think it a bit fast! I've taken a suite for you at Garborough's Hotel—most respectable family hotel."

"When was it built?"

"Built? Built? When was it built? Good heavens, I don't know, madame. I should suppose about 1840."

"Well, that's all I want to know. But go ahead."

Mr. Turner's car left the station to a slight rustle of cheering from Terry's youthful admirers and to earnest questions from the reporters as to how many cocktails American boys of ten usually consume before dinner. But after that, there was no sign that London knew it was entertaining another king.

Fog packed in about them. The sooty house fronts disappeared in saffron-gray. The roar of Trafalgar Square seemed louder, more menacing, than Los Angeles or even New York. Bessie thrust out her hand with a gesture of timid affection which she rarely used toward that rare and golden goose, Terry.

The living room of their suite at Garborough's Hotel was brown and dingy. To Bessie, accustomed to hotel rooms the size of a railroad terminal, the room was shockingly small. It was but little bigger than the entire cottage she had occupied four years before.

She sniffed. And quite rightly.

And the bedrooms had wardrobes instead of proper closets.

She sniffed again. She rang for the room waiter.

"Dry Martini," said Bessie.

"Eek?" gasped the room waiter.

"Dry Martini! Cocktail! Licker!" snarled Bessie.

"I beg pardon, madame, but we do not serve cocktails."

"You don't——" In the hurt astonishment of it Bessie sat down, hard. "Say, what kind of a dump is this? What kind of a bunch do you get here?"

"His Grace, the Duke of Ightham, has been coming here for sixty years."

"Ever since you were a boy of forty! All right, bring me a highball."

"A high ball, madame?"

"A highball! A whisky and soda! A lightning and cloud-burst!"

"Very well, madame."

After the waiter's stately exit, Bessie whimpered, "And they said I'd like these old ruins!"

For the moment she looked beaten. "Maybe it ain't going to be as easy to be buddies with Maximilian and Sidonie as I thought. I wish I'd brought old Rabbit!" Her depression vanished; she sprang up like a war horse. "How I'd bawl him out! Come on, Bess! Here's where we show this old run-down Europe what an honest-to-goodness American lady can do!"

They had arrived at Garborough's at three of the afternoon. At five, in a black velvet costume which made her look like a vamp—as far up as her chin—Bessie was stalking into the lobby of the Hotel Picardie.

The reception clerk at Garborough's had been a stringy young woman in black alpaca and a state of disapproval, but at the Picardie he was a young Spanish count in a morning coat.

"I want," she said, "the best suite you have."

"Certainly, madame; at once."

The clerk leaped into action and brought out from a glass-enclosed holy of holies an assistant manager who was more dapperly mustached, more sleekly frock-coated, more soapily attentive than himself.

"May I inquire how large a suite Madame would desire? And—uh—is Madame's husband with Madame?"

"No. I'm the mother of Terry Tait, the movie, I mean cinema, star. I'm here with him; just us two. I'd like a parlor and coupla of bedrooms and a few private dining rooms. I guess you need references here." For a second Bessie again sounded a little hopeless. "Probably if you called up the American ambassador he would know about us."

"Oh, no, madame; of course we are familiar with the pictures of Master Tait. May I show you some suites?"

The first suite that he showed was almost as large, it had almost as much gilt, paneling, omelet-marble table tops, telephone extensions, water taps and Persian rugs as a hotel in Spokane, Schenectady, or St. Petersburg, Florida.

"This is more like it. But look here, I heard somewhere that Queen Sidonie and her boy are staying here."

"Yes, quite so, madame."

"Well, look: I'd like to be on their floor."

"Sorry, madame, but that is impossible. We have reserved the entire floor for Their Majesties and their suite."

"But there must be some rooms empty on it."

"Sorry, madame, but that is quite impossible. The police

would be very nasty if we even attempted such a thing."

Bessie unhappily recalled the days when she had first gone to Hollywood with Terry and tried to persuade a castiron-faced guard to let them through to the casting director. Not since then had anyone spoken to her so firmly. It was a dejected Bessie Tait from Mechanicville who besought, "Well, then, I'd like to be on the floor right above them or below them. I'll make it worth your while, manager. Oh, I know I can't bribe you, but I don't like to bother anybody without I pay for their trouble, and it would be worth ten of your pounds, or whatever you callum, to have a nice suite just above Their Majesties."

The assistant manager hesitated. From her gold-link purse Bessie drew out the edge of a ten-pound note. At that beautiful sight the assistant manager sighed, and murmured respectfully, "I'll see what can be done, madame."

Ten minutes later Bessie had a voluptuous suite guaranteed to be just above that of Queen Sidonie.

Someone had informed Bessie Tait that English people dined as late as eight in the evening. It scarcely seemed possible. But, "I'll try anything once," said Bessie.

At eight, she sat in a corner of the Renaissance Salon of the Hotel Picardie, in a striking white tulle frock with gold sequins, and with her was Master Tait, in full evening clothes.

She noticed that the other guests stared at him considerably.

"They know who we are!" she rejoiced, as she picked up the menu. It was in French, but if the supercilious captain of waiters expected the American lady not to understand French, he was mistaken, for in eighteen lessons at Poppy Peaks she had learned not only the vocabulary of food but also the French for "I should like to take a horse-back ride on a horse tomorrow," "How much costs a hat of this fashion?" and "Where obtains one the tickets of the first class for Holland?"

She said rapidly to the captain, "*Donnyma deh pottage German one order crevettes and one wheats, deh rosbifs, pom de terres, and some poissons—no, pois—and deh fois ice cream and hustle it will you, please?*"

"*Perfaitment!*" said the French captain and, continuing in his delightful native tongue, he commanded a waiter, "*Jetz mach' schnell, du, Otto!*"

At nine, Bessie commanded again the presence of the assistant manager who had found her suite.

"I want you," she suggested, "to get me some good English servants. First I want a valet for my son. I want Terry should have a high-class English valet—and I don't want none that talks bad English, neither."

"Certainly, madame."

"And I want a maid that can fix my hair."

"Certainly, madame."

"And then I want a refined lady secretary."

"Refined?"

"Yes, she's gotta be refined. I never could stand dames that aren't refined."

"I know a young lady, madame, Miss Tingle, the daughter of a most worthy Low Church clergyman, and formerly secretary to Lady Frisbie."

"Lady Frisbie? Oh, in the nobility?"

"Why—uh—practically. Her husband, Sir Edward Frisbie, was a linen draper, and mayor of Bournemouth. Oh, yes, you'll find Miss Tingle most refined."

"Grand! That's what I'm always telling these rough-necks in Hollywood—like when they wanted Terry to play a comic part, bell boy in a harem—'No, sir,' I said,

'Terry's got a refined father and mother, and he'll be refined himself or I'll bust his head!' Well, shoot in your valet and maid and Miss Tingle—have 'em here by noon."

The assistant manager promised. After his going, Bessie received Mr. Turner and Mr. Clapham of the Anglo-Jupiter Corporation.

"We have decided——" said Mr. Clapham gently.

"Yes, we have quite decided," said Mr. Turner with firmness.

"—that it would be indiscreet for you to seek an audience with King Maximilian at all."

"Oh, you have!" murmured Bessie. "It's nice to have things decided for you."

"Yes, we hoped you would be pleased. We have, in fact, gone into the matter most thoroughly. I rang up a gentleman connected with the press, and he assured me that the proper way would be for you to apply to your ambassador, and that doubtless the matter could be arranged in a year or two—doubtless you would have to go to Slovaria."

"Well, that's splendid. Just a year or two! That's fine! Mighty kind of you."

"So pleased to do any little thing that I can. Now Mr. Turner and I have talked it over, and it seems to both of us that it would be better to have a little subtler publicity. So if you care to have him do so, your son will address the Lads' Brigade of St. Crispin's, Golder's Green, next Thursday evening—the papers will give several paragraphs to this interesting occasion. And then—I do a bit in the literary way, you know—I have ventured to write an interview with you which I hope to have used by one of the papers. It goes as follows:

"'Well, I swow! Say, dod gast my cats, this yere is by gosh all whillikens one big burg,' was the first remark of Mrs. Tait, mother of the well-known juvenile cinema star,

Terry Tait, upon arrival in London yesterday. 'Yes-sir-ree-bob,' she continued, 'out thar in the broad bosom of the Golden West, out where the handclasp grows a little warmer, we get some mighty cute burgs, but nothing like this yere ant heap.'"

"Isn't that nice?" sighed Bessie. "And that's the American language you've written it in, isn't it?"

"Yes. I'm often taken for an American when I wish."

"I'm sure you must be."

Left alone by Turner and Clapham, with the promise that within a few days they would arrange other feats of publicity at least equal to the chance to address the Lads' Brigade of Golder's Green, Bessie sat down and sighed. But the next morning she resolutely marched into Terry's modest 24 x 42 bedroom, where he was reading *Treasure Island,* and she ordered, "Come on, son; we're going out and buy the town. Toys."

"I don't want any toys. I hate toys!"

"You heard what I said! Think I'm going to have a lot of kings dropping into your room and seeing you without a lot of swell toys?"

"But Mother, I'd rather have books."

"Say, if you keep on like this, you'll turn out nothing but an author working for one-fifty a week. Books never did nobody no good. Come on!"

By suggestion of the concierge, they took a taxi for an enormous Toy Bazaar on Oxford Street. Bessie firmly bought for Terry an electric train, an electric Derby game, a portable chemical laboratory, a set of boxing gloves, and a choice article in the way of a model of the Colosseum in which electric lions devoured electric Early Christians.

"There! I bet none of these boy kings has got a better set of toys than that!" remarked Bessie.

As they emerged from the Toy Bazaar, Terry saw, next to it, an animal shop.

Ever since they had left Poppy Peaks, Terry had mourned for the disgraceful mongrel which the English quarantine regulations had compelled him to leave at home, and he cried now, "Oh, Mother, I want a dog!"

"If I get you one, will you play nicely with the electric toys?"

"I'll try; honestly I will."

"And will you address these Lad Brigands or whatever it is in this Golden Green or wherever it is? I'll have this bird Clapham write your speech."

"Yes. But a jolly dog!"

"I wish," said Bessie, in her most refined way, as they entered the animal shop, "to look at a line of dogs. What have you got good today?"

"This, madame, is a very superior animal." And the clerk brought out an object as thin as paper, as long as Saturday morning, as gloomy as a cameraman. "This is an Imperial Russian wolfhound, a genuine borzoi—you will recognize the typical borzoi touch, madame—it's brother of a hound which we sold just yesterday to the Earl of Tweepers for his daughter, Lady Ann—no doubt you know her ladyship, madame."

"H-how much?" faltered Bessie.

"To close out this line, madame, we should be willing to let you have this animal for a hundred guineas."

The inner, the still Mechanicvillized Bessie Tait was calculating, "Great grief—that's five hundred bucks for a pooch!" but the outer, the newly refined Mrs. T. Benescoten Tait was remarking evenly, "Rather a lot, but I might consider—— Does it please you, Terry?"

She could keep up the strain of refinement no longer; and most briskly, much more happily, she remarked to the clerk, "This is my son, Terry Tait. You've probably seen him in the movies. They call him the King of Boy Comedians."

"Oh, Mother, please!" protested Terry, but the clerk was trumpeting, "Oh, yes, madame. We are honored in being allowed to serve you."

And with that the canine blotter would have been sold, but for one accident. Terry sighed, "Mother, I don't like him."

"But *dar*ling, this is the kind of dog that all nobility get their pictures taken with. But if you don't like him——"

While Bessie grew momently more impatient, Terry was offered, and declined, such delightful pets as a Pekingese that looked like a misanthropic bug and an Airedale like a rolled-up doormat. Then he stopped before a cage and, his hands clasped in ecstasy, exulted, "Oh, there's the dog I want!"

The clerk looked shocked; Bessie, seeing his expression, looked shockeder.

Terry's choice was a canine social error. He was, probably, a cross between a police dog and a collie, with a little Scotch terrier and a trace of cocker spaniel. He had bright eyes, a wide and foolish mouth, and paws so enormous that he resembled a pup on snowshoes. And he had none of the dignity and aloof tolerance of the pedigreed dogs whom Terry had rejected; he laughed at them and wagged at them and barked an ill-bred joyful bark.

"That," objected the clerk, "is a mongrel, I'm afraid. We are exhibiting him only out of deference to the widow of a country customer. I really shouldn't care to recommend him."

"But he's a sweet dog!" wailed Terry. "He's the one I want!"

"Very well, then, my fine young gentleman, you get no

dog at all, if you're going to be so dog-gone *common!*"
raged Bessie, and she dragged the protesting Terry from
the shop and hastened to the Hotel Picardie.

Bessie telephoned to those unseen powers that somewhere in the mysterious heart of every hotel regulate all
human destinies, "Will you please send up a bell boy at
once?"

"A bell boy? Oh, a page!"

"Well, whatever you want to call him."

There appeared at her suite a small boy whom she immediately longed to put on the stage. He was red-headed,
freckle-faced, and he carried his snub nose high and cockily. He wore a skin-tight blue uniform with a row of brass
buttons incredibly close together, and on the corner of his
head rode an impudent pill-box cap of soldierly scarlet.

"Yes, madame?" He was obviously trying not to grin,
in pure good fellowship, and when Terry grinned, the
page's cockney mug was wreathed with smiling.

"What is your name?" demanded Bessie.

"Bundock, madame."

"Heavens, you can't call a person Bundock! What are
you called at home?"

"Ginger, madame."

"Well, Ginger, this is my son, Master Terry Tait, the
movie—the cinema star."

"Oh, madame, we were told below that Master Tait was
'ere, but I didn't know I'd 'ave the pleasure of seeing him!
I'm familiar with Master Tait in the pictures, if I may say
so, madame."

"All right. Play."

"I beg your pardon?"

"I said play. Play! You are to play with Master Terry."

While Ginger looked dazed, she led the two boys into

Terry's bedroom, pointed an imperial forefinger at the new toys which she had brought home in the taxicab, and loftily left them.

"Gosh, I think it's the limit that this playing business is wished onto you, too!" sighed Terry. "I guess she'll want us to play with the electric train. Do you mind playing with an electric train?"

"I've never before 'ad the opportunity, sir."

"Oh, golly, don't call me 'sir.'"

"Very well, sir."

"What did you play with at home?"

"Well, sir——"

"Terry! Not sir!"

"Well, Master Terry, sir, I 'ad a very nice cricket bat that my uncle 'Ennery made for me, and a wagon made out of a Bass' Ale box, sir, but it didn't go so very well, sir —permit me!"

Terry had begun to open the case containing the electric train. Ginger sprang to help him. As he lifted out an electric locomotive, a dozen railroad carriages which represented the Flying Scotsman in miniature, a station on whose platform a tiny station master waved a flag when the set was connected with the electric-light socket, a tunnel through a conveniently portable mountain, and an even more miraculously portable bridge across a mighty tin river three feet long, Ginger muttered, "I'll be jiggered."

"Do you like them?" marveled Terry.

"Oh! *Like* them, sir!"

"Well, you wouldn't if they gave you one every birthday and Christmas, and you had to run 'em while a bunch of gin-hounds stood around and watched you and said, 'isn't he cute!'"

But Terry was impressed by the admiration of this obviously competent Ginger, this fortunate young man who was allowed to wear brass buttons and live in the joyous informality of kitchens and linen closets. Within fifteen minutes, unanimously elected president and general manager of the Hollywood & Pasadena R. R., Terry was excitedly giving orders to the vice president and traffic manager; trains were darting through tunnels and intelligently stopping at stations; and once there was a delightful accident in which the train ran off the curve, to the anguish of sixteen unfortunate passengers.

"Gee, I do like it when I've got somebody to play with!" marveled Terry. "Say, I wish you could see my dog back home. He's a dandy dog. His name is Corn Beef and Cabbage."

"Really, sir? What breed is 'e?"

"Well, he's kind of an Oklahoma wolfhound, my dad says."

"Oh, yes. Okaloma wolf'ound. I've 'eard of that breed, sir. I say! Let's put one of the passengers on the track, and then the train runs into 'im and we could 'ave a funeral."

"Slick!"

Miss Tingle, the refined lady secretary recommended by the hotel, had arrived at noon, and had been engaged.

"Can you go to work right now?" demanded Bessie. "I'm going to grab off a king!"

"Grab off—a king, madame?"

"Oh, gosh, I don't know why it is! Back in Hollywood, I thought I could sling the King's English all right, but in England, seems like every time I say anything they repeat what I say and register astonishment! I guess I'm kind of a lady Buffalo Bill. Well, let's get to it. Now listen."

She explained the scheme for the capture of publicity by making Terry and King Maximilian chums.

"And just between you and I, I wouldn't kick and holler

much if I got to be buddies with Queen Sidonie. Of course
Terry's publicity comes first. I just sacrifice everything to
that boy. But same time I've seen pictures of Sidonie.
Somehow I just feel (Do you believe in the Higher
Thought?—you know there's a lot of these instincts and
hunches and all like that that you just can't explain by
material explanations)—and somehow I feel that she and
I would be great pals, if we had the chance. Oh, dear!"

Bessie sighed the gentle sigh of a self-immolating
mother.

"It's just fierce the way I've had to submerge my own
personality for my husband and son. But I guess unselfish-
ness never goes unrewarded. So look. We'll just write her a
little letter and send it down by hand. Of course I want to
enclose a card, so's she'll know whom I am. Which of these
cards would do the trick better, do you think?"

One of the two cards was a highly restrained document:
merely "Mrs. T. Benescoten Tait," in engraved script.
But the other card was baroque. It was impressive. It announced:

> *Mr. & Mrs. T. Benescoten Tait*
> *Pop and Mom of*
> *TERRY TAIT*
> *The King of Boy Comedians*
> *Star of "Kids Is Kids," "Wee Waifs o' Dockland,"*
> *"A Child of the Midnight," etc.*
>
> *Castello Marino*　　　　　　　　　　　*Poppy Peaks, Cal.*

It was embossed in red, blue, silver, and canary-yellow,
and while it was slightly smaller than a motor-license plate,
it was much more striking.

"Now maybe this colored one ain't as society as the
other, but don't you think Her Majesty would be more
likely to notice it?" said Bessie anxiously.

Miss Tingle was terrified yet fascinated. "I've never,"

she gasped, "had the privilege of communicating with a queen, but if I may say so, I fancy the plainer card would be more suitable, madame."

"Oh, I suppose so. But the big card cost a lot of money. Well, now, will you take dictation on a letter? I suppose the old gal reads English?"

"Oh, I understand that Their Majesties write and speak six languages."

"Well, I'd be satisfied with one. When I get back home I'm going to hire some Britisher to learn me to talk snooty. Well, here goes. Take this down:

"Her Majesty, the Queen of Slovaria.
"Dear Madame:
"I guess you will be surprised at receiving this letter from a total stranger, but I am a neighbor of yours, having the suite right above yours here in the hotel. And probably you have heard of my son, Mr. Terry Tait, the well-known boy actor in the movies—no, make that cinema, Miss Tingle—and I hope that maybe your boy, King Maximilian, has seen him in some of his celebrated films, such as 'Please Buy a Paper,' or 'Give Me a Penny, Mister.'

"He is here with me in London, and every hour he says to me, 'Ma, I'm just crazy to meet this boy king, Maximilian, he being my own age, which is ten, etc.'

"As your boy is a king, and as folks in many lands have been kind enough to call Terry the King of Boy Actors, I thought maybe it would be nice if the two could get together and compare notes, etc. I would be very pleased to give him and you lunch or tea or dinner or a cocktail or whatever would be convenient for you and though of course Terry has many dates, having to lecture to the Lads' Brigade, etc., we would try to keep any date that you might set.

"But I am afraid we'll have to make it in the next few days, as Terry's Public in Paris is begging for him.

"So if you could just ring me up here in Suite Five-B any time that's handy for you, we can arrange details, etc.

"Hoping you are in the best of health, I am Yours sincerely.

"As soon as you get that typed—I've had 'em bring up a machine and stick it in my bedroom—get a bell boy to hustle it right down to Siddy's suite. We gotta get action. Shoot!"

And Bessie scampered happily out to the foyer to hire a maid, and to engage for Terry a lugubrious valet.

His name was Humberstone. He had, of course, never served anyone of lesser degree than a duke, and he would require two pounds extra a week to associate with Americans. He got it. He was worth it. Even a boy king from Slovaria would be impressed by Humberstone's egg-shaped head.

Bessie proudly let this four-pounds-a-week worth of noble valet into the bedroom. On the floor, extremely linty, sat two small boys whom Humberstone eyed with malevolence. Ginger quaked. Terry looked irritated.

"Sonny dear, this is your new valet," crooned Bessie, with a maternal sweetness alarming to her well-trained son.

Humberstone eyed the railwaymen with the eye of an ogre who liked little boys nicely fried, with onion sauce. Under that smug glare, the first excited gayety that Terry had shown these many weeks died out.

"Oh, I don't need a valet, Mother!"

"And who, Master Smarty, do you think is going to look out for your clothes? You certainly don't expect me to, I hope! Humberstone, you can sleep here in this dressing room. Now get busy and press Master Terry's clothes."

When Humberstone had gone out with an armful of clothes and when Bessie had left them, the two playmates sat on a couch, too dispirited to go on happily wrecking trains.

"Gee, that's fierce, that man-eating valet," confided Terry.

"Right you are. 'E's 'orrible," said his friend Ginger.

"He's a big stiff!"

"'E is that! 'E's an old buffins."

"It's fierce, Ginger. We won't stand it!"

"It is that, Terry. We won't!"

"We'll run away. To Poppy Peaks!"

"Is that your ranch?"

Now when Terry comes to Heaven's gate and has to explain to Saint Peter the extreme untruth of what he said about bears and the wild free life of the ranches, let us trust that the wise old saint will understand that Terry had long been overadmired for silly things like having cherubic lips and silky hair, and never been admired for the proper things, such as the ability to ride mustangs, lasso steers and shoot Indians, which, unquestionably, he would have demonstrated if only he had ever been nearer a ranch than Main Street, Los Angeles.

"Yes, sure, it's our ranch. Gee, I'm going to get Mother to invite you there. We live in a big log cabin, and every night, gee, you can hear the grizzly bears howling!"

"My word! I say, did you ever shoot a grizzly bear?"

"Oh, not awful many, but couple of times."

"Tell me about it. Were you with Will Rogers or Hoot Gibson?"

"Both of them. There was Bill and Hoot and Doug Fairbanks and—uh—and there was Will Beebe, the nachalist, and we all went up camping in the—uh—in the Little Bighorn Valley—that's on our ranch, Poppy Peaks—and one night I was sleeping out in the sagebrush, all rolled up in my blankets, and I woke up and I heard something going snuffle-snuffle-snuffle, and I looked up and there was a great, big, tall, huge figger——"

"My 'at!"

"—just like a great, big, enormous man, only twict as big, and like he had an awful' thick fur coat, and gee,

I was scared, but I reached out my hand and I grabbed my dad's rifle, and I aimed—I just took a long careful aim——"

"My word!"

"—and I let her go, *bang!* and the bear he fell—no, at first he didn't fall right down dead, but he kind of staggered like he was making for me——"

"My aunt!"

"—but my shot'd woke up everybody, and Harold Lloyd, no, Richard Bart'lemess it was—he grabbed up his gun and he shot and the bear fell down right beside me, with its awful hot breath stirring my hair, and then it just flopped a couple of times and *bing!* it was dead!"

"My!"

"But I bet you've had some adventures, Ginger. Don't all English kids go to sea as cabin boys?"

"Well, me, I never 'ad time to, not exactly. But me uncle, Uncle 'Ennery Bundock, now there's a man, Terry, that's after your own 'eart. Adventures? Why, Uncle 'Ennery 'as 'ad more adventures than the Prince of Wales! 'E was a cabin boy, 'e was! Why, one time 'e was out in the South Seas and the ship 'e was on was wrecked, it was, it ran into a w'ale, a monstrous big w'ale, and it busted the forward keelson, and that wessel, it began to sink immejitly, oh, something shocking, and me uncle swam ashore, four miles it was, through them seas simply infected with sharks, and 'e come ashore, only me own age, twelve, 'e was then, but many's the time 'e's told me, six foot 'e stood in 'is stocking feet.

"And there on shore was a fee-rocious band of nekked savages but—well, 'e 'ad a burning glass in 'is clothes, and 'e 'eld it up, and them poor ignorant savages, they didn't know what it was, and then 'e acted like 'e didn't even see 'em, and 'e stuck that burning glass over a pile of driftwood, and the wood caught fire, and them savages all gave one 'orrible shriek, and they all ran away, and so that's 'ow 'e got to be their king."

"Is he still their king?"

"'Im? Uncle 'Ennery? No fear! 'E 'ad other things to do, 'e 'ad, and when 'e got tired of being king, 'e up and made 'isself a canoe out of a log and sailed away and—and 'e stood for Parliament in the Sandwich Islands!"

"Tell me some more!" cried Terry.

But their ardor was interrupted by the return of the formidable Humberstone, and then Bessie whisked in with, "You can go now, Ginger. Terry! Wash your hands. Lunch."

"Mother! I want Ginger to come play with me every day!"

"Well, perhaps; we'll see. Now be snappy. This afternoon we might—we might have some important visitors. Most important!"

For two days Bessie awaited a reply to her note to Queen Sidonie, but from the royal fastnesses she had no murmur.

London mildly discovered that the King of Boy Comedians was in town. A special writer from a newspaper which had been Americanized came to interview Terry on the contrasting spiritual values of baseball vs. cricket, his favorite poem, and the cooking of Brussels sprouts.

He addressed the Lads' Brigade, and that was nothing to write about. And he received six hundred and eighteen letters from people who were willing to let him pay for their mortgages and their surgical operations.

But for most of the two days he sneaked into corners and tried to look inconspicuous while, in the living room of the suite, Bessie stalked and glared, and in his bedroom Humberstone the valet glared and stalked. Ginger was sum-

moned to play, but Bessie so raged at their noise that the
two infants made a pirates' den behind Terry's bed, where
Ginger chronicled his uncle 'Ennery Bundock's adventures
as steward and bartender to a celebrated arctic expedition
—"'Bring me a whisky-soda, me man,' says Sir John
Peary, and Uncle 'Ennery brings it, and standing there
Sir John drinks a toast to the North Pole, and 'e says to
me uncle, ''Ennery, we'd never 've discovered it but for your
splendid service'"—and 'Ennery's astonishing experiences
during the Great War when, as a British spy, he reached
the Imperial Palace in Berlin and talked with the Kaiser,
who, such was Uncle 'Ennery's cunning, took him for a
Turkish ally.

If anything more than Ginger's freckled grin had been
needed to make Terry adore him, it would have been the
privilege of meeting the relative of so spirited a hero as
Uncle 'Ennery Bundock.

With Terry in Ginger's care, Bessie was able to give herself up whole-heartedly to worrying about failure to receive an answer from Queen Sidonie, to worrying about
what Rabbit might be doing by his lone wicked self in
Hollywood, and to being manicured, massaged, dress-
fitted, hat-fitted, and generally enjoying herself. On the
afternoon of the second day, she fretted only a little when
Terry, with Ginger, seemed to be missing. But when they
had been missing for two hours, she realized with sudden
horror that Terry was lost in the wilds.

It was some comfort to think that there would be front-
page stories even in the London papers, which have their
first pages on the third page, but she did hope he wouldn't
be late for dinner. With all the devotion of a mother and
the efficiency of a true American, she telephoned first to
the newspapers and second to Scotland Yard.

Just as the happy reporters and cameramen arrived,

she heard a slight squealing back in Terry's room and dashed out to find that Terry had sheepishly sneaked in the back way, accompanied by a yet more sheepish Ginger and by a very sheep of sheeps—a large irregular-shaped dog of a predominating hue of brown, streaked and striped and spotted with black, white, yellow, and plain dirt. He had a broad back, built for boys to ride upon, a tail that wagged foolishly, and an eye that looked with fond ecstasy upon the two boys, but with alarm upon the ineffable Humberstone.

"Good heavens!" wailed Bessie. "That's that horrible animal I told you you couldn't have!"

"Oh, no, Mother! *That*"—with vast scorn—"was just a collie-police-dog, with terrier blood, but this is a pure-bred Margate Wader. The man *said* so! And his name is Josephus. The dog's. And the man wanted to charge me ten shillings, but Ginger got him for me for eighteen-pence and that autographed picture of Fred Stone."

"Oh," groaned Bessie, "to think that I should have a son that's common! It's funny, but you're just like your father. But I haven't got time to talk about that now. Listen! The reporters are here! You were lost! You gotta tell 'em—a man tried to kidnap you, but Ginger—he'd happened to see you once in the hotel, and of course he knew who you were, and he was coming along, and he persuaded you not to go with this man—he looked like a Bolshevik. Get that? Snappy now!"

With maternal pride, she heard Terry admit to the reporters how reckless he had been in wandering through the foggy city. Ginger, called on for further details, loyally brought in his uncle 'Ennery Bundock—it seemed that Uncle 'Ennery Bundock had once served in the Czar's Imperial Guard, and was an authority on Bolsheviks; it was he who had recognized the Soviet spy and rescued Terry.

The reporters raised their eyebrows and went away, most politely. Next morning, Bessie was up at seven, clamoring for all the newspapers. Terry's awful escape was mentioned in only one of them, in the column of Mr. Swannen Haffer:

After, so it is asserted, frequently associating with gunmen and like underworld characters of San Francisco, Bangor, and other western cities of the United States, Terence Tate, the American boy cinema actor, discovered that Brighter London is delightfully beginning to realize the perils of his native land. Strolling from his hotel yesterday, Master Tate, whose mother has interestingly compared his art to that of Sir Henry Irving, Sir Johnston Forbes-Robertson, and Eleonora Duse, contrived so thoroughly to lose himself in the trackless wilds of Pall Mall that it was necessary to send out an expedition of hotel servants, equipped with wireless, ice axes, and tinned walrus meat, to discover and rescue him.

Master Tate, with that shrewd perception which has so endeared all Yankee filmaturgy to the naïve British heart, discovered a band of red Indians encamped in front of the Carlton Club, and a band of Bolshevik spies, disguised as bishops but concealing bombs under their aprons, lurking on the roof of the Atheneum. Master Tate's horrendous discoveries have been conveyed to Scotland Yard, and it is to be hoped that thanks to the young hero—who is only six years old; in fact, so young that his mother permits him to have only three motor cars—London will presently be made almost as safe as his native Chicago.

Bessie spoke for half an hour without stopping. It did not soothe her particularly to find, in every newspaper, a two-column account of the children's party given by the little Princess Elizabeth, with King Maximilian of Slovaria as honor guest, and the announcement that within a week Sidonie and Maximilian were to accompany the

British Royal Family to Sandringham Hall, in Norfolk.

The house party, said the announcement, would be informal, and limited to intimate friends of the Family.

Somehow—she could not explain why—that seemed to Bessie Tait, of Poppy Peaks, to shut her out more than any account of a grand public entertainment.

A week! She was desperate.

And if the British press wasn't to be roused by Terry's ghastly kidnaping, what could a lady do? All day she galloped up and down her suite, raging at her maid, at Humberstone, even at Miss Tingle, the refined lady secretary. The cheerful sounds of Terry, Ginger, and Josephus the Margate Wader, from Terry's room, the sound of yelps and giggles and tremendous chasings after a tennis ball, irritated her the more; made her forget the small voice within her that whispered, "Now be careful, Bess—don't monkey with the buzz saw."

"Oh, shut up!" she said to the alarmed mentor and, sending Miss Tingle to buy stationery which she didn't need, the maid to buy hair nets which she never used, and Humberstone to go back to his room and continue doing nothing save look impressive, she dashed to the telephone and snarled, "I want to speak to Suite Four-B."

"I'm sorry, madame, but I can't connect you with that apartment. It's taken by the Queen of Slovaria."

"Good Lord, don't you suppose I know that? The Queen and I are great friends."

"Very sorry, madame, but I have my orders. I can connect you with the bureau of Count Elopatak, Her Majesty's equerry."

Bessie was puzzled as to why one should be connected telephonically with a bureau, an object which to her was firmly associated with Mr. Rabbit Tait's collars and pink silk undergarments, and equally puzzled as to what an equerry did for a living. "Sounds like a horse—and at that, I guess a horse is about the only bird connected with Her Maj that I'm going to get to talk to," she reflected tragically, but she said meekly, "Very well, I'll speak to his countship."

She then spoke in turn, so far as she could later make out, with an American who was breeches buyer for Eglantine, Katz and Kominsky, of Cleveland, Ohio, and who seemed to have no connection whatever with the Royal House of Slovaria; with an Englishwoman who appeared to be the stenographer to the secretary of the equerry; to the secretary of the equerry; to an indignant Englishman who asserted that he was no Slovarian equerry but, on the contrary, a coffee planter from British Guiana; to Count Elopatak, and at last to a man with a swart and bearded voice who admitted to being the secretary of Queen Sidonie.

But he didn't seem to care for telephoning. He kept making sounds as though he were about to hang up, and Bessie held him only by a string of such ejaculations as, "Now you must get this clear!" and "This is very important!"

Hadn't Her Majesty, Bessie demanded, received the letter from Mrs. T. Benescoten Tait, of California, mother of the celebrated——

Yes, the secretary seemed to remember some such letter but of course letters from strangers were never considered.

Well, then, she was willing to take the matter up over the phone.

Take up *what* matter? There were no matters, thank heaven, which had to be taken up!

But had they asked His Young Majesty whether he might not like to meet the celebrated boy——

His Majesty cared to meet no one and really, if Madame would be so kind, there were innumerable affairs of the most pressing necessity and—click!

This time Bessie expressed her opinion in a subdued manner. "But I'm not licked yet. I've got an Idea!"

When Mrs. T. Benescoten Tait had an Idea, Hollywood sat up and looked nervous, but the gray welter of city beyond the windows of the Hotel Picardie looked strangely indifferent.

"Of course, none of her hired men—equerries or whatever fancy names they want to call themselves—would understand it, but I'll bet Sidonie herself would be tickled pink to get some high-class publicity! It's just a matter of getting to her and explaining it," considered Bessie. "And we'd have such a nice time talking about our boys. Well, then, on the job—get past all these darn watchdogs."

She marched into Terry's bedroom. She chased Ginger out of the room, shut Josephus the Margate Wader in Humberstone's room, and remarked to Terry with a maternal sweetness which caused him to look alarmed and suspicious, "Come, my little mannie, put on your Fauntleroy suit; we're going to see Queen Sidonie!"

Now deep and dark and terrible as was Terry's hatred for the polo costume, it was as love and loyalty compared with his detestation of the Little Lord Fauntleroy suit, with its velvet jacket, velvet breeches, buckled slippers and lace collar. He protested. He wailed, while from beyond the door Josephus wailed with him—and furiously started to chew Humberstone's respectable slippers.

With a considerable drop in tenderness, Bessie snarled, "Now, we'll have no more out of you! Good Lord! I work myself to the bone trying to give you a chance in life! I work and slave to have you meet the real *bon ton*, like kings and queens, and not a lot of these Hollywood bums, and then you won't act nice like I tell you to! Terry Tait, I haven't punished you for some time, but unless you put on the nice Fauntleroy suit, and act nice and gentlemanly, why, I'll just nachly snatch you bald-headed, jhear me?"

In the case of Mr. Rabbit Benescoten Tait, Terry had seen his mother's rare ability to snatch people bald-headed and, sobbing slightly, he took off the honest boy-town tweed suit he was wearing and began to force himself into the abomination of lace and black velvet.

Out of the door, down the corridor, about to meet a queen—about to meet the first woman who might prove to be her own equal—marched Mrs. T. Benescoten Tait.

Bessie had, in a week of London, learned that really cultured and cosmopolitan people called candy "sweets," called trolley cars "trams," called hotel clerks "reception clerks," called six bits "three bob," and, most especially, called an elevator a "lift." Thus it was no common and uneducated elevator but an exotic lift that they took, and it was to a lift attendant that Bessie murmured charmingly, with just a touch of a Mechanicville French accent, "We'll stop at the *catriem étage*—oh, how fonny!—I mean the fourt' floor, please."

"Very sorry, madame, but that floor is reserved. I am not permitted to stop there."

"Say, don't you suppose I know it's reserved for the Slovarian royal party? It's them I'm going to see!"

The lift attendant had stopped the lift (or elevator or *ascenseur*) just below the fourth floor. He was a bright lift boy of sixty-five. He said unhappily, "I'm sorry, madame, but I'm not permitted to let anyone off on the fourth floor unless they are recognized or are accompanied by someone from the royal entourage."

"Rats! I tell you they're expecting me! Look at this!"

This was a pound note. The lift attendant looked on it regretfully, but he sighed. "Very sorry, madame—much as my position is worth," and shot the lift down to the ground floor.

"All right, then; you can take us back to the fifth floor," said Bessie.

Terry turned toward their suite, but his mother snapped, "Where do you think you're going?" and marched him toward the onyx-and-crystal front staircase from their floor down to the fourth, the royal floor.

As they elegantly emerged on the sacred corridor, they were confronted by one of the largest, tallest, most ruddy-faced bobbies in the entire British police force. He too was sorry, and he too explained that he could not let strangers approach Their Majesties.

Bessie wasted no words on so rude a fellow. She marched upstairs again. "If they think they can stop *me!* There's nothing I won't do for the sake of my poor little son!" she moaned and, grabbing the poor little son, she marched him to the east end of their corridor.

Now at the east end Bessie had noted a flight of slate-tread stairs, presumably intended for servants and as a fire escape.

At the foot of the stairs stood the same bobby whom she had just met.

"Now then! 'Ave I got to run you in?" he growled.

With one proud glance she marched back upstairs.

For half an hour she cried on her bed, raging at the tyrants who insulted a mother who was trying to give her son a chance to get along in the world. Then she rose, powdered, and stalked into Terry's room, where he had already changed from the nice Fauntleroy suit into khaki shirt and shorts. He sat behind a couch, arguing with Josephus.

"Now look here, young man, I'm going out, and if you

stir one foot out of this suite, you and me will have a little talk this evening, jhear me!"

She marched out, singularly like the Fifth Cavalry on the trail of the Apaches.

Terry telephoned for Ginger. In blessed quiet and lack of maternal care, the two small boys and the one large dog became happy again. Liberally interpreting the boundaries of the suite, which Terry was not to leave, as including the corridor, they laid out the electric railway from Edinburgh (opposite Room 597) to South Africa (overlooking the canyon of the back stairs).

And while they reveled, Bessie was at the American Embassy, successively failing to see the ambassador, the counselor, the first and second secretaries, and finally, with indignation at this neglect of her Rights as an American Citizen, hearing the third secretary murmur:

"I greatly sympathize with you, but I'm afraid it would be hard to get the chief to feel that you have been insulted and that the State Department ought to cable Slovaria. Suppose some complete stranger were to come to your studio in Hollywood while Terry was making the most important scenes of a new picture, and should want to go right in—would he be admitted?"

"But that's entirely different! Terry isn't a stranger!"

"But he might be to the Slovarians."

"Well, I've heard a lot about how ignorant these Europeans are, but you can't make me believe that even the Slovarians haven't heard about Terry Tait, the King of Boy Comedians!"

The third secretary rose with a manner which was familiar to Bessie from her first job-hunting days in Los Angeles. He observed silkily, "Dreadfully sorry, but I'm afraid we can't do a thing in this matter. But if we can help you about passports . . ."

As Bessie walked disconsolately away from the Embassy she groaned, "I guess the game's up! We ain't going to meet any queen. My poor little boy! They won't raise him to four grand a week, after all. And I won't be able to buy that steam yacht! . . . The dirty snobs, that care more for red tape than for a mother's heart! Say, why wouldn't that make a swell title for Terry's next movie after 'His Majesty, Junior'? 'A Mother's Heart'!"

Terry, Ginger, and Josephus, the managers of the Edinburgh, South Africa and Peking R. R., were repairing a wreck and gleefully counting the temporarily dead passengers beside the slaty African caverns of what would, to unenlightened adult eyes, have seemed the back stairs.

Up those crevasses crept a small boy, obviously English, a boy with black hair, a cheery nose of a cocky Irish tilt, and gray flannels. He was of Terry's age.

"Hello!" he said.

"'Ello yourself," observed Ginger grandly.

"I'm going up to the top floor and I'm going to slide down all the banisters all the way down," confided the stranger.

"You better be careful on the floor below this. Some king's got it. There's a lot of cops there. How'd you ever get by 'em?" demanded Terry.

"I waited till they weren't looking, and slipped past 'em. Oh, I say, what a lovely train!"

He seemed a nice lad, and with much cordiality Terry urged, "Wouldn't you like to play train with us?"

"Oh, I'd love it!" cried the stranger. "I say, this is ripping! I've run away from my family. They want me to go to parties and have my picture taken."

"Isn't it fierce!" sympathized Terry.

"If you must 'ave your picture taken," Ginger remarked

oracularly, "you just tell your old lady to take you to Gumbridge's, on Great St. Jever Street, Whitechapel; 'e'll do you 'andsome—six bob a dozen."

"Oh, thank you very much indeed. I'll tell my mother. May I—would you mind if I started the train just once?"

The new boy was so enthusiastic about the signal system, he so fervently enjoyed the most sanguinary wrecks, that Ginger and Terry adopted him as a third musketeer, and Terry urged, "If you like it, come into my room. I've got some other things there."

The new boy gazed in awe at the electrical Derby race and the electrical Colosseum with the lions charmingly devouring Early Christians.

"I've just never *seen* such things," he sighed.

"What do you play with at home?" asked Terry.

"Why, we live in the country most of the year, and I ride and swim and play tennis and—and—that's about all. You see, I have ever such a stern tutor, and he keeps me at work so much. But—oh, I have a bicycle, too!"

Ginger and Terry exchanged glances of pity for their unfortunate new friend, and Terry said comfortingly, "But still, it must be slick to ride horseback on these English roads—not get jounced all to pieces like I do when I ride on the ranch."

"You ride on a ranch? I *thought* you were American!"

"Yes. I'm in the movies."

The stranger startled them with his scream: "Now I know! I knew you looked familiar! You're Terry Tait! I've seen you in the pictures. I loved 'em! Oh, I am so glad to meet you!"

The boys shook hands, while Ginger beamed and Josephus wagged with appreciation, and Terry said generously, "But you Englishers don't care for my stuff like they do at home. I guess I ain't so much as——"

"But honestly, Terry—if I may call you that?"

"Sure, kid."

"But I'm not English—at least only an eighth English. I'm Slovarian."

"With that Slovarian bunch with King Maximilian downstairs?"

"Yes. I'm Maximilian."

"Oh, go-*wan!* You don't look like a king! You look like a regular kid!"

"Blimey!" groaned Ginger, "I believe 'e is the king, Terry! I seen 'is pictures!"

"Gee," wailed Terry, "and I thought kings always wore tights and carried swords!"

"I'm frightfully sorry, Terry. Honestly, I hate being a king! It's just beastly! I have to learn six languages, and all about taxation and diplomacy and history and all those things—and I just want to play and be let alone! And they're always trying to assassinate me!"

"Jiminy! Honest?" breathed Terry.

"Yes; I've been shot at three times this year, and really, I don't like it a bit."

"Say, gee, Your Majesty has got to excuse me if I got fresh with you."

"Oh, please, won't you call me 'Max'?"

"Thunder! You can't call a king 'Max.' You call him 'Your Majesty,' or 'Sire.'"

"No, you don't! Not in private life."

"Well, gosh, I ought to know! I've read *A Gentleman of France* and a lot like that."

"Well, I ought to know. I'm a king!"

"But you haven't been a king long!"

"That's so. But anyway—oh, please call me 'Max.' Honestly, Terry, I'm so frightfully pleased to have met you. I've always been eager to know you ever since I saw you as the cabin boy in 'The Burning Deck.' I say! That was simply ripping where you had that idea about dropping one end of the hose in the ocean and putting out the fire whence all but you had fled. Jove, you must have led the most perilous life!"

"Oh. That! That scene with the hose was taken in the studio. The fire wasn't nothing but some oily waste in pails. No. I never did anything dangerous. Dog-gone it! My mother won't let me!"

"Oh, Terry! Look! When we grow up, and I get to be a *real* king, and my mother and Sebenéco (he's the prime minister) and Professor Michelowsky (he's my tutor)—when I'm of age and they can't govern me any longer, will you be my Commander in Chief?"

"Well, I wouldn't mind, Max." In a sudden consideration of his own troubles, it is to be feared that Terry forgot he was addressing a king. "Anyway, I'd certainly like to get out of the movies. You talk about your troubles—say, you don't know how turble it is to be a movie star. Awful!

"I have to give interviews, and every time I go out of the house somebody is there horning in, trying to photograph me, and I have to wear trick clothes—oh, horrible clothes!—and old ladies come and stroke my hair, and I have to listen while they tell me what a dandy actor I am—and honest, Max, I'm fierce, and now I've got to meet the king of—— Oh, golly, I forgot! You *are* the king!"

"Yes, hang it!"

"It's fierce!"

"It is, by Jove!" mourned Maximilian.

"I wish we could run away and find some nice farmhouse and just be kids there, and feed the pigs!"

"Rather! Wouldn't I like to!"

So engrossed was Terry in Maximilian that he had not realized that Ginger was standing stiffly at attention.

"Oh, jiminy, I forgot to introduce Mr. Ginger Bundock, Max—Your Majesty."

Then Ginger was kneeling, kissing Maximilian's hand.

"Oh, I say, please don't do that!" begged Maximilian.

"An Englishman, sir, knows wot's befitting to a Royal Majesty!" protested Ginger.

"Oh, chuck it, will you!"

"Right you are, sir!"

And the three small boys, actor and king and page, started to play with the delightful assassinations of the Early Christians in the model of the Colosseum and, aside from a profuse buttering of the conversation with "sirs," Ginger was not uncomfortably obsequious to these great men. Indeed, apropos of Terry's further complaint that it was awful to have to retake a scene twenty times, Ginger complained darkly, "If I may say so, sir, an 'otel page 'asn't too cheery a time, you know. There's old gentlemen that get very drunk, sir, and expects you to bounce out and buy 'em clean shirts after all the shops is closed, and there's old ladies that gets you into their rooms and asks you, 'Are you saved?' and——"

Maximilian interrupted, "Then we ought all three to run away and——"

"And be pirates!"

"Splendid!" said Maximilian.

"Uncle 'Ennery Bundock used to be a pirate!" yearned Ginger.

From the next room flared a voice, "Good heavens, Marie, I *told* you to send that dress down to be pressed."

Maximilian quaked, "Oh, it's my mother! She's looking for me."

"No," said Terry, looking pale. "It's mine."

"Erp!" said Josephus.

Bessie entered the room swiftly, glanced at Maximilian

and cried, "Good heavens, can't I leave you for one moment without your picking up a lot of ragtag and bobtail? Who's this brat? Send him home. We're going to pack and go to Paris."

"Mother! This is King Maximilian of Slovaria!"

Bessie's eyes darted like humming birds. From her fluttered expression it might be judged that she was recalling the rotogravure pictures of the boy king. She gasped at Maximilian, "Oh, I'm so sorry I spoke mean to you! Honestly, are you the king?"

"I'm afraid so!"

"I guess I ought to call you 'Your Majesty,' but I met you so sort of sudden and—uh—— Did your mother know you were coming up here, King?"

"I'm afraid not. I rather ran away."

"Oh, my gracious, then she'll be worried to death. I must take you right down to her. But we'd be real pleased to have you come up here and play whenever you get the time. Come on, Terry; we'll go down with His Majesty. And you, Ginger—you beat it!"

Hesitatingly, glancing at each other like conspirators but ruled by Bessie's clanging voice, the two royalties sheepishly followed her, not to the surreptitious back stairs but to the haughty flight in front. At her former enemy, the bobby, on guard on the floor below, Bessie snarled, "I'm with His Majesty," and stalked past him.

"I guess I better take you right to your mother, King, so's she'll know you're all safe," beamed Bessie.

"Oh, I'm—— Honestly, I'm afraid she might not like it. Mother always has a massage and rests from tea time to dinner, and she doesn't like to be disturbed. Thank you very much for coming with me, but I can take care of myself now."

"Well, I thought, seeing I'm right here—it won't be a bit of trouble; I have a few minutes to spare, and maybe we won't go to Paris tomorrow, after all—I thought it might be nice if I could arrange for you to play with Terry again."

"Oh, I would like that! Perhaps we'd better see Count Elopatak. He's in charge of most of my arrangements. He'll be here in Room 416."

Bessie saw that along the corridor doors were opening, curious heads popping out. A tremendous functionary in plush breeches, yellow waistcoat and powdered wig was bearing down. Seizing Terry's hand, she followed Maximilian into 416. It was a bedroom converted into an office. At a desk was a tall, black-mustached man with a monocle.

He spoke to Maximilian in a strange tongue; the king answered.

Coming out from behind the desk, the monocled one bowed and observed, "It is very kind of you, Madame Tait, to have brought back His Majesty. And now if I may haf the pleasure of escorting you upstairs—— My name is Elopatak; I am a gentleman-in-waiting to Their Majesties."

"I'm pleased to meet you, Count. I think I've talked to you on the phone."

"I believe I do remember having that pleasure!" Very dryly.

Elopatak looked embarrassed as Bessie ardently shook his hand and crowed, "I want you to meet my boy, Terry. You've probably seen him in the cinema."

"Oh! Oh, yes. Quite."

"Terry and His Majesty got along just lovely, and I thought it was nice, both of them being famous like they

are, to get together like this. You had a good time, didn't
you, King?"

"Oh, thank you very much."

"And I thought it would be just lovely—both boys
would prize it so much in after years—if we had a news
photographer take a few nice pictures of 'em playing together. I guess both their Publics would be tickled to see
'em."

Elopatak cried, all in one word, "Butmydearmadame-
thatwouldbequiteimpossibleohquite!"

"But look here! They like each other."

"My dear madame, I'm afraid you cannot possibly
understand that a royal personage has to consider many
things besides his own preferences, and while I am sure
His Majesty found your son delightful, as he is, you see he
must represent Slovaria, and to be paraded in the cinema
would not be dignified. . . .

"Maximilian! I hope you have not forgotten that you
are to be taken to a Workmen's Club this afternoon by
Prince Henry. I'm very sorry, but it's your mother's request, and I'm afraid you must dash in and dress for it at
once!"

The king looked patiently melancholy. He shook hands
with Bessie and with Terry; he murmured, "I do hope
I shall see you again," and marched slowly out.

Bessie was clamoring, "But look here! Queen Sidonie
would understand how I mean. After all, there's only one
heart that can understand and do for a small boy, and
that's his mother, so if I could see her and explain——"

"Her Majesty is resting, and she has every moment
filled until Their Majesties go to Sandringham next Saturday. So if I may escort you upstairs——"

This time Elopatak did not offer his arm to Bessie; he
took hers, firmly. Bessie saw that there was danger of a

scene which might get into the papers, might ruin her. Stiffly she said, "Thanks; I can find my own way. *Good day!*"

As she clumped upstairs she was touchingly ignorant of what Maximilian and Terry had whispered to each other while she had been talking to Elopatak.

"I hate it all! Now I'll have to go and make b'lieve I'm a king for a lot of people in the East End. I wish I could run away with you!" groaned Maximilian.

"Look, Max! Let's *do* it! I hate being a star. News reels! Having to pose. Let's go be cabin boys on a pirate ship."

"Really? Really run away?"

"Sure; you bet. Look, Max, they watch you all day, but can't you sneak away good and early in the morning? I'll meet you tomorrow morning, by the back stairs, and we'll make plans."

"Yes! I will! But what do you mean by early?"

"Oh, before anybody's up. Eight-thirty. Or is that too early for you? What time do they get you up at home— I mean at the palace?"

"Six."

"What? Six? In the morning? Why, you poor kid!"

"Then I have to ride an hour before breakfast, and have a cold bath."

"Why, you poor *kid!* Gee, that's fierce! Gosh, I guess being kings is even worse 'n being actors! But I bet you eat one darn' big breakfast after that."

"Oh, yes. Cocoa and sometimes three rolls!"

"Don't you get any ham and eggs?"

"For *breakfast?* Oh, one couldn't eat eggs for breakfast!"

"Say, in Poppy Peaks I eat six flapjacks and about six steen millions of gallons of maplsirup!"

"But," in rather a worried way, "I'm afraid they'll make us get up very early on a pirate ship."

"Naw! Didn't I see 'em making 'Yo, Ho, Ho'? Pirates always drink rum all night, and they wear silk, and they don't get up till noon anyway. Look! Quick! I'll be there—back stairs—six tomorrow."

Max was politely shaking hands with the Taits and making exit; but his hands were held behind him and he was showing six fingers.

Bessie was cross and hopeless-looking, all that evening. They were to have gone to the theater, but Bessie said shortly that they would stay home—she had some plans she had to think about.

Terry's chief difficulty that evening was getting hold of Ginger. His mother had explained, adequately, that Ginger was a roughneck, if indeed not an alley cat, and it was *time* she *did* something about Terry's taste for low *company* and where he *got* it, she couldn't *see*—and his father was *just* as bad.

By bribing the chambermaid to call Ginger, Terry was able to meet him for a second at the elevator.

"Look! Ginger! Be up here tomorrow, six in the morning. Max'll be here. We're going to run away; going to be pirates. Understand—*six!*"

"I'll be there, Gaffer! I'm not on duty till eight—I live out—but I'll sleep in a linen closet 'ere tonight, swelp me Bob!"

It was only because his mind was charged with the thought that he was going to run away now and lead the jaunty life of a pirate that Terry managed to awake at a quarter to six. He slipped into blue knickers and a blue jacket, creeping softly about the fog-dimmed room that he might not awaken the snorting Humberstone in the room beyond; he tiptoed down the corridor, followed by Josephus the hound, just as Ginger emerged from an ele-

vator which he had run himself, and as Maximilian slipped
up the darkness of the back stairs.

Terry whispered feverishly, "We *are* going to run away.
Now swear it!"

"I swear!" muttered Maximilian and Ginger.

"Swert!" said Josephus.

"Till death do us part, by jiminy Christmas!"

"Till death do us part!"

"And," croaked Terry, suddenly inspired, "we're going
to start right now."

"Oh, I say, Terry, we couldn't do that! Not—not right
now, without making plans. Boys always make plans before they run away. Lookit Tom Sawyer and Huck," protested Max.

"Am I the boss of this gang?"

Maximilian said humbly, admiringly, "Yes, Terry,
but——"

"Am I, Ginger; am I, hey?"

"Ra-ther!"

"Didn't you," Terry demanded of Maximilian, "have
some trouble getting up here this morning?"

"Yes. I did. I met a policeman patrolling the hall. He
didn't dare say anything, but I know he watched me. I'm
afraid he'll go wake old Elopatak."

"Do you see? Just as I've told you," crowed Terry.
"Next time we may not be able to get together at all.
We'll start right now, this minute. Bimeby we'll write nice
letters to our mothers—and my, they'll be proud as anything when we come back from pirating and give 'em par-
rots and ivory and Spanish doubloons and all like that."

"I've got no mother nor no father but I'll give me Spanish doubloons to me uncle 'Ennery—'e used to be a pirate
'isself—'e says it's a rare life. I fancy we'll find a good
pirate ship at Bristol," said Ginger, in a judicious way.

"Come! We'll start! Ginger'll take us down to the basement and show us how to sneak out," commanded Terry.

"But I *say*," protested Maximilian, "we have no money."

"Haven't we, though?" Terry jeered. "Lookit! Here's fifty pounds Mother gave me. I was to give it to the Infants' Charitable and Rehabilitation Institution today . . . It *would* be good publicity, at that. Pictures of me giving each kid a pound. Still, I guess pirates don't go out for publicity much. Not anyway when they're running away from their mothers. Come on, *will* you?"

And the resolute Terry was followed down the hall, into the elevator, through monastic cellars and corridors and fog-choked areaways, by the uneasy Maximilian and the triumphant Ginger. But as they came out on Berkeley Square, in a wet dawn smelling of coal smoke, broken only by the sound of a one-lunged taxicab, as Maximilian realized that he had escaped from the ardors of kinghood without being captured, while at the same time Ginger realized that he had given up an excellent job and was committing a felony, to wit, stealing and abstracting a valuable piece of property, to wit, one blue uniform, the property of the Hotel Picardie Co., Inc., London W. 1, their attitudes changed. Ginger became uneasy, looking back, trying to whistle, while Max strode on, rising into song, breathing this damp exciting air, peering into this mysterious fog, for the first time an adventurer in a land of boundless freedom, safe from the respectfully disapproving people who every moment watched him.

And as for Josephus, he rushed hither and yon with all the excitement of an honest alley dog who has been released from a satin suite.

Ginger stopped them to hiss, "We must disguise ourselves! Directly the alarm is given, any bobby will know

us. I'm in me uniform, and anyone can see that you two
are gentry."

"Why, Max and I have on awful' simple suits! Nobody
would ever notice 'em," insisted Terry.

For once, Ginger was pleasantly able to be superior.
"Simple, me eye! You may know all about courts and the
likes of that, but I know the bobbies." The other two
looked at him humbly, regretting their ignorance, and
Ginger crowed: "I know a place where we can get some
simply 'orrid old clothes. Oh, beautiful! And the man 'e
knows me uncle 'Ennery, and I think I can get 'im to exchange our clothes for old ones without charging us a bob.
Come *on!*"

Ginger led them into the mediterranean mysteries of
Soho. Here, in streets that ran like wounded snakes, was a
world of Italians, Greeks, Spaniards, with a sprinkling of
Chinese and Syrians, dwelling in gloomy low-windowed
flats over restaurants or over sinister-looking chemist
shops with signs in strange peppery languages.

Josephus went hysterical over rubbish piles and push-
carts. Ginger stopped at an old-clothes bazaar on Greek
Street, but at the door he looked terrified.

"Crickey! The lad will remember me uniform! 'E
mustn't see me. You two must get some clothes for me, too;
I'll meet you down at the next alley, and change in the
court be'ind."

Ginger vanished, running. Terry and Maximilian
glanced at each other nervously; nervously they called the
valiant Josephus and stroked him. They could not confess
that they were such weaklings, but neither had ever been
allowed to go into a shop by himself, unwatched.

"Oh, hang it, I'm not afraid!" snarled Terry. Max
looked grimly courageous.

The proprietor, a gentleman from the sunny lands of

Syria, was eying them from the window. He rubbed his hands when they came in, and simpered.

"I want two old suits, quite old, for this boy and me," said Max. "We're—uh—going camping. And another suit for a boy about two inches taller than me."

"Erggg," said Josephus, in a tone of positive dislike.

While the proprietor fetched them, Maximilian muttered, "Do you suppose he has a decent dressing room here? Really, the place seems dirty!"

"No!" urged Terry. "We mustn't change here and leave our things—Scotland Yard might trace us by our clothes if we left 'em."

"Oh!" Maximilian seemed distinctly flattered. "I've read about Scotland Yard—detective stories I borrow from an English gardener at the palace at home. Do you suppose we'll have a real inspector hunting for us? *Clues?* How ripping! Do you *really* think so?"

"Oh, rather. At least I should think they'd search for a king, wouldn't you?"

"Oh, yes; I suppose they would. You see, I've been a king so short a time that I don't quite know. But think of a Scotland Yard inspector hunting for you—microscope and bloodstains and everything. I say, I do like this! It's so much more practical than Latin."

The old-clothes man was coming with three suits which were as beautifully 'orrid as Ginger had promised. All three of them were gray along the seams, they were greasy, and the buttons hung wearily on worn threads. The three were worth, as masquerade costumes, six shillings altogether, but anyone with fancies about sanitation would have demanded five pounds to touch them.

"Just the thing for an outing, young gentlemen!"exulted the dealer. "Three quid for the lot—and your own clothes, of course. Swelp me, I'm giving 'em away."

LET'S PLAY KING 61

The greenhorn Terry was roused to irritation. Three quid—he had learned from the scholarly Ginger that a quid was a pound. He snorted, "Don't be silly! I'll give you a pound and a half—what'd you call it, thirty shillings?—and we'll keep our own clothes."

As he spoke, he had brought out his roll of notes, the fifty pounds that were to see them to Bristol and the gay free life of piracy. The dealer's eyes popped, and he said crooningly:

"You're an American, aren't you, matey? And a fine little fellow, you and your little friend." Then, savagely, grasping Terry's shoulders, his yellow teeth showing evilly, "And where did you steal your fine clothes? I'll take *four* quid, and keep quiet—else I'll call in the police and we'll find out what a couple of American stowaways, blinkin' young tramps that've stole their clothes, are doing in my shop at seven in the morning!"

Josephus had, on sight, fallen out of love with the old-clothes dealer; he had growled when the man seized Terry; now, with enthusiasm, he grabbed the man's trousers leg and began to tear. The man leaped back, barricaded himself behind a rack of old coats. Terry snatched up the bundles of clothes, dropped a pound note on the counter, shooed Max and Josephus outside.

"He'll have us arrested!" quaked Max.

"Huh! He'll never call the police, now he's got his quid. The less he sees of the police, the better he'll like it. I ain't afraid!" said Terry boldly—while inside he was fully as calm as a cat chased up a tree by a pack of dogs.

They reached the alley mouth and the waiting Ginger, and Ginger drove them through the alley, a courtyard, another alley, and a blind area way behind a shop. They undressed madly, while Terry told of their misadventure.

"I'll 'ave my uncle 'Ennery scrag 'im!" raged Ginger. "'E eats men alive, Uncle 'Ennery does."

Dressed, they were as scandalously soiled a trio as was to be found in greater London. Ginger insisted on tearing the caps and stockings of his two heroes; on rubbing dirt over their faces.

He himself was capless. But now, free of his skin-tight uniform, he chucked his fears away with it, and cried, "Righto, me brave lads! 'Tis off to the boundin' blue—as Uncle 'Ennery says. What about a bit of breakfast?"

To avoid the old-clothes man, after hiding their proper clothes in a garbage can, he led them through further alleys and courts to a restaurant which he guaranteed to be the best twopenny dive in London. Relieved of worried relatives who insisted on nice porridge with nice cream, Terry and Max joyfully smeared themselves with a breakfast of fried fish, apple tart, pink cakes, and jam.

Josephus had a voluptuous bone, and as for Ginger, he breakfasted on tea and fish. He was a pal, he said, of the assistant pastry cook at the Hotel Picardie, and he could have all the cakes he wanted, any time.

"You can eat all the cakes you want? Any time? And nobody stops you?" gasped H.R.M. Maximilian III.

"All you want?" marveled Terry.

"Ra-ther!" said Ginger superciliously.

Mr. Ginger Bundock knew that Max was a real king, that Terry was a famous actor, but he couldn't believe it. They looked like two dirty small boys, and while they seemed to have read books, which had never been a habit in the Bundock family, they were so ignorant of his London that he couldn't help feeling superior. And over the fish and pink cakes he was rather sniffy with them about reaching Bristol and the haunts of pirate ships.

"It's west of London. Right away west," he said authoritatively.

"How far?" asked Terry.

"How far? Oh, a long way. Seventy-five miles. Or per'aps three 'undred."

"Pooh! That's not far!" Terry was trying to regain the scornfulness of leadership. "My dad and I drove from Los Angeles to San Francisco in one day, and that's five hundred miles!"

"Oh, I dare say! You Americans! An Englishman wouldn't care to go barging about like that, you know!"

"I think," hinted Max, "we ought to be taking a train at once, before they find we're missing."

"A train?" grumbled Ginger. "Oh, I say now, don't be balmy, Max—I mean, Your Majesty."

"Oh, I like being called Max. Please call me Max, Ginger. We're all fellow pirates now, you know."

"Aw, Max sounds Dutch," reflected Terry. "Let's call him 'Mix.'"

"Mix?" queried Maximilian.

"You bet! That's the name of one of the swellest cow-punchers in the movie game, ain't it, Ginger?"

"Oh, that would be nice. 'Mix.' And then of course as a pirate I suppose I *would* have to have a *nom de guerre*."

"A wot?" demanded Ginger.

"He's swallowed a dictionary!" protested Terry.

"Oh, I am sorry!" wailed Maximilian. He wasn't sure what he had done to offend these superior representatives of the Anglo-Saxon race, but he was ready to apologize for anything or for nothing to keep their comradeship.

"'T'sall right, Mixie," said Terry generously; then abruptly, to Ginger, "Anyway, why shouldn't we take a train?"

Ginger recognized his master's voice. More humbly: "W're d'you suppose they'd look for us first? On trains, of course! We must walk. *Besides!* Did you ever 'ear of pirates taking trains?"

"Don't you think we ought to carry swords, though?" worried Terry. "Pirates always carry swords."

"Oh, I don't believe modern ones do," said Max. "I fancy they just carry revolvers and six-shooters and things like that, and I don't believe we need buy them till we reach Bristol."

"Well, maybe; but when we get to Bristol, we ought to buy sabers *and* guns, so when we find a pirate ship and go aboard, they won't think we're a lot of tenderfeet," insisted Terry.

"That's right," Ginger agreed. "Now as I say, we must walk, and I think we ought to go up to 'Ampstead 'Eath and practice being tramps—you know, meeting savage dogs, and sleeping under 'edges, and telling the direction by the bark on the trees, and making fires by rubbing sticks together."

"That's so; we must learn that," agreed Captain Terry, and the three boys, solemnly starting for the Spanish Main by way of Hampstead Heath, made a gallant beginning by finding a Number 24 bus.

The morning fog was gone when they reached the heath; the broad wastes of that tamed moorland were bright with sun and wind, in whose exhilaration the three boys forgot that they were king and star and expert hotel page, and chased one another, yowled and whistled like any other three small boys, while Josephus went earnestly mad, snapping at royal heels with loving painfulness.

Max remembered from his English history that the heath had once been the favorite scene of highway robbery, and the four of them played highwaymen. Josephus, unhappily harnessed by Terry's belt, was the faithful coach horse, Terry was the driver, Ginger the haughty and noble passenger, and Max was permitted the grandest rôle of all, that of the robber.

Old Jim Dangerfield, the gallant coachman of the Yorkshire Flyer, was apprehensive. He clucked cheerily enough to his stout team of dappled mares, Jo and Sephus, and hummed a careless little tune ("My Toil and Strife Has Gotta Eye on We, Ba-by"), but when his passengers were not looking, brave Old Jim shuddered, hunched down within his many-caped cloak, now whitened with flying snowflakes.

On the seat beside him was a mysterious man in the old, ancient costume of the day. He had refused to give his name, but he was Lord Montmorency. Old Jim knew nothing of this, however.

And so they went on across the heath when all of a sudden a cloaked and masked man, riding a huge great big black horse, leaped out from behind a tree and leveling his pistol cried, "Your money or your life!"

Old Jim reached for his own pistol, but the villain shot him dead and he expired all over the ground, while the faithful Jo and Sephus licked his face—after craftily sneaking out of their harness.

But the brave Lord Montmorency was not to be quelled by anybody. Crying, "Come one, come all! I defy the blooming lot o' ye!" he leaped from the coach, drawing his trusty sword and, knocking the pistol from the wicked highwayman's hand, he engaged him in mortal combat.

It lasted a long time. In fact, it lasted till Old Jim Dangerfield protested, "Oh, that ain't fair—you two going on swording for hours and hours when I'm dead! I'm going to come to life!"

In the argument with Lord Montmorency and the robber as to whether a pistoled coachman could prove to be merely playing possum, they forgot the game and, panting, lay on the grass.

"My uncle 'Ennery was a 'ighwayman once," mused Ginger.

"Oh, didn't they arrest him?" fretted Terry.

"No, 'e wasn't *that* kind of a 'ighwayman. 'E gave all 'e robbed to the poor."

"Where was this?" Terry sounded suspicious.

"Hey, quit scattering dust all over me, will you, Mixy?" was Ginger's adequate answer. "Excuse me, Your Majesty, but honestly, it gets in me eyes."

"When we go back—I mean, if we hadn't gone off to be pirates, I'd ask my mother to invite your uncle Henry to the palace," considered Max. "He must be a wonderful man. I don't like my uncles so much. But I had some lovely ancestors. I'm descended from Genghis Khan!"

"Oh, I've seen 'im. 'E's that banker from New York. 'E often stays at the Picardie," condescended Ginger.

"I think that must be another Khan," Max said doubtfully. "I think Genghis lived years and years ago. And my grandfather had an estate with two hundred thousand acres of land!"

"Huh! That's nothing," said Terry. "I know a movie actor in California that's got a million acres."

"Oh, he has not!" protested Max.

"He has, too. And I'm going to have a million million acres and grow bees, when I grow up."

"Oh, you will not!" complained Max. "Besides, I'll mobilize my army and conquer Roumania and Bulgaria and a lot of countries, and then I'll have a million trillion billion acres! And another of my ancestors was Seljuk."

"Never heard of him. Jever hear of Seljuk, Ginger?"

"Now! Never 'eard of 'im!"

"And one of my ancestors," continued Terry, "was sheriff of Cattaraugus County, New York!"

"Me uncle 'Ennery was a sergeant major in Boolgaria," Ginger confided.

"Oh, say, let's play soldiers!" cried Terry. "Which of you has the most military training?"

"I almost joined the Boy Scouts once. There was a curate ast me to join 'em," reflected Ginger. "But you, Mixy, a king must 'ave bushels of military training."

Max confessed, "Not really. Just fencing and riding as yet. Oh, I am a field marshal in the Slovarian Army, and I'm a colonel in the British Army, and in Italy I'm an admiral and a general, but I wouldn't say I was a soldier."

"I know all about militaries. I saw 'em making some of the film of 'The Big Parade,'" boasted Terry; and Max, who had been faintly irritated at their ignorance of his renowned ancestor, Seljuk, rose again to admiration for his hero, the great Terry Tait, and murmured, "Oh, I saw that picture. And you saw them *making* it? That must have been priceless! You be the captain on one side, and Ginger can be it on the other."

And that was a very nice war. There were any number of hand-to-hand combats, as well as a devastating machine gun produced by Ginger's winding his 3/6 watch and remarking, "Brrrrrrr!"

When the war ended they lay in the long grass again while Ginger modestly admitted that during the World War his uncle 'Ennery had single-handed captured sixteen Germans.

Terry interrupted, to shout, "Oh, I've got a dandy game. Let's play king!"

"Oh, that's no fun!" protested Max.

"I don't mean like any of these ole kings they got today —I mean like there used to be in the Olden Times. I'll show you. You'll like it, Mixy. I'll be king, and Ginger, you're Lord High Executioner."

"Kings don't have Lord High Executioners!" protested Max.

"They do too! Anyway, they always usta have! And Ginger is my Lord High Executioner, and you're a rebel, Mixy; you're leading a band of brigands."

"Who's the brigands?" said Max darkly.

"Josephus, of course, you poor boob. Now, look. See, here's my throne." Terry had found a beautiful rock on the heath.

H.R.M. Terry sat down, very royal, his left hand on his hip, his right waving an object which resembled a weed but which to him was a golden scepter.

"Now, you and Josephus go and hide off there over the hill," he ordered Max, "and begin to sneak up on us. You're a band of rebellious peasants. And you, Ginger, you're my Commander in Chief."

"But you said I was Lord Executioner, 'ooever 'e is!"

"You're going to be, later, stupid! Now you beat it, Max! That's it, hide!"

As Max and Josephus began a most realistic creep through the grass, glaring their hatred of all monarchial institutions, King Terry reasonably addressed his Commander in Chief, together with hordes of other courtiers who were standing behind the commander:

"What ho, my lieges! Trusty messengers, coming apace, do give me informations that hell is let loose in our mountaineous domains and a band of rebels is now approaching. Gwan out, then, my brave troops, and capture 'em. Seek to the nor-nor-east, I bid thee. . . . Now you go capture 'em, Ginger; but you put up a fierce battle, Max."

Fierce battle.

During it, King Terry bounced with excitement, demanding, "Lookit, Ginger, you gotta keep running in—you're a messenger—telling me how the battle is going; see, I'm standing up here at the window of a tower looking across my royal plains."

The trusty commander brought in the rebels, and despite a plaintive "Ouch!" from Max, cast them roughly down before the king, who climbed from the tower (which resembled a hummock of grass), seated himself on his throne again, and addressed the traitor:

"Villain, art guilty?"

"What do I say? I've never played this game before," begged Max.

"Neither have I, stupid! Haven't you got any imagination? What *would* a villain say if a king bawled him out like that?"

"I don't know. Oh, I fancy he'd say, 'No, I aren't.'"

"You are too! Commander in Chief, *isn't* he guilty? Didn't you catch him treasoning?"

"Ra-ther!"

"Then—— (Now you're Lord High Executioner.) Then off with his head!"

"Oh, I say!" protested Max. "Kings can't have people's heads cut off!"

"Of course they can! Don't be silly. Maybe they can't in Slovaria, but lots and lots of places they can."

"Can they, honest?" admired Max. "I wish I could! By Jove, I'd have old Michelowsky's head off in two twos! He's my tutor—a horrid man!"

"Dry up! You hadn't ought to interrupt a king, don't you know that? Now you get your head cut off. And Josephus, too. Now you form a procession. See, I walk in front, and then you and Josephus, and Ginger in behind with the headsman's sword—here, you can take my skepter for sword, Ginger."

And they marched to the sweetly solemn tune of "Onward, Christian Soldiers," chanted by Terry, and the noble tragedy of the event was only a little marred by Ginger's peeping at his 3/6 watch just before he dealt the awful blow, and exclaiming, "It's one o'clock! We must find a bit of lunch. I'm not going to start pirating on an empty stomach!"

Bessie Tait, whenever she felt depressed and put upon, slept late in the morning, waking only to think of the broiling letters she would write to her enemies, and to doze off again. This morning, at ten, she was still sunk among the little pink-and-white lace pillows with which she had adorned the Hotel Picardie bed when she was roused by her maid and her secretary, crying, "Oh, madame, there's a lady; I think it's——"

As Bessie sat up, iron-jawed and furious in her mosquito-netting nightgown, the maid and secretary were thrust aside by a woman who dashed into the room raging, "What have you done with my son?"

She was a tall woman, not unlike Bessie herself, and if her voice was not so harsh, she was more voluble. "If you have kidnaped him, if you have let him go off with your brat——"

"Are you crazy? Get out of here! Miss Tingle, call a policeman!" wailed Bessie.

"Oh, madame, it's Queen Sidonie of Slovaria!" whimpered the secretary.

"Queen!... Sidonie!... Oh, my Lord!" howled Bessie, capsizing among the pillows.

The queen flew to the bed, savagely seized her arm. "Where is he? Is he here?"

"Your son? The king?"

"Naturally, idiot! I know you lured him here yesterday——"

"Now, you can't talk to me like that, queen or no queen! How do I know where the boys are? I don't get up in the dawn! We'll see."

Bessie huddled into a dressing gown that was like the froth on sparkling Burgundy. Hoping, in her agitation at this somewhat unexpected way of meeting royalty, that Queen Sidonie was noticing her superior chic, she led Sidonie quickly through the living room, into Terry's room.

And it was empty.

In the room beyond, Humberstone, the valet whom Bessie had hired just for this purpose of impressing Sidonie, slumbered in a fume of gin, and instead of an edifying morning coat he exhibited the top of a red flannel nightgown.

If Sidonie had landed on Bessie somewhat precipitately, it had been a lover's greeting compared with the way in which Bessie hailed the valet, seizing an ear in each hand. The tempestuous Sidonie, for a generation the storm cloud of the Balkans, looked almost admiringly at Bessie's vocabulary, and the flower of English Service quaked as he stated that, because of his neuralgia, he had overslept, and of Master Terry and of all kings whatsoever he knew nothing.

Bessie flew at Terry's cupboard. "His blue suit is gone!" She flew at the telephone. "Ginger—that's the no-'count bell boy Terry plays with—he's missing, they say downstairs. Oh, Queen! He's missing! My little boy! And I been so hard on him! Oh, you may love your kid, the king, a lot, but you don't love him one bit more than I do mine and——"

And two women, Her Majesty of Slovaria and Mrs. Rabbit Tait of Mechanicville, sobbed on each other's shoulders.

It took Bessie exactly six minutes to dress—Sidonie

drove out the trembling maid and herself helped Bessie. In six and a half minutes they were in the royal suite below —and Bessie, beside the queen, stalked past the agitated Count Elopatak with the air of a Persian cat. She scarcely noticed the perfumedness and powderiness of the queen's own rooms, or the weeping maids.

Sidonie had the manager of the hotel, its three detectives, and all the policemen on duty, in her room instantly. The policemen now on guard had gone on duty at eight; they had seen nothing of the king. No servant in the hotel had seen anything of him since yesterday. Elopatak was, meantime, calling Scotland Yard. In a few minutes he had a report from one of the policemen who had been on duty in the corridor through the night that he had seen Maximilian playing ball in the corridor early, about six, he thought; he didn't know whether Maximilian had returned to his room or had gone upstairs.

Just then Scotland Yard had a report from the London garbage-collecting department that two good suits of boys' clothing and a Hotel Picardie uniform had been found in an alley off Greek Street, Soho.

Bessie and Queen Sidonie identified the clothes from the descriptions.

"They've run off together! It's that cursed bell boy's doing! Come on, Queen, let's grab a taxi and start right out from that alley looking for 'em!"

"Yes!" cried Sidonie, to the stupefaction of her suite, and she fled toward the door, arm in arm with Bessie Tait. At the door she shouted back, "I'll telephone every few minutes! Tell the Home Secretary to see that hundreds of policemen start right off to look for His Majesty." She slammed the door; she jerked it open to add, "And for Terry. Hundreds, do you hear? Hundreds!"

While the alarm went out to every policeman in Greater

London, while the newspaper offices went wild with the news that even Royalty could not keep from them, two anxious women, very chummy, sadly patting each other's hands and calling each other "My dear," rode through all the tangled streets and byways of Soho, stopping to ask every policeman for three small boys and an undistinguished dog who was, for twenty-four hours, to become the most famous dog in the world.

Because of their free and joyful play—and perhaps because of the agreeable menu of pork pie, vealnam pie, steak and kidney pudding, sausage and mashed, strawberry tart, vanilla ice, chocolate ice and little mince pies—the three musketeers were curiously sleepy after luncheon at a "cocoa room" near the Heath. They agreed that they ought to be starting for Bristol and the wild life, oh! immediately, but perhaps they would do better if they rested a bit—by attending a movie, which promised something nice in the way of a drama about a poisoner.

Terry had become used to tackling shopkeepers. With the loftiest confidence he engaged a greengrocer to keep Josephus during the movie, and bought the most expensive seats.

It was a pleasant and elevating picture, and moral, as the poisoner died in tremendous agony.

They came out of the theater at four, to find the streets littered with newspaper placards shrieking, "Disappearance of Boy King and Yank Cinema Star."

"Jiminy!" whispered Terry. He hastily bought each of the evening papers and led his pirate band into the darkest, least conspicuous back corner of an A.B.C. tea room, to read the news.

The first paper announced that Terry, who, though but eight years old, had been a celebrated character in Chicago before he became a film star (which was a neat way of saying that he was a gunman, and still avoiding the libel law), was believed to have persuaded His Majesty, to whom he had been presented at a well-known West End hotel, to run away. There was no proof that Terry was connected with the notorious Lisbon gang of counterfeiters and kidnapers, but still, the police were looking into it.

The second paper spoke of the sinister disappearance of a red-headed hotel page named Alf Bundock, whose record the police were examining.

The third came out bluntly and proved that it was a crime of the Bolsheviki, and demanded that the government renounce its dastardly policy of permitting Bolshevik spies to roam around innocent England—kidnaping kings this way.

All the newspapers contained enormous biographies of King Maximilian and much sketchier accounts of Terry, who was, according to the three versions, eight, fourteen, and four years of age. And all three had pictures, lots of pictures—Maximilian in the uniform of a Czechoslovakian Horse Marine; Maximilian opening the Museum of Osteothermodynamics in Tzetokoskavar, capital of Slovaria; Terry in the rôle of the Poor Little Blind Boy (he recovered his sight, of course, when the Kind Rich Lady and the Big-hearted Surgeon got hold of him) in the film "Out of the Night"; Terry gardening at Poppy Peaks—Terry was known to be as fond of gardening as Presidential candidates are of haymaking; the Hotel Picardie—X marks the spot; and sixteen lovely portraits of Queen Sidonie.

But the *Evening Era* had the greatest triumph of all—an account of Josephus the Hound, with a photograph furnished by the courtesy of the Bond Street Dog and Animal Shop. Only it was the photograph of a greyhound. But Terry was slightly comforted by a full-page advertisement

of his film "Kiddies Kourageous," which the enterprising
Halcyon Theater was going to revive.

The three boys crouched over the papers; even Josephus
was crouching, under the table.

"All the 'tecs in the United Kingdom will be looking
for us. We must cut and run," moaned Ginger. Then, with
such concentration as he had never given to any intellectual problem, even the question of transmuting a shilling
tip into two-and-six, he considered, "No, we must 'ide.
They'll be watching even the roads. We'll lay up for a
couple of days, and then start out by midnight. Yuss. 'Ide
under 'edges."

"Splendid. Just like escaping from German prison
camps!" gloated Terry. "But where shall we hide till——
Oh! At your uncle Henry's! You said he lived in London.
And he'll tell us all about pirates. You said he was a pirate
once, didn't——"

Ginger looked dark-browed; Ginger looked distressed.
"Now. Can't be done. Me uncle 'Ennery and me isn't on
speaking terms."

"Then you'll just have to get on speaking terms! It's the
only place we've got."

"Now. Can't."

"Nonsense!" It was Max, very vigorous. "Of course
an old pirate would be glad to greet young ones. You'll
take us there at once, Ginger."

"I will not!"

"Do you hear me, Bundock?" Terry and Ginger stared
equally at the change in the amiable Max's voice. "I'm not
requesting it; I'm giving a command. Do you happen to
remember who I am?"

Ginger looked more scared than ever; he snapped back
into his training as a hotel servant; he quivered, "Very
well, sir, but I don't advise it; not Uncle 'Ennery I don't."

But he led them, sneaking through alleys, craftily taking roundabout bus lines, shivering every time they fancied a policeman was looking at them, across the river and into the district of Bermondsey. It was, to Max and Terry, a London altogether different from the city of Palladian clubs, snug Georgian houses about tranquil squares, haughty shops and immaculate streets that they had known. They were bewildered by a waste of houses, two stories high, made of stone or a grimy grayish-yellow brick, set side by side, without grass or trees—miles of brick dog kennels, broken only by bristling railroad tracks, warehouses like prisons, innumerable public houses that smelled of stale beer, and vast streets that were as disordered as they were noisy.

They left a bus on Abbey Road, and Ginger guided them up a side street full of little shops. It was six o'clock now, with smoke-streaked fog settling down again; the bars were open and into them streamed navvies with trousers tied above the ankles, old charwomen in shawls and aprons, scrawny children with beer cans. They were all contemptuously indifferent to a stray American small boy, these thirsty workers.

"Let's hurry to your uncle's," Terry begged.

"You won't like 'im," said Ginger darkly.

"But you said he was so jolly! That time he sang 'Knocked 'Em in the Old Kent Road' to the Empress of Japan."

"Oh. *That* time," observed Ginger.

His steps slackened. For all their urging, for all Josephus' cheerful leaping, Ginger loitered, till they came to a hand laundry and, pointing through a steamy window at a small squirrel-toothed narrow-shouldered man who was turning a wringer, Ginger muttered, "That's 'im; that's Uncle 'Ennery."

Terry and Max stared, feeling empty at the stomach. They said nothing. They didn't need to. They simultaneously doubted whether Uncle 'Ennery had ever captured sixteen Germans at once, or been more than just engaged to the princess of the South Seas isle.

"You *would* barge in!" complained Ginger and, inching open the door of the laundry, he whimpered, "Uncle 'Ennery!"

Uncle 'Ennery lifted his head, rubbed the back of his neck as though it hurt, peered through the steam at Ginger, and remarked, "Ow, it's you, you little beggar! Get out of this! Coming around in your 'otel uniform, making mock of your betters, and they your own relations! And now you're in the gutter again; you're in ragsantatters again, and I'm glad of it, I am. Get out of this!"

"I ayn't in the gutter! I'm just on me 'oliday," protested Ginger.

"Yes, a fine 'oliday, as'll end in the workus. Get out!"

"Give me three bob to show 'im," Ginger whispered to Terry and, displaying the money, smiling a false sugar-sweet smile, he crooned, "Me and me friends are going tramping. We'll give you this three bob if you'll let us sleep 'ere tonight."

"Let's see the money!" demanded Uncle 'Ennery. He turned the shillings over and over. Looking slightly disappointed that they seemed to be genuine, he grunted, "I ought to 'orsewhip you, you young misbegotten, but I'll let you stay. Only you goes out and gets your own supper."

Without further welcome, he led the three boys and Josephus among the tubs in the back room of the laundry, up an outside stairway to a chaste establishment consisting of one room (Uncle 'Ennery was a widower and childless) with one bed, unmade, a fireplace stove, a chair and a cupboard.

"You can sleep on the floor," he snarled. "The dog—'e goes out in the areaway."

Terry looked indignant but—they were alone, fugitives, hunted by the entire British police force. . . . What was the penalty for kidnaping a king? Hanging, or life imprisonment? He sighed and stood drooping, a very lonely little boy.

Somewhat comforted at being taken in by his loving uncle, Ginger piped, "Cheer-o! We'll go 'ave a bite to eat. There's a love-ly fried-fish shop on the corner."

He walked ahead of his comrades in crime, rather defiantly. Behind him, Terry whispered to Max, "I don't believe his uncle Henry ever was a deep-sea diver!"

"No; and I don't believe he was a sergeant major in the Bulgarian Army—hardly more than a private," Max said.

"Or an aviator!"

"Or an African explorer!"

Ginger pretended that it didn't matter that he had lost now the Uncle 'Ennery whose exploits had been the one glory by which he had been able to shine beside a king. Most boisterously he ushered them into the fried-fish shop with, "If you toffs ayn't too good for it, 'ere's the best bloaters in London."

And through supper he contradicted them, laughed at their ignorance of such fundamental matters of culture as the standing of the Middlesex cricket team and the record of the eminent middleweight, Mr. Jem Blurry. So Max and Terry became refined. They were sickeningly polite. Their silence shouted that they regarded him as low.

When they had reluctantly returned to the mansion of Uncle 'Ennery, their host was sitting on the one chair, his shoes out on the one bed, reading an evening paper. He glared at them, but the beer in which he had invested their

three shillings had warmed his not over-philanthropic
heart, and he condescended to Ginger, "'Ere's a funny go,
and at your 'otel. This king a-missing, along of a Yark
actor. Goings-on!"

Now, for the many weary years of his life, Ginger had
singularly failed to impress his uncle. Now he had his
chance to startle this exalted relative.

"And did you 'appen to notice who was the third boy
went with 'em?" he mocked.

"A third one? Now. Ayn't read all the article yet."

Ginger—while Terry and Max wildly shook their heads
at him—loftily pointed out a paragraph in the paper.
Uncle 'Ennery spelled out, "It is sus-pec-ted that wif them
was a pyge nymed Alf Bundock who——" He leaped up,
terrified. "Bundock? Is that you, you young murdering
blighter?"

Ginger laughed like the villainess making exit after tying
the heroine to the circular saw.

Uncle 'Ennery looked at Max and Terry with a wild
surmise, silent upon a peak in Little West Poultry Street,
S. E. He pointed a terrified finger at Terry. "You, there!
Speak, will yer?"

"What's the trouble with you?" snapped Terry.

"My eye! It's true!" wailed Uncle 'Ennery. "You're an
American—or some sort of sanguinary foreigner! You three
get out of 'ere! I'll have nothing to do with it! Bringing
down the police on me! Get out of 'ere, all of you, kings
or no kings!"

Uncle 'Ennery was in a panic, his eyes insane, his hands
waving. He drove them down the stairs, through the courtyard—when Terry stopped to call Josephus he almost hit
them—and through the laundry into the street. He could
be heard slamming the door, bolting it.

"Uncle 'Ennery never did like the police," reflected

Ginger. "Well, I'll find you a nice bit of 'ay in a ware-'ouse."

In a pile of wet and soggy hay, among vile-smelling boxes and carboys, between a warehouse and tracks along which freight trains shrieked all night long, the three boys crept together and shivered and wept—and went fast asleep.

All day they had searched, Bessie Tait and Queen Sidonie, wherever two adventurous boys seemed likely to be. They had so far forgotten any social differences between them that not only did they exchange anecdotes about their boys' incomparable naughtiness in the matter of sugar on porridge, but also, as they sat exhausted at tea in Sidonie's boudoir, Bessie gave and Sidonie gratefully noted down a splendid recipe for baked Virginia ham with peaches.

"And if you come to America, you simply must come and stay with Mr. Tait and me, and don't let any of these millionaire producers pinch you off!"

"I *will* come and stay with you, my friend! And Terry and my boy shall play together!" promised H.R.M. "And you will come to us in Slovaria?"

"Well, if I can find time, I'll certainly try to, Sidonie," consented Bessie Tait, and the two women—so alike, save that Bessie had the better dressmaker—leaned wearily back and smoked their cigarettes, and glared when the terrified Count Elopatak came in to announce that Prince Sebenéco, Prime Minister of Slovaria, had left for London by airplane.

"The old fool!" murmured Sidonie.

Then she tried to look haughty, but it ended in the two tired female warriors, grinning at each other as Elopatak elegantly slunk out.

"Elopatak's misfortune," confided Sidonie, "is that he has no calm. He permits the gross material to rule him. He would be calm like myself, if he would only take up Higher Thought."

Bessie leaned forward excitedly. "Oh! Have you taken up Higher Thought, too? So have I! Isn't it just lovely! There's the livest Higher Thought teacher in Los Angeles that I go to every week—such a fine, noble-looking man, with the loveliest wavy black hair!

"Before I went to him, I used to lose my temper—people are *such* fools!—and I used to try to exercise my selfish will on them, but now whenever I get sore at some poor idiot, I just say, 'All is mystery and 'tis a smile that unlocks the eternal kinship of man to man,' and then I get just as placid and nice as can be. Such a help!"

"*Isn't* it! We have just the same sentence in Higher Thought at home—only it doesn't sound quite the same, being in Slovarian. And isn't that curious: my healer is also a handsome man, with such won-derful hair! Of course, in my position I have to belong to the State Church, but it's out of Higher Thought I've learned that any man is as good as I am, even when he obviously isn't.

"And now I never lose my temper any more. I just say, 'I am Calmness, therefore I am calm.' If I could only get Elopatak and Prince Sebenéco—the filthy swine! Oh, Bessie, you don't know what meeting you means to me! Somehow, in Slovaria and here in England, they don't seem to understand how sensitive I am!"

All evening the two mothers raged and roamed, but by one of the morning, Bessie was asleep, exhausted. A few hours later it was she who (saluted by bobbies and guards and aides as she stalked down the royal corridor) awoke Sidonie early—and with her she was dragging a scared Ginger Bundock.

This was twelve hours after Ginger, Terry, and Max had lain tearfully down in the damp hay by the warehouse in Bermondsey.

The management of the Picardie had excitedly telephoned to Bessie that Ginger had returned; that he knew the whereabouts of the two kings. They brought him in, like a prisoner, and Bessie dragged him to Queen Sidonie.

In Sidonie's bedroom, with its tall bed, scarlet-draped and surmounted by a vast golden crown, its purple carpet and a vista of little tables, deep chairs, vast dressing gowns and long mirrors, Sidonie sat up in bed, looking scraggly and care-channeled, smoking a cigarette nervously, while Bessie, in her foamy dressing gown, paced wildly. And to this dreadful audience Ginger told his story.

"It isn't my fault, Your Majesty. 'Is Majesty and Master Tait, they wanted me to go along. They said they were just going for a stroll. They said it would be fun to dress up in old clothes. I don't know what they did with me uniform and their clothes, but we changed in an alley off Greek Street, Soho. Then we went to play on 'Ampstead 'Eath. Then they wanted to go into the country and we walked west——"

Now the warehouse where, so far as Ginger knew, Max and Terry were still sleeping, was southeast.

"—walked west, far into the country. Oh, we walked far into the night, we did, and I think we came almost to 'Arrow on the 'Ill, and we slept under a 'edge. And when I woke this morning, they were gone. So I 'opped a lorry and came right in to tell you, ma'am. Swelp me, it was none of my doing! And I 'eard 'em say something last night about going to Scotland, so if you searches all the roads north and west——"

Already Sidonie was shrieking for Elopatak; already she was telephoning to Scotland Yard.

"And of course the 'otel never give me my place again, Your Majesty, but oh, please, could you persuade the police not to arrest me?"

"Certainly. They shan't arrest you," glowed Sidonie. "Of course, if young gentlemen like His Majesty and Master Terry told you to accompany them, there was nothing else to do but recognize your place and obey them. I quite understand, and I'm thankful for your being so brave as to come to us. I don't suppose the hotel will want you, after this, but we might need you. You go up to Terry's room and stay till we call you. I'll see the police."

"That's the idea," said Bessie amiably, and to Ginger, "Skip . . . Sidonie! Breakfast! Quick! We'll start for Harrow."

"Right you are! We'll have the little fiends—the darlings!—in two hours. Oh, I'm so relieved!" said Sidonie of Tzetokoskavar to her friend Bessie of Mechanicville.

Terry woke only enough to know that he was awake, that he was miserable, that he was rather wet and extremely cold. He opened his eyes stupidly, amazed to find himself curled in filthy hay, between two boxes, looking out on a foggy welter of freight cars.

He wanted his warm bed, and cocoa coming, and his mother's voice. He had a feeling of loss and disaster—no excitement that he was free of photographers and press agents and about to become a rollicking pirate.

There was something comfortable about life, however, and he awoke enough to sit up and discover that it was the muzzle of Josephus, tucked in beside his knee. Josephus roused to lick his hand and to whine hungrily.

"Poor pup! I'll get you something," asserted Terry. Then his sympathy for Josephus widened enough to take in Max, curled with both hands beneath one cheek, hayseed spotting his filthy clothes. "Poor kid!" muttered Terry, and a horrible doubt crept into him.

Were they really going to enjoy being pirates?

He realized that Ginger was not there and that a note, scratched in pencil on a muddy sheet of wrapping paper, had been thrust through Josephus' collar. Terry anxiously snatched it out, to read:

Dear Friends Yr. Majesty & Terry:

I haven't been any help to you I am awful sorry Im just in the way I made believe I didn't care the way my Uncle acted but he was turble and I think the best thing I can do for you is to go away am going back to hotel and hope can do this for you, will tell them you are going different way from way you are going so through then off the sent they will not know you are going the way you are going I appresheate your taking me along hope have not been too disrespekt- full when you get to be pirates maybe you will give me a chance to come join you am sure you will sune be Orficers. Must close now yrs respectfly Ginger PS I lied about my Uncle he wasn't never no pirate, sodger ettc.

When Max had been awakened and had read the note, he quavered, "I'm not sure we can get along without Ginger. We don't know about tramping and all that. Do you think we'd better go home now? We could take a taxi."

"Never!" said the valiant Terry. "Go home, where you have to wash all the time, and they won't let you have any pink cakes, and there's newspaper reporters asking you questions, and you have to act like you liked it when hor- rible old maids pat you on the head? When we could be pirates and sail the bounding main?"

But he didn't sound very defiant, and feeble was Max's "Well, perhaps."

"Come on, Mixy; come on, you, Josephibus!" caroled Terry, with false heartiness. It was suddenly disheartized by a cockney voice beside them.

"Come out of that, you! Wot d'yer think ye're doing, sleeping there? Get out!"

It was a large man in a watchman's uniform, and the criminals slunk most ingloriously out of the railroad yards. Josephus slunk after them. They found a mean and dirty tea shop.

Terry wanted the corn flakes, Max desired the porridge, at which they had scoffed twenty-four hours before. The waitress told them they could have fried eggs, boiled eggs, bloaters, or kippers.

They sighed, and had fried eggs.

"I wonder," said Max, suddenly excited, "if we dare drink tea. I've always wanted to drink tea. But my mother and Professor Michelowsky never would let me. Do you suppose we dare?"

"Oh, let's! No matter what our mothers say! A pirate can't always be thinking about what his mother says!"

And daringly, taking the first step into lives of dissipation, they ordered tea.

Now it may be true, as envious foreigners assert, that the British Empire is founded on four things: tea, beer, calico, and diplomacy. But this uncheering cup at the den in Bermondsey was not the sort of tea on which empires are likely to be founded. It was bitter. It was lukewarm.

Max tasted it, and shook his head. "I don't understand why people drink it," he mused. "And I don't understand why I have to study Latin. And I don't understand why Mother is so cross with me when I tell her I want to be a farmer. Oh, dear, I'm"—his voice quavered—"I'm glad we're going to be pirates! They don't drink tea. They drink rum. And that must be nice!"

Very slightly cheered by breakfast, they started for Bristol.

Bristol, Ginger had said, was west. Very well, they would walk westward.

The waitress told them which direction was west, and they trudged for miles. They kept on gallantly—stopping only to keep Josephus out of a dog fight and keep the other dogs in it; to buy large and indigestible balls of hard candy; to watch a back-yard cricket game; to dally with a light mid-morning refreshment of toffee, sugar buns, cocoa, tongue, strawberry tart, and shortbread.

Toward noon they came out on a stretch of railroad tracks which barred their advance. While they were looking for a crossing, Terry started, and whimpered, "Look, Mixy! There's where we slept last night! We've gone in a circle!"

"Oh, fiddle!" raged Max the Pirate.

They sat disconsolately on a box, Josephus abashed at their feet.

"I guess," Terry suggested, after a gloomy pause, "we better take a taxi till we get out of London. Then we can follow a road west. Let's see how much money we got left. Gimme that two shillings I lent you and we'll count up."

They gravely spread all their notes, their silver and copper, between them on the box, and counted them. Of Terry's fifty pounds, together with the fifteen-pence which had been Max's pocket money, they now had left forty-seven pounds and a penny.

"Oh, we can do lots with that!" gloated Terry. "We could buy a lady dog, to go with Josephus. He must get lonely."

"But he might not like her."

"Oh, gee, *that's* easy! Lookit. We'd go into a dog store, see, and I'd say to the clerk, 'Look,' I'd say, 'I want to find a lady dog for my dog Josephus,' I'd say, 'and I want him to look around and see which lady dog he likes,' I'd say, and then Josephus would look around at all the cages they got dogs in——"

"Honestly, I think it's a shame to keep dogs in cages."

"So do I. I wouldn't like to live in no cage. Gee, I read once, it was in a book of stories, there was this man that had been a revolution, and they put him in a cage—oh, yes, it was in China——"

"Oh, I would like to go to China. Let's go to China!"

"Sure; you betcha. Pirates always go to China, I think they do, and——"

"You don't suppose we'd have to do any murders or anything nasty like that, do you, Terry, when we're pirates?"

"Oh, not *now;* they just did that in the Old Days. Now they just stop ships that belong to rich merchants and take silk and all like that, and then they give a lot to the poor——"

"And bleedin' nice of 'em I calls it!" said a new voice, a dripping and slimy voice behind them, and a filthy hand swooped upon their money.

They looked back, gasping, at a man with a hard little nut of a face under a greasy cap. Instantly the hand had tumbled them off the box, to right and left; a foot in a broken shoe had caught Josephus under the jaw as he leaped up growling; the filthy hand had scooped up every penny of their horde; and the thief was galloping away.

They followed, Josephus followed, but they could not find the robber.

They crouched again on the box. For five minutes they could not quite comprehend that they had no money whatever; nothing for lunch, nothing for movies.

"But nobody can't down us! We'll work our way!" flared Terry.

It did not sound too convincing, and Max answered

nothing whatever. They started off again silent. By repeatedly asking, they managed to keep going westward and, after their competent mid-morning lunch, they were not too hungry till three o'clock. Terry felt hungry enough then, and Max's face seemed to him thin and taut.

"I guess we better work for some grub now," he muttered. "Let's ask 'em here in this news shop. There's a nice, kind-looking old lady in there."

To the nice, kind-looking old lady, in the dusty recesses of the shop, he confided, "We're very hungry. Could we do some work for you?" And, winningly: "Your shop needs cleaning."

The nice, kind-looking old lady said never a word. She inspected them benevolently. Then she hurled an old paper-bound book at them, and at last she spoke: "Get along with you!"

They asked for work at an ironmonger's, at a surgery, at a fish market, at three restaurants and coffee stalls, but nowhere did they find it. Toward evening, in a terrifying dimness over unknown streets that stretched endlessly toward nowhere, Terry confessed:

"We can't do it. We'll have to give ourselves up. But we'll study to be tramps and pirates and everything! We'll be able to do it next time!"

"Yes!"

They tramped on till they found a policeman, a jolly, cheerful policeman.

"And what do you gents want?" he chuckled.

"Please, officer, I'm an American cinema star and this is the King of Slovaria. We're missing. We should like to give ourselves up, please!"

The policeman roared with joy. "And w'ere is Douglas Fairbanks and the Queen of Rooshia? 'Ave you 'idden 'em around the corner?" Seriously: "You lads ought to be ashamed of yourselves, telling such lies! That's wot comes of the likes of you reading the papers. The King and the Yankee lad, I 'ear, were captured at 'Arrow this afternoon. So cut along now. Scat!"

And they scatted, on feet that felt like hot sponges, utterly frightened, overwhelmed by dusk in a forest of petty streets, certain that they would have to go forever till they starved.

"We ought to try to go back to our hotel," sighed Max.

"But it's so far. And I don't believe they'd let us through that gosh-awful gold lobby."

"That's so."

As they crept on, they passed hundreds of agitated newspaper posters which told the world that Their Majesties were still lost. The placards gave Terry his idea.

"Lookit! I guess the papers are always hunting for news. I guess maybe if we went to a newspaper office and told who we were, they might help us get back home. Especially if we went to the London office of an American paper. I can talk American good, anyway! And I know the office of the New York *Venture* is on Fleet Street."

"I tell you, Terry! Let's find a drinking trough and wash ourselves as well as we can, and then per*haps* some taxi driver will take us and wait for his fare."

Terry looked at him with hurt astonishment. "Clean up? And lose all that publicity, when they'll be taking our photographs? Why, Mixy!"

"What's publicity?" asked Max humbly.

Discouraged by such ignorance, too tired to explain the metaphysical doctrine, Terry merely grunted, "Come on, we'll start for Fleet Street."

A dozen times they stopped to rest. Once they bathed

their feet in a fountain. But at nine that evening, they climbed the stairs to the office of the London bureau of the New York *Venture*.

They found a reception room littered with newspapers and with an office boy who snapped, "Now *get* along!"

But Terry now was Terry Tait again. "Get along, rats! I want to see the boss!" he clamored.

"What's all this?" from an inner door, where stood a sleepy young man in shirt sleeves. His voice was American.

"I'm Terry Tait. This is the King of Slovaria."

The sleepy young man came awake with vigor. He seized Terry's shoulder; peered at him; glanced at Max.

"And I believe you are!" he shouted. "Have you been back to the Picardie?"

"No. We're too dirty. We came here first. We ran away to be pirates, and a man robbed us in Bermondsey of all our money, and we been wandering around there all day, and we came here because my father always reads the *Venture* and—we're hungry!"

"Wait! For heaven's sake!" The man threw a ten-shilling note at the gaping office boy. "Beat it! Get some food! Beans! Ice cream! Champagne! Anything! But make it snappy! Come in here, you kids—I mean, Your Majesty, and you, Terry." He hustled them into his office, threw two chairs in their general direction, and was bellowing into the telephone receiver the number of the central cable office.

Three minutes later a wild telegraph operator slapped on the desk of the news editor of the *Venture*, in New York, a dispatch reading:

FLASH TAIT KING SLOVARIA GIVE SELVES UP LON-
DON BUREAU VENTURE RUNAWAY BE PIRATES
BULLETIN IMMEDIATELY

And sixteen minutes after that newsboys were racing out of the *Venture* building bellowing, "Terry Tait and King found! Terry and King found!"

And half an hour after that, the complete story, with "exclusive interviews" with Terry Tait and H.R.M. the King of Slovaria, was being eagerly read, in various tongues, by excited journalists in Rutland and Raleigh, Barcelona and Budapest, Manila and Madrid.

But the most famous two boys in the world, and the most famous dog, almost, in history, were quietly and unctuously eating ham and cold chicken and sally lunns, while a wide-awake young man called the Picardie and desired to speak to the suite of the Queen of Slovaria.

In the boudoir of Her Majesty, the Queen of Slovaria, was a scene at once impressive enough for the movies and humble enough for—well, humble enough for the movies.

On Her Majesty's lap sat an American small boy, recently and drastically scrubbed, clad in pajamas and a dressing gown, beatifically eating a most unhygienic and delightful cream roll. Beside them, beaming up at this Madonna scene, was another small boy, also scrubbed, also in dressing gown, also cramming into his mouth the luscious gooey cream. He was petting a woolly dog—a pure-bred Margate Wader—whose tongue lolled out with idiotic contentment.

Facing them was Bessie, smiling over her cigarette. And rushing around faithfully doing nothing in particular was a young Englishman, name of Bundock, who was to be Max's valet in two or three years, after he had been properly trained in the household of Sidonie's dear friend, the Duchess of Twickenham.

Now begins, after the pleasant homeliness, the impressiveness. The duchess began it. She was staring at the family scene; she was tall and gray; she wore rusty black; and within her powerful brain she was obviously meditating, "This is what comes of treating Slovarians and Americans and all suchlike colonials, no matter how highly placed, as though they were gentry!"

The second touch of impressiveness was given by Prince Sebenéco, Prime Minister of Slovaria.

He was a tall man with a black beard. He was protesting, "But, ma'am, I quite appreciate that it would be an honor for us to entertain Madame Tait and her charming son, but your people, ma'am; they were highly agitated by His Majesty's disappearance, and I fear they would resent your bringing His Majesty's associate in this idiot—I mean, in this adventure. How alarmed I was you may deduce from my having taken an airplane. Eeee! A nasty device! I was very sick!"

The same assistant manager who had once found Bessie her room was ushered in, bowing, timidly venturing, "A cablegram for you, Madame Tait."

Bessie opened the cablegram. She smiled slightly, and sniffed.

"Sebenéco!" said Sidonie.

"Ma'am?"

"You're a fool!"

"I?"

"Exactly.... Bessie, my friend, Terry and you will come to Slovaria. He will be educated by my son's tutors. You will both become Slovarian citizens. Some day he will be a general. We will bestow on him a title. Good! In two weeks we start for Tzetokoskavar. Do you play piquet, Bessie? I am very fond of piquet."

"Well, that's real nice of you, Sidonie," yawned Bessie, "and some day Terry and I will sure be glad to come over and visit you, but now we've got to beat it back to California. Just had a cablegram from Abe Granville, our manager. Well, I guess everybody better go to bed."

In their room she showed Terry the cablegram from Granville.

CONGRATULATIONS SWELLEST PUBLICITY EVER PULLED GIVE YOU CONTRACT FOUR HUNDRED THOUSAND A YEAR HUSTLE BACK START MAKING MAJESTY JUNIOR EIGHTEENTH ABE

.   .   .   .

In the Hollywood studio of the Jupiter-Triumph-Tait Film Corporation they were shooting "His Majesty, Junior," which was to be the first realistic, intimate, low-down picture of the inside life of royalty that had ever been made.

His Majesty, Terry, sat on a throne at the end of a vast room, and before him stood a squadron of guards, saluting.

The director was outlining the opening scene to Terry. "You sit on a throne in the throne room, see? The prime minister stands beside you, see, he's the comedy character, see, and there's a big gang of guards in fur hats, saluting. You don't like the way one of them acts and you say, 'Off with his head.'"

"Aw, thunder; kings can't say, 'Off with his head,'" complained Terry.

"Now, you, Terence Tait, will you kindly shut up and do what you're told?" said Bessie. "Here we work and slave and try to educate you, and then you just go on being so iggorent!"

"Listen, will you?" demanded the director, while Terry wistfully stroked the head of a broad-backed mongrel dog. "You wear a regular king's uniform, see—red tights and a jacket with fur—and you carry a sword."

And the splendid labor of making a great realistic movie went on—while seven thousand miles away a lonely small boy in a palace garden studied Latin and meditated on the day when Terry and he would both be twenty-one, when they would escape from the awful respectability of being kings and celebrities.

Out on the lot, Mr. T. Benescoten Tait was talking to an obsequious extra man. Mr. Tait was wearing a sulphur-colored topcoat and a salmon-colored tie which his wife had brought him from London.

"Yes, sir!" chanted Mr. Tait. "We wouldn't let the newspapers have the real low-down on Terry's chummin' around with the King of Slovaria. You see, this-here is a democratic country, this United States, I mean, and folks might not like it if they knew that their heroes, like Terry, was just like this with royalty. But fact is, this was all bunk about him and the King bumming around in old clothes. Fact is, they was introduced in London by special request of Queen Sidonie—she's always been crazy about Terry's pictures. And then the two kids, they were taken up to this Sandelham Castle by King George of England—yes, sir, that's the real fact."

At the same moment, on the same lot, two other extra men were discoursing, and one of them was explaining:

"Terry and the King! Say, lissen, where was you brought up? Gosh, you certainly are an easy mark! Mean to say you believe all this stuff about this Tait kid being chummy with a king? Say, that was all just publicity. I *know*.

"Wiggins, the press agent, told me so himself. Don't tell anybody—I wouldn't tell anybody but you; I don't want this to go any further—but the fact is, Terry and this kid king never met at all.

"These pictures you see of the two of 'em together, in

them dirty clothes, is all fake! Wiggins was there in London, and he got hold of a kid that looked like this king, and had him and Terry photographed together." /

"Gee, life's cer'nly different from what you'd expect," said his companion.

"Ain't it, though? You said it!"

THE WILLOW WALK

THE WILLOW WALK

From the drawer of his table Jasper Holt took a pane of window glass. He laid a sheet of paper on the glass and wrote, "Now is the time for all good men to come to the aid of their party." He studied his round business-college script, and rewrote the sentence in a small finicky hand, that of a studious old man. Ten times he copied the words in that false pinched writing. He tore up the paper, burned the fragments in his large ash tray and washed the delicate ashes down his stationary washbowl. He replaced the pane of glass in the drawer, tapping it with satisfaction. A glass underlay does not retain an impression.

Jasper Holt was as nearly respectable as his room, which, with its frilled chairs and pansy-painted pincushion, was the best in the aristocratic boarding house of Mrs. Lyons. He was a wiry, slightly bald, black-haired man of thirty-eight, wearing an easy gray flannel suit and a white carnation. His hands were peculiarly compact and nimble. He gave the appearance of being a youngish lawyer or bond salesman. Actually he was senior paying teller in the Lumber National Bank in the city of Vernon.

He looked at a thin expensive gold watch. It was six-thirty, on Wednesday—toward dusk of a tranquil spring day. He picked up his hooked walking stick and his gray silk gloves and trudged downstairs. He met his landlady in the lower hall and inclined his head. She effusively commented on the weather.

"I shall not be there for dinner," he said amiably.

"Very well, Mr. Holt. My, but aren't you always going out with your swell friends though! I read in the *Herald* that you were going to be a star in another of those society plays in the Community Theater. I guess you'd be an actor if you wasn't a banker, Mr. Holt."

"No, I'm afraid I haven't much temperament." His voice was cordial, but his smile was a mere mechanical sidewise twist of the lip muscles. "You're the one that's got the stage presence. Bet you'd be a regular Ethel Barrymore if you didn't have to take care of us."

"My, but you're such a flatterer!"

He bowed his way out and walked sedately down the street to a public garage. Nodding to the night attendant, but saying nothing, he started his roadster and drove out of the garage, away from the center of Vernon, toward the suburb of Rosebank. He did not go directly to Rosebank. He went seven blocks out of his way, and halted on Fandall Avenue—one of those petty main thoroughfares which, with their motion-picture palaces, their groceries, laundries, undertakers' establishments and lunch rooms, serve as local centers for districts of mean residences. He got out of the car and pretended to look at the tires, kicking them to see how much air they had. While he did so he covertly looked up and down the street. He saw no one whom he knew. He went into the Parthenon Confectionery Store.

The Parthenon Store makes a specialty of those in-

genious candy boxes that resemble bound books. The back
of the box is of imitation leather, with a stamping simulat-
ing the title of a novel. The edges are apparently the edges
of a number of pages. But these pages are hollowed out,
and the inside is to be filled with candy.

Jasper gazed at the collection of book boxes and chose
the two whose titles had the nearest approach to dignity—
Sweets to the Sweet and The Ladies' Delight. He asked
the Greek clerk to fill these with the less expensive grade of
mixed chocolates, and to wrap them.

From the candy shop he went to the drugstore that
carried an assortment of reprinted novels, and from these
picked out two of the same sentimental type as the titles
on the booklike boxes. These also he had wrapped. He
strolled out of the drugstore, slipped into a lunchroom, got
a lettuce sandwich, doughnuts, and a cup of coffee at the
greasy marble counter, took them to a chair with a table
arm in the dim rear of the lunchroom and hastily devoured
them. As he came out and returned to his car he again
glanced along the street.

He fancied that he knew a man who was approaching.
He could not be sure. From the breast up the man seemed
familiar, as did the customers of the bank whom he viewed
through the wicket of the teller's window. When he saw
them in the street he could never be sure of them. It
seemed extraordinary to find that these persons, who to
him were nothing but faces with attached arms that held
out checks and received money, could walk about, had
legs and a gait and a manner of their own.

He walked to the curb and stared up at the cornice of
one of the stores, puckering his lips, giving an impersonation of a man inspecting a building. With the corner of
an eye he followed the approaching man. The man ducked
his head as he neared, and greeted him, "Hello, Brother

Teller." Jasper seemed startled; gave the "Oh! Oh, how are you!" of sudden recognition; and mumbled, "Looking after a little bank property."

The man passed on.

Jasper got into his car and drove back to the street that would take him out to the suburb of Rosebank. As he left Fandall Avenue he peered at his watch. It was five minutes to seven.

At a quarter past seven he passed through the main street of Rosebank and turned into a lane that was but little changed since the time when it had been a country road. A few jerry-built villas of freckled paint did shoulder upon it, but for the most part it ran through swamps spotted with willow groves, the spongy ground covered with scatterings of dry leaves and bark. Opening on this lane was a dim-rutted grassy private road which disappeared into one of the willow groves.

Jasper sharply swung his car between the crumbly gate posts and along on the bumpy private road. He made an abrupt turn, came in sight of an unpainted shed and shot the car into it without cutting down his speed, so that he almost hit the back of the shed with his front fenders. He shut off the engine, climbed out quickly and ran back toward the gate. From the shield of the bank of alder bushes he peered out. Two clattering women were going down the public road. They stared in through the gate and half halted.

"That's where that hermit lives," said one of them.

"Oh, you mean the one that's writing a religious book, and never comes out till evening? Some kind of a preacher?"

"Yes, that's the one. John Holt, I think his name is. I guess he's kind of crazy. He lives in the old Beaudette

house. But you can't see it from here—it's clear through
the block, on the next street."

"I heard he was crazy. But I just saw an automobile go
in here."

"Oh, that's his cousin or brother or something—lives
in the city. They say he's rich, and such a nice fellow."

The two women ambled on, their clatter blurring with
distance. Standing behind the alders Jasper rubbed the
palm of one hand with the fingers of the other. The palm
was dry with nervousness. But he grinned.

He returned to the shed and entered a brick-paved walk
almost a block long, walled and sheltered by overhanging
willows. Once it had been a pleasant path; carved wooden
benches were placed along it, and it widened to a court
with a rock garden, a fountain and a stone bench. The
rock garden had degenerated into a riot of creepers sprawling over the sharp stones; the paint had peeled from the
fountain, leaving its iron cupids and naiads eaten with
rust. The bricks of the wall were smeared with lichens and
moss and were untidy with windrows of dry leaves and
caked earth. Many of the bricks were broken; the walk
was hilly in its unevenness. From willows and bricks and
scuffled earth rose a damp chill. But Jasper did not seem
to note the dampness. He hastened along the walk to the
house—a structure of heavy stone which, for this newish
Midwestern land, was very ancient. It had been built by a
French fur trader in 1839. The Chippewas had scalped
a man in its dooryard. The heavy back door was
guarded by an unexpectedly expensive modern lock. Jasper
opened it with a flat key and closed it behind him. It locked
on a spring. He was in a crude kitchen, the shades of which
were drawn. He passed through the kitchen and dining
room into the living room. Dodging chairs and tables in

the darkness as though he was used to them he went to each of the three windows of the living room and made sure that all the shades were down before he lighted the student lamp on the game-legged table. As the glow crept over the drab walls Jasper bobbed his head with satisfaction. Nothing had been touched since his last visit.

The room was musty with the smell of old green rep upholstery and leather books. It had not been dusted for months. Dust sheeted the stiff red velvet chairs, the uncomfortable settee, the chill white marble fireplace, the immense glass-fronted bookcase that filled one side of the room.

The atmosphere was unnatural to this capable business man, this Jasper Holt. But Jasper did not seem oppressed. He briskly removed the wrappers from the genuine books and from the candy-box imitations of books. One of the two wrappers he laid on the table and smoothed out. Upon this he poured the candy from the two boxes. The other wrapper and the strings he stuffed into the fireplace and immediately burned. Crossing to the bookcase he unlocked one section on the bottom shelf. There was a row of rather cheap-looking novels on this shelf, and of these at least six were actually such candy boxes as he had purchased that evening.

Only one shelf of the bookcase was given over to anything so frivolous as novels. The others were filled with black-covered, speckle-leaved, dismal books of history, theology, biography—the shabby-genteel sort of books you find on the fifteen-cent table at a secondhand bookshop. Over these Jasper pored for a moment as though he was memorizing their titles.

He took down *The Life of the Rev. Jeremiah Bodfish* and read aloud: "In those intimate discourses with his family that followed evening prayers I once heard Brother Bodfish observe that Philo Judaeus—whose scholarly career always calls to my mind the adumbrations of Melanchthon upon the essence of rationalism—was a mere sophist——"

Jasper slammed the book shut, remarking contentedly, "That'll do. Philo Judaeus—good name to spring."

He relocked the bookcase and went upstairs. In a small bedroom at the right of the upper hall an electric light was burning. Presumably the house had been deserted till Jasper's entrance, but a prowler in the yard might have judged from this ever-burning light that someone was in the residence. The bedroom was Spartan—an iron bed, one straight chair, a washstand, a heavy oak bureau. Jasper scrambled to unlock the bottom drawer of the bureau, yank it open, take out a wrinkled shiny suit of black, a pair of black shoes, a small black bow tie, a Gladstone collar, a white shirt with starched bosom, a speckly brown felt hat and a wig—an expensive and excellent wig with artfully unkempt hair of a faded brown.

He stripped off his attractive flannel suit, wing collar, blue tie, custom-made silk shirt and cordovan shoes, and speedily put on the wig and those gloomy garments. As he donned them the corners of his mouth began to droop. Leaving the light on and his own clothes flung on the bed he descended the stairs. He was obviously not the same Jasper, but less healthy, less practical, less agreeable, and decidedly more aware of the sorrow and long thoughts of the dreamer. Indeed it must be understood that now he was not Jasper Holt, but Jasper's twin brother, John Holt, hermit and religious fanatic.

II

John Holt, twin brother of Jasper Holt, the bank teller, rubbed his eyes as though he had for hours been absorbed in study, and crawled through the living room, through the tiny hall, to the front door. He opened it, picked up a couple of circulars that the postman had dropped through the letter slot in the door, went out and locked the door behind him. He was facing a narrow front yard, neater than the willow walk at the back, on a suburban street more populous than the straggly back lane.

A street arc illuminated the yard and showed that a card was tacked on the door. John touched the card, snapped it with a nail of his finger to make sure it was securely tacked. In that light he could not read it, but he knew that it was inscribed in a small finicky hand: "Agents kindly do not disturb, bell will not be answered, occupant of the house engaged in literary work."

John stood on the doorstep until he made out his neighbor on the right—a large stolid commuter, who was walking before his house smoking an after-dinner cigar. John poked to the fence and sniffed at a spray of lilac blossoms till the neighbor called over, "Nice evening."

"Yes, it seems to be pleasant."

John's voice was like Jasper's but it was more guttural, and his speech had less assurance.

"How's the story going?"

"It is—it is very difficult. So hard to comprehend all the inner meanings of the prophecies. Well, I must be hastening to Soul Hope Hall. I trust we shall see you there some Wednesday or Sunday evening. I bid you good-night, sir."

John wavered down the street to the drugstore. He purchased a bottle of ink. In a grocery that kept open evenings he got two pounds of cornmeal, two pounds of flour, a pound of bacon, a half pound of butter, six eggs and a can of condensed milk.

"Shall we deliver them?" asked the clerk.

John looked at him sharply. He realized that this was a

new man, who did not know his customs. He said rebuk-
ingly: "No, I always carry my parcels. I am writing a
book. I am never to be disturbed."

He paid for the provisions out of a postal money order
for thirty-five dollars, and received the change. The
cashier of the store was accustomed to cashing these money
orders, which were always sent to John from South Vernon, by one R. J. Smith. John took the bundle of food and
walked out of the store.

"That fellow's kind of a nut, isn't he?" asked the new
clerk.

The cashier explained: "Yep. Doesn't even take fresh
milk—uses condensed for everything! What do you think
of that! And they say he burns up all his garbage—never
has anything in the ashcan except ashes. If you knock at
his door, he never answers it, fellow told me. All the time
writing this book of his. Religious crank, I guess. Has a
little income though—guess his folks were pretty well
fixed. Comes out once in a while in the evening and pokes
round town. We used to laugh about him, but we've kind
of got used to him. Been here about a year, I guess it
is."

John was serenely passing down the main street of
Rosebank. At the dingier end of it he turned in at a hallway marked by a lighted sign announcing in crude house-
painter's letters: "Soul Hope Fraternity Hall. Experience
Meeting. All Welcome."

It was eight o'clock. The members of the Soul Hope cult
had gathered in their hall above a bakery. Theirs was a
tiny, tight-minded sect. They asserted that they alone
obeyed the scriptural tenets; that they alone were certain
to be saved, that all other denominations were damned
by unapostolic luxury, that it was wicked to have organs
or ministers or any meeting places save plain halls. The

members themselves conducted the meetings, one after another rising to give an interpretation of the scriptures or to rejoice in gathering with the faithful, while the others commented with "Hallelujah!" and "Amen, brother, amen!" They were plainly dressed, not overfed, somewhat elderly, and a rather happy congregation. The most honored of them all was John Holt.

John had come to Rosebank only eleven months before. He had bought the Beaudette house with the library of the recent occupant, a retired clergyman, and had paid for them in new one-hundred-dollar bills. Already he had great credit in the Soul Hope cult. It appeared that he spent almost all his time at home, praying and reading and writing a book. The Soul Hope Fraternity were excited about the book. They had begged him to read it to them. So far he had only read a few pages, consisting mostly of quotations from ancient treatises on the Prophecies. Nearly every Sunday and Wednesday evening he appeared at the meeting and in a halting and scholarly way lectured on the world and the flesh.

Tonight he spoke polysyllabically of the fact that one Philo Judaeus had been a mere sophist. The cult were none too clear as to what either a Philo Judaeus or a sophist might be, but with heads all nodding in a row, they murmured: "You're right, brother! Hallelujah!"

John glided into a sad earnest discourse on his worldly brother Jasper, and informed them of his struggles with Jasper's itch for money. By his request the fraternity prayed for Jasper.

The meeting was over at nine. John shook hands all round with the elders of the congregation, sighing: "Fine meeting tonight, wasn't it? Such a free outpouring of the Spirit!" He welcomed a new member, a servant girl just come from Seattle. Carrying his groceries and the bottle of ink he poked down the stairs from the hall at seven minutes after nine.

At sixteen minutes after nine John was stripping off his brown wig and the funereal clothes in his bedroom. At twenty-eight after, John Holt had become Jasper Holt, the capable teller of the Lumber National Bank.

Jasper Holt left the light burning in his brother's bedroom. He rushed downstairs, tried the fastening of the front door, bolted it, made sure that all the windows were fastened, picked up the bundle of groceries and the pile of candies that he had removed from the booklike candy boxes, blew out the light in the living room and ran down the willow walk to his car. He threw the groceries and candy into it, backed the car out as though he was accustomed to backing in this bough-scattered yard, and drove along the lonely road at the rear.

When he was passing a swamp he reached down, picked up the bundle of candies, and steering with one hand removed the wrapping paper with the other hand and hurled out the candies. They showered among the weeds beside the road. The paper which had contained the candies, and upon which was printed the name of the Parthenon Confectionery Store, Jasper tucked into his pocket. He took the groceries item by item from the labeled bag containing them, thrust that bag also into his pocket, and laid the groceries on the seat beside him.

On the way from Rosebank to the center of the city of Vernon, he again turned off the main avenue and halted at a goat-infested shack occupied by a crippled Norwegian. He sounded the horn. The Norwegian's grandson ran out.

"Here's a little more grub for you," bawled Jasper.

"God bless you, sir. I don't know what we'd do if it wasn't for you!" cried the old Norwegian from the door.

But Jasper did not wait for gratitude. He merely

shouted "Bring you some more in a couple of days," as he started away.

At a quarter past ten he drove up to the hall that housed the latest interest in Vernon society—The Community Theater. The Boulevard Set, the "best people in town," belonged to the Community Theater Association, and the leader of it was the daughter of the general manager of the railroad. As a well-bred bachelor Jasper Holt was welcome among them, despite the fact that no one knew much about him except that he was a good bank teller and had been born in England. But as an actor he was not merely welcome: he was the best amateur actor in Vernon. His placid face could narrow with tragic emotion or puff out with comedy, his placid manner concealed a dynamo of emotion. Unlike most amateur actors he did not try to act —he became the thing itself. He forgot Jasper Holt, and turned into a vagrant or a judge, a Bernard Shaw thought, a Lord Dunsany symbol, a Noel Coward man-about-town.

The other one-act plays of the next program of the Community Theater had already been rehearsed. The cast of the play in which Jasper was to star were all waiting for him. So were the ladies responsible for the staging. They wanted his advice about the blue curtain for the stage window, about the baby-spot that was out of order, about the higher interpretation of the rôle of the page in the piece—a rôle consisting of only two lines, but to be played by one of the most popular girls in the younger set. After the discussions, and a most violent quarrel between two members of the play-reading committee, the rehearsal was called. Jasper Holt still wore his flannel suit and a wilting carnation; but he was not Jasper; he was the Duc de San Saba, a cynical, gracious, gorgeous old man, easy of gesture, tranquil of voice, shudderingly evil of desire.

"If I could get a few more actors like you!" cried the professional coach.

The rehearsal was over at half-past eleven. Jasper drove his car to the public garage in which he kept it, and walked home. There, he tore up and burned the wrapping paper bearing the name of the Parthenon Confectionery Store and the labeled bag that had contained the groceries.

The Community Theater plays were given on the following Wednesday. Jasper Holt was highly applauded, and at the party at the Lakeside Country Club, after the play, he danced with the prettiest girls in town. He hadn't much to say to them, but he danced fervently, and about him was a halo of artistic success.

That night his brother John did not appear at the meeting of the Soul Hope Fraternity out in Rosebank.

On Monday, five days later, while he was in conference with the president and the cashier of the Lumber National Bank, Jasper complained of a headache. The next day he telephoned to the president that he would not come down to work—he would stay home and rest his eyes, sleep and get rid of the persistent headache. That was unfortunate, for that very day his twin brother John made one of his frequent trips into Vernon and called at the bank.

The president had seen John only once before, and by a coincidence it had happened on this occasion also Jasper had been absent—had been out of town. The president invited John into his private office.

"Your brother is at home; poor fellow has a bad headache. Hope he gets over it. We think a great deal of him here. You ought to be proud of him. Will you have a smoke?"

As he spoke the president looked John over. Once or twice when Jasper and the president had been out at lunch Jasper had spoken of the remarkable resemblance between himself and his twin brother. But the president told himself that he didn't really see much resemblance. The features of the two were alike, but John's expression of chronic spiritual indigestion, his unfriendly manner, and his hair—unkempt and lifeless brown, where Jasper's was sleekly black about a shiny bald spot—made the president dislike John as much as he liked Jasper.

And now John was replying: "No, I do not smoke. I can't understand how a man can soil the temple with drugs. I suppose I ought to be glad to hear you praise poor Jasper, but I am more concerned with his lack of respect for the things of the spirit. He sometimes comes to see me, at Rosebank, and I argue with him, but somehow I can't make him see his errors. And his flippant ways——!"

"We don't think he's flippant. We think he's a pretty steady worker."

"But he's play-acting! And reading love stories! Well, I try to keep in mind the injunction, 'Judge not, that ye be not judged.' But I am pained to find my own brother giving up immortal promises for mortal amusements. Well, I'll go and call on him. I trust that some day we shall see you at Soul Hope Hall, in Rosebank. Good day, sir."

Turning back to his work, the president grumbled: "I am going to tell Jasper that the best compliment I can hand him is that he is not like his brother."

And on the following day, another Wednesday, when Jasper reappeared at the bank, the president did make this jesting comparison, and Jasper sighed, "Oh, John is really a good fellow, but he's always gone in for metaphysics and Oriental mysticism and Lord knows what all, till he's kind of lost in the fog. But he's a lot better than I am. When I murder my landlady—or say, when I rob the bank, Chief—you go get John, and I bet you the best lunch in town that he'll do his best to bring me to justice. That's how square he is!"

"Square, yes—corners just sticking out! Well, when you do rob us, Jasper, I'll look up John. But do try to keep from robbing us as long as you can. I'd hate to have to associate with a religious detective in a boiled shirt!"

Both men laughed, and Jasper went back to his cage. His head continued to hurt, he admitted. The president advised him to lay off for a week. He didn't want to, he said. With the new munition industries due to the war in Europe there was much increase in factory pay rolls, and Jasper took charge of them.

"Better take a week off than get ill," argued the president late that afternoon.

Jasper did let himself be persuaded to go away for at least a week-end. He would run up north, to Wakamin Lake, the coming Friday, he said; he would get some black-bass fishing, and be back on Monday or Tuesday. Before he went he would make up the pay rolls for the Saturday payments and turn them over to the other teller. The president thanked him for his faithfulness, and as was his not infrequent custom, invited Jasper to his house for the evening of the next day—Thursday.

That Wednesday evening Jasper's brother John appeared at the Soul Hope meeting in Rosebank. When he had gone home and magically turned back into Jasper this Jasper did not return the wig and garments of John to the bureau but packed them in a suitcase, took the suitcase to his room in Vernon and locked it in his wardrobe.

Jasper was amiable at dinner at the president's house on Thursday, but he was rather silent, and as his head still throbbed he left the house early—at nine-thirty. Sedately carrying his gray silk gloves in one hand and pompously swinging his stick with the other, he walked from the president's house on the fashionable boulevard back to the center of Vernon. He entered the public garage in which he stored his car. He commented to the night attendant, "Head aches. Guess I'll take the 'bus out and get some fresh air."

He drove away at not more than fifteen miles an hour. He headed south. When he had reached the outskirts of the city he speeded up to a consistent twenty-five miles an hour. He settled down in his seat with the unmoving steadiness of the long-distance driver; his body quiet except for the tiny subtle movements of his foot on the accelerator, of his hand on the steering wheel—his right hand across the wheel, holding it at the top, his left elbow resting easily on the cushioned edge of his seat and his left hand merely touching the wheel.

He drove down in that southern direction for fifteen miles—almost to the town of Wanagoochie. Then by a rather poor side road he turned sharply to the north and west, and making a huge circle about the city drove toward the town of St. Clair. The suburb of Rosebank, in which his brother John lived, is also north of Vernon. These directions were of some importance to him; Wanagoochie eighteen miles south of the mother city of Vernon; Rosebank, on the other hand, eight miles north of Vernon, and St. Clair twenty miles north—about as far north of Vernon as Wanagoochie is south.

On his way to St. Clair, at a point that was only two miles from Rosebank, Jasper ran the car off the main road into a grove of oaks and maples and stopped it on a long-unused woodland road. He stiffly got out and walked through the woods up a rise of ground to a cliff overlooking a swampy lake. The gravelly farther bank of the cliff rose perpendicularly from the edge of the water. In that wan light distilled by stars and the earth he made out the reedy expanse of the lake. It was so muddy, so tangled with sedge grass that it was never used for swimming, and as its inhabitants were only slimy bullheads few people ever tried to fish there. Jasper stood reflective. He was remembering the story of the farmer's team which had run away, dashed over this cliff and sunk out of sight in the mud bottom of the lake.

Swishing his stick he outlined an imaginary road from the top of the cliff back to the sheltered place where his car was standing. Once he hacked away with a large pocketknife a mass of knotted hazel bushes which blocked that projected road. When he had traced the road to his car he smiled. He walked to the edge of the woods and looked up and down the main highway. A car was approaching. He waited till it had passed, ran back to his own car, backed it out on the highway, and went on his northward course toward St. Clair, driving about thirty miles an hour.

On the edge of St. Clair he halted, took out his kit of tools, unscrewed a spark plug, and sharply tapping the plug on the engine block, deliberately cracked the porcelain jacket. He screwed the plug in again and started the car. It bucked and spit, missing on one cylinder, with the short-circuited plug.

"I guess there must be something wrong with the ignition," he said cheerfully.

He managed to run the car into a garage in St. Clair. There was no one in the garage save an old negro, the night washer, who was busy over a limousine with sponge and hose.

"Got a night repair man here?" asked Jasper.

"No, sir; guess you'll have to leave it till morning."

"Hang it! Something gone wrong with the carburetor or the ignition. Well, I'll have to leave it then. Tell him—— Say will you be here in the morning when the repair man comes on?"

"Yes, sir."

"Well, tell him I must have the car by tomorrow noon. No, say by tomorrow at nine. Now, don't forget. This will help your memory."

He gave a quarter to the negro, who grinned and shouted: "Yes, sir; that'll help my memory a lot!" As he tied a storage tag on the car the negro inquired: "Name?"

"Uh—my name? Oh, Hanson. Remember now, ready about nine tomorrow."

Jasper walked to the railroad station. It was ten minutes of one. Jasper did not ask the night operator about the next train into Vernon. Apparently he knew that there was a train stopping here at St. Clair at one-thirty-seven. He did not sit in the waiting room but in the darkness outside, on a truck behind the baggage room. When the train came in he slipped into the last seat of the last car, and with his soft hat over his eyes either slept or appeared to sleep. When he reached Vernon he got off and came to the garage in which he regularly kept his car. He stepped inside. The night attendant was drowsing in a large wooden chair tilted back against the wall in the narrow runway which formed the entrance to the garage.

Jasper jovially shouted to the attendant: "Certainly ran into some hard luck. Ignition went wrong—I guess it was the ignition. Had to leave the car down at Wanagoochie."

"Yuh, hard luck, all right," assented the attendant.

"Yump. So I left it at Wanagoochie," Jasper emphasized as he passed on.

He had been inexact in this statement. It was not at Wanagoochie, which is south, but at St. Clair, which is north, that he had left his car.

He had returned to his boarding house, slept beautifully, hummed in his morning shower bath. Yet at breakfast he complained of his continuous headache, and announced that he was going up north, to Wakamin, to get some bass fishing and rest his eyes. His landlady urged him to go.

"Anything I can do to help you get away?" she queried.

"No, thanks. I'm just taking a couple of suitcases, with some old clothes and some fishing tackle. Fact, I have 'em all packed already. I'll probably take the noon train north if I can get away from the bank. Pretty busy now, with these pay rolls for the factories that have war contracts for the Allies. What's it say in the paper this morning?"

Jasper arrived at the bank, carrying the two suitcases and a neat, polite, rolled silk umbrella, the silver top of which was engraved with his name. The doorman, who was also the bank guard, helped him to carry the suitcases inside.

"Careful of that bag. Got my fishing tackle in it," said Jasper, to the doorman, apropos of one of the suitcases which was heavy but apparently not packed full. "Well, I think I'll run up to Wakamin today and catch a few bass."

"Wish I could go along, sir. How is the head this morning? Does it still ache?" asked the doorman.

"Rather better, but my eyes still feel pretty rocky. Guess I've been using them too much. Say, Connors, I'll try to catch the train north at eleven-seven. Better have a taxicab here for me at eleven. Or no; I'll let you know a little before eleven. Try to catch the eleven-seven north, for Wakamin."

"Very well, sir."

The president, the cashier, the chief clerk—all asked Jasper how he felt; and to all of them he repeated the statement that he had been using his eyes too much, and that he would catch a few bass at Wakamin.

The other paying teller, from his cage next to that of Jasper, called heartily through the steel netting: "Pretty soft for some people! You wait! I'm going to have the hay fever this summer, and I'll go fishing for a month!"

Jasper placed the two suitcases and the umbrella in his cage, and leaving the other teller to pay out current money he himself made up the pay rolls for the next day—Saturday. He casually went into the vault—a narrow, unimpressive, unaired cell with a hard linoleum floor, one unshaded electric bulb, and a back wall composed entirely of steel doors of safes, all painted a sickly blue, very unimpressive, but guarding several millions of dollars in cash and securities. The upper doors, hung on large steel arms and each provided with two dials, could be opened only by two officers of the bank, each knowing one of the two combinations. Below these were smaller doors, one of which Jasper could open, as teller. It was the door of an insignificant steel box, which contained one hundred and seventeen thousand dollars in bills and four thousand dollars in gold and silver.

Jasper passed back and forth, carrying bundles of currency. In his cage he was working less than three feet from the other teller, who was divided from him only by the bands of the steel netting.

While he worked he exchanged a few words with this other teller.

Once, as he counted out nineteen thousand dollars, he commented: "Big pay roll for the Henschel Wagon Works this week. They're making gun carriages and truck bodies for the Allies, I understand."

"Uh-huh!" said the other teller, not much interested.

Mechanically, unobtrusively going about his ordinary routine of business, Jasper counted out bills to amounts agreeing with the items on a typed schedule of the pay rolls. Apparently his eyes never lifted from his counting and from the typed schedule which lay before him. The bundles of bills he made into packages, fastening each with a paper band. Each bundle he seemed to drop into a small black leather bag which he held beside him. But he did not actually drop the money into these pay-roll bags.

Both the suitcases at his feet were closed and presumably fastened, but one was not fastened. And though it was heavy it contained nothing but a lump of pig iron. From time to time Jasper's hand, holding a bundle of bills, dropped to his side. With a slight movement of his foot he opened that suitcase and the bills slipped from his hand down into it.

The bottom part of the cage was a solid sheet of stamped steel, and from the front of the bank no one could see this suspicious gesture. The other teller could have seen it, but Jasper dropped the bills only when the other teller was busy talking to a customer or when his back was turned. In order to delay for such a favorable moment Jasper frequently counted packages of bills twice, rubbing his eyes as though they hurt him.

After each of these secret disposals of packages of bills Jasper made much of dropping into the pay-roll bags the rolls of coin for which the schedule called. It was while he was tossing these blue-wrapped cylinders of coin into the bags that he would chat with the other teller. Then he would lock up the bags and gravely place them at one side.

Jasper was so slow in making up the pay rolls that it was five minutes of eleven before he finished. He called the doorman to the cage and suggested, "Better call my taxi now."

He still had one bag to fill. He could plainly be seen dropping packages of money into it, while he instructed the assistant teller: "I'll stick all the bags in my safe and you can transfer them to yours. Be sure to lock my safe. Lord, I better hurry or I'll miss my train! Be back Tuesday morning, at latest. So long; take care yourself."

He hastened to pile the pay-roll bags into his safe in the vault. The safe was almost filled with them. And except for the last one not one of the bags contained anything except a few rolls of coin. Though he had told the other teller to lock his safe, he himself twirled the combination —which was thoughtless of him, as the assistant teller would now have to wait and get the president to unlock it.

He picked up his umbrella and two suitcases, bending over one of the cases for not more than ten seconds. Waving good-by to the cashier at his desk down front and hurrying so fast that the doorman did not have a chance to help him carry the suitcases, he rushed through the bank, through the door, into the waiting taxicab, and loudly enough for the doorman to hear he cried to the driver, "M. & D. Station."

At the M. & D. R. R. Station, refusing offers of redcaps to carry his bags, he bought a ticket for Wakamin, which is a lake-resort town one hundred and forty miles north-west of Vernon, hence one hundred and twenty beyond St. Clair. He had just time to get aboard the eleven-seven train. He did not take a chair car, but sat in a day coach near the rear door. He unscrewed the silver top of his umbrella, on which was engraved his name, and dropped it into his pocket.

When the train reached St. Clair, Jasper strolled out to the vestibule, carrying the suitcases but leaving the top-less umbrella behind. His face was blank, uninterested. As the train started he dropped down on the station platform and gravely walked away. For a second the light of adventure crossed his face, and vanished.

At the garage at which he had left his car on the evening before he asked the foreman: "Did you get my car fixed —Mercury roadster, ignition on the bum?"

"Nope! Couple of jobs ahead of it. Haven't had time to touch it yet. Ought to get at it early this afternoon."

Jasper curled his tongue round his lips in startled vexation. He dropped his suitcases on the floor of the garage and stood thinking, his bent forefinger against his lower lip.

Then: "Well, I guess I can get her to go—sorry—can't wait—got to make the next town," he grumbled.

"Lot of you traveling salesmen making your territory by motor now, Mr. Hanson," said the foreman civilly, glancing at the storage check on Jasper's car.

"Yep. I can make a good many more than I could by train."

He paid for overnight storage without complaining, though since his car had not been repaired this charge was unjust. In fact, he was altogether prosaic and inconspicuous. He thrust the suitcases into the car and drove away, the motor spitting. At another garage he bought another spark plug and screwed it in. When he went on, the motor had ceased spitting.

He drove out of St. Clair, back in the direction of Vernon—and of Rosebank where his brother lived. He ran the car into that thick grove of oaks and maples only two miles from Rosebank, where he had paced off an imaginary road to the cliff overhanging the reedy lake. He parked his car in a grassy space beside the abandoned woodland road. He laid a light robe over the suitcases. From beneath the seat he took a can of deviled chicken, a box of biscuits, a canister of tea, a folding cooking kit and a spirit lamp. These he spread on the grass—a picnic lunch.

He sat beside that lunch from seven minutes past one

in the afternoon till dark. Once in a while he made a pretense of eating. He fetched water from the brook, made tea, opened the box of biscuits and the can of chicken. But mostly he sat still and smoked cigarette after cigarette.

Once, a Swede, taking this road as a short cut to his truck farm, passed by and mumbled, "Picnic, eh?"

"Yuh, takin' the day off," said Jasper dully.

The man went on without looking back.

At dusk Jasper finished a cigarette down to the tip, crushed out the light and made the cryptic remark:

"That's probably Jasper Holt's last smoke. I don't suppose you can smoke, John—damn you!"

He hid the two suitcases in the bushes, piled the remains of the lunch into the car, took down the top of the car, and crept down to the main road. No one was in sight. He returned. He snatched a hammer and a chisel from his tool kit, and with a few savage cracks he so defaced the number of the car stamped on the engine block that it could not be made out. He removed the license numbers from fore and aft, and placed them beside the suitcases. Then, when there was just enough light to see the bushes as cloudy masses, he started the car, drove through the woods and up the incline to the top of the cliff, and halted, leaving the engine running.

Between the car and the edge of the cliff which overhung the lake there was a space of about one hundred and thirty feet, fairly level and covered with straggly red clover. Jasper paced off this distance, returned to the car, took his seat in a nervous, tentative way and put her into gear, starting on second speed and slamming her into third. The car bolted toward the edge of the cliff. He instantly swung out on the running board. Standing there, headed directly toward the sharp drop over the cliff, steering with his left hand on the wheel, he shoved the hand throttle up—up—up with his right. He safely leaped down from the running board.

Of itself, the car rushed forward, roaring. It shot over the edge of the cliff. It soared twenty feet out into the air, as though it were a thick-bodied aeroplane. It turned over and over, with a sickening drop toward the lake. The water splashed up in a tremendous noisy circle. Then silence. In the twilight the surface of the lake shone like milk. There was no sign of the car on the surface. The concentric rings died away. The lake was secret and sinister and still. "Lord!" ejaculated Jasper, standing on the cliff; then: "Well, they won't find that for a couple of years anyway."

He turned to the suitcases. Squatting beside them he took from one the wig and black garments of John Holt. He stripped, put on the clothes of John, and packed those of Jasper in the bag. With the cases and the motor-license plates he walked toward Rosebank, keeping in various groves of maples and willows till he was within half a mile of the town. He reached the stone house at the end of the willow walk and sneaked in the back way. He burned Jasper Holt's clothes in the grate, melted down the license plates in the stove, and between two rocks he smashed Jasper's expensive watch and fountain pen into an unpleasant mass of junk, which he dropped into the cistern for rain water. The silver head of the umbrella he scratched with a chisel till the engraved name was indistinguishable.

He unlocked a section of the bookcase and taking a number of packages of bills in denominations of one, five, ten and twenty dollars from one of the suitcases he packed them into those empty candy boxes which, on the shelves, looked so much like books. As he stored them he counted the bills. They came to ninety-seven thousand five hundred and thirty-five dollars.

The two suitcases were new. There were no distinguishing marks on them. But taking them out to the kitchen he kicked them, rubbed them with lumps of blacking, raveled their edges and cut their sides, till they gave the appearance of having been long and badly used in traveling. He took them upstairs and tossed them up into the low attic.

In his bedroom he undressed calmly. Once he laughed: "I despise those pretentious fools—bank officers and cops. I'm beyond their fool law. No one can catch me—it would take me myself to do that!"

He got into bed. With a vexed "Hang it!" he mused, "I suppose John would pray, no matter how chilly the floor was."

He got out of bed and from the inscrutable Lord of the Universe he sought forgiveness—not for Jasper Holt, but for the denominations who lacked the true faith of Soul Hope Fraternity.

He returned to bed and slept till the middle of the morning, lying with his arms behind his head, a smile on his face.

Thus did Jasper Holt, without the mysterious pangs of death, yet cease to exist, and thus did John Holt come into being not merely as an apparition glimpsed on Sunday and Wednesday evenings but as a being living twenty-four hours a day, seven days a week.

III

The inhabitants of Rosebank were familiar with the occasional appearances of John Holt, the eccentric recluse, and they merely snickered about him when on the Saturday evening following the Friday that has been chronicled he was seen to come out of his gate and trudge down to a news and stationery shop on Main Street.

He purchased an evening paper and said to the clerk: "You can have the *Morning Herald* delivered at my house every morning—27 Humbert Avenue."

"Yuh, I know where it is. Thought you had kind of a grouch on newspapers," said the clerk pertly.

"Ah, did you indeed? The *Herald*, every morning, please. I will pay a month in advance," was all John Holt said, but he looked directly at the clerk, and the man cringed.

John attended the meeting of the Soul Hope Fraternity the next evening—Sunday—but he was not seen on the streets again for two and a half days.

There was no news of the disappearance of Jasper Holt till the following Wednesday, when the whole thing came out in a violent, small-city, front-page story, headed:

PAYING TELLER

SOCIAL FAVORITE—MAKES GET-AWAY

The paper stated that Jasper Holt had been missing for four days, and that the officers of the bank, after first denying that there was anything wrong with his accounts, had admitted that he was short one hundred thousand dollars—two hundred thousand, said one report. He had purchased a ticket for Wakamin, this state, on Friday and a trainman, a customer of the bank, had noticed him on the train, but he had apparently never arrived at Wakamin.

A woman asserted that on Friday afternoon she had seen Holt driving an automobile between Vernon and St. Clair. This appearance near St. Clair was supposed to be merely a blind, however. In fact, our able chief of police had proof that Holt was not headed north, in the direction of St. Clair, but south, beyond Wanagoochie—probably for Des Moines or St. Louis. It was definitely known that on the previous day Holt had left his car at Wanagoochie, and with their customary thoroughness and promptness the police were making search at Wanagoochie. The chief had already communicated with the police in cities to the south, and the capture of the man could confidently be expected at any moment. As long as the chief appointed by our popular mayor was in power, it went ill with those who gave even the appearance of wrongdoing.

When asked his opinion of the theory that the alleged fugitive had gone north the chief declared that of course Holt had started in that direction, with the vain hope of throwing pursuers off the scent, but that he had immediately turned south and picked up his car. Though he would not say so definitely the chief let it be known that he was ready to put his hands on the fellow who had hidden Holt's car at Wanagoochie.

When asked if he thought Holt was crazy the chief laughed and said: "Yes, he's crazy two hundred thousand dollars' worth. I'm not making any slams, but there's a lot of fellows among our political opponents who would go a whole lot crazier for a whole lot less!"

The president of the bank, however, was greatly distressed, and strongly declared his belief that Holt, who was a favorite in the most sumptuous residences on the Boulevard, besides being well known in local dramatic circles, and who bore the best of reputations in the bank, was temporarily out of his mind, as he had been distressed by pains in the head for some time past. Meantime the bonding company, which had fully covered the employees of the bank by a joint bond of two hundred thousand dollars, had its detectives working with the police on the case.

As soon as he had read the paper John took a trolley

into Vernon and called on the president of the bank.
John's face drooped with the sorrow of the disgrace. The
president received him. John staggered into the room,
groaning: "I have just learned in the newspaper of the
terrible news about my brother. I have come——"

"We hope it's just a case of aphasia. We're sure he'll
turn up all right," insisted the president.

"I wish I could believe it. But as I have told you,
Jasper is not a good man. He drinks and smokes and play-
acts and makes a god of stylish clothes——"

"Good Lord, that's no reason for jumping to the con-
clusion that he's an embezzler!"

"I pray you may be right. But meanwhile I wish to give
you any assistance I can. I shall make it my sole duty to
see that my brother is brought to justice if it proves that
he is guilty."

"Good o' you," mumbled the president. Despite this
example of John's rigid honor he could not get himself to
like the man. John was standing beside him, thrusting his
stupid face into his.

The president pushed his chair a foot farther away and
said disagreeably: "As a matter of fact, we were thinking
of searching your house. If I remember, you live in Rosebank?"

"Yes. And of course I shall be glad to have you search
every inch of it. Or anything else I can do. I feel that I
share fully with my twin brother in this unspeakable sin.
I'll turn over the key of my house to you at once. There
is also a shed at the back where Jasper used to keep his
automobile when he came to see me." He produced a
large, rusty, old-fashioned door key and held it out, add-
ing: "The address is 27 Humbert Avenue, Rosebank."

"Oh, it won't be necessary, I guess," said the president,
somewhat shamed, irritably waving off the key.

"But I just want to help somehow! What can I do? Who is—in the language of the newspapers—who is the detective on the case? I'll give him any help——"

"Tell you what you do: Go see Mr. Scandling, of the Mercantile Trust and Bonding Company, and tell him all you know."

"I shall. I take my brother's crime on my shoulders— otherwise I'd be committing the sin of Cain. You are giving me a chance to try to expiate our joint sin, and, as Brother Jeremiah Bodfish was wont to say, it is a blessing to have an opportunity to expiate a sin, no matter how painful the punishment may seem to be to the mere physical being. As I may have told you I am an accepted member of the Soul Hope Fraternity, and though we are free from cant and dogma it is our firm belief——"

Then for ten dreary minutes John Holt sermonized; quoted forgotten books and quaint, ungenerous elders; twisted bitter pride and clumsy mysticism into fanatical spider web. The president was a churchgoer, an ardent supporter of missionary funds, for forty years a pew-holder at St. Simeon's Church, but he was alternately bored to a chill shiver and roused to wrath against this self-righteous zealot.

When he had rather rudely got rid of John Holt he complained to himself: "Curse it, I oughtn't to, but I must say I prefer Jasper the sinner to John the saint. Uff! What a smell of damp cellars the fellow has! He must spend all his time picking potatoes. Say! By thunder, I remember that Jasper had the infernal nerve to tell me once that if he ever robbed the bank I was to call John in. I know why, now! John is the kind of egotistical fool that would muddle up any kind of a systematic search. Well, Jasper, sorry, but I'm not going to have anything more to do with John than I can help!"

John had gone to the Mercantile Trust and Bonding Company, had called on Mr. Scandling, and was now wearying him by a detailed and useless account of Jasper's early years and recent vices. He was turned over to the detective employed by the bonding company to find Jasper. The detective was a hard, noisy man, who found John even more tedious. John insisted on his coming out to examine the house in Rosebank, and the detective did so—but sketchily, trying to escape. John spent at least five minutes in showing him the shed where Jasper had sometimes kept his car.

He also attempted to interest the detective in his precious but spotty books. He unlocked one section of the case, dragged down a four-volume set of sermons and started to read them aloud.

The detective interrupted: "Yuh, that's great stuff, but I guess we aren't going to find your brother hiding behind those books!"

The detective got away as soon as possible, after insistently explaining to John that if they could use his assistance they would let him know.

"If I can only expiate——"

"Yuh, sure, that's all right!" wailed the detective, fairly running toward the gate.

John made one more visit to Vernon that day. He called on the chief of city police. He informed the chief that he had taken the bonding company's detective through his house, but wouldn't the police consent to search it also? He wanted to expiate—— The chief patted John on the back, advised him not to feel responsible for his brother's guilt and begged: "Skip along now—very busy."

As John walked to the Soul Hope meeting that evening, dozens of people murmured that it was his brother who had robbed the Lumber National Bank. His head was bowed with the shame. At the meeting he took Jasper's sin upon himself, and prayed that Jasper would be caught and receive the blessed healing of punishment. The others begged John not to feel that he was guilty—was he not one of the Soul Hope brethren who alone in this wicked and perverse generation were assured of salvation?

On Thursday, on Saturday morning, on Tuesday and on Friday, John went into the city to call on the president of the bank and the detective. Twice the president saw him, and was infinitely bored by his sermons. The third time he sent word that he was out. The fourth time he saw John, but curtly explained that if John wanted to help them the best thing he could do was to stay away.

The detective was out all four times.

John smiled meekly and ceased to try to help them. Dust began to gather on certain candy boxes on the lower shelf of his bookcase, save for one of them, which he took out now and then. Always after he had taken it out a man with faded brown hair and a wrinkled black suit, a man signing himself R. J. Smith, would send a fair-sized money order from the post office at South Vernon to John Holt, at Rosebank—as he had been doing for more than six months. These money orders could not have amounted to more than twenty-five dollars a week, but that was even more than an ascetic like John Holt needed. By day John sometimes cashed these at the Rosebank post office, but usually, as had been his custom, he cashed them at his favorite grocery when he went out in the evening.

In conversation with the commuter neighbor, who every evening walked about and smoked an after-dinner cigar in the yard at the right, John was frank about the whole lamentable business of his brother's defalcation. He wondered, he said, if he had not shut himself up with his studies too much, and neglected his brother. The neighbor ponderously advised John to get out more. John let himself be persuaded, at least to the extent of taking a short walk every afternoon and of letting his literary solitude be disturbed by the delivery of milk, meat, and groceries. He also went to the public library, and in the reference room glanced at books on Central and South America—as though he was planning to go south some day.

But he continued his religious studies. It may be doubted if previous to the embezzlement John had worked very consistently on his book about Revelation. All that the world had ever seen of it was a jumble of quotations from theological authorities. Presumably the crime of his brother shocked him into more concentrated study, more patient writing. For during the year after his brother's disappearance—a year in which the bonding company gradually gave up the search and came to believe that Jasper was dead—John became fanatically absorbed in somewhat nebulous work. The days and nights drifted together in meditation in which he lost sight of realities, and seemed through the clouds of the flesh to see flashes from the towered cities of the spirit.

It has been asserted that when Jasper Holt acted a rôle he veritably lived it. No one can ever determine how great an actor was lost in the smug bank teller. To him were imperial triumphs denied, yet he was not without material reward. For playing his most subtle part he received ninety-seven thousand dollars. It may be that he earned it. Certainly for the risk entailed it was but a fair payment. Jasper had meddled with the mystery of personality, and was in peril of losing all consistent purpose, of becoming a Wandering Jew of the spirit, a strangled body walking.

IV

The sharp-pointed willow leaves had twisted and fallen, after the dreary rains of October. Bark had peeled from the willow trunks, leaving gashes of bare wood that was a wet and sickly yellow. Through the denuded trees bulked the solid stone of John Holt's house. The patches of earth were greasy between the tawny knots of grass stems. The bricks of the walk were always damp now. The world was hunched up in this pervading chill.

As melancholy as the sick earth seemed the man who in a slaty twilight paced the willow walk. His step was slack, his lips moved with the intensity of his meditation. Over his wrinkled black suit and bleak shirt bosom was a worn overcoat, the velvet collar turned green. He was considering.

"There's something to all this. I begin to see—I don't know what it is I do see! But there's lights—supernatural world that makes food and bed seem ridiculous. I am—I really am beyond the law! I make my own law! Why shouldn't I go beyond the law of vision and see the secrets of life? But I sinned, and I must repent—some day. I need not return the money. I see now that it was given me so that I could lead this life of contemplation. But the ingratitude to the president, to the people who trusted me! Am I but the most miserable of sinners, and as the blind? Voices—I hear conflicting voices—some praising me for my courage, some rebuking——"

He knelt on the slimy black surface of a wooden bench beneath the willows, and as dusk clothed him round about he prayed. It seemed to him that he prayed not in words but in vast confusing dreams—the words of a language larger than human tongues. When he had exhausted himself he slowly entered the house. He locked the door. There was nothing definite of which he was afraid, but he was never comfortable with the door unlocked.

By candle light he prepared his austere supper—dry toast, an egg, cheap green tea with thin milk. As always—as it had happened after every meal, now, for eighteen months —he wanted a cigarette when he had eaten, but did not take one. He paced into the living room and through the long still hours of the evening he read an ancient book, all footnotes and cross references, about The Numerology of the Prophetic Books, and the Number of the Beast. He tried to make notes for his own book on Revelation—that scant pile of sheets covered with writing in a small finicky hand. Thousands of other sheets he had covered; through whole nights he had written; but always he seemed with tardy pen to be racing after thoughts that he could never quite catch, and most of what he had written he had savagely burned.

But some day he would make a masterpiece! He was feeling toward the greatest discovery that mortal man had encountered. Everything, he had determined, was a symbol—not just this holy sign and that, but all physical manifestations. With frightened exultation he tried his new power of divination. The hanging lamp swung tinily. He ventured: "If the arc of that moving radiance touches the edge of the bookcase, then it will be a sign that I am to go to South America, under an entirely new disguise, and spend my money."

He shuddered. He watched the lamp's unbearably slow swing. The moving light almost touched the bookcase. He gasped. Then it receded.

It was a warning; he quaked. Would he never leave this place of brooding and of fear, which he had thought so clever a refuge? He suddenly saw it all.

"I ran away and hid in a prison! Man isn't caught by justice—he catches himself!"

Again he tried. He speculated as to whether the number of pencils on the table was greater or less than five. If greater, then he had sinned; if less, then he was veritably beyond the law. He began to lift books and papers, looking for pencils. He was coldly sweating with the suspense of the test.

Suddenly he cried, "Am I going crazy?"

He fled to his prosaic bedroom. He could not sleep. His brain was smoldering with confused inklings of mystic numbers and hidden warnings.

He woke from a half sleep more vision-haunted than any waking thought, and cried: "I must go back and confess! But I can't! I can't, when I was too clever for them! I can't go back and let them win. I won't let those fools just sit tight and still catch me!"

It was a year and a half since Jasper had disappeared. Sometimes it seemed a month and a half; sometimes gray centuries. John's will power had been shrouded with curious puttering studies; long, heavy-breathing sittings with the ouija board on his lap, midnight hours when he had fancied that tables had tapped and crackling coals had spoken. Now that the second autumn of his seclusion was creeping into winter he was conscious that he had not enough initiative to carry out his plans for going to South America. The summer before he had boasted to himself that he would come out of hiding and go South, leaving such a twisty trail as only he could make. But—oh, it was too much trouble. He hadn't the joy in play-acting which had carried his brother Jasper through his preparations for flight.

He had killed Jasper Holt, and for a miserable little pile of paper money he had become a moldy recluse!

He hated his loneliness, but still more did he hate his only companions, the members of the Soul Hope Fraternity—that pious shrill seamstress, that surly carpenter, that tight-lipped housekeeper, that old shouting man with the unseemly frieze of whiskers. They were so unimaginative. Their meetings were all the same; the same persons rose in the same order and made the same intimate announcements to the Deity that they alone were his elect.

At first it had been an amusing triumph to be accepted as the most eloquent among them, but that had become commonplace, and he resented their daring to be familiar with him, who was, he felt, the only man of all men living who beyond the illusions of the world saw the strange beatitude of higher souls.

It was at the end of November, during a Wednesday meeting at which a red-faced man had for a half hour maintained that he couldn't possibly sin, that the cumulative ennui burst in John Holt's brain. He sprang up.

He snarled: "You make me sick, all of you! You think you're so certain of sanctification that you can't do wrong. So did I, once! Now I know that we are all miserable sinners—really are! You all say you are, but you don't believe it. I tell you that you there that have just been yammering, and you, Brother Judkins, with the long twitching nose, and I—I—I, most unhappy of men, we must repent, confess, expiate our sins! And I will confess right now. I st-stole——"

Terrified he darted out of the hall, and hatless, coatless, tumbled through the main street of Rosebank, nor ceased till he had locked himself in his house. He was frightened because he had almost betrayed his secret, yet agonized because he had not gone on, really confessed, and gained the only peace he could ever know now—the peace of punishment.

He never returned to Soul Hope Hall. Indeed for a week he did not leave his house save for midnight prowling

in the willow walk. Quite suddenly he became desperate
with the silence. He flung out of the house, not stopping
to lock or even close the front door. He raced uptown, no
topcoat over his rotting garments, only an old gardener's
cap on his thick brown hair. People stared at him. He
bore it with resigned fury.

He entered a lunch room, hoping to sit inconspicuously
and hear men talking normally about him. The attendant
at the counter gaped. John heard a mutter from the cashier's desk: "There's that crazy hermit!"

All of the half-dozen young men loafing in the place
were looking at him. He was so uncomfortable that he
could not eat even the milk and sandwich he had ordered.
He pushed them away and fled, a failure in the first attempt to dine out that he had made in eighteen months;
a lamentable failure to revive that Jasper Holt whom he
had coldly killed.

He entered a cigar store and bought a box of cigarettes.
He took joy out of throwing away his asceticism. But
when, on the street, he lighted a cigarette it made him so
dizzy that he was afraid he was going to fall. He had to
sit down on the curb. People gathered. He staggered to his
feet and up an alley.

For hours he walked, making and discarding the most
contradictory plans—to go to the bank and confess, to
spend the money riotously and never confess.

It was midnight when he returned to his house.

Before it he gasped. The front door was open. He
chuckled with relief as he remembered that he had not
closed it. He sauntered in. He was passing the door of the
living room, going directly up to his bedroom, when his
foot struck an object the size of a book, but hollow sound-
ing. He picked it up. It was one of the booklike candy
boxes. And it was quite empty. Frightened, he listened.

There was no sound. He crept into the living room and lighted the lamp.

The doors of the bookcase had been wrenched open. Every book had been pulled out on the floor. All of the candy boxes, which that evening had contained almost ninety-six thousand dollars, were in a pile, and all of them were empty. He searched for ten minutes, but the only money he found was one five-dollar bill, which had fluttered under the table. In his pocket he had one dollar and sixteen cents. John Holt had six dollars and sixteen cents, no job, no friends—and no identity.

V

When the president of the Lumber National Bank was informed that John Holt was waiting to see him he scow1ᵔd.

"Lord, I'd forgotten that minor plague! Must be a year since he's been here. Oh, let him—— No, hanged if I will! Tell him I'm too busy to see him. That is, unless he's got some news about Jasper. Pump him, and find out."

The president's secretary sweetly confided to John:

"I'm so sorry, but the president is in conference just now. What was it you wanted to see him about? Is there any news about—uh—about your brother?"

"There is not, miss. I am here to see the president on the business of the Lord."

"Oh! If that's all I'm afraid I can't disturb him."

"I will wait."

Wait he did, through all the morning, through the lunch hour—when the president hastened out past him—then into the afternoon, till the president was unable to work with the thought of that scarecrow out there, and sent for him.

"Well, well! What is it this time, John? I'm pretty busy. No news about Jasper, eh?"

"No news, sir, but—Jasper himself! I am Jasper Holt! His sin is my sin."

"Yes, yes, I know all that stuff—twin brothers, twin souls, share responsibility——"

"You don't understand. There isn't any twin brother. There isn't any John Holt. I am Jasper. I invented an imaginary brother, and disguised myself—— Why, don't you recognize my voice?"

While John leaned over the desk, his two hands upon it, and smiled wistfully, the president shook his head and soothed: "No, I'm afraid I don't. Sounds like good old religious John to me! Jasper was a cheerful, efficient sort of crook. Why, his laugh——"

"But I can laugh!" The dreadful croak which John uttered was the cry of an evil bird of the swamps. The president shuddered. Under the edge of the desk his fingers crept toward the buzzer by which he summoned his secretary.

They stopped as John urged: "Look—this wig—it's a wig. See, I am Jasper!"

He had snatched off the brown thatch. He stood expectant, a little afraid.

The president was startled, but he shook his head and sighed.

"You poor devil! Wig, all right. But I wouldn't say that hair was much like Jasper's!"

He motioned toward the mirror in the corner of the room.

John wavered to it. And indeed he saw that his hair had turned from Jasper's thin sleek blackness to a straggle of damp gray locks writhing over a yellow skull.

He begged pitifully: "Oh, can't you see I am Jasper?

I stole ninety-seven thousand dollars from the bank. I
want to be punished! I want to do anything to prove——
Why, I've been at your house. Your wife's name is Evelyn.
My salary here was——"

"My dear boy, don't you suppose that Jasper might
have told you all these interesting facts? I'm afraid the
worry of this has—pardon me if I'm frank, but I'm afraid
it's turned your head a little, John."

"There isn't any John! There isn't! There isn't!"

"I'd believe that a little more easily if I hadn't met you
before Jasper disappeared."

"Give me a piece of paper. You know my writing——"

With clutching claws John seized a sheet of bank stationery and tried to write in the round script of Jasper. During
the past year and a half he had filled thousands of pages
with the small finicky hand of John. Now, though he tried
to prevent it, after he had traced two or three words in
large but shaky letters the writing became smaller, more
pinched, less legible.

Even while John wrote the president looked at the sheet
and said easily: "Afraid it's no use. That isn't Jasper's
fist. See here, I want you to get away from Rosebank—
go to some farm—work outdoors—cut out this fuming
and fussing—get some fresh air in your lungs." The
president rose and purred: "Now, I'm afraid I have some
work to do."

He paused, waiting for John to go.

John fiercely crumpled the sheet and hurled it away.
Tears were in his weary eyes.

He wailed: "Is there nothing I can do to prove I am
Jasper?"

"Why, certainly! You can produce what's left of the
ninety-seven thousand!"

John took from his ragged waistcoat pocket a five-dollar

bill and some change. "Here's all there is. Ninety-six thousand of it was stolen from my house last night."

Sorry though he was for the madman, the president could not help laughing. Then he tried to look sympathetic, and he comforted: "Well, that's hard luck, old man. Uh, let's see. You might produce some parents or relatives or somebody to prove that Jasper never did have a twin brother."

"My parents are dead, and I've lost track of their kin —I was born in England—Father came over when I was six. There might be some cousins or some old neighbors, but I don't know. Probably impossible to find out, in these wartimes, without going over there."

"Well, I guess we'll have to let it go, old man." The president was pressing the buzzer for his secretary and gently bidding her: "Show Mr. Holt out, please."

From the door John desperately tried to add: "You will find my car sunk——"

The door had closed behind him. The president had not listened.

The president gave orders that never, for any reason, was John Holt to be admitted to his office again. He telephoned to the bonding company that John Holt had now gone crazy; that they would save trouble by refusing to admit him.

John did not try to see them. He went to the county jail. He entered the keeper's office and said quietly: "I have stolen a lot of money, but I can't prove it. Will you put me in jail?"

The keeper shouted: "Get out of here! You hoboes always spring that when you want a good warm lodging for the winter! Why the devil don't you go to work with a shovel in the sand pits? They're paying two-seventy-five a day."

"Yes, sir," said John timorously. "Where are they?"

THE CAT OF THE STARS

THE CAT OF THE STARS

THE fatalities have been three thousand, two hundred and ninety-one, to date, with more reported in every cable from San Coloquin, but it is not yet decided whether the ultimate blame is due to the conductor of Car 22, to Mrs. Simmy Dolson's bland selfishness, or to the fact that Willis Stodeport patted a sarsaparilla-colored kitten with milky eyes.

It was a hypocritical patting. Willis had been playing pumpum-pullaway all afternoon, hence was hungry, and desirous of winning favor with his mother by his nice attitude toward our dumb friends. Willis didn't actually care for being nice to the dumb friend. What he wanted was cookies. So slight was his esteem for the kitten—whose name was Adolphus Josephus Mudface—that afterward he took it out to the kitchen and tried to see if it would drown under the tap of the sink.

Yet such is the strange and delicate balance of nature, with the lightest tremor in the dream of a terrestrial baby affecting the course of suns ten million light-years away, that the patting of Adolphus Josephus Mudface has started a vicious series of events that will be felt forever in star beyond mounting star. The death of exiled Napoleon made a few old men stop to scratch their heads and dream. The fall of Carthage gave cheap bricks to builders of dumpy huts. But the false deed of Willis Stodeport has changed history.

Mrs. Simmy Dolson was making an afternoon call upon the mother of this portentous but tow-headed Willis, who resides upon Scrimmins Street, in the Middle-Western city of Vernon. The two matrons had discussed the price of butter, the iniquities of the fluffy-headed new teacher in Public School 17, and the idiocy of these new theories about bringing up young ones. Mrs. Dolson was keeping an ear on the car line, for the Oakdale cars run only once in eighteen minutes, and if she missed the next one she would be too late to prepare supper. Just as she heard it coming, and seized her hat, she saw young Willis edge into the room and stoop to pat the somnolent Adolphus Josephus Mudface.

With a hatpin half inserted Mrs. Dolson crooned, "My, what a dear boy! Now isn't that sweet!"

Willis's mother forgot that she had intended to have words with her offspring in the matter of the missing knob of the flour bin. She beamed, and to Willis she gurgled, "Do you like the kittie, dearie?"

"Yes, I love our kittie; can I have a cookie?" young Machiavelli hastened to get in; and Aldebaran, the crimson star, throbbed with premonition.

"Now isn't that sweet!" Mrs. Dolson repeated—then remembered her car and galloped away.

She had been so delayed by the admiration of daily deeds of kindness that when she reached the corner the Oakdale car was just passing. It was crowded with tired business men in a fret to get home to the outskirts of Vernon, but Mrs. Simmy Dolson was one of those plump, amiably selfish souls who would keep a whole city waiting while she bought canary seed. She waved at the car and made deceptive motions of frantic running.

The conductor of the car, which was Number 22, was a kind-hearted family man, and he rang for a stop halfway down the block. Despite the growling of the seventy passengers he held the car till Mrs. Dolson had wheezed aboard, which made them two minutes late. That was just enough to cause them to miss the switch at Seven Corners; and they had to wait while three other cars took the switch before them.

By that time Car 22 was three and three-quarters minutes late.

Mr. Andrew Discopolos, the popular proprietor of the Dandy Barber Shop, was the next step in the tragedy. Mr. Discopolos was waiting for this same Oakdale car. He had promised his wife to go home to supper, but in his bacchanalian soul he desired to sneak down to Barney's for an evening of poker. He waited one minute, and was tremendously moral and determined to eschew gambling. He waited for two minutes, and began to see what a martyr he was. There would never be another Oakdale car. He would have to walk home. His wife expected too darn much of him, anyway! He waited for three minutes, and in rose tints and soft gold he remembered the joys of playing poker at Barney's.

Seven seconds before the delayed Oakdale car turned the corner Mr. Discopolos gave up the struggle, and with outer decorum and inner excitement he rushed up an alley, headed for Barney's. He stopped at the Southern Café for a Denver sandwich and cuppacoffee. He shook for the cigars at the Smoke House, and won three-for's, which indicated to him how right he had been in not going home. He reached Barney's at seven-thirty. He did not leave Barney's till one-thirty in the morning, and when he did leave he was uncertain of direction, but very vigorous of motion, due to his having celebrated the winning of four dollars by buying a quart of rye.

Under a dusty and discouraged autumn moon Mr. Discopolos weaved home. Willis Stodeport and Mrs. Simmy Dolson and the conductor of Car 22 were asleep now; even the disreputable Adolphus Josephus Mudface had, after a charming fight behind the Smiths' garbage can, retired to innocent slumbers on the soft folds of the floor mop in the corner of the back porch where he was least likely to be disturbed by mice. Only Mr. Discopolos was awake, but he was bearing on the torch of evil destiny; and on one of the planets of the sun that is called Procyon there were floods and earthquakes.

When Mr. Discopolos awoke in the morning his eyes were filmy and stinging. Before he went to his shop he had three fingers of pick-me-up, which so exhilarated him that he stood on the corner, swaying and beaming. Normally he had pride in his technic as a barber, but now all his more delicate artistry was gone in a roving desire for adventure. With a professional eye he noted the haircut of a tough young man loafing in front of the drug store. It was a high haircut, leaving the neck and the back of the head bald clear up to the crown. "Be a joke on some fellow to cut his hair that way!" giggled Mr. Discopolos.

It was the first time in a year that he had needed, or taken, a drink before afternoon. Chuckling Fate sent to him the next torchbearer, Mr. Palmer McGee.

Palmer McGee was one of Vernon's most promising young men. He lived at the University Club; he had two suits of evening clothes; and he was assistant to the president of the M. & D. R. R. He was a technical-school graduate and a Spanish scholar as well as a business-system expert; and his club-grill manners were as accurate as his knowledge of traffic routing. Today was his hour of greatness. He had, as the result of long correspondence, this morning received a telegram inviting him to come to New York to see the president and directors of the Citrus and Southern Steamship Company about the position of Buenos Aires manager for the company. He had packed in ten minutes. But he had an hour before his train, with the station only twenty minutes away by trolley. Instead of taking a taxi he exuberantly walked from the club to Selden Street to catch a car.

One door from the corner he beheld the barber shop of Mr. Discopolos, which reminded him that he needed a haircut. He might not have time to get one in New York before he saw the steamship directors. The shop was bright, and Mr. Discopolos, by the window in a white jacket, was clean and jolly.

Palmer McGee popped into the shop and caroled "Haircut; medium." Magnetized by Mr. Discopolos' long light fingers he closed his eyes and dreamed of his future.

About the middle of the haircut the morning's morning of Mr. Discopolos rose up and jostled him and dimmed his eyes, with the result that he cut too deep a swath of hair across the back of Mr. McGee's sleek head. Mr. Discopolos sighed, and peeped at the victim to see if he was aware of the damage. But Mr. McGee was sitting with eyes tight, lips apart, already a lord of ocean traffic, giving orders to Singhalese planters and to traders in the silent northern pines.

Mr. Discopolos remembered the high-shaved neck of the corner loafer, and imitated that model. He ruthlessly con-

cealed the too-deep slash by almost denuding the back of
Mr. McGee's head. That erstwhile polite neck stood out
as bare as an ostrich.

Being an artist, Mr. Discopolos had to keep the sym-
metry—the rhythm—correct, so he balanced the back by
also removing too much hair from in front—from above
Mr. McGee's Yalensian ears.

When the experiment was complete, Mr. McGee looked
like a bald young man with a small wig riding atop his
head. He looked like a wren's nest on top of a clothes
pole. He looked painstakingly and scientifically skinned.
At least it was thus that he saw himself in the barber's
mirror when he opened his eyes.

He called on a number of deities; he said he wanted to
assassinate Mr. Discopolos. But he hadn't time for this
work of mercy. He had to catch his train. He took his mal-
treated head into a taxi, feeling shamefully that the taxi
driver was snickering at his haircut.

Left behind, untipped and much berated, Mr. Discopolos grumbled, "I did take off a little too much; but rats,
he'll be all right in couple of weeks. What's couple of
weeks? Believe I'll go get a drink."

Thus, as ignorant as they of taking any part in a pro-
gressive tragedy, Mr. Discopolos joined Willis Stodeport,
Adolphus Josephus, Mrs. Dolson and the too-generous
conductor of Car 22, in the darkness of unimportance,
while Palmer McGee was on the Pullman—and extremely
wretched.

He fancied that everyone from the porter to the silken
girl across the aisle was snickering at his eccentric coiffure.
To Mr. McGee, queerness of collar or hair or slang was
more wicked than murder. He had rigidly trained himself
to standards in everything. There were, for example, only
three brands of whisky on which a gentleman could de-

cently get edged. He was the most dependable young man
in the general offices of the M. & D. R. R., and before that
he had been so correctly pleasant to the right fellows and so
correctly aloof with the wrong fellows, so agreeably pipe-
smoking and laudatory of athletics, that he had made both
junior and senior societies at Yale. He had had no experience to teach him to bear up under this utter disgrace of a
variation from the standard of haircutting.

As the train relentlessly bore him on toward New York
he now and then accumulated courage to believe that his
haircut couldn't be so bad as he knew it was. He would
stroll with noble casualness into the smoking compart-
ment, and the instant it was free of other passengers he
would dart at the mirror. Each time he made the same
quaking discovery that he was even more ridiculous than
he remembered.

By day, trying to read or scan the scenery or impress
fellow smokers, by night, folded in his swaying berth—he
could think of nothing else. He read only one paragraph
of the weighty book which all persons carry on all Pullmans
in the hope that they will be forced to finish it because they
have nothing else to read. He grew more and more sensitive. Every time he heard a laugh he was sure that it was
directed at him; and because he so uncomfortably looked
away from the absent-minded gaze of fellow passengers he
made them gaze the harder.

The beautiful self-confidence which had always concealed Mr. McGee's slight defects from himself and had
helped him to rise to the position of assistant to the railroad president was torn away, and he began to doubt himself, began to feel that others must doubt him. When he
finally crept up the cement incline in the New York station, after a writhing glance at the redcaps, to see if New
Yorkers would notice his ludicrousness as much as people

had on the way through, he wondered if he could not return to Vernon and wire the steamship directors that he was ill.

He was not exaggerating about the importance of this trip to New York. The directors of the Citrus and Southern Line really were waiting for him. They needed him.

It is a curious fact of psychological economics that there are almost as many large employers waiting and praying for the chance to pay tens of thousands a year to dependable young men as there are dependable young men waiting and praying for the chance to earn a thousand a year. The president of the Citrus and Southern, the pouchy blob-nosed dean of South American and West Indian shipping, had been in the hospital for six months, after peritonitis. From his bed he had vaguely directed the policies of the company. Things had run well enough, with the old clerks working mechanically. But a crisis had come. The company had either to expand or break.

The Green Feather Line, weary of litigation, wanted to sell all its ships to the Citrus and Southern, which if it bought them might double its business. If some other company bought them and vigorously increased competition, the Citrus and Southern might be ruined.

The Citrus and Southern held a five months' option. By the end of that period they hoped to have found the man who could connect the sick president's brain with the general office's body—and they believed that in Palmer McGee they had found that man.

McGee did not know how carefully he had been watched. He had never met one of the directors or officers of the Citrus and Southern, had never seen one of them, and their correspondence had been polite but not exciting. But the two suave gentlemen who had been poking about Vernon lately had been commercial secret agents of the

Titanic Rating and Credit Company; and they knew all about McGee, from the number of drinks he had at the club to the amount of his bank account and his manner of listening to the stories of the chief shippers of the M. & D. R. R.

The Citrus and Southern chiefs were certain that they had found their man. McGee was to be sent to Buenos Aires, but only on test. If he was as good as they thought, he would in three months be brought back as vice president at a salary nearly four times as large as the one he had received in Vernon. In this crisis they had the generosity of despair.

They were to meet McGee in the president's suite at the hospital at four-thirty; and the train got in at three-fifteen.

McGee went to a hotel, and sat still, scared, looking at himself in a dressing-table mirror. He became momently more rustic, more tough, more skinned and awkward in his own eyes.

He called up the hospital, got the president. "Th-this is McGee. I—I'm coming right over," he quavered.

"Huh! That fellow sounds kind of lightwaisted. Not much self-confidence," complained the president to his old friend, the chairman of the board of directors. "Here, prop me up, Billy. We must give him a thorough look-over. Can't take any chances."

The note of doubt was a germ which instantly infected the chairman. "That's too bad. The Rating and Credit people reported he was a find. But still—of course——"

When Palmer McGee faced the president, the first vice president and a committee of four directors, three of the six had already turned from welcoming eagerness to stilly doubt. He felt that doubt. But he interpreted it thus:

"They think I'm a complete boob to have a haircut like

this. Think I don't know any better. And I can't explain. Mustn't admit that I know there's anything wrong— mustn't admit I was an easy mark and let a drunken barber carve me up."

He was so busy with these corroding reflections that he did not quite catch the sharp question which the president fired at him:

"McGee, what's your opinion of the future of the competition between Australian wheat and the Argentine crop?"

"I—I—I didn't quite understand you, sir," lamented poor McGee, victim of the cat of the trembling stars.

The president thought to himself: "If he can't get as dead simple a question as that—— Wonder if the first vice president wouldn't do, after all? No. Too old-fogyish."

While he meditated he was repeating the query without much interest; and without interest he heard McGee's thorough but shaky answer.

And McGee forgot to put in his usual information about the future of New Zealand grain.

Two hours later the president and directors decided that McGee "wouldn't quite do"; which meant that he wouldn't do at all; and they wearily began to talk of other candidates for the position. None of the others were satisfactory.

Four months later they decided that they would have to go slow; wait for the president to recover. They could find no one adaptable enough to coördinate the president and the working management. So they gave up their option on the steamers of the Green Feather Line.

The best of the jest was that Palmer McGee had looked rather well in his flippant haircut. Because the Chapel Street barber had started cutting his hair a certain length when he had been a Freshman in Yale he had kept up that mode, which was respectable but dull. But the semi-shave had brought out his energetic neck muscles. Never had he looked so taut and trim. Though dozens of people between the Vernon barber shop and the New York hospital had noticed his uneasiness none of them had considered his coiffure queer—they had merely wondered whether he was an embezzler or a forger.

McGee returned to Vernon broken, and General Coreos y Dulce, ex-president of the Central American republic of San Coloquin, entered the train of victims of Willis Stodeport, of Scrimmins Street.

The general had colonized Ynez Island, lying off the coast of San Coloquin. Fields of cane and coffee he had created, and he was happily expropriating ten thousand melodious natives. The general was a merry and easy ruler. When he had accepted the presidency of San Coloquin, after certain military misunderstandings, he hadn't even executed anybody—except a cousin or two, merely for politeness' sake.

His colony on Ynez Island was served by the steamers of the Green Feather Line. The business was not yet sufficient to warrant a regular stop, but General Dulce had a private agreement with the manager of the Green Feather, as well as one with the sick president of the Citrus and Southern, which later agreement was to take effect if the company took over the Green Feather boats.

But when the Citrus and Southern gave up their option the Green Feather fleet was bought, not by another Atlantic line but by a Seattle firm, for their Alaskan and Siberian trade. Consequently the general had to depend for service on a tin-can line which ran out of San Coloquin.

The owner of that line hated the general; had hated him when the general had been president, and had added to that hate with every meditative gin rickey he had sipped in the long years since. The general's fruit spoiled aboard the creaky old steamers; it was always too late to catch the boat north. His coffee was drenched, and his sugar short weight. When the general desperately bought a freighter of his own it was mysteriously burned.

Poverty and failure closed in on Ynez Island. The colonists hadn't enough to eat. When the influenza reached the island the weakened natives died in hordes. Some of them fled to the mainland, carrying the disease. The number of fatalities that would probably have been prevented by comfort and proper food and a supply of drugs has been estimated by Dr. Prof. Sir Henry Henson Sturgis at three thousand two hundred and ninety. One of the last to die was the broken-hearted general.

Before he died the wheel of Fate had turned past him and stopped at a certain European monarch. The general had in all his colonizing and his financial schemes been merely the secret agent of that monarch. The king was uncomfortable on his throne. It rocked and squeaked and threatened to give way at the seat. It was kept together only by many fees for repairs—jolly gifts to the duke who hypocritically led the opposition party, to a foreign agent, to certain clerics and editors and professors, even to the ostensible leader of the left wing of the radical party.

Five years before Willis Stodeport had patted Adolphus Josephus Mudface, the king had realized that he was in danger of using up all his private estate. He had speculated. He had called General Coreos y Dulce from Central America; and it was royalty's own money that had developed the colonization of Ynez Island.

It had been impossible for the king to keep in touch with the details of the colonization. Had he learned of the loss of the Green Feather service he might have raised funds for the purchase of the whole fleet when the Citrus and Southern gave up the option. But the proud, dogged general, with his sky-climbing mustachios and his belief that one Castilian was cleverer than four Andalusians or eight gringos, had been certain that he could pull through without help from the royal master.

It was not till the approach of death that he sent the coded cablegram which informed the king that he could expect no income from Ynez Island. Then the monarch knew that he could not keep his promises to certain peers and ministers; that his wordiest supporters would join the republican movement; that the gold-crusted but shaky-legged throne would at any moment be kicked out from beneath him by rude persons in mechanics' boots.

So it came to pass that at a certain hour the farthest stars quivered with mystic forces from the far-off fleck of dust called Earth, forces which would, just for a sketchy beginning, change all the boundaries and customs of Southern Europe. The king had at that hour desperately called in the two ministers and the one foreign emissary whom he trusted, and with that famous weak smile had murmured: "Gentlemen, it is the end. Shall I flee or— or—— You remember they didn't give my cousin the funeral even of a private gentleman."

At that hour, in a hovel in the Jamaica negro quarter of the capital of San Coloquin, General Coreos y Dulce, friend of composers and masters of science, was dying of nothing at all but sick hope and coldly creeping fear, and a belief that he had pneumonia.

A thousand and more miles away the president of the Citrus and Southern Steamship Company was writing his resignation. His old friend, the chairman of the board of directors, again begged: "But this means the ruin of the company, Ben. We can't go on without you."

"I know, Billy," the president sighed, "but I'm all in.

If we could have found someone to carry out my ideas I could have pulled through—and the company could have. Shame we were fooled about that McGee fellow. If we hadn't wasted so much time looking him over we might have had time to find the right man, and he'd have taken enough worry off my shoulders so that—— Well, I'll about pass out in three months, I reckon, old man. Let's have one more go at pinochle. I have a hunch I'm going to get double pinochle."

About half an hour after that, and half a continent away, Palmer McGee left the home of the president of the M. & D. R. R. He walked as one dreaming. The railroad president had said: "I don't know what the trouble is, my boy, but you haven't been worth a hang for quite a while now. And you're drinking too much. Better go off some place and get hold of yourself."

McGee crawled to the nearest telegraph office that was open, and sent a wire to the Buffalo & Bangor, accepting their offer in the purchasing department. The salary was not less than the one he had been receiving, but there was little future. Afterward he had a cocktail, the fourth that evening.

It cannot be authoritatively determined whether it was that evening or the one before that a barber named Discopolos first actually struck his wife, and she observed, "All right, I'll leave you." The neighbors say that though this was the first time he had mauled her, things had been going badly with them for many months. One of them asserts that the trouble started on an evening when Discopolos had promised to come home to supper but had not shown up till one-thirty in the morning. It seems that, though he had forgotten it, this had been her birthday, and she, poor mouse, had prepared a feast for them.

But it is certainly known that at the same hour on the

same evening there was much peace and much study of the newspaper comics in the house of the Stodeports on Scrimmins Street.

Willis stooped to pull the tail of Adolphus Josephus Mudface, now a half-grown cat. Mrs. Stodeport complained: "Now, Willie, do let that cat alone! He might scratch you, and you'll get fleas and things. No telling what-all might happen if you go patting and fooling with——"

Mr. Stodeport yawningly interrupted: "Oh, let the child alone! Way you go on, might think something dreadful would happen, just because he strokes a cat. I suppose probably he might get one of these germs, and spread it, and before he got through with it, maybe be the cause of two-three people taking sick! Ha, ha, ha! Or maybe he might make somebody rob a bank or something just awful! Ha, ha, ha! You better hold in your imagination, Mamma! We-ell——"

Mr. Stodeport yawned, and put the cat out, and yawned, and wound the clock, and yawned, and went up to bed, still chuckling over his fancy about Willis having a mysterious effect on persons five or six blocks away.

At exactly that moment in a medieval castle about five thousand miles from Willis Stodeport, the king of an ancient nation sighed to the Right Honorable the Earl of Arden, K. C. B., special and secret emissary of the British throne: "Yes, it is the twilight of the gods. I take some little pride in saying that even in my downfall I can see clearly the mysteries of Fate. I know definitely that my misfortune is a link in a chain of events that impressively started with——"

"—with the loss of thousands of lives and millions of pounds, in San Coloquin," mused Lord Arden.

"No! No! No! Nothing so earthy and petty. I have

long been a student of astrology. My astrologer and I have determined that this evil chance of myself and my poor people is but the last act in a cosmic tragedy that started with an esoteric change in the magnetism of Azimech, the cold and virgin star. At least it is comforting to know that my sorrows originated in nothing trivial, but have been willed by the brooding stars in the farthest abysses of eternal night, and that——"

"Um. Oh, yes. Yes, I see," said the Earl of Arden.

LAND

LAND

He was named Sidney, for the sake of elegance, just as his parents had for elegance in their Brooklyn parlor a golden-oak combination bookcase, desk, and shield-shaped mirror. But Sidney Dow was descended from generations of Georges and Johns, of Lorens and Lukes and Nathans.

He was little esteemed in the slick bustle of his city school. He seemed a loutish boy, tall and heavy and slow-spoken, and he was a worry to his father. For William Dow was an ambitious parent. Born on a Vermont farm, William felt joyously that he had done well in the great city of Brooklyn. He had, in 1885, when Sidney was born, a real bathroom with a fine tin tub, gas lights, and a handsome phaeton with red wheels, instead of the washtub in the kitchen for Saturday-night baths, the kerosene lamps, and the heavy old buggy which his father still used in Vermont. Instead of being up at 5:30, he could loll abed till a quarter of seven, and he almost never, he chuckled in gratification at his progress, was in his office before a quarter to eight.

But the luxury of a red-wheeled carriage and late lying did not indicate that William's Yankee shrewdness had been cozened by urban vice, or that he was any less solid and respectable than old George, his own father. He was a deacon in the Universalist church, he still said grace before meals, and he went to the theater only when Ben-Hur was appearing.

For his son, Sidney, William Dow had even larger ambitions. William himself had never gone to high school, and his business was only a cautious real-estate and insurance agency, his home a squatting two-story brick house in a red, monotonous row. But Sidney—he should go to college, he should be a doctor or a preacher or a lawyer, he should travel in Europe, he should live in a three-story graystone house in the Forties in Manhattan, he should have a dress suit and wear it to respectable but expensive hops!

William had once worn dress clothes at an Odd Fellows' ball, but they had been rented.

To enable Sidney to attain all these graces, William toiled and sacrificed and prayed. American fathers have always been as extraordinary as Scotch fathers in their heroic ambitions for their sons—and sometimes as unscrupulous and as unwise. It bruised William and often it made him naggingly unkind to see that Sidney, the big slug, did not "appreciate how his parents were trying to do for him and give him every opportunity." When they had a celebrated Columbia Heights physician as guest for dinner, Sidney merely gawked at him and did not at all try to make an impression.

"Suffering cats! You might have been one of your uncles still puttering around with dirty pitchforks back on the farm! What are you going to do with yourself, anyway?" raged William.

"I guess maybe I'd like to be a truck driver," mumbled
Sidney.

Yet, even so, William should not have whipped him. It
only made him sulkier.

To Sidney Dow, at sixteen, his eagerest memories were
of occasional weeks he had spent with his grandfather and
uncles on the Vermont farm, and the last of these was
seven years back now. He remembered Vermont as an enchanted place, with curious and amusing animals—cows,
horses, turkeys. He wanted to return, but his father seemed
to hate the place. Of Brooklyn, Sidney liked nothing save
livery stables and occasional agreeable gang fights, with
stones inside iced snowballs. He hated school, where he
had to cramp his big knees under trifling desks, where irritable lady teachers tried to make him see the importance
of A's going more rapidly than B to the town of X, a town
in which he was even less interested than in Brooklyn—
school where hour on hour he looked over the top of his
geography and stolidly hated the whiskers of Longfellow,
Lowell, and Whittier. He hated the stiff, clean collar and
the itchy, clean winter underwear connected with Sunday
school. He hated hot evenings smelling of tarry pavements,
and cold evenings when the pavements were slippery.

But he didn't know that he hated any of these things.
He knew only that his father must be right in saying that
he was a bad, disobedient, ungrateful young whelp, and
in his heart he was as humble as in his speech he was sullen.

Then, at sixteen, he came to life suddenly, on an early
June morning, on his grandfather's farm. His father had
sent him up to Vermont for the summer, had indeed exiled
him, saying grimly, "I guess after you live in that tumble-
down big old shack and work in the fields and have to get

up early, instead of lying abed till your majesty is good and ready to have the girl wait on you—I guess that next fall you'll appreciate your nice home and school and church here, young man!" So sure of himself was his father that Sidney was convinced he was going to encounter hardship on the farm, and all the way up, in the smarting air of the smoker on the slow train, he wanted to howl. The train arrived at ten in the evening, and he was met by his uncle Rob, a man rugged as a pine trunk and about as articulate.

"Well! Come for the summer!" said Uncle Rob; and after they had driven three miles: "Got new calf—yeh, new calf"; and after a mile more: "Your pa all right?" And that was all the conversation of Uncle Rob.

Seven years it was since Sidney had been in any country wilder than Far Rockaway, and the silent hills of night intimidated him. It was a roaring silence, a silence full of stifled threats. The hills that cut the stars so high up on either side the road seemed walls that would topple and crush him, as a man would crush a mosquito between his two palms. And once he cried out when, in the milky light from the lantern swung beneath the wagon, he saw a porcupine lurch into the road before them. It was dark, chill, unfriendly and, to the boy, reared to the lights and cheery voices of the city, even though he hated them, it was appallingly lonely.

His grandfather's house was dark when they arrived. Uncle Rob drove into the barn, jerked his thumb at a ladder up to the haymow and muttered, "Y'sleep up there. Not allowed t' smoke. Take this lantern when we've unharnessed. Sure to put it out. No smoking in the barn. Too tired to help?"

Too tired? Sidney would have been glad to work till daylight if Uncle Rob would but stay with him. He was in a

panic at the thought of being left in the ghostly barn
where, behind the pawing of horses and the nibble of
awakened cows, there were the sounds of anonymous wild
animals—scratchings, squeaks, patterings overhead. He
made the task as slow as possible, though actually he was
handy with horses, for the livery stables of Brooklyn had
been his favorite refuge and he had often been permitted
to help the hostlers, quite free.

"Gee, Uncle Rob, I guess I'm kind of all thumbs about
unharnessing and like that. Seven years since I been here
on the farm."

"That so? G'night. Careful of that lantern now. And no
smoking!"

The barn was blank as a blind face. The lantern was
flickering, and in that witching light the stalls and the heap
of sleighs, plows, old harness, at the back wall of the barn
were immense and terrifying. The barn was larger than his
whole house in Brooklyn, and ten times as large it seemed
in the dimness. He could not see clear to the back wall, and
he imagined abominable monsters lurking there. He dashed
at the ladder up to the haymow, the lantern handle in his
teeth and his imitation-leather satchel in one hand.

And the haymow, rising to the darkness of its hand-hewn
rafters, seemed vaster and more intimidating than the
space below. In one corner a space had been cleared of hay
for a cot, with a blanket and a pea-green comforter, and
for a chair and a hinged box. Sidney dashed at the cot and
crawled into it, waiting only to take off his shoes and
jacket. Till the lantern flame died down to a red rim of
charred wick, he kept it alight. Then utter darkness leaped
upon him.

A rooster crowed, and he startled. Past him things
scampered and chittered. The darkness seemed to swing

in swift eddies under the rafters, the smell of dry hay
choked him—and he awoke to light slipping in silver darts
through cracks in the roof, and to jubilant barn swallows
diving and twittering.

"Gee, I must have fell asleep!" he thought. He went
down the ladder, and now, first, he saw the barn.

Like many people slow of thought and doubtful of
speech, Sidney Dow had moments of revelation as complete as those of a prophet, when he beheld a scene or a
person or a problem in its entirety, with none of the confusing thoughts of glibber and more clever people with
their minds forever running off on many tracks. He saw
the barn—really saw it, instead of merely glancing at it,
like a normal city boy. He saw that the beams, hand-hewn,
gray with sixty years, were beautiful; that the sides of the
stalls, polished with rubbing by the shoulders of cattle
dead these fifty years, were beautiful; that the harrow,
with its trim spikes kept sharp and rustless, was beautiful;
that most beautiful of all were the animals—cows and
horses, chickens that walked with bobbing heads through
the straw, and a calf tethered to the wall. The calf capered
with alarm as he approached it; then stood considering
him with great eyes, letting him stroke its head and at last
licking his hand. He slouched to the door of the barn and
looked down the valley. More radiant in that early morning light than even the mountain tops covered with maples
and hemlock were the upland clearings with white houses
and red barns.

"Gosh, it looks nice! It's—it's sort of—it looks nice! I
didn't hardly get it when I was here before. But gee"—
with all the scorn of sixteen—"I was just a kid then!"

With Uncle Rob he drove the cows to pasture; with
Uncle Ben he plowed; with his grandfather, sourly philan-

thropic behind his beard, he split wood. He found an even
greater menagerie than in the barn—turkeys, geese, ducks,
pigs and, in the woods and mowings, an exciting remnant
of woodchucks, chipmunks, rabbits, and infrequent deer.
With all of them—uncles and grandfather, beasts, wild or
tame—he felt at home. They did not expect him to chatter
and show off, as had his gang in Brooklyn; they accepted
him. That, perhaps, more than any ancestral stoutness,
more than the beauty of the land, made a farmer of him.
He was a natural hermit, and here he could be a hermit
without seeming queer.

And a good farmer he was—slow but tireless, patient,
unannoyed by the endless work, happy to go to bed early
and be up at dawn. For a few days his back felt as though
he were burning at the stake, but after that he could lift
all day in the hayfield or swing the scythe or drive the
frisky young team. He was a good farmer, and he slept at
night. The noises which on his first night had fretted his
city-tortured nerves were soporific now, and when he heard
the sound of a distant train, the barking of a dog on the
next farm, he inarticulately told himself that they were
lovely.

"You're pretty fair at working," said Uncle Rob, and
that was praise almost hysterical.

Indeed, in one aspect of labor, Sidney was better than
any of them, even the pine-carved Uncle Rob. He could endure wet dawns, wild winds, all-day drenching. It seems to
be true that farmers are more upset by bad weather than
most outdoor workers—sailors, postmen, carpenters,
brakemen, teamsters. Perhaps it is because they are less
subject to higher authority; except for chores and getting
in the hay, they can more nearly do things in their own
time, and they build up a habit of taking shelter on nasty
days. Whether or no, it was true that just the city crises

that had vexed Sidney, from icy pavements to sudden fire alarms, had given him the ability to stand discomforts and the unexpected, like a little Cockney surprisingly stolid in the trenches.

He learned the silent humor of the authentic Yankee. Evenings he sat with neighbors on the bench before the general store. To a passing stranger they seemed to be saying nothing, but when the stranger had passed, Uncle Rob would drawl, "Well, if I had fly nets on my hosses, guess I'd look stuck-up too!" and the others would chuckle with contempt at the alien.

This, thought Sidney, was good talk—not like the smart gabble of the city. It was all beautiful, and he knew it, though in his vocabulary there was no such word as "beautiful," and when he saw the most flamboyant sunset he said only, "Guess going to be clear tomorrow."

And so he went back to Brooklyn, not as to his home but as to prison, and as a prison corridor he saw the narrow street with little houses like little cells.

Five minutes after he had entered the house, his father laughed. "Well, did you get enough of farming? I guess you'll appreciate your school now! I won't rub it in, but I swear, how Rob and Ben can stand it——"

"I kind of liked it, Dad. I think I'll be a farmer. I—kind of liked it."

His father had black side whiskers, and between them he had thin cheeks that seemed, after Uncle Rob and Uncle Ben, pallid as the under side of a toadstool. They flushed now, and William shouted:

"You're an idiot! What have I done to have a son who is an idiot? The way I've striven and worked and economized to give you a chance to get ahead, to do something worth while, and then you want to slip right back and be ordinary, like your uncles! So you think you'd like it!

You're a fool! Sure you like it in summer, but if you knew it like I do—rousted out to do the chores five o'clock of a January morning, twenty below zero, and maybe have to dig through two feet of snow to get to the barn! Have to tramp down to the store, snowstorm so thick you can't see five feet in front of you!"

"I don't guess I'd mind it much."

"Oh, you don't! Don't be a fool! And no nice company like here—go to bed with the chickens, a winter night, and no nice lodge meeting or church supper or lectures like there is here!"

"Don't care so much for those things. Everybody talking all the while. I like it quiet, like in the country."

"Well, you will care so much for those things, or I'll care you, my fine young man! I'm not going to let you slump back into being a rube like Ben, and don't you forget it! I'll make you work at your books! I'll make you learn to appreciate good society and dressing proper and getting ahead in the world and amounting to something! Yes, sir, amounting to something! Do you think for one moment that after the struggle I've gone through to give you a chance—the way I studied in a country school and earned my way through business college and went to work at five dollars a week in a real-estate office and studied and economized and worked late, so I could give you this nice house and advantages and opportunity—— No, sir! You're going to be a lawyer or a doctor or somebody that amounts to something, and not a rube!"

It would have been too much to expect of Sidney's imagination that he should have seen anything fine and pathetic in William's fierce ambition. That did not move him, but rather fear. He could have broken his father in two, but the passion in this blenched filing-case of a man was such that it hypnotized him.

For days, miserably returned to high school, he longed for the farm. But his mother took him aside and begged: "You mustn't oppose your father so, dearie. He knows what's best for you, and it would just break his heart if he thought you were going to be a common person and not have something to show for all his efforts."

So Sidney came to feel that it was some wickedness in him that made him prefer trees and winds and meadows and the kind cattle to trolley cars and offices and people who made little, flat, worried jokes all day long.

He barely got through high school. His summer vacations he spent in warehouses, hoisting boxes. He failed to enter medical school, botched his examinations shockingly—feeling wicked at betraying his father's ambitions —and his father pushed him into a second-rate dental school with sketchy requirements, a school now blessedly out of existence.

"Maybe you'd be better as a dentist anyway. Requires a lot of manipulation, and I will say you're good with your hands," his father said, in relief that now Sidney was on the highway to fortune and respectability.

But Sidney's hands, deft with hammer and nails, with reins or hoe or spade, were too big, too awkward for the delicate operations of dentistry. And in school he hated the long-winded books with their queer names and shocking colored plates of man's inwards. The workings of a liver did not interest him. He had never seen a liver, save that of a slain chicken. He would turn from these mysteries to a catalogue of harvesting machinery or vegetable seed. So with difficulty he graduated from this doubtful school, and he was uneasy at the pit of his stomach, even when his father, much rejoicing now, bought for him a complete dental outfit, and rented an office, on the new frontier of the Bronx, in the back part of a three-story red-brick apartment house.

His father and mother invited their friends over from Brooklyn to admire the office, and served them coffee and cake. Not many of them came, which was well, for the office was not large. It was really a single room, divided by a curtain to make a reception hall. The operating room had pink-calcimined walls and, for adornment, Sidney's diploma and a calendar from a dental supply house which showed, with no apparent appropriateness, a view of Pike's Peak.

When they had all gone, mouthing congratulations, Sidney looked wistfully out on the old pasture land which, fifteen years later, was to be filled solidly with tall, cheap apartment houses and huge avenues with delicatessen shops and movie palaces. Already these pastures were doomed and abandoned. Cows no longer grazed there. Gaunt billboards lined the roads and behind their barricades were unkempt waste lands of ashes and sodden newspapers. But they were open grass, and they brought back the valleys and uplands of Vermont. His great arms were hungry for the strain of plowing, and he sighed and turned back to his shining new kit of tools.

The drill he picked up was absurd against his wide red palm. All at once he was certain that he knew no dentistry, and that he never would; that he would botch every case; that dreadful things would happen—suits for malpractice——

Actually, as a few and poorly paying neighborhood patients began to come in, the dreadful things didn't happen. Sidney was slow, but he was careful; if he did no ingenious dental jeweling, he did nothing wrong. He learned early what certain dentists and doctors never learn—that nature has not yet been entirely supplanted by the professions. It was not his patients who suffered; it was he.

All day long to have to remain indoors, to stand in one place, bent over gaping mouths, to fiddle with tiny instruments, to produce unctuous sounds of sympathy for cranks who complained of trivial aches, to try to give brisk and confident advice which was really selling talk—all this tortured him.

Then, within one single year, his mother died, his grandfather died on the Vermont farm, Uncle Rob and Uncle Ben moved West, and Sidney met the most wonderful girl in the world. The name of this particular most wonderful girl in the world, who unquestionably had more softness and enchantment and funny little ways of saying things than Helen of Troy, was Mabelle Ellen Pflugmann, and she was cultured; she loved the theater, but rarely attended it; loved also the piano, but hadn't time, she explained, to keep up her practice, because, her father's laundry being in a state of debility, for several years she had temporarily been cashier at the Kwiturwurry Lunch.

They furnished a four-room apartment and went to Vermont for their honeymoon. His grandfather's farm—Sidney wasn't quite sure just who had bought it—was rented out to what the neighborhood considered foreigners—that is, Vermonters from way over beyond the Ridge, fifteen miles away. They took in Sidney and Mabelle. She enjoyed it. She told how sick she had become of the smell and dish clatter of the ole lunch and the horrid customers who were always trying to make love to her. She squealed equally over mountains and ducklings, sunsets and wild strawberries, and as for certain inconveniences—washing with a pitcher and bowl, sleeping in a low room smelling of the chicken run, and having supper in the kitchen with the menfolks in shirt sleeves—she said it was just too darling for words—it was, in fact, sweet. But after ten days of the fortnight on which they had planned, she thought perhaps they had better get back to New York and make sure all the furniture had arrived.

They were happy in marriage. Mabelle saw him, and made him see himself, as a man strong and gallant but shy and blundering. He needed mothering, she said, and he got it and was convinced that he liked it. He was less gruff with his patients, and he had many more of them, for Mabelle caused him to be known socially. Till marriage he had lived in a furnished room, and all evening he had prowled alone, or read dentistry journals and seed catalogues. Now Mabelle arranged jolly little parties—beer and Welsh rabbit and a game of five hundred. If at the Kwiturwurry Lunch she had met many light fellows, West Farms Lotharios, she had also met estimable but bohemian families of the neighborhood—big traveling men whose territory took them as far west as Denver, assistant buyers from the downtown department stores, and the office manager of a large insurance agency.

Mabelle, a chatelaine now, wanted to shine among them, and wanted Sidney to shine. And he, feeling a little cramped in a new double-breasted blue serge coat, solemnly served the beer, and sometimes a guest perceived that here was an honest and solid dentist upon whom to depend. And once they gave a theater party—six seats at a vaudeville house.

Yet Sidney was never, when he awoke mornings, excited about the adventure of standing with bent, aching shoulders over patients all this glorious coming day.

They had two children in three years and began to worry a little about the rent bill and the grocery bill, and

Sidney was considerably less independent with grumbling patients than he had been. His broad shoulders had a small stoop, and he said quite humbly, "Well, I'll try my best to fix 'em to your satisfaction, Mrs. Smallberg," and sometimes his thick fingers tapped nervously on his chin as he talked. And he envied now, where once he had despised them, certain dental-school classmates who knew little of dentistry, but who were slick dressers and given to verbal chuckings under the chin, who had made money and opened three-room offices with chintz chairs in the waiting room. Sidney still had his old office, with no assistant, and the jerry-built tenement looked a little shabby now beside the six-story apartment houses of yellow brick trimmed with marble which had sprung up all about it.

Then their children, Rob and Willabette, were eight and six years old, and Mabelle began to nag Sidney over the children's lack of clothes as pretty as those of their lovely little friends at school.

And his dental engine—only a treadle affair at that— was worn out. And his elbows were always shiny. And in early autumn his father died.

His father died, muttering, "You've been a good boy, Sid, and done what I told you to. You can understand and appreciate now why I kept you from being just a farmer and gave you a chance to be a professional man. I don't think Mabelle comes from an awful good family, but she's a spunky little thing, and real bright, and she'll keep you up to snuff. Maybe some day your boy will be a great, rich banker or surgeon. Keep him away from his Vermont relations—no ambition, those folks. My chest feels so tight! Bless you, Sid!"

He was his father's sole heir. When the will was read in the shabby lawyer's office in Brooklyn, he was astonished to find that his father had still owned—that he himself now owned—the ancestral Vermont home. His slow-burning imagination lighted. He was touched by the belief that his father, for all his pretended hatred of the place, had cherished it and had wanted his son to own it. Not till afterward did he learn from Uncle Rob that William, when his own father had died, had, as eldest son, been given the choice of the farm or half the money in the estate, and had taken the farm to keep Sidney away from it. He had been afraid that if his brothers had it they would welcome Sidney as a partner before he became habituated as a dentist. But in his last days, apparently, William felt that Sidney was safely civilized now and caught. With the farm Sidney inherited some three thousand dollars—not more, for the Brooklyn home was mortgaged.

Instantly and ecstatically, while the lawyer droned senseless advice, Sidney decided to go home. The tenant on his farm—his!—had only two months more on his lease. He'd take it over. The three thousand dollars would buy eight cows—well, say ten—with a cream separator, a tractor, a light truck, and serve to put the old buildings into condition adequate for a few years. He'd do the repairing himself! He arched his hands with longing for the feel of a hammer or a crowbar.

In the hall outside the lawyer's office, Mabelle crowed: "Isn't it—oh, Sid, you do know how sorry I am your father's passed on, but won't it be just lovely! The farm must be worth four thousand dollars. We'll be just as sensible as can be—not blow it all in, like lots of people would. We'll invest the seven thousand, and that ought to give us three hundred and fifty dollars a year—think of it, an extra dollar every day! You can get a dress suit now, and at last I'll have some decent dresses for the evening, and we'll get a new suit for Rob right away—how soon can you get the money? did he say?—and I saw some lovely little dresses for Willabette and the cutest slippers, and now we can get a decent bridge table instead of that rickety old thing, and——"

As she babbled, which she did, at length, on the stairs down from the office, Sidney realized wretchedly that it was going to take an eloquence far beyond him to convert her to farming and the joys of the land. He was afraid of her, as he had been of his father.

"There's a drug store over across. Let's go over and have an ice-cream soda," he said mildly. "Gosh, it's hot for September! Up on the farm now it would be cool, and the leaves are just beginning to turn. They're awful pretty —all red and yellow."

"Oh, you and your old farm!" But in her joy she was amiable.

They sat at the bright-colored little table in the drug store, with cheery colored drinks between them. But the scene should have been an ancient castle at midnight, terrible with wind and lightning, for suddenly they were not bright nor cheery, but black with tragedy.

There was no manner of use in trying to cajole her. She could never understand how he hated the confinement of his dental office; she would say, "Why, you get the chance of meeting all sorts of nice, interesting people, while I have to stay home," and not perceive that he did not want to meet nice, interesting people. He wanted silence and the smell of earth! And he was under her spell as he had been under his father's. Only violently could he break it. He spoke softly enough, looking at the giddy marble of the soda counter, but he spoke sternly:

"Look here, May. This is our chance. You bet your sweet life we're going to be sensible and not blow in our stake! And we're not going to blow it in on a lot of clothes and a lot of fool bridge parties for a lot of fool folks that don't care one red hoot about us except what they get out of us! For that matter, if we were going to stay on in New York——"

"Which we most certainly are, young man!"

"Will you listen to me? I inherited this dough, not you! Gee, I don't want to be mean, May, but you got to listen to reason, and as I'm saying, if we were going to stay in the city, the first thing I'd spend money for would be a new dental engine—an electric one.

"Need it like the mischief—lose patients when they see me pumping that old one and think I ain't up-to-date—which I ain't, but that's no skin off their nose!"

Even the volatile Mabelle was silent at the unprecedented length and vigor of his oration.

"But we're not going to stay. No, sir! We're going back to the old farm, and the kids will be brought up in the fresh air instead of a lot of alleys. Go back and farm it——"

She exploded then, and as she spoke she looked at him with eyes hot with hatred, the first hatred he had ever known in her:

"Are you crazy? Go back to that hole? Have my kids messing around a lot of manure and dirty animals and out working in the hayfield like a lot of cattle? And attend a little one-room school with a boob for a teacher? And play with a lot of nitwit brats? Not on your life they won't! I've got some ambition for 'em, even if you haven't!"

"Why, May, I thought you liked Vermont and the farm! You were crazy about it on our honeymoon, and you said——"

"I did not! I hated it even then. I just said I liked it to make you happy. That stifling little bedroom, and kerosene lamps, and bugs, and no bathroom, and those fools of farmers in their shirt sleeves——Oh, it was fierce! If you go, you go without the kids and me! I guess I can still earn a living!

And I guess there's still plenty of other men would like to marry me when I divorce you! And I mean it!"

She did, and Sidney knew she did. He collapsed as helplessly as he had with his father.

"Well, of course, if you can't stand it——" he muttered.

"Well, I'm glad you're beginning to come to your senses! Honest, I think you were just crazy with the heat! But listen, here's what I'll do: I won't kick about your getting the electric dental doodingus if it don't cost too much. Now how do you go about selling the farm?"

There began for this silent man a secret life of plotting and of lies. Somehow—he could not see how—he must persuade her to go to the farm. Perhaps she would die—— But he was shocked at this thought, for he loved her and believed her to be the best woman living, as conceivably she may have been. But he did not obey her and sell the farm. He lied. He told her that a Vermont real-estate dealer had written that just this autumn there was no market for farms, but next year would be excellent. And the next year he repeated the lie, and rented the farm to Uncle Rob, who had done well enough on Iowa cornland but was homesick for the hills and sugar groves and placid maples of Vermont. Himself, Sidney did not go to the farm. It was not permitted.

Mabelle was furious that he had not sold, that they had only the three thousand—which was never invested—for clothes and bridge prizes and payments on the car and, after a good deal of irritated talk, his electric dental engine.

If he had always been sullenly restless in his little office, now he was raging. He felt robbed. The little back room, the view—not even of waste land now, but of the center of a cheap block and the back of new tenements—the anguish of patients, which crucified his heavy, unspoken sympathy for them, and that horrible, unending series of wide-

stretched mouths and bad molars and tongues—it was
intolerable. He thought of meadows scattered with daisies
and devil's-paintbrush, of dark, healing thundershowers
pouring up the long valley. He must go home to the land!

From the landlord who owned his office he got, in the
spring a year and a half after his father's death, the right
to garden a tiny patch amid the litter and cement areaways
in the center of the block. Mabelle laughed at him, but he
stayed late every evening to cultivate each inch of his
pocket paradise—a large man, with huge feet, setting them
carefully down in a plot ten feet square.

The earth understood him, as it does such men, and
before the Long Island market gardeners had anything to
display, Sidney had a row of beautiful radish plants. A
dozen radishes, wrapped in a tabloid newspaper, he took
home one night, and he said vaingloriously to Mabelle,
"You'll never get any radishes like these in the market!
Right out of our own garden!"

She ate one absently. He braced himself to hear a jeer-
ing "You and your old garden!" What he did hear was,
in its uncaring, still worse: "Yes, they're all right, I guess."

He'd show her! He'd make her see him as a great farmer!
And with that ambition he lost every scruple. He plotted.
And this was the way of that plotting:

Early in July he said, and casually, "Well, now we got
the darn car all paid for, we ought to use it. Maybe we
might take the kids this summer and make a little tour
for a couple weeks or so."

"Where?"

She sounded suspicious, and in his newborn guile he
droned, "Oh, wherever you'd like. I hear it's nice up
around Niagara Falls and the Great Lakes. Maybe come
back by way of Pennsylvania, and see Valley Forge and all
them famous historical sites."

"Well, yes, perhaps. The Golheims made a tour last summer and—they make me sick!—they never stop talking about it."

They went. And Mabelle enjoyed it. She was by no means always a nagger and an improver; she was so only when her interests or what she deemed the interests of her children were threatened. She made jokes about the towns through which they passed—any community of less than fifty thousand was to her New Yorkism a "hick hole"— and she even sang jazz and admired his driving, which was bad.

They had headed north, up the Hudson. At Glens Falls he took the highway to the right, instead of left toward the Great Lakes, and she, the city girl, the urban rustic, to whom the only directions that meant anything were East Side and West Side as applied to New York, did not notice, and she was still unsuspicious when he grumbled. "Looks to me like I'd taken the wrong road." Stopping at a filling station, he demanded, "How far is it to Lake George? We ought to be there now."

"Well, stranger, way you're headed, it'll be about twenty-five thousand miles. You're going plumb in the wrong direction."

"I'll be darned! Where are we? Didn't notice the name of the last town we went through."

"You're about a mile from Fair Haven."

"Vermont?"

"Yep."

"Well, I'll be darned! Just think of that! Can't even be trusted to stay in one state and not skid across the border line!"

Mabelle was looking suspicious, and he said with desperate gayety, "Say, do you know what, May? We're only forty miles from our farm! Let's go have a look at it."

Mabelle made a sound of protest, but he turned to the children, in the back seat amid a mess of suitcases and tools and a jack and spare inner tubes, and gloated, "Wouldn't you kids like to see the farm where I worked as a kid—where your grandfather and great-grandfather were born? And see your Granduncle Rob? And see all the little chicks, and so on?"

"Oh, yes!" they shrilled together.

With that enthusiasm from her beloved young, with the smart and uniformed young filling-station attendant listening, Mabelle's talent for being righteous and indignant was gagged. Appearances! She said lightly to the filling-station man, "The doctor just doesn't seem to be able to keep the road at all, does he? Well, Doctor, shall we get started?"

Even when they had gone on and were alone and ready for a little sound domestic quarreling, she merely croaked, "Just the same, it seems mighty queer to me!" And after another mile of brooding, while Sidney drove silently and prayed: "Awfully queer!"

But he scarcely heard her. He was speculating, without in the least putting it into words, "I wonder if in the early summer evenings the fireflies still dart above the meadows? I wonder if the full moon, before it rises behind the hemlocks and sugar maples along the Ridge, still casts up a prophetic glory? I wonder if sleepy dogs still bark across the valley? I wonder if the night breeze slips through the mowing? I, who have for fortress and self-respect only a stuffy office room—I wonder if there are still valleys and stars and the quiet night? Or was that all only the dream of youth?"

They slept at Rutland, Sidney all impatient of the citified hotel bedroom. It was at ten in the morning—he drove in twenty minutes the distance which thirty years ago had taken Uncle Rob an hour and a half—that he drove up to the white house where, since 1800, the Dows had been born.

He could see Uncle Rob with the hayrake in the south mowing, sedately driving the old team and ignoring the visitors.

"I guess he prob'ly thinks we're bootleggers," chuckled Sidney. "Come on, you kids! Here's where your old daddy worked all one summer! Let's go! . . . Thirsty? Say, I'll give you a drink of real spring water—not none of this chlorinated city stuff! And we'll see the menagerie."

Before he had finished, Rob and Willabette had slipped over the rear doors of the car and were looking down into the valley with little sounds of excitement. Sidney whisked out almost as quickly as they, while Mabelle climbed down with the dignity suitable to a dweller in the Bronx. He ignored her. He clucked his children round the house to the spring-fed well and pumped a bucket of water.

"Oh, it's so cold, Daddy. It's swell!" said Rob.

"You bet your life it's cold and swell. Say! Don't use words like 'swell'! They're common. But hell with that! Come on, you brats! I'll show you something!"

There were kittens, and two old, grave, courteous cats. There was a calf—heaven knows by how many generations it was descended from the calf that on a June morning, when Sidney was sixteen, had licked his fingers. There were ducklings, and young turkeys with feathers grotesquely scattered over their skins like palm trees in a desert, and unexpected more kittens, and an old, brown-and-white, tail-wagging dog, and a pen of excited little pigs.

The children squealed over all of them until Mabelle caught up, puffing a little.

"Well," she said, "the kits are kind of cute, ain't they?"

Then, darkly: "Now that you've got me here, Sid, with your plans and all!"

Uncle Rob crept up, snarling, "What you folks want? ... By gracious, if it ain't Sid! This your wife and children? Well, sir!"

It was, Sidney felt, the climax of his plot, and he cried to his son, "Rob! This is your granduncle, that you were named for. How'd you like to stay here on the farm instead of in New York?"

"Hot dog! I'd love it! Them kittens and the li'l' ducks! Oh, they're the berries! You bet I'd like to stay!"

"Oh, I'd love it!" gurgled his sister.

"You would not!" snapped Mabelle. "With no bathroom?"

"We could put one in," growled Sidney.

"On what? On all the money you'd make growing orchids and bananas here, I guess! You kids—how'd you like to walk two miles to school, through the snow, in winter?"

"Oh, that would be slick! Maybe we could kill a deer," said young Rob.

"Yes, and maybe a field mouse could kill you, you dumb-bell! Sure! Lovely! All evening with not a dog-gone thing to do after supper!"

"Why, we'd go to the movies! Do you go to the movies often, Granduncle Rob?"

"Well, afraid in winter you wouldn't get to go to the movies at all. Pretty far into town," hesitated Uncle Rob.

"Not—go—to—the—movies?" screamed the city children, incredulous. It was the most terrible thing they had ever heard of.

Rob, Jr., mourned, "Oh, gee, that wouldn't be so good! Say, how do the hicks learn anything if they don't go to the movies? But still, we could go in the summer, Ma, and in the winter it would be elegant, with sliding and hunting and everything. I'd love it!"

Mabelle cooked supper, banging the pans a good deal and emitting opinions of a house that had no porcelain sink, no water taps, no refrigerator, no gas or electricity. She was silent through supper, silent as Sidney, silent as Uncle Rob. But Sidney was exultant. With the children for allies, he would win. And the children themselves, they were hysterical. Until Mabelle screamed for annoyance; they leaped up from the table, to come back with the most unspeakable and un-Bronxian objects—a cat affectionately carried by his hind leg, but squealing with misunderstanding of the affection, a dead mole, an unwiped oil can, a muck-covered spade.

"But, Mother," they protested, "in the city you never find anything, except maybe a dead lemon."

She shooed them off to bed at eight; herself, sniffily, she disappeared at nine, muttering to Sidney, "I hope you and your boy friend, Uncle Rob, chew the rag all night and get it out of your systems!"

He was startled, for indeed the next step of his plot did concern Uncle Rob and secret parleys.

For half an hour he walked the road, almost frightened by the intensity of stillness. He could fancy catamounts in the birch clumps. But between spasms of skittish city nerves he stretched out his arms, arched back his hands, breathed consciously. This was not just air, necessary meat for the lungs; it was a spirit that filled him.

He knew that he must not tarry after 9:30 for his intrigue with Uncle Rob. Uncle Rob was seventy-five, and in seventy-five times three hundred and sixty-five evenings he had doubtless stayed up later than 9:30 o'clock several times—dancing with the little French Canuck

girls at Potsdam Forge as a young man, sitting up with a
sick cow since then, or stuck in the mud on his way back
from Sunday-evening meeting. But those few times were
epochal. Uncle Rob did not hold with roistering and staying up till all hours just for the vanities of the flesh.

Sidney crept up the stairs to Uncle Rob's room.

Mabelle and Sidney had the best bedroom, on the
ground floor; young Rob and Bette had Grampa's room,
on the second; Uncle Rob lived in the attic.

City folks might have wondered why Uncle Rob, tenant
and controller of the place, should have hidden in the attic,
with three good bedrooms below him. It was simple. Uncle
Rob had always lived there since he was a boy.

Up the narrow stairs, steep as a rock face, Sidney crept,
and knocked.

"Who's there!" A sharp voice, a bit uneasy. How many
years was it since Uncle Rob had heard anyone knock at
his bedroom door?

"It's me, Rob—Sid."

"Oh, well—well, guess you can come in. Wait 'll I unlock the door."

Sidney entered his uncle's room for the first time in his
life. The hill people, anywhere in the world, do not intrude
or encourage intrusion.

Perhaps to fastidious and alien persons Uncle Rob's
room would have seemed unlovely. It was lighted by a
kerosene lamp, smoking a little, with the wick burned
down on one side. There was, for furniture, only a camp
cot, with a kitchen chair, a washstand and a bureau. But
to make up for this paucity, the room was rather littered.
On the washstand, beside a pitcher dry from long disuse,
there were a mail-order catalogue, a few packets of seed,
a lone overshoe, a ball of twine, a bottle of applejack, and

a Spanish War veteran's medal. The walls and ceiling were of plaster so old that they showed in black lines the edges of every lath.

And Sidney liked it—liked the simplicity, liked the freedom from neatness and order and display, liked and envied the old-bach quality of it all.

Uncle Rob, lying on the bed, had prepared for slumber by removing his shoes and outer clothing. He blinked at Sidney's amazing intrusion, but he said amiably enough, "Well, boy?"

"Uncle Rob, can't tell you how glad I am to be back at the old place!"

"H'm."

"Look, I—— Golly, I feel skittish as a young colt! Hardly know the old doc, my patients wouldn't! Rob, you got to help me. Mabelle don't want to stay here and farm it—maybe me and you partners, eh? But the kids and I are crazy to. How I hate that ole city! So do the kids."

"Yeh?"

"Sure they do. Didn't you hear how they said they wouldn't mind tramping to school and not having any movies?"

"Sid, maybe you'll understand kids when you get to be a granddad. Kids will always agree with anything that sounds exciting. Rob thinks it would be dandy to hoof it two miles through the snow to school. He won't! Not once he's done it!" Uncle Rob thrust his hands behind his skinny, bark-brown old neck on the maculate pillow. He was making perhaps the longest oration of his life. The light flickered, and a spider moved indignantly in its web in a corner. "No," said Uncle Rob, "he won't like it. I never did. And the schoolmaster used to lick me. I hated it, crawling through that snow and then get licked because you're late. And jiminy—haven't thought of it for thirty years, I guess, maybe forty, but I remember how some big fellow would dare you to put your tongue to your lunch pail, and it was maybe thirty below, and your tongue stuck to it and it took the hide right off! No, I never liked any of it, especially chores."

"Rob, listen! I'm serious! The kids will maybe kind of find it hard at first, but they'll get to like it, and they'll grow up real folks and not city saps. It'll be all right with them. I'll see to that. It's Mabelle. Listen, Rob, I've got a swell idea about her, and I want you to help me. You get hold of the ladies of the township—the Grange members and the Methodist ladies and like that. You tell 'em Mabelle is a swell city girl, and it would be dandy for the neighborhood if they could get her to stay here. She's grand, but she does kind of fall for flattery, and in the Bronx she ain't so important, and if these ladies came and told her they thought she was the cat's pajamas, maybe she'd fall for it, and then I guess maybe she might stay, if the ladies came——"

"They wouldn't!"

Uncle Rob had been rubbing his long and prickly chin and curling his toes in his gray socks.

"What do you mean?"

"Well, first place, the ladies round here would be onto your Mabelle. They ain't so backwoods as they was in your time. Take Mrs. Craig. Last three winters, her and her husband, Frank, have packed up the flivver and gone to Florida. But that ain't it. Fact is, Sid, I kind of sympathize with Mabelle."

"What do you mean?"

"Well, I never was strong for farming. Hard life, Sid. Always thought I'd like to keep store or something in the city. You forget how hard the work is here. You with your easy job, just filling a few teeth! No, I can't help you, Sid."

"I see. All right. Sorry for disturbing you."

As he crept downstairs in bewilderment, Sidney prayed —he who so rarely prayed—"O Lord, doesn't anybody but me love the land any more? What is going to happen to us? Why, all our life comes from the land!"

He knew that in the morning he would beg Mabelle to stay for a fortnight—and that she would not stay. It was his last night here. So all night long, slow and silent, he walked the country roads, looking at hemlock branches against the sky, solemnly shaking his head and wondering why he could never rid himself of this sinfulness of longing for the land; why he could never be grown-up and ambitious and worthy, like his father and Mabelle and Uncle Rob.

A LETTER FROM THE QUEEN

A LETTER FROM THE QUEEN

DOCTOR SELIG was an adventurer. He did not look it, certainly. He was an amiable young bachelor with thin hair. He was instructor in history and economics in Erasmus College, and he had to sit on a foolish little platform and try to coax some fifty young men and women, who were interested only in cuddling and four-door sedans, to become hysterical about the law of diminishing returns.

But at night, in his decorous boarding house, he sometimes smoked a pipe, which was viewed as obscene in the religious shades of Erasmus, and he was boldly writing a book which was to make him famous.

Of course everyone is writing a book. But Selig's was different. It was profound. How good it was can be seen from the fact that with only three quarters of it done, it already had fifteen hundred footnotes—such lively comments as "*Vid.* J. A. S. H. S. VIII, 234 *et seq.*" A real book, nothing flippant or commercialized.

It was called *The Influence of American Diplomacy on the Internal Policies of Paneuropa.*

"Paneuropa," Selig felt, was a nice and scholarly way of saying "Europe."

It would really have been an interesting book if Doctor Selig had not believed that all literature is excellent in proportion as it is hard to read. He had touched a world romantic and little known. Hidden in old documents, like discovering in a desert an oasis where girls laugh and fountains chatter and the market place is noisy, he found the story of Franklin, who in his mousy fur cap was the Don Juan of Paris, of Adams fighting the British Government to prevent their recognizing the Confederacy, of Benjamin Thompson, the Massachusetts Yankee who in 1791 was chief counselor of Bavaria, with the title of Count Rumford.

Selig was moved by these men who made the young America more admired than she is today. And he was moved and, in a most unscholarly way, he became a little angry as he reviewed the story of Senator Ryder.

He knew, of course, that Lafayette Ryder had prevented war between England and America in the first reign of Grover Cleveland; he knew that Ryder had been Secretary of State, and Ambassador to France, courted by Paris for his wisdom, his manners, his wit; that as Senator he had fathered (and mothered and wet-nursed) the Ryder-Hanklin Bill, which had saved our wheat markets; and that his two books, *Possibilities of Disarmament* and *The Anglo-American Empire*, were not merely glib propaganda for peace, but such inspired documents as would have prevented the Boer War, the Spanish-American War, the Great War, if there had been in his Victorian world a dozen men with minds like his. This Selig knew, but he could not remember when Ryder had died.

Then he discovered with aghast astonishment that Senator Ryder was not dead, but still alive at ninety-two, forgotten by the country he had helped to build.

Yes, Selig felt bitterly, we honor our great men in

America—sometimes for as much as two months after the particular act of greatness that tickles us. But this is a democracy. We mustn't let anyone suppose that because we have given him an (undesired) parade up Broadway and a (furiously resented) soaking of publicity on March first, he may expect to be taken seriously on May second.

The Admiral Dewey whom the press for a week labeled as a combination of Nelson, Napoleon, and Chevalier Bayard, they later nagged to his grave. If a dramatist has a success one season, then may the gods help him, because for the rest of his life everyone will attend his plays only in the hope that he will fail.

But sometimes the great glad-hearted hordes of boosters do not drag down the idol in the hope of finding clay feet, but just forget him with the vast, contemptuous, heavy indifference of a hundred and twenty million people.

So felt Doctor Selig, angrily, and he planned for the end of his book a passionate resurrection of Senator Ryder. He had a shy hope that his book would appear before the Senator's death, to make him happy.

Reading the Senator's speeches, studying his pictures in magazine files, he felt that he knew him intimately. He could see, as though the Senator were in the room, that tall ease, the contrast of long thin nose, gay eyes, and vast globular brow that made Ryder seem a combination of Puritan, clown, and benevolent scholar.

Selig longed to write to him and ask—oh, a thousand things that only he could explain; the proposals of Lionel Sackville-West regarding Colombia; what Queen Victoria really had said in that famous but unpublished letter to President Harrison about the Newfoundland fisheries. Why couldn't he write to him?

No! The man was ninety-two, and Selig had too much reverence to disturb him, along with a wholesome suspicion that his letter would be kicked out by the man who had once told Gladstone to go to the devil.

So forgotten was the Senator that Selig could not, at first, find where he lived. Who's Who gave no address. Selig's superior, Professor Munk, who was believed to know everything in the world except the whereabouts of his last-season's straw hat, bleated, "My dear chap, Ryder is dwelling in some cemetery! He passed beyond, if I remember, in 1901."

The mild Doctor Selig almost did homicide upon a venerable midwestern historian.

At last, in a bulletin issued by the Anti-Prohibition League, Selig found among the list of directors: "Lafayette Ryder (form. U. S. Sen., Sec'y State), West Wickley, Vermont." Though the Senator's residence could make no difference to him, that night Selig was so excited that he smoked an extra pipe of tobacco.

He was planning his coming summer vacation, during which he hoped to finish his book. The presence of the Senator drew him toward Vermont, and in an educational magazine he found the advertisement: "Sky Peaks, near Wickley, Vt., woodland nook with peace and a library—congenial and intellectual company and writers—tennis, handball, riding—nightly Sing round Old-time Bonfire—fur. bung. low rates."

That was what he wanted: a nook and a library and lots of low rates, along with nearness to his idol. He booked a fur. bung. for the summer, and he carried his suitcase to the station on the beautiful day when the young fiends who through the year had tormented him with unanswerable questions streaked off to all parts of the world and for three tremendous months permitted him to be a private human being.

When he reached Vermont, Selig found Sky Peaks an

old farm, redecorated in a distressingly tea-roomy fashion. His single bungalow, formerly an honest corncrib, was now painted robin's-egg blue with yellow trimmings and christened "Shelley." But the camp was on an upland, and air sweet from hayfield and spruce grove healed his lungs, spotted with classroom dust.

At his first dinner at Sky Peaks, he demanded of the host, one Mr. Iddle, "Doesn't Senator Ryder live somewhere near here?"

"Oh, yes, up on the mountain, about four miles south."

"Hope I catch a glimpse of him some day."

"I'll run you over to see him any time you'd like."

"Oh, I couldn't do that! Couldn't intrude!"

"Nonsense! Of course he's old, but he takes quite an interest in the countryside. Fact, I bought this place from him and—— Don't forget the Sing tonight."

At eight that evening Iddle came to drag Selig from the security of his corncrib just as he was getting the relations of the Locarno Pact and the Versailles Treaty beautifully coördinated.

It was that kind of Sing. "The Long, Long Trail," and "All God's Chillun Got Shoes." (God's Chillun also possessed coats, pants, vests, flivvers, and watermelons, interminably.) Beside Selig at the campfire sat a young woman with eyes, a nose, a sweater, and an athletic skirt, none of them very good or particularly bad. He would not have noticed her, but she picked on him:

"They tell me you're in Erasmus, Doctor Selig."

"Um."

"Real attention to character. And after all, what benefit is there in developing the intellect if the character isn't developed to keep pace with it? You see, I'm in educational work myself—oh, of course nothing like being on a college faculty, but I teach history in the Lincoln High School at

Schenectady—my name is Selma Swanson. We must
have some good talks about teaching history, mustn't
we!"

"Um!" said Selig, and escaped, though it was not till
he was safely in his corncrib that he said aloud, "We must
not!"

For three months he was not going to be a teacher, or
heed the horrors of character-building. He was going to
be a great scholar. Even Senator Ryder might be excited
to know how powerful an intellect was soothing itself to
sleep in a corncrib four miles away!

He was grinding hard next afternoon when his host,
Iddle, stormed in with: "I've got to run in to Wickley
Center. Go right near old Ryder's. Come on. I'll introduce
you to him."

"Oh, no, honestly!"

"Don't be silly: I imagine he's lonely. Come on!"

Before Selig could make up his mind to get out of Iddle's
tempestuous flivver and walk back, they were driving up
a mountain road and past marble gateposts into an estate.
Through a damp grove of birches and maples they came
out on meadows dominated by an old brick house with a
huge porch facing the checkered valley. They stopped
with a dash at the porch, and on it Selig saw an old man
sunk in a canvas deck chair and covered with a shawl. In
the shadow the light seemed to concentrate on his bald
head, like a sphere of polished vellum, and on long blood-
less hands lying as in death on shawl-draped knees. In
his eyes there was no life nor desire for it.

Iddle leaped out, bellowing, "Afternoon, Senator!
Lovely day, isn't it? I've brought a man to call on you.
This is Mr. Selig of—uh—one of our colleges. I'll be back
in an hour."

He seized Selig's arm—he was abominably strong—and

almost pulled him out of the car. Selig's mind was one
wretched puddle of confusion. Before he could dredge any
definite thought out of it, Iddle had rattled away, and
Selig stood below the porch, hypnotized by the stare of
Senator Ryder—too old for hate or anger, but not too old
for slow contempt.

Not one word Ryder said.

Selig cried, like a schoolboy unjustly accused:

"Honestly, Senator, the last thing I wanted to do was
to intrude on you. I thought Iddle would just introduce
us and take me away. I suppose he meant well. And perhaps subconsciously I did want to intrude! I know your
Possibilities of Disarmament and *Anglo-American Empire*
so well——"

The Senator stirred like an antediluvian owl awakening
at twilight. His eyes came to life. One expected him to
croak, like a cynical old bird, but his still voice was fastidious:

"I didn't suppose anyone had looked into my books
since 1910." Painful yet gracious was the gesture with
which he waved Selig to a chair. "You are a teacher?"

"Instructor in a small Ohio college. Economics and
history. I'm writing a monograph on our diplomacy, and
naturally—— There are so many things that only you
could explain!"

"Because I'm so old?"

"No! Because you've had so much knowledge and
courage—perhaps they're the same thing! Every day,
literally, in working on my book I've wished I could con-
sult you. For instance—— Tell me, sir, didn't Secretary
of State Olney really want war with England over Vene-
zuela? Wasn't he trying to be a tin hero?"

"No!" The old man threw off his shawl. It was somehow a little shocking to find him not in an ancient robe

laced with gold, but in a crisp linen summer suit with a smart bow tie. He sat up, alert, his voice harsher. "No! He was a patriot. Sturdy. Honest. Willing to be conciliatory but not flinching. Miss Tully!"

At the Senator's cry, out of the wide fanlighted door of the house slid a trained nurse. Her uniform was so starched that it almost clattered, but she was a peony sort of young woman, the sort who would insist on brightly mothering any male, of any age, whether or not he desired to be mothered. She glared at the intruding Selig; she shook her finger at Senator Ryder, and simpered:

"Now I do hope you aren't tiring yourself, else I shall have to be ever so stern and make you go to bed. The doctor said——"

"Damn the doctor! Tell Mrs. Tinkham to bring me down the file of letters from Richard Olney, Washington, for 1895—O-l-n-e-y—and hustle it!"

Miss Tully gone, the Senator growled, "Got no more use for a nurse than a cat for two tails! It's that mutton-headed doctor, the old fool! He's seventy-five years old, and he hasn't had a thought since 1888. Doctors!"

He delivered an address on the art of medicine with such vigorous blasphemy that Selig shrank in horrified admiration. And the Senator didn't abate the blazing crimson of his oration at the entrance of his secretary, Mrs. Tinkham, a small, narrow, bleached, virginal widow.

Selig expected her to leap off the porch and commit suicide in terror. She didn't. She waited, she yawned gently, she handed the Senator a manila envelope, and gently she vanished.

The Senator grinned. "She'll pray at me tonight! She daren't while you're here. There! I feel better. Good cussing is a therapeutic agent that has been forgotten in these degenerate days. I could teach you more about cussing than about diplomacy—to which cussing is a most valuable aid. Now here is a letter that Secretary Olney wrote me about the significance of his correspondence with England."

It was a page of history. Selig handled it with more reverence than he had given to any material object in his life.

He exclaimed, "Oh, yes, you used—of course I've never seen the rest of this letter, and I can't tell you, sir, how excited I am to see it. But didn't you use this first paragraph —it must be about on page 276 of your *Anglo-American Empire?*"

"I believe I did. It's not my favorite reading!"

"You know, of course, that it was reprinted from your book in the *Journal of the American Society of Historical Sources* last year?"

"Was it?" The old man seemed vastly pleased. He beamed at Selig as at a young but tested friend. He chuckled, "Well, I suppose I appreciate now how King Tut felt when they remembered him and dug him up. . . . Miss Tully! Hey! Miss Tully, will you be so good as to tell Martens to bring us whisky and soda, with two glasses? Eh? Now you look here, young woman; we'll fight out the whole question of my senile viciousness after our guest has gone. Two glasses, I said! . . . Now about Secretary Olney. The fact of the case was . . ."

Two hours later, Senator Ryder was still talking and in that two hours he had given Selig such unrecorded information as the researcher could not have found in two years of study.

Selig had for two hours walked with presidents and ambassadors; he had the dinner conversation of foreign ministers, conversations so private, so world-affecting, that they never had been set down, even in letters. The Senator had revealed his friendship with King Edward, and the predictions about the future World War the King had made over a glass of mineral water.

The mild college instructor, who till this afternoon had never spoken to anyone more important than the president of a prairie college, was exalted with a feeling that he had become the confidant of kings and field marshals, of Anatole France and Lord Haldane, of Sarah Bernhardt and George Meredith.

He had always known but till now he had never understood that in private these great personages were plain human beings, like Doctor Wilbur Selig of Erasmus. It made him feel close to King Edward to hear (though the Senator may have exaggerated) that the King could not pronounce his own name without a German accent; it made him feel a man of the world to learn the details of a certain not very elevating party at which an English duke and a German prince and a Portuguese king, accompanied by questionable ladies, had in bibulous intimacy sung to Senator Ryder's leadership the lyric, "How Dry I Am."

During that two hours, there had been ten minutes when he had been entirely off in a Conan Doyle spirit world. His notion of prodigious alcoholic dissipation was a bottle of home-brewed beer once a month. He had tried to mix himself a light whisky and soda—he noted, with some anxiety about the proper drinking-manners in diplomatic society, that he took approximately one third as much whisky as the Senator.

But while the old man rolled his drink in his mouth and shook his bald head rapturously and showed no effect, Selig was suddenly lifted six million miles above the earth, through pink-gray clouds shot with lightning, and at that altitude he floated dizzily while below him the Senator discoursed on the relations of Cuban sugar to Colorado beets.

And once Iddle blatted into sight, in his dirty flivver, suggested taking him away, and was blessedly dismissed by the Senator's curt, "Doctor Selig is staying here for dinner. I'll send him back in my car."

Dinner . . . Selig, though he rarely read fiction, had read in some novel about "candle-flames, stilled in the twilight and reflected in the long stretch of waxed mahogany as in a clouded mirror—candles and roses and old silver." He had read, too, about stag horns and heraldic shields and the swords of old warriors.

Now, actually, the Senator's dining room had neither stag horn nor heraldic shield nor sword, and if there were still candle-flames, there was no mahogany to reflect them, but instead a silver stretch of damask. It was a long room, simple, with old portraits against white panels. Yet Selig felt that he was transported into all the romance he had ever read.

The dinner was countrylike. By now, Selig expected peacocks' tongues and caviar; he got steak and cantaloupe and corn pudding. But there were four glasses at each plate, and along with water, which was the familiar drink at Erasmus, he had, and timidly, tasted sherry, Burgundy, and champagne.

If Wilbur Selig of Iowa and Erasmus had known anything, it was that champagne was peculiarly wicked, associated with light ladies, lewd talk, and losses at roulette invariably terminating in suicide. Yet it was just as he was nibbling at his very first glass of champagne that Senator Ryder began to talk of his delight in the rise of Anglo-Catholicism.

No. It was none of it real.

If he was exhilarated that he had been kept for dinner, he was ecstatic when the Senator said, "Would you care to come for dinner again day after tomorrow? Good. I'll send Martens for you at seven-thirty. Don't dress."

In a dream phantasmagoria he started home, driven by Martens, the Senator's chauffeur-butler, with unnumbered things that had puzzled him in writing his book made clear.

When he arrived at the Sky Peaks camp, the guests were still sitting about the dull campfire.

"My!" said Miss Selma Swanson, teacher of history. "Mr. Iddle says you've spent the whole evening with Senator Ryder. Mr. Iddle says he's a grand person—used to be a great politician."

"Oh, he was kind enough to help me about some confused problems," murmured Selig.

But as he went to bed—in a reformed corncrib—he exulted, "I bet I could become quite a good friend of the Senator! Wouldn't that be wonderful!"

Lafayette Ryder, when his visitor—a man named Selig or Selim—was gone, sat at the long dining table with a cigarette and a distressingly empty cognac glass. He was meditating, "Nice eager young chap. Provincial. But mannerly. I wonder if there really are a few people who know that Lafe Ryder once existed?"

He rang, and the crisply coy Miss Tully, the nurse, waltzed into the dining room, bubbling, "So we're all ready to go to bed now, Senator!"

"We are not! I didn't ring for you; I rang for Martens."

"He's driving your guest."

"Humph! Send in cook. I want some more brandy."

"Oh, now, Daddy Ryder! You aren't going to be naughty, are you?"

"I am! And who the deuce ever told you to call me 'Daddy'? Daddy!"

"You did. Last year."

"I don't—this year. Bring me the brandy bottle."

"If I do, will you go to bed then?"

"I will not!"

"But the doctor——"

"The doctor is a misbegotten hound with a face like a fish. And other things. I feel cheerful tonight. I shall sit up late. Till All Hours."

They compromised on eleven-thirty instead of All Hours, and one glass of brandy instead of the bottle. But, vexed at having thus compromised—as so often, in ninety-odd years, he had been vexed at having compromised with Empires—the Senator was (said Miss Tully) very naughty in his bath.

"I swear," said Miss Tully afterward, to Mrs. Tinkham, the secretary, "if he didn't pay so well, I'd leave that horrid old man tomorrow. Just because he was a politician or something, once, to think he can sass a trained nurse!"

"You would not!" said Mrs. Tinkham. "But he *is* naughty."

And they did not know that, supposedly safe in his four-poster bed, the old man was lying awake, smoking a cigarette and reflecting:

"The gods have always been much better to me than I have deserved. Just when I thought I was submerged in a flood of women and doctors, along comes a man for companion, a young man who seems to be a potential scholar, and who might preserve for the world what I tried to do. Oh, stop pitying yourself, Lafe Ryder! . . . I wish I could sleep."

Senator Ryder reflected, the next morning, that he had probably counted too much on young Selig. But when Selig came again for dinner, the Senator was gratified to see how quickly he was already fitting into a house probably more elaborate than any he had known. And quite easily he told of what the Senator accounted his uncivilized farm boyhood, his life in a state university.

"So much the better that he is naïve, not one of these third-secretary cubs who think they're cosmopolitan because they went to Groton," considered the Senator. "I must do something for him."

Again he lay awake that night, and suddenly he had what seemed to him an inspired idea.

"I'll give young Selig a lift. All this money and no one but hang-jawed relatives to give it to! Give him a year of freedom. Pay him—he probably earns twenty-five hundred a year; pay him five thousand and expenses to arrange my files. If he makes good, I'd let him publish my papers after I pass out. The letters from John Hay, from Blaine, from Choate! No set of unpublished documents like it in America! It would *make* the boy!"

Mrs. Tinkham would object. Be jealous. She might quit. Splendid! Lafe, you arrant old coward, you've been trying to get rid of that woman without hurting her feelings for three years! At that, she'll probably marry you on your dying bed!"

He chuckled, a wicked, low, delighted sound, the old man alone in darkness.

"Yes, and if he shows the quality I think he has, leave him a little money to carry on with while he edits the letters. Leave him—let's see."

It was supposed among Senator Ryder's lip-licking relatives and necessitous hangers-on that he had left of the Ryder fortune perhaps two hundred thousand dollars. Only his broker and he knew that he had by secret investment increased it to a million, these ten years of dark, invalid life.

He lay planning a new will. The present one left half his fortune to his university, a quarter to the town of Wickley for a community center, the rest to nephews and nieces, with ten thousand each for the Tully, the Tinkham, Martens, and the much-badgered doctor, with a grave proviso that the doctor should never again dictate to any patient how much he should smoke.

Now to Doctor Selig, asleep and not even dream-warned in his absurd corncrib, was presented the sum of twenty-five thousand dollars, the blessings of an old man, and a store of historical documents which could not be priced in coin.

In the morning, with a headache, and very strong with Miss Tully about the taste of the aspirin—he suggested that she had dipped it in arsenic—the Senator reduced Selig to five thousand, but that night it went back to twenty-five.

How pleased the young man would be.

Doctor Wilbur Selig, on the first night when he had unexpectedly been bidden to stay for dinner with Senator Ryder, was as stirred as by—— What *would* most stir Doctor Wilbur Selig? A great play? A raise in salary? An Erasmus football victory?

At the second dinner, with the house and the hero less novel to him, he was calmly happy, and zealous about getting information. The third dinner, a week after, was agreeable enough, but he paid rather more attention to the squab in casserole than to the Senator's revelations about the Baring panic, and he was a little annoyed that the Senator insisted (so selfishly) on his staying till midnight, instead of going home to bed at a reasonable hour like ten—with, perhaps, before retiring, a few minutes of chat with that awfully nice bright girl, Miss Selma Swanson.

And through that third dinner he found himself reluctantly critical of the Senator's morals.

Hang it, here was a man of good family, who had had a chance to see all that was noblest and best in the world, and why did he feel he had to use such bad language, why did he drink so much? Selig wasn't (he proudly reminded himself) the least bit narrow-minded. But an old man like this ought to be thinking of making his peace; ought to be ashamed of cursing like a stableboy.

He reproved himself next morning, "He's been mighty nice to me. He's a good old coot—at heart. And of course a great statesman."

But he snapped back to irritation when he had a telephone call from Martens, the chauffeur: "Senator Ryder would like you to come over for tea this afternoon. He has something to show you."

"All right, I'll be over."

Selig was curt about it, and he raged, "Now, by thunder, of all the thoughtless, selfish old codgers! As if I didn't have anything to do but dance attendance on him and amuse him! And here I'd planned to finish a chapter this afternoon! 'Course he does give me some inside information, but still—as if I needed all the tittle-tattle of embassies for my book! Got all the stuff I need now. And how am I to get over there? The selfish old hound never thinks of that! Does he suppose I can afford a car to go over? I'll have to walk! Got half a mind not to go!"

The sulkiness with which he came to tea softened when the Senator began to talk about the Queen Victoria letter.

Historians knew that during the presidency of Benjamin Harrison, when there was hostility between America and Britain over the seizure by both sides of fishing boats, Queen Victoria had written in her own hand to President Harrison. It was believed that she deplored her royal inability to appeal directly to Parliament, and suggested his first taking the difficulty up with Congress. But precisely what was in this unofficial letter, apparently no one knew.

This afternoon Senator Ryder said placidly, "I happen to have the original of the letter in my possession."

"*What?*"

"Perhaps some day I'll give you a glimpse of it. I think I have the right to let you quote it."

Selig was electrified. It would be a sensation—*he* would be a sensation! He could see his book, and himself, on the front pages. But the Senator passed on to a trivial, quite improper anecdote about a certain Brazilian ambassador and a Washington milliner, and Selig was irritable again. Darn it, it was indecent for a man of over ninety to think of such things! And why the deuce was he so skittish and secretive about his old letter? If he was going to show it, why not do it?

So perhaps Doctor Selig of Erasmus was not quite so gracious as a Doctor Selig of Erasmus should have been when, at parting, the old man drew from under his shawl a worn blue-gray pamphlet, and piped:

"I'm going to give you this, if you'd like it. There's only six copies left in the world, I believe. It's the third one of my books—privately printed and not ordinarily listed with the others. It has, I imagine, a few things in it the historians don't know; the real story of the Paris commune."

"Oh, thanks," Selig said brusquely and, to himself, in the Senator's car, he pointed out that it showed what an egotistic old codger Ryder was to suppose that just because he'd written something, it must be a blooming treasure!

He glanced into the book. It seemed to have information. But he wasn't stirred, for it was out of line with what he had decided were the subjects of value to Doctor Selig and, therefore, of general interest.

After tea, now, it was too late for work before dinner, and he had Ryder's chauffeur set him down at Tredwell's General Store, which had become for members of the Sky Peaks camp a combination of department store, post office and café, where they drank wild toasts in lemon pop.

Miss Selma Swanson was there, and Selig laughingly treated her to chewing gum, Attaboy Peanut Candy Rolls, and seven fishhooks. They had such a lively time discussing that funny Miss Elkington up at the camp.

When he started off, with Miss Swanson, he left the Senator's book behind him in the store. He did not miss it till he had gone to bed.

Two days afterward, the Senator's chauffeur again telephoned an invitation to tea for that afternoon, but this time Selig snapped, "Sorry! Tell the Senator I unfortunately shan't be able to come!"

"Just a moment, please," said the chauffeur. "The Senator wishes to know if you care to come to dinner tomorrow evening—eight—he'll send for you."

"Well—— Yes, tell him I'll be glad to come."

After all, dinner here at Sky Peaks was pretty bad, and he'd get away early in the evening.

He rejoiced in having his afternoon free for work. But the confounded insistence of the Senator had so bothered him that he banged a book on his table and strolled outside.

The members of the camp were playing One Old Cat, with Selma Swanson, very jolly in knickerbockers, as cheer leader. They yelped at Selig to join them and, after a stately refusal or two, he did. He had a good time. Afterward he pretended to wrestle with Miss Swanson—she had the supplest waist and, seen close up, the moistest eyes. So he was glad that he had not wasted·his afternoon listening to that old bore.

The next afternoon, at six, a splendid chapter done, he went off for a climb up Mount Poverty with Miss Swanson. The late sun was so rich on pasture, pine clumps, and distant meadows, and Miss Swanson was so lively in tweed skirt and brogues—but the stockings were silk—that he regretted having promised to be at the Senator's at eight.

"But of course I always keep my promises," he reflected proudly.

They sat on a flat rock perched above the valley, and he observed in rather a classroom tone, "How remarkable that light is—the way it picks out that farmhouse roof, and then the shadow of those maples on the grass. Did you ever realize that it's less the shape of things than the light that gives a landscape beauty?"

"No, I don't think I ever did. That's so. It's the light! My, how observant you are!"

"Oh, no, I'm not. I'm afraid I'm just a bookworm."

"Oh, you are not! Of course you're tremendously scholarly—my, I've learned so much about study from you —but then, you're so active—you were just a circus playing One Old Cat yesterday. I do admire an all-round man."

At seven-thirty, holding her firm hand, he was saying, "But really, there's so much that I lack that—— But you do think I'm right about it's being so much manlier not to drink like that old man? By the way, we must start back."

At a quarter to eight, after he had kissed her and apologized and kissed her, he remarked, "Still, he can wait a while—won't make any difference."

At eight: "Golly, it's so late! Had no idea. Well, I better not go at all now. I'll just phone him this evening and say I got balled up on the date. Look! Let's go down to the lake and dine on the wharf at the boathouse, just you and I."

"Oh, that would be grand!" said Miss Selma Swanson

Lafayette Ryder sat on the porch that, along with his dining room and bedroom, had become his entire world, and waited for the kind young friend who was giving back to him the world he had once known. His lawyer was coming from New York in three days, and there was the matter of the codicil to his will. But—the Senator stirred impatiently—this money matter was grubby; he had for Selig something rarer than money—a gift for a scholar.

He looked at it and smiled. It was a double sheet of thick bond, with "Windsor Castle" engraved at the top. Above this address was written in a thin hand: "To my friend L. Ryder, to use if he ever sees fit. Benj. Harrison."

The letter began, "To His Excellency, the President," and it was signed, "Victoria R." In a few lines between inscription and signature there was a new history of the great Victoria and of the Nineteenth Century. . . . Dynamite does not come in large packages.

The old man tucked the letter into a pocket down beneath the rosy shawl that reached up to his gray face.

Miss Tully rustled out, to beg, "Daddy, you won't take more than one cocktail tonight? The doctor says it's so bad for you!"

"Heh! Maybe I will and maybe I won't! What time is it?"

"A quarter to eight."

"Doctor Selig will be here at eight. If Martens doesn't have the cocktails out on the porch three minutes after he gets back, I'll skin him. And you needn't go looking for the cigarettes in my room, either! I've hidden them in a brand-new place, and I'll probably sit up and smoke till dawn. Fact; doubt if I shall go to bed at all. Doubt if I'll take my bath."

He chuckled as Miss Tully wailed, "You're so naughty!"

The Senator need not have asked the time. He had groped down under the shawl and looked at his watch every five minutes since seven. He inwardly glared at himself for his foolishness in anticipating his young friend, but—all the old ones were gone.

That was the devilishness of living so many years. Gone, so long. People wrote idiotic letters to him, still, begging for his autograph, for money, but who save this fine young Selig had come to him? . . . So long now!

At eight, he stirred, not this time like a drowsy old owl, but like an eagle, its lean head thrusting forth from its pile of hunched feathers, ready to soar. He listened for the car.

At ten minutes past, he swore, competently. Confound that Martens!

At twenty past, the car swept up the driveway. Out of it stepped only Martens, touching his cap, murmuring, "Very sorry, sir. Mr. Selig was not at the camp."

"Then why the devil didn't you wait?"

"I did, sir, as long as I dared."

"Poor fellow! He may have been lost on the mountain. We must start a search!"

"Very sorry, sir, but if I may say so, as I was driving back past the foot of the Mount Poverty trail, I saw Mr. Selig with a young woman, sir, and they were talking and laughing and going away from the camp, sir. I'm afraid ——"

"Very well. That will do."

"I'll serve dinner at once, sir. Do you wish your cocktail out here?"

"I won't have one. Send Miss Tully."

When the nurse had fluttered to him, she cried out with alarm. Senator Ryder was sunk down into his shawl. She bent over him to hear his whisper:

"If it doesn't keep you from your dinner, my dear, I think I'd like to be helped up to bed. I don't care for anything to eat. I feel tired."

While she was anxiously stripping the shawl from him, he looked long, as one seeing it for the last time, at the darkening valley. But as she helped him up, he suddenly became active. He snatched from his pocket a stiff double sheet of paper and tore it into fragments which he fiercely scattered over the porch with one sweep of his long arm.

Then he collapsed over her shoulder.

THE GHOST PATROL

THE GHOST PATROL

Donald PATRICK DORGAN had served forty-four years on the police force of Northernapolis, and during all but five of that time he had patrolled the Forest Park section.

Don Dorgan might have been a sergeant, or even a captain, but it had early been seen at headquarters that he was a crank about Forest Park. For hither he had brought his young wife, and here he had built their shack; here his wife had died, and here she was buried. It was so great a relief in the whirl of department politics to have a man who was contented with his job that the Big Fellows were glad of Dorgan, and kept him there where he wanted to be, year after year, patrolling Forest Park.

For Don Pat Dorgan had the immense gift of loving people, all people. In a day before anyone in Northernapolis had heard of scientific criminology, Dorgan believed that the duty of a policeman with clean gloves and a clean heart was to keep people from needing to be arrested. He argued with drunken men and persuaded them to hide out in an alley and sleep off the drunk. When he did arrest them it was because they were sedately staggering home

intent on beating up the wives of their bosoms. Any homeless man could get a nickel from Dorgan and a road-map
of the doss-houses. To big bruisers he spoke slowly, and
he beat them with his nightstick where it would hurt the
most but injure the least. Along his beat, small boys might
play baseball, provided they did not break windows or get
themselves in front of motor cars. The pocket in his coat-
tail was a mine; here were secreted not only his midnight
sandwiches, his revolver and handcuffs and a comic supple-
ment, but also a bag of striped candy and a red rubber ball.

When the Widow Maclester's son took to the booze, it
was Don Dorgan who made him enlist in the navy. Such
things were Don's work—his art. Joy of his art he had
when Kitty Silva repented and became clean-living; when
Micky Connors, whom Dorgan had known ever since
Micky was a squawking orphan, became a doctor, with a
large glass sign lettered J. J. Connors, M.D., and a nurse
to let a poor man in to see the great Doctor Connors!

Dorgan did have for one boy and girl a sneaking fond-
ness that transcended the kindliness he felt toward the
others. They were Polo Magenta, son of the Italian-
English-Danish jockey who had died of the coke, and
Effie Kugler, daughter of that Jewish delicatessen man
who knew more of the Talmud than any man in the Ghetto
—Effie the pretty and plump, black-haired and quick-
eyed, a perfect armful for anyone.

Polo Magenta had the stuff of a man in him. The boy
worshiped motors as his father had worshiped horses. At
fourteen, when his father died, he was washer at Mc-
Manus' Garage; at eighteen he was one of the smoothest
taxi-drivers in the city. At nineteen, dropping into Kugler's Delicatessen for sausages and crackers for his midnight lunch, he was waited upon by Effie.

Thereafter he hung about the little shop nightly, till old

Kugler frowned upon them—upon Polo, the gallantest lad in Little Hell, supple in his chauffeur's uniform, straight-backed as the English sergeant who had been his grand-father, pale-haired like a Dane, altogether a soldierly figure, whispering across the counter to blushing Effie.

Kugler lurked at the door and prevented Polo from driving past and picking her up. So Effie became pale with longing to see her boy; Polo took to straight Bourbon, which is not good for a taxi-driver racing to catch trains. He had an accident, once; he merely smashed the fenders of another car; but one more of the like, and the taxi-company would let him out.

Then Patrolman Don Dorgan sat in on the game. He decided that Polo Magenta should marry Effie. He told Polo that he would bear a message from him to the girl, and while he was meticulously selecting a cut of sausage for sandwich, he whispered to her that Polo was waiting, with his car, in the alley off Minnis Place. Aloud he bawled: "Come walk the block with me, Effie, you little divvle, if your father will let you. Mr. Kugler, it isn't often that Don Dorgan invites the ladies to go a-walking with him, but it's spring, and you know how it is with us wicked cops. The girl looks as if she needed a breath of fresh air."

"That's r-r-r-right," said Kugler. "You go valk a block with Mr. Dorgan, Effie, and mind you come r-r-r-right back."

Dorgan stood like a lion at the mouth of the alley where, beside his taxi, Polo Magenta was waiting. As he caught the cry with which Effie came to her lover, he remembered the evenings long gone when he and his own sweetheart had met in the maple lane that was now the scrofulous Minnis Place.

"Oh, Polo, I've just felt dead, never seeing you no-where."

"Gee, it hurts, kid, to get up in the morning and have everything empty, knowing I won't see you any time. I could run the machine off the Boulevard and end everything, my heart's so cold without you."

"Oh, is it, Polo, is it really?"

"Say, we only got a couple minutes. I've got a look in on a partnership in a repair shop in Thornwood Addition. If I can swing it, we can beat it and get hitched, and when your old man sees I'm prospering——"

While Dorgan heard Polo's voice grow crisp with practical hopes, he bristled and felt sick. For Kugler was coming along Minnis Place, peering ahead, hunched with suspicion. Dorgan dared not turn to warn the lovers, nor even shout.

Dorgan smiled. "Evening again," he said. "It was a fine walk I had with Effie. Is she got back yet?"

He was standing between Kugler and the alley-mouth, his arms akimbo.

Kugler ducked under his arm, and saw Effie cuddled beside her lover, the two of them sitting on the running-board of Polo's machine.

"Effie, you will come home now," said the old man. There was terrible wrath in the quietness of his graybeard voice.

The lovers looked shamed and frightened.

Dorgan swaggered up toward the group. "Look here, Mr. Kugler: Polo's a fine upstanding lad. He ain't got no bad habits—to speak of. He's promised me he'll lay off the booze. He'll make a fine man for Effie——"

"Mr. Dorgan, years I have respected you, but—Effie, you come home now," said Kugler.

"Oh, what will I do, Mr. Dorgan?" wailed Effie. "Should I do like Papa wants I should, or should I go off with Polo?"

Dorgan respected the divine rights of love, but also he had an old-fashioned respect for the rights of parents with their offspring.

"I guess maybe you better go with your papa, Effie. I'll talk to him——"

"Yes, you'll talk, and everybody will talk, and I'll be dead," cried young Polo. "Get out of my way, all of you."

Already he was in the driver's seat and backing his machine out. It went rocking round the corner.

Dorgan heard that Polo had been discharged by the taxi-company for speeding through traffic and smashing the tail-lights of another machine; then that he had got a position as private chauffeur in the suburbs, been discharged for impudence, got another position and been arrested for joy-riding with a bunch of young toughs from Little Hell. He was to be tried on the charge of stealing his employer's machine.

Dorgan brushed his citizen's clothes, got an expensive haircut and shampoo and went to call on the employer, who refused to listen to maundering defenses of the boy.

Dorgan called on Polo in his cell.

"It's all right," Polo said. "I'm glad I was pinched. I needed something to stop me, hard. I was going nutty, and if somebody hadn't slammed on the emergency, I don't know what I would have done. Now I've sat here reading and thinking, and I'm right again. I always gotta do things hard, booze or be good. And now I'm going to think hard, and I ain't sorry to have the chanct to be quiet."

Dorgan brought away a small note in which, with much misspelling and tenderness, Polo sent to Effie his oath of deathless love. To the delivery of this note Dorgan devoted one bribery and one shocking burglarious entrance.

Polo was sentenced to three years in prison, on a charge of grand larceny.

That evening Dorgan climbed, panting, to the cathedral, and for an hour he knelt with his lips moving, his spine cold, as he pictured young Polo shamed and crushed in prison, and as he discovered himself hating the law that he served.

One month later Dorgan reached the age-limit, and was automatically retired from the Force, on pension. He protested; but the retirement rule was inviolable.

Dorgan went to petition the commissioner himself. It was the first time in five years, except on the occasions of the annual police parades, that he had gone near headquarters, and he was given a triumphal reception. Inspectors and captains, reporters and aldermen, and the commissioner himself, shook his hand, congratulated him on his forty-five years of clean service. But to his plea they· did not listen. It was impossible to find a place for him. They heartily told him to rest, because he had earned it.

Dorgan nagged them. He came to headquarters again and again, till he became a bore, and the commissioner refused to see him. Dorgan was not a fool. He went shamefacedly back to his shack, and there he remained.

For two years he huddled by the fire and slowly became melancholy mad—gray-faced, gray-haired, a gray ghost of himself.

From time to time, during his two years of hermitage, Dorgan came out to visit his old neighbors. They welcomed him, gave him drinks and news, but they did not ask his advice. So he had become a living ghost before two years had gone by, and he talked to himself, aloud.

During these two years the police force was metropolitanized. There were a smart new commissioner and smart new inspectors and a smart new uniform—a blue military uniform with flat cap and puttees and shaped coats. After his first view of that uniform, at the police parade, Dorgan went home and took down from behind the sheet-iron stove a photograph of ten years before—the Force of that day, proudly posed on the granite steps of the city hall. They had seemed efficient and impressive then, but—his honest soul confessed it—they were like rural constables beside the crack corps of today.

Presently he took out from the redwood chest his own uniform, but he could not get himself to put on its shapeless gray coat and trousers, its gray helmet and spotless white gloves. Yet its presence comforted him, proved to him that, improbable though it seemed, the secluded old man had once been an active member of the Force.

With big, clumsy, tender hands he darned a frayed spot at the bottom of the trousers and carefully folded the uniform away. He took out his nightstick and revolver and the sapphire-studded star the Department had given him for saving two lives in the collapse of the Anthony building. He fingered them and longed to be permitted to carry them. . . . All night, in a dream and half-dream and tossing wakefulness, he pictured himself patrolling again, the father of his people.

Next morning he again took his uniform, his nightstick and gun and shield out of the redwood chest, and he hung them in the wardrobe, where they had hung when he was off duty in his days of active service. He whistled cheerfully and muttered: "I'll be seeing to them Tenth Street devils, the rotten gang of them."

Rumors began to come into the newspaper offices of a "ghost-scare" out in the Forest Park section. An old man had looked out of his window at midnight and seen a dead man, in a uniform of years before, standing on nothing at all. A stranger to the city, having come to his apartment-hotel, the Forest Arms, some ten blocks above Little Hell, at about two in the morning, stopped to talk with a strange-looking patrolman whose face he described as a drift of fog about burning, unearthly eyes. The patrolman had courteously told him of the building up of Forest Park, and at parting had saluted, an erect, somewhat touching figure. Later the stranger was surprised to note that the regulation uniform was blue, not gray.

After this there were dozens who saw the "Ghost Patrol," as the *Chronicle* dubbed the apparition; some spoke to him, and importantly reported him to be fat, thin, tall, short, old, young, and composed of mist, of shadows, of optical illusions and of ordinary human flesh.

Then a society elopement and a foreign war broke, and Ghost Patrol stories were forgotten.

One evening of early summer the agitated voice of a woman telephoned to headquarters from the best residence section of Forest Park that she had seen a burglar entering the window of the house next door, which was closed for the season. The chief himself took six huskies in his machine, and they roared out to Forest Park and surrounded the house. The owner of the agitated voice stalked out to inform the chief that just after she had telephoned, she had seen another figure crawling into the window after the burglar. She had thought that the second figure had a revolver and a policeman's club.

So the chief and the lieutenant crawled nonchalantly through an unquestionably open window giving on the pantry at the side of the house. Their electric torches showed the dining room to be a wreck—glass scattered and broken, drawers of the buffet on the floor, curtains torn down. They remarked "Some scrap!" and shouted:

"Come out here, whoever's in this house. We got it surrounded. Kendall, are you there? Have you pinched the guy?"

There was an unearthly silence, as of someone breathing in terror, a silence more thick and anxious than any mere absence of sound. They tiptoed into the drawing room, where, tied to a davenport, was that celebrated character, Butte Benny.

"My Gawd, Chief," he wailed, "get me outa this. De place is haunted. A bleeding ghost comes and grabs me and ties me up. Gee, honest, Chief, he was a dead man, and he was dressed like a has-been cop, and he didn't say nawthin' at all. I tried to wrastle him, and he got me down; and oh, Chief, he beat me crool, he did, but he was dead as me great-grandad, and you could see de light t'rough him. Let's get outa this—frame me up and I'll sign de confession. Me for a nice, safe cell for keeps!"

"Some amateur cop done this, to keep his hand in. Ghost me eye!" said the chief. But his own flesh felt icy, and he couldn't help looking about for the unknown.

"Let's get out of this, Chief," said Lieutenant Saxon, the bravest man in the strong-arm squad; and with Butte Benny between them they fled through the front door, leaving the pantry window still open. They didn't handcuff Benny. They couldn't have lost him!

Next morning when a captain came to look over the damages in the burglarized house he found the dining room crudely straightened up and the pantry window locked.

When the baby daughter of Simmons, the plumber of Little Hell, was lost, two men distinctly saw a gray-faced figure in an old-time police helmet leading the lost girl through unfrequented back alleys. They tried to follow, but the mysterious figure knew the egresses better than they did; and they went to report at the station house.

Meantime there was a ring at the Simmons' door, and Simmons found his child on the doormat, crying but safe. In her hand, tight clutched, was the white-cotton glove of a policeman.

Simmons gratefully took the glove to the precinct station. It was a regulation service glove; it had been darned with white-cotton thread till the original fabric was almost overlaid with short, inexpert stitches; it had been whitened with pipe-clay, and from one slight brown spot it must have been pressed out with a hot iron. Inside it was stamped, in faded rubber stamping: Dorgan, Patrol, 9th Precinct. The chief took the glove to the commissioner, and between these two harsh, abrupt men there was a pitying silence surcharged with respect.

"We'll have to take care of the old man," said the chief at last.

A detective was assigned to the trail of the Ghost Patrol. The detective saw Don Dorgan come out of his shack at three in the morning, stand stretching out his long arms, sniff the late-night dampness, smile as a man will when he starts in on the routine of work that he loves. He was erect; his old uniform was clean-brushed, his linen collar spotless; in his hand he carried one lone glove. He looked to right and left, slipped into an alley, prowled through the darkness, so fleet and soft-stepping that the shadow almost lost him. He stopped at a shutter left open and prodded it shut with his old-time long nightstick. Then he stole back to his shack and went in.

The next day the chief, the commissioner, and a self-appointed committee of inspectors and captains came calling on Don Dorgan at his shack. The old man was a slovenly figure, in open-necked flannel shirt and broken-backed slippers. Yet Dorgan straightened up when they came, and faced them like an old soldier called to duty.

The dignitaries sat about awkwardly, while the commissioner tried to explain that the Big Fellows had heard Dorgan was lonely here, and that the department fund was, unofficially, going to send him to Dr. Bristow's Private Asylum for the Aged and Mentally Infirm—which he euphemistically called "Doc Bristow's Home."

"No," said Dorgan, "that's a private booby-hatch. I don't want to go there. Maybe they got swell rooms, but I don't want to be stowed away with a bunch of nuts."

They had to tell him, at last, that he was frightening the neighborhood with his ghostly patrol and warn him that if he did not give it up they would have to put him away some place.

"But I got to patrol!" he said. "My boys and girls here, they need me to look after them. I sit and I hear voices—voices, I tell you, and they order me out on the beat. . . . Stick me in the bughouse. I guess maybe it's better. Say, tell Doc Bristow to not try any shenanigans wit' me, but let me alone, or I'll hand him something; I got a wallop like a probationer yet—I have so, Chief."

The embarrassed committee left Captain Luccetti with him, to close up the old man's shack and take him to the asylum in a taxi. The Captain suggested that the old uniform be left behind.

Dr. Davis Bristow was a conscientious but crotchety man who needed mental easement more than did any of his patients. The chief had put the fear of God into him, and he treated Dorgan with respect at first.

The chief had kind-heartedly arranged that Dorgan was to have a "rest," that he should be given no work about the farm; and all day long Dorgan had nothing to do but pretend to read, and worry about his children.

Two men had been assigned to the beat, in succession,

since his time; and the second man, though he was a good officer, came from among the respectable and did not understand the surly wistfulness of Little Hell. Dorgan was sure that the man wasn't watching to lure Matty Carlson from her periodical desire to run away from her decent, patient husband.

So one night, distraught, Dorgan lowered himself from his window and ran, skulking, stumbling, muttering across the outskirts and around to Little Hell. He didn't have his old instinct for concealing his secret patrolling. A policeman saw him, in citizen's clothes, swaying down his old beat, trying doors, humming to himself. And when they put him in the ambulance and drove him back to the asylum, he wept and begged to be allowed to return to duty.

Dr. Bristow telephoned to the chief of police, demanding permission to put Dorgan to work, and set him at gardening.

This was very well indeed. For through the rest of that summer, in the widespread gardens, and half the winter, in the greenhouses, Dorgan dug and sweated and learned the names of flowers. But early in January he began to worry once more. He told the super that he had figured out that, with good behavior, Polo Magenta would be out of the pen now, and need looking after. "Yes, yes—well, I'm busy; sometime you tell me all about it," Dr. Bristow jabbered, "but just this minute I'm very busy."

One day in mid-January Dorgan prowled uneasily all day long—the more uneasy as a blizzard blew up and the world was shut off by a curtain of weaving snow. He went up to his room early in the evening. A nurse came to take away his shoes and overcoat, and cheerily bid him go to bed.

But once he was alone he deliberately tore a cotton

blanket to strips and wound the strips about his thin slippers. He wadded newspapers and a sheet between his vest and his shirt. He found his thickest gardening cap. He quietly raised the window. He knocked out the light wooden bars with his big fist. He put his feet over the windowsill and dropped into the storm, and set out across the lawn. With his gaunt form huddled, his hands rammed into his coat pockets, his large feet moving slowly, certainly, in their moccasinlike covering of cloth and thin slippers, he plowed through to the street and down toward Little Hell.

Don Dorgan knew that the blizzard would keep him from being traced by the asylum authorities for a day or two, but he also knew that he could be overpowered by it. He turned into a series of alleys, and found a stable with a snowbound delivery wagon beside it. He brought hay from the stable, covered himself with it in the wagon, and promptly went to sleep. When he awoke the next afternoon the blizzard had ceased and he went on.

He came to the outskirts of Little Hell. Sneaking through alleys, he entered the back of McManus' red-light-district garage.

McManus, the boss, was getting his machines out into the last gasps of the storm, for the street-car service was still tied up, and motors were at a premium. He saw Dorgan and yelled: "Hello there, Don. Where did you blow in from? Ain't seen you these six months. T'ought you was living soft at some old-folks' home or other."

"No," said Dorgan, with a gravity which forbade trifling, "I'm a—I'm a kind of a watchman. Say, what's this I hear, young Magenta is out of the pen?"

"Yes, the young whelp. I always said he was no good, when he used to work here, and——"

"What's become of him?"

"He had the nerve to come here when he got out, looking for a job; suppose he wanted the chanct to smash up a few of my machines too! I hear he's got a job wiping, at the K. N. roundhouse. Pretty rough joint, but good enough for the likes o' him. Say, Don, things is slow since you went, what with these dirty agitators campaigning for prohibition——"

"Well," said Dorgan, "I must be moseying along, John."

Three men of hurried manner and rough natures threw Dorgan out of three various entrances to the roundhouse, but he sneaked in on the tender of a locomotive and saw Polo Magenta at work, wiping brass—or a wraith of Polo Magenta. He was thin, his eyes large and passionate. He took one look at Dorgan, and leaped to meet him.

"Dad—thunder—you old son of a gun."

"Sure! Well, boy, how's it coming?"

"Rotten."

"Well?"

"Oh, the old stuff. Keepin' the wanderin' boy tonight wanderin'. The warden gives me good advice, and I thinks I've paid for bein' a fool kid, and I pikes back to Little Hell with two bucks and lots of good intentions and—they seen me coming. The crooks was the only ones that welcomed me. McManus offered me a job, plain and fancy driving for guns. I turned it down and looks for decent work, which it didn't look for me none. There's a new cop on your old beat. Helpin' Hand Henry, he is. He gets me up and tells me the surprisin' news that I'm a desprit young jailbird, and he's onto me—see; and if I chokes any old women or beats up any babes in arms, he'll be there with the nippers—see: so I better quit my career of murder.

"I gets a job over in Milldale, driving a motor-truck, and he tips 'em off I'm a forger and an arson and I dunno what all, and they lets me out—wit' some more good advice. Same wit' other jobs."

"Effie?"

"Ain't seen her yet. But say, Dad, I got a letter from her that's the real stuff—says she'll stick by me till her dad croaks, and then come to me if it's through fire. I got it here—it keeps me from going nutty. And a picture postcard of her. You see, I planned to nip in and see her before her old man knew I was out of the hoosegow, but this cop I was tellin' you about wises up Kugler, and he sits on the doorstep with the Revolutionary musket loaded up with horseshoes and cobblestones, and so—get me? But I gets a letter through to her by one of the boys."

"Well, what are you going to do?"

"Search me. . . . There ain't nobody to put us guys next, since you got off the beat, Dad."

"I ain't off it! Will you do what I tell you to?"

"Sure."

"Then listen: You got to start in right here in Northern-apolis, like you're doing, and build up again. They didn't sentence you to three years but to six—three of 'em here, getting folks to trust you again. It ain't fair, but it is. See? You lasted there because the bars kep' you in. Are you man enough to make your own bars, and to not have 'em wished onto you?"

"Maybe."

"You are! You know how it is in the pen—you can't pick and choose your cell or your work. Then listen: I'm middlin' well off, for a bull—savin's and pension. We'll go partners in a fine little garage, and buck John McManus —he's a crook, and we'll run him out of business. But you got to be prepared to wait, and that's the hardest thing a man can do. Will you?"

"Yes."

"When you get through here, meet me in that hallway behint Mullins' Casino. So long, boy."

"So long, Dad."

When Polo came to him in the hallway behind Mullins' Casino, Dorgan demanded: "I been thinking; have you seen old Kugler?"

"Ain't dared to lay an eye on him, Dad. Trouble enough without stirrin' up more. Gettin' diplomatic."

"I been thinking. Sometimes the most diplomatic thing a guy can do is to go right to the point and surprise 'em. Come on."

They came into Kugler's shop, without parley or trembling; and Dorgan's face was impassive, as befits a patrolman, as he thrust open the door and bellowed "Evenin'!" at the horrified old Jewish scholar and the maid.

Don Dorgan laid his hands on the counter and spoke.

"Kugler," said he, "you're going to listen to me, because if you don't, I'll wreck the works. You've spoiled four lives. You've made this boy a criminal, forbidding him a good, fine love, and now you're planning to keep him one. You've kilt Effie the same way—look at the longing in the poor little pigeon's face! You've made me an unhappy old man. You've made yourself, that's meanin' to be good and decent, unhappy by a row with your own flesh and blood. Some said I been off me nut, Kugler, but I know I been out beyont, where they understand everything and forgive everything—and I've learnt that it's harder to be bad than to be good, that you been working harder to make us all unhappy than you could of to make us all happy."

Dorgan's gaunt, shabby bigness seemed to swell and fill the shop; his voice boomed and his eyes glowed with a will unassailable.

The tyrant Kugler was wordless, and he listened with respect as Dorgan went on, more gently:

"You're a godly man among the sinners, but that's made you think you must always be right. Are you willing to kill us all just to prove you can't never be wrong? Man, man, that's a fiendish thing to do. And oh, how much easier it would be to give way, onct, and let this poor cold boy creep home to the warmness that he do be longing so for, with the blizzard bitter around him, and every man's hand ag'in' him. Look—look at them poor, good children!"

Kugler looked, and he beheld Polo and Effie—still separated by the chill marble counter—with their hands clasped across it, their eyes met in utter frankness.

"Vell——" said Kugler wistfully.

"So!" said Patrolman Dorgan. "Well, I must be back on me beat—at the asylum . . . There's things that'd bear watching there!"

THINGS

THINGS

Τ<small>HIS</small> is not the story of Theodora Duke and Stacy Lindstrom, but of a traveling bag with silver fittings, a collection of cloisonné, a pile of ratty school-books, and a fireless cooker that did not cook.

Long before these things were acquired, when Theo was a girl and her father, Lyman Duke, was a so-so dealer in cut-over lands, there was a feeling of adventure in the family. They lived in a small brown house which predicated children and rabbits in the back yard, and a father invariably home for supper. But Mr. Duke was always catching trains to look at pine tracts in northern Minnesota. Often his wife went along and, in the wilds, way and beyond Grand Marais and the steely shore of Lake Superior, she heard wolves howl and was unafraid. The Dukes laughed much those years, and were eager to see mountains and new kinds of shade trees.

Theo found her own freedom in exploring jungles of five-foot mullein weeds with Stacy Lindstrom. That pale, stolid little Norwegian she chose from her playmates because he was always ready to try new games.

The city of Vernon was newer then—in 1900. There were no country clubs, no fixed sets. The pioneers from Maine and York State who had appropriated lumber and flour were richer than the newly come Buckeyes and Hoosiers and Scandinavians, but they were friendly. As they drove their smart trotters the leading citizens shouted "Hello, Heinie," or "Evenin', Knute," without a feeling of condescension. In preferring Stacy Lindstrom to Eddie Barnes, who had a hundred-dollar bicycle and had spent a year in a private school, Theo did not consider herself virtuously democratic. Neither did Stacy!

The brown-haired, bright-legged, dark-cheeked, glowing girl was a gorgeous colt, while he was a fuzzy lamb. Theo's father had an office, Stacy's father a job in a planing mill. Yet Stacy was the leader. He read books, and he could do things with his hands. He invented Privateers, which is a much better game than Pirates. For his gallant company of one privateers he rigged a forsaken dump cart, in the shaggy woods on the Mississippi bluffs, with sackcloth sails, barrel-hoop cutlasses, and a plank for victims to walk. Upon the request of the victims, who were Theo, he added to the plank a convenient handrail.

But anyone could play Ship—even Eddie Barnes. From a territorial pioneer Stacy learned of the Red River carts which, with the earthquaking squawk of ungreased wheels and the glare of scarlet sashes on the buckskin-shirted drivers, used to come plodding all the redskin-haunted way from the outposts of the Free Trappers, bearing marten and silver fox for the throats of princesses. Stacy changed the privateers' brigantine into a Red River cart. Sometimes it was seven or ten carts, and a barricade. Behind it Stacy and Theo kept off hordes of Dakotas.

After voyaging with Stacy, Theo merely ya-ah'd at Eddie Barnes when he wanted her to go skating. Eddie

considered a figure eight, performed on the ice of a safe
creek, the final accomplishment of imaginative sport,
while Stacy could from immemorial caverns call the Wiz-
ard Merlin as servitor to a little playing girl. Besides, he
could jump on ski! And mend a bike! Eddie had to take
even a dirty sprocket to the repair shop.

The city, and Theo, had grown less simple-hearted when
she went to Central High School. Twenty-five hundred
boys and girls gathered in those tall gloomy rooms, which
smelled of water pails and chalk and worn floors. There
was a glee club, a school paper, a debating society and
dress-up parties. The school was brisk and sensible, but it
was too large for the intimacy of the grade buildings. Eddie
Barnes was conspicuous now, with his energy in managing
the athletic association, his beautifully combed hair and
his real gold watch. Stacy Lindstrom was lost in the mass.

It was Eddie who saw Theo home from parties. He was a
man of the world. He went to Chicago as calmly as you or
I would go out to the St. Croix River to spear pickerel.

Stacy rarely went to parties. Theo invited him to her
own, and the girls were polite to him. Actually he danced
rather better than Eddie. But he couldn't talk about Chicago. He couldn't talk at all. Nor did he sing or go out for
sports. His father was dead. He worked Saturdays and
three nights a week in an upholstery shop—a dingy, lint-
blurred loft, where two old Swedes kept up as a permanent
institution a debate on the Lutheran Church versus the
Swedish Adventist.

"Why don't you get a good live job?" Eddie patron-
izingly asked Stacy at recess, and Theo echoed the question; but neither of them had any suggestions about
specific good live jobs.

Stacy stood from first to fifth in every class. But what,
Eddie demanded, was the use of studying unless you were

going to be a school teacher? Which he certainly was not!
He was going to college. He was eloquent and frequent on
this topic. It wasn't the darned old books, but the association with the fellows, that educated you, he pointed out.
Friendships. Fraternities. Helped a fellow like the dickens,
both in society and business, when he got out of college.

"Yes, I suppose so," sighed Theo.

Eddie said that Stacy was a longitudinal, latitudinous,
isothermic, geologic, catawampaboid Scandahoofian.
Everybody admired the way Eddie could make up long
words. Theo's older sister, Janet, who had cold, level eyes,
said that Theo was a fool to let a shabby, drabby nobody
like that Stacy Lindstrom carry her books home from
school. Theo defended Stacy whenever he was mentioned.
There is nothing which so cools young affection as having
to defend people.

After high school Eddie went East to college, Stacy was
a clerk in the tax commissioner's department of the railroad—and the Dukes became rich, and immediately ceased
to be adventurous.

Iron had been found under Mr. Duke's holdings in
northern Minnesota. He refused to sell. He leased the land
to the iron-mining company, and every time a scoop
brought up a mass of brown earth in the open pit the company ran very fast and dropped twenty-five cents in Mr.
Duke's pocket. He felt heavy with silver and importance;
he bought the P. J. Broom mansion and became the abject
servant of possessions.

The Broom mansion had four drawing rooms, a heraldic
limestone fireplace and a tower and a half. The half tower
was merely an octagonal shingle structure with a bulbous
Moorish top; but the full tower, which was of stone on a
base of brick, had cathedral windows, a weather vane, and

a metal roof down which dripped decorative blobs like
copper tears. While the mansion was being redecorated the
Duke senior took the grand tour from Miami to Port Said,
and brought home a carload of treasures. There was a
ready-made collection of cloisonné, which an English baron
had spent five years in gathering in Japan and five hours
in losing at Monte Carlo. There was a London traveling
bag, real seal, too crammed with silver fittings to admit
much of anything else, and too heavy for anyone save a
piano mover to lift. There were rugs, and books, and hand-
painted pictures, and a glass window from Nuremberg,
and ushabti figures from Egypt, and a pierced brass lamp
in the shape of a mosque.

All these symbols of respectability the Dukes installed
in the renovated Broom mansion, and settled down to
watch them.

Lyman Duke was a kindly man, and shrewd, but the
pride of ownership was a germ, and he was a sick man.
Who, he meditated, had such a lamp? Could even the
Honorable Gerard Randall point to such glowing rods of
book backs?

Mrs. Duke organized personally conducted excursions
to view the Axminster rug in the library. Janet forgot that
she had ever stood brushing her hair before a pine bureau.
Now she sat before a dressing table displaying candle-
sticks, an eyelash pencil, and a powder-puff box of gold
lace over old rose. Janet moved graciously, and invited
little sister Theo to be cordially unpleasant to their grubby
friends of grammar-school days.

The accumulation of things to make other people envious is nothing beside their accumulation because it's the
thing to do. Janet discovered that life would be unendur-
able without an evening cloak. At least three evening

cloaks were known to exist within a block of the Broom
mansion. True, nobody wore them. There aren't any balls
or plays except in winter, and during a Vernon winter you
don't wear a satin cloak—you wear a fur coat and a muf-
fler and a sweater and arctics, and you brush the frozen
breath from your collar, and dig out of your wraps like a
rabbit emerging from a brush pile. But if everybody had
them Janet wasn't going to be marked for life as one
ignorant of the niceties. She used the word "niceties" frequently and without quailing.

She got an evening cloak. Also a pair of fifteen-dollar
pumps, which she discarded for patent leathers as soon as
she found that everybody wore those—everybody being a
girl in the next block, whose house wasn't anywhere near
as nice as "ours."

II

Theo was only half glad of their grandeur. Oh, undoubtedly she was excited about the house at first, and mentioned it to other girls rather often, and rang for maids she
didn't need. But she had a little pain in the conscience. She
felt that she hadn't kept up defending Stacy Lindstrom
very pluckily.

She was never allowed to forget Stacy's first call at
the mansion. The family were settled in the house. They
were anxious for witnesses of their nobility. The bell rang
at eight one Saturday evening when they were finishing
dinner. It was hard to be finishing dinner at eight. They
had been used to starting at six-thirty-one and ending the
last lap, neck and neck, at six-fifty-two. But by starting
at seven, and having a salad, and letting Father smoke his
cigar at the table, they had stretched out the ceremony to
a reasonably decent length.

At the sound of the buzz in the butler's pantry Janet

squeaked: "Oh, maybe it's the Garlands! Or even the Randalls!" She ran into the hall.

"Janet! Jan-et! The maid will open the door!" Mrs. Duke wailed.

"I know, but I want to see who it is!"

Janet returned snapping: "Good heavens, it's only that Stacy Lindstrom! Coming at this early hour! And he's bought a new suit, just to go calling. It looks like sheet iron."

Theo pretended she had not heard. She fled to the distant library. She was in a panic. She was ashamed of herself, but she didn't trust Stacy to make enough impression. So it was Mr. Duke who had the first chance at the audience:

"Ah, Stacy, glad to see you, my boy. The girls are round some place. Theo!"

"Lyman! Don't shout so! I'll send a maid to find her," remonstrated Mrs. Duke.

"Oh, she'll come a-running. Trust these girls to know when a boy's round!" boomed Mr. Duke.

Janet had joined Theo in the library. She veritably hissed as she protested: "Boys-s-s-s-s! We come running for a commonplace railway clerk!"

Theo made her handkerchief into a damp, tight little ball in her lap, smoothed it out, and very carefully began to tear off its border.

Afar Mr. Duke was shouting: "Come see my new collection while we're waiting."

"I hate you!" Theo snarled at Janet, and ran into the last of the series of drawing rooms. From its darkness she could see her father and Stacy. She felt that she was protecting this, her brother, from danger; from the greatest of dangers—being awkward in the presence of the stranger, Janet. She was aware of Janet slithering in beside her.

"Now what do you think of that, eh?" Mr. Duke was demanding. He had unlocked a walnut cabinet, taken out an enameled plate.

Stacy was radiant. "Oh, yes. I know what that stuff is. I've read about it. It's cloysoan." He had pronounced it to rime with moan.

"Well, not precisely! Cloysonnay, most folks would call it. Culwasonnay, if you want to be real highbrow. But cloysoan, that's pretty good! Mamma! Janet! The lad says this is cloysoan! Ha, ha! Well, never mind, my boy. Better folks than you and I have made that kind of a mistake."

Janet was tittering. The poisonous stream of it trickled through all the rooms. Stacy must have heard. He looked about uneasily.

Suddenly Theo saw him as a lout, in his new suit that hung like wood. He was twisting a button and trying to smile back at Mr. Duke.

The cloisonné plate was given to Stacy to admire. What he saw was a flare of many-colored enamels in tiny compartments. In the center a dragon writhed its tongue in a field of stars, and on the rim were buds on clouds of snow, a flying bird, and amusing symbols among willow leaves.

But Mr. Duke was lecturing on what he ought to have seen:

"This is a *sara*, and a very fine specimen. Authorities differ, but it belonged either to the *Shi sinwo* or the *Monzeki*—princely monks, in the monastery of *Nin-na-ji*. Note the extreme thinness of the cloisons, and the pastes are very evenly vitrified. The colors are remarkable. You'll notice there's slate blue, sage green, chrome yellow, and—uh—well, there's several other colors. You see the ground shows the *kara kusa*. That bird there is a *ho-ho* in flight above the branches of the *kiri* tree."

Stacy had a healthy suspicion that a few months before

Mr. Duke had known no more about Oriental art than Stacy Lindstrom. But he had no Japanese words for repartee, and he could only rest his weight on the other foot and croak "Well, well!"

Mr. Duke was beatifically going on: "Now this *chatsubo*, you'll notice, is not cloisonné at all, but champlevé. Very important point in studying *shippo* ware. Note the unusually fine *kiku* crest on this *chawan*."

"I see. Uh—I see," said Stacy.

"Just a goat, that's all he is, just a giddy goat," Janet whispered to Theo in the dark room beyond, and pranced away.

It was five minutes before Theo got up courage to rescue Stacy. When she edged into the room he was sitting in a large leather chair and fidgeting. He was fidgeting in twenty different but equally irritating ways. He kept recrossing his legs, and every time he crossed them the stiff trousers bagged out in more hideous folds. Between times he tapped his feet. His fingers drummed on the chair. He looked up at the ceiling, licking his lips, and hastily looked down, with an artificial smile in acknowledgment of Mr. Duke's reminiscences of travel.

Theo swooped on Stacy with hands clapping in welcome, with a flutter of white muslin skirts about young ankles.

"Isn't the house comfy? When we get a pig we can keep him under that piano! Come on, I'll show you all the hidey holes," she crowed.

She skipped off, dragging him by the hand—but she realized that she was doing altogether too much dragging. Stacy, who had always been too intent on their games to be self-conscious, was self-conscious enough now. What could she say to him?

She besought: "I hope you'll come often. We'll have lots of fun out of——"

"Oh, you won't know me any more, with a swell place like this," he mumbled.

As women do she tried to bandage this raw, bruised moment. She snapped on the lights in the third drawing room, and called his attention to the late Mr. P. J. Broom's coat of arms carved on the hulking stone fireplace. "I got the decorator to puzzle it out for me, and as far as he could make out, if Pat Broom was right he was descended from an English duke, a German general and a Serbian undertaker. He didn't miss a trick except——"

"Well, it's a pretty fine fireplace," Stacy interrupted. He looked away, his eyes roving but dull, and dully he added: "Too fine for me, I guess."

Not once could she get him to share her joy in the house. He seemed proud of the virtue of being poor. Like a boast sounded his repeated "Too darned fine for me—don't belong in with all these doo-dads." She worked hard. She showed him not only the company rooms but the delightful secret passage of the clothes chute which led from an upstairs bedroom to the laundry; the closet drawers which moved on rollers and could be drawn out by the little finger; the built-in clock with both Trinity and Westminster chimes; the mysterious spaces of the basement, with the gas drier for wet wash, and the wine cellar which —as it so far contained only a case of beer and seven bottles of ginger ale—was chiefly interesting to the sense of make-believe.

Obediently he looked where she pointed; politely he repeated that everything was "pretty fine"; and not once was he her comrade. The spirit of divine trust was dead, horribly mangled and dead, she panted, while she caroled in the best nice-young-woman tone she could summon: "See, Stace. Isn't this cun-ning?"

It is fabled that sometimes the most malignant ghosts

are souls that in life have been the most kindly and beloved. Dead though this ancient friendship seemed, it had yet one phase of horror to manifest. After having implied that he was a plain honest fellow and glad of it, Stacy descended to actual boasting. They sat uneasily in the smallest of the drawing rooms, their eyes fencing. Theo warned herself that he was merely embarrassed. She wanted to be sorry for him. But she was tired—tired of defending him to others, tired of fighting to hold his affection.

"I certainly am eating the work in the tax commissioner's office. I'm studying accounting systems and banking methods evenings, and you want to watch your Uncle Stacy. I'll make some of these rich fellows sit up! I know the cashier at the Lumber National pretty well now, and he as much as said I could have a job there, at better money, any time I wanted to."

He did not say what he wished to put into the railroad and the bank—only what he wished to get out of them. He had no plans, apparently, to build up great institutions for Vernon, but he did have plans to build up a large salary for Stacy Lindstrom.

And one by one, as flustered youth does, he dragged in the names of all the important men he had met. The conversation had to be bent distressingly, to get them all in.

He took half an hour in trying to make an impressive exit.

"I hate him! He expects me to be snobbish! He made it so hard for me to apologize for being rich. He—— Oh, I hate him!" Theo sobbed by her bed.

III

Not for a week did she want to see the boy again; and not for a month did he call. By that time she was used to doing without him. Before long she was used to doing without most people. She was left lonely. Janet had gone East to a college that wasn't a college at all, but a manicurist's buffer of a school, all chamois, celluloid, and pink powder—a school all roses and purring and saddle horses and pleasant reading of little manuals about art. Theo had admired her older sister. She had been eager when Janet had let her wash gloves and run ribbons. She missed the joy of service. She missed too the conveniences of the old brown house—the straw-smelling dog house in the back yard, with the filthy, agreeable, gentlemanly old setter who had resided there; and the tree up which a young woman with secret sorrows could shin resentfully.

Not only Janet and Eddie Barnes but most of Theo's friends had escaped domestic bliss and gone off to school. Theo wanted to follow them, but Mrs. Duke objected: "I wouldn't like to have both my little daughters desert me at once." At the age halfway between child and independent woman Theo was alone. She missed playing; she missed the achievements of housework.

In the old days, on the hired girl's night out, Theo had not minded splashing in rainbow-bubbled suds and polishing the water glasses to shininess. But now there was no hired girl's night out, and no hired girls. There were maids instead, three of them, with a man who took care of the furnace and garden and put on storm windows. The eldest of the maids was the housekeeper-cook, and she was a straight-mouthed, carp-eyed person named Lizzie. Lizzie had been in the Best Houses. She saw to it that neither the other servants nor the Dukes grew slack. She would have fainted at the sight of Sunday supper in the kitchen or of Theo washing dishes.

Mr. Duke pretended to be glad that they had a furnace man; that he no longer had to put on overalls and black leather gloves to tend the furnace and sift the ashes. That had been his before-supper game at the shabby brown house. As a real-estate man, he had been mediocre. As a furnace man, he had been a surgeon, an artist. He had operated on the furnace delicately, giving lectures on his technic to a clinic of admiring young. You mustn't, he had exhorted, shake for one second after the slivers of hot coal tumble through the grate. You must turn off the draft at exactly the moment when the rose-and-saffron flames quiver above the sullen mound of coal.

His wife now maintained that he had been dreadfully bored and put upon by chores. He didn't contradict. He was proud that he no longer had to perch on a ladder holding a storm window or mightily whirling the screw driver as the screws sunk unerringly home. But with nothing to do but look at the furnace man, and gaze at his collections of jugs and bugs and rugs, he became slow of step and foggy of eye, and sometimes, about nothing in particular, he sighed.

Whenever they had guests for dinner he solemnly showed the cloisonné and solemnly the guests said, "Oh," and "Really?" and "Is it?" They didn't want to see the cloisonné, and Mr. Duke didn't want to show it, and of his half-dozen words of Japanese he was exceedingly weary. But if one is a celebrated collector one must keep on collecting and showing the collections.

These dinners and private exhibits were part of a social system in which the Dukes were entangled. It wasn't an easy-fitting system. It was too new. If we ever have professional gentlemen in this country we may learn to do nothing and do it beautifully. But so far we want to do things. Vernon society went out for businesslike activities. There was much motoring, golf and the discussion of golf, and country-club dances at which the men's costumes ran from full evening dress through dinner coats to gray suits with tan shoes.

Most of the men enjoyed these activities honestly. They danced and motored and golfed because they liked to; because it rested them after the day in the office. But there was a small exclusive set in Vernon that had to spend all its time in getting recognized as a small exclusive set. It was social solitaire. By living in a district composed of a particular three blocks on the Boulevard of the Lakes Mr. Duke had been pushed into that exclusive set—Mrs. Duke giving a hand in the pushing.

Sometimes he rebelled. He wanted to be back at work. He had engaged a dismayingly competent manager for his real-estate office, and even by the most ingenious efforts to find something wrong with the books or the correspondence he couldn't keep occupied at the office for more than two hours a day. He longed to discharge the manager, but Mrs. Duke would not have it. She enjoyed the ownership of a leisure-class husband.

For rich women the social system in Vernon does provide more games than for men. The poor we have always with us, and the purpose of the Lord in providing the poor is to enable us of the better classes to amuse ourselves by investigating them and uplifting them and at dinners telling how charitable we are. The poor don't like it much. They have no gratitude. They would rather be uplifters themselves. But if they are taken firmly in hand they can be kept reasonably dependent and interesting for years.

The remnants of the energy that had once taken Mrs. Duke into the woods beyond the end of steel now drove her into poor-baiting. She was a committeewoman five deep. She had pigeonholes of mysteriously important correspondence, and she hustled about in the limousine.

When her husband wanted to go back and do real work
she was oratorical:

"That's the trouble with the American man. He really
likes his sordid office. No, dearie, you just enjoy your
leisure for a while yet. As soon as we finish the campaign
for censoring music you and I will run away and take a
good trip—San Francisco and Honolulu."

But whenever she actually was almost ready to go even
he saw objections. How ridiculous to desert their adorable
house, the beds soft as whipped cream, the mushrooms and
wild rice that only Lizzie could cook, for the discomforts of
trains and hotels! And was it safe to leave the priceless
collections? There had been a burglar scare—there always
has just been a burglar scare in all cities. The Dukes didn't
explain how their presence would keep burglars away, but
they gallantly gave up their lives to guarding the cloisonné
while they talked about getting a caretaker, and never
tried to get him.

Thus at last was Lyman Duke become a prison guard
shackled to the things he owned, and the longest journey
of the man who had once desired new peaks and softer air
was a slow walk down to the Commercial Club for lunch.

IV

When Janet and Eddie Barnes and the rest of Theo's
friends came back from college; when the sons went into
their fathers' wholesale offices and clubs, and the daughters
joined their mothers' lecture courses and societies, and
there was an inheriting Younger Set and many family
plans for marriages—then Theo ceased to be lonely, and
remembered how to play. She had gone to desultory dances
during their absence, but only with people too old or too

young. Now she had a group of her own. She danced with a hot passion for music and movement; her questioning about life disappeared in laughter as she rose to the rushing of people and the flashing of gowns.

Stacy Lindstrom was out of existence in this colored world. Stacy was now chief clerk in the railroad tax commissioner's office, and spoken of as future assistant cashier in the Lumber National Bank. But he was quite insignificant. He was thin—not slim. He was silent—not reserved. His clothes were plain—not cleverly inconspicuous. He wore eyeglasses with a gold chain attached to a hoop over one ear; and he totally failed to insist that he was bored by the vaudeville which everybody attended and everybody sneered at. Oh, he was ordinary, through and through.

Thus with boarding-school wisdom Janet dissected the unfortunate social problem known as Stacy Lindstrom. Theo didn't protest much. It was not possible for youth to keep on for five years very ardently defending anybody who changed as little as Stacy. And Theo was busy.

Not only to dances did Janet lead her, but into the delights of being artistic. Janet had been gapingly impressed by the Broom mansion when the family had acquired it, but now, after vacation visits to Eastern friends, she saw that the large brown velvet chairs were stuffy, and the table with the inlaid chessboard of mother-of-pearl a horror. What Janet saw she also expressed.

In one of the manuals the girls had been tenderly encouraged to glance through at Janet's college it was courageously stated that simplicity was the keynote in decoration. At breakfast, dinner, and even at suppers personally abstracted from the ice box at two A. M., Janet clamored that their ratty old palace ought to be refurnished. Her parents paid no attention. That was just as well.

Otherwise Janet would have lost the chance to get into her portable pulpit and admonish: "When I have a house it will be absolutely simple. Just a few exquisite vases, and not one chair that doesn't melt into the environment. Things—things—things—they are so dreadful! I shan't have a thing I can't use. Use is the test of beauty."

Theo knew that the admirable Janet expressed something which she had been feeling like a dull, unplaced pain. She became a member of an informal art association consisting of herself, Janet, Eddie Barnes, and Harry McPherson, Janet's chief suitor. It is true that the art association gave most of its attention to sitting together in corners at dances and giggling at other people's clothes, but Janet did lead them to an exhibit at the Vernon Art Institute, and afterward they had tea and felt intellectual and peculiar and proud.

Eddie Barnes was showing new depths. He had attended a great seaboard university whose principal distinction, besides its athletics, was its skill in instructing select young gentlemen to discuss any topic in the world without having any knowledge of it whatever. During Janet's pogrom against the Dukes' mosque-shaped brass lamp Eddie was heard to say a number of terribly good things about the social value of knowing wall sconces.

When Janet and Harry McPherson were married Eddie was best man, Theo bridesmaid.

Janet had furnished her new house. When Theo had accompanied Janet on the first shopping flight she had wanted to know just what sort of chairs would perform the miracle of melting into the environment. She wondered whether they could be found in department stores or only in magic shops. But Janet led her to a place only too familiar—the Crafts League, where Mrs. Duke always bought candle shades and small almond dishes.

Janet instantly purchased a hand-tooled leather box for playing cards, and a desk set which included a locked diary in a morocco cover and an ingenious case containing scissors, magnifying glass, pencil sharpener, paper cutter, steel ink eraser, silver penknife. This tool kit was a delightful toy, and it cost thirty-seven dollars. The clerk explained that it was especially marked down from forty-five dollars, though he did not explain why it should be especially marked down.

Theo wailed: "But those aren't necessary! That last thingumajig has four different kinds of knives, where you only need one. It's at least as useless as Papa's cloisonné."

"I know, but it's so amusing. And it's entirely different from Papa's old stuff. It's the newest thing out!" Janet explained.

Before she had bought a single environment-melting chair Janet added to her simple and useful furnishings a collection of glass fruit for table centerpiece, a set of Venetian glass bottles, a traveling clock with a case of gold and platinum and works of tin. For her sensible desk she acquired a complicated engine consisting of a tiny marble pedestal, on which was an onyx ball, on which was a cerise and turquoise china parrot, from whose back, for no very clear anatomical reason, issued a candlestick. But not a stick for candles. It was wired for electricity.

As she accepted each treasure Janet rippled that it was so amusing. The clerk added "So quaint," as though it rimed with amusing. While Theo listened uncomfortably they two sang a chorus of disparagement of Mid-Victorian bric-a-brac and praise of modern clever bits.

When Janet got time for the miraculous chairs——

She had decided to furnish her dining room in friendly, graceful Sheraton, but the clerk spoke confidentially of French lacquer, and Theo watched Janet pledge her troth to a frail red-lacquered dining-room set of brazen angles. The clerk also spoke of distinguished entrance halls, and wished upon Janet an enormous Spanish chair of stamped leather upholstery and dropsical gilded legs, with a mirror that cost a hundred and twenty dollars, and a chest in which Janet didn't intend to keep anything.

Theo went home feeling that she was carrying on her shoulders a burden of gilded oak; that she would never again run free.

When Janet's house was done it looked like a sale in a seaside gift shop. Even her telephone was covered with a brocade and china doll. Theo saw Janet spending her days vaguely endeavoring to telephone to living life through brocade dolls.

After Janet's marriage Theo realized that she was tired of going to parties with the same group; of hearing the same Eddie tell the same stories about the cousin of the Vanderbilts who had almost invited him to go yachting. She was tired of Vernon's one rich middle-aged bachelor; of the bouncing girl twins who always rough-housed at dances. She was peculiarly weary of the same salads and ices which all Vernon hostesses always got from the same caterer. There was one kind of cake with rosettes of nuts which Theo met four times in two weeks—and expected to meet till the caterer passed beyond. She could tell beforehand how any given festivity would turn out. She knew at just what moment after a luncheon the conversation about babies would turn into uneasy yawns, and the hostess would, inevitably, propose bridge. Theo desired to assassinate the entire court of face cards.

Stacy Lindstrom had about once a year indicated a shy desire to have her meet his own set. He told her that they went skiing in winter and picnicking in summer; he hinted how simply and frankly they talked at dinners. Theo went gladly with him to several parties of young married people and a few unmarried sisters and cousins. For three times she enjoyed the change in personnel. As she saw the bright new flats, with the glassed-in porches, the wicker furniture, the colored prints and the davenports; as she heard the people chaff one another; as she accompanied them to a public skating rink and sang to the blaring band—she felt that she had come out of the stupidity of stilted social sets and returned to the naturalness of the old brown house.

But after three parties she knew all the jokes of the husbands about their wives, and with unnecessary thoroughness she knew the opinions of each person upon movies, Chicago, prohibition, the I. W. W., Mrs. Sam Jenkins' chronic party gown, and Stacy's new job in the Lumber National. She tried to enliven the parties. She worked harder than any of her hostesses. She proposed charades, music. She failed. She gave them one gorgeous dance, and disappeared from their group forever.

She did go with Stacy on a tramp through the snow, and enjoyed it—till he began to hint that he, too, might have a great house and many drawing rooms some day. He had very little to say about what he hoped to do for the Lumber National Bank in return.

Then did Theo feel utterly deserted. She blamed herself. Was something wrong with her that she alone found these amusements so agonizingly unamusing? And feeling thus why didn't she do something about it? She went on helping her mother in the gigantic task of asking Lizzie what orders Lizzie wanted them to give her. She went on planning that some day she would read large books and know all about world problems, and she went on forgetting to buy the books. She was twenty-six, and there was no man to marry except the chattering Eddie Barnes. Certainly she could not think romantically about that Stacy Lind-

strom whose ambition seemed to be to get enough money
to become an imitation chattering Eddie Barnes.

Then America entered the war.

V

Eddie Barnes went to the first officers' training camp,
and presently was a highly decorative first lieutenant in a
hundred-dollar uniform. Stacy Lindstrom made his sav-
ings over to his mother, and enlisted. While Eddie was still
stationed at a cantonment as instructor Stacy was writing
Theo ten-word messages from France. He had become a
sergeant, and French agriculture was interesting, he wrote.

Stacy's farewell had been undistinguished. He called—
a slight, commonplace figure in a badly fitting private's
uniform. He sat on the piano stool and mouthed: "Well,
I have a furlough. Then we get shipped across. Well—
don't forget me, Theo."

At the door Stacy kissed her hand so sharply that his
teeth bruised her skin, and ran down the steps, silent.

But Eddie, who came up from the cantonment at least
once a month, at least that often gave a long, brave farewell to Theo. Handsome, slim, erect, he invariably paced
the smallest drawing room, stopped, trembled, and said in
a military tone, tenor but resolute: "Well, old honey, this
may be the last time I see you. I may get overseas service
any time now. Theo dear, do you know how much I care?
I shall take a picture of you in my heart, and it may be the
last thing I ever think of. I'm no hero, but I know I shall
do my duty. And, Theo, if I don't come back——"

The first two times Theo flared into weeping at this
point, and Eddie's arm was about her, and she kissed him.
But the third, fourth and fifth times he said good-by forever she chuckled, "Cheer up, old boy." It was hard for

her to feel tragic about Eddie's being in the service, because she was in the service herself.

At last there was work that needed her. She had started with three afternoons a week at Red Cross; chatty afternoons, with her mother beside her, and familiar neighbors stopping in the middle of surgical dressings to gurgle: "Oh, did you hear about how angry George Bangs was when Nellie bought a case of toilet soap at a dollar a cake? Think of it. A dollar! When you can get a very nice imported soap at twenty-five cents."

Theo felt that there was too much lint on the conversation and too little on their hands. She found herself one with a dozen girls who had been wrens and wanted to be eagles. Two of them learned motor repairing and got across to France. Theo wanted to go, but her mother refused. After a dignified protest from Mrs. Duke, Theo became telephone girl at Red Cross headquarters, till she had learned shorthand and typing, and was able to serve the head of the state Red Cross as secretary. She envied the motor-corps women in their uniforms, but she exulted in power—in being able to give quick, accurate information to the distressed women who came fluttering to headquarters.

Mrs. Duke felt that typing was low. Theo was protected by her father.

"Good thing for the girl to have business training," he kept insisting, till the commanding officer of the house impatiently consented.

It was the American Library Association collection which turned Theo from a dim uneasiness about the tyranny of possessions to active war. She bounced into the largest drawing room one dinner time, ten minutes late, crying: "Let's go over all our books tonight and weed out a dandy bunch for the soldiers!"

Mrs. Duke ruled: "Really, my dear, if you would only try to be on time for your meals! It's hard enough on Lizzie and myself to keep the house running——"

"Come, come, come! Get your hat off and comb your hair and get ready for dinner. I'm almost starved!" grumbled Mr. Duke.

Theo repeated the demand as soon as she was seated. The soldiers, she began, needed——

"We occasionally read the newspapers ourselves! Of course we shall be very glad to give what books we can spare. But there doesn't seem to be any necessity of going at things in this—this—hit-or-a-miss! Besides, I have some letters to write this evening," stated Mrs. Duke.

"Well, I'm going over them anyway!"

"I wish to see any books before you send them away!"

With Theo visualizing herself carrying off a carload of books, the Dukes ambled to the library after finishing dinner—and finishing coffee, a cigar and chocolate peppermints, and a discussion of the proper chintz for the shabby chairs in the guest room. Theo realized as she looked at the lofty, benign, and carefully locked bookcases that she hadn't touched one of the books for a year; that for six months she hadn't seen anyone enter the room for any purpose other than sweeping.

After fifteen minutes spent in studying every illustration in a three-volume history Mrs. Duke announced: "Here's something I think we might give away, Lym. Nobody has ever read it. A good many of the pages are uncut."

Mr. Duke protested: "Give that away? No, sir! I been meaning to get at that for a long time. Why, that's a valuable history. Tells all about modern Europe. Man ought to read it to get an idea of the sources of the war."

"But you never will read it, Papa," begged Theo.

"Now, Theo," her mother remonstrated in the D. A. R.

manner, "if your father wishes to keep it that's all there is to be said, and we will make no more words about it." She returned the three volumes to the shelf.

"I'll turn it over to you just as soon as I've read it," her father obliged. Theo reflected that if any soldiers in the current conflict were to see the history they would have to prolong the war till 1950.

But she tried to look grateful while her father went on: "Tell you what I was thinking, though, Mother. Here's these two shelves of novels—none of 'em by standard authors—all just moonshine or blood and thunder. Let's clear out the whole bunch."

"But those books are just the thing for a rainy day—nice light reading. And for guests. But now this—this old book on saddlery. When we had horses you used to look at it, but now, with motors and all——"

"I know, but I still like to browse in it now and then."

"Very well."

Theo fled. She remembered piles of shabby books in the attic. While the Dukes were discovering that after all there wasn't one of the four hundred volumes in the library which they weren't going to read right away Theo heaped the dining-room table with attic waifs. She called her parents. The first thing Mrs. Duke spied was a Tennyson, printed in 1890 in a type doubtless suitable to ants, small sand-colored ants, but illegible to the human eye. Mrs. Duke shrieked: "Oh! You weren't thinking of giving that handsome Tennyson away! Why, it's a very handsome edition. Besides, it's one of the first books your father and I ever had. It was given to us by your Aunt Gracie!"

"But Moth-er dear! You haven't even seen the book for years!"

"Well, I've thought of it often."

"How about all these Christmas books?"

"Now, Theodora, if you wouldn't be so impatient, but kindly give your father and me time to look them over,——"

Two hours and seventeen minutes after dinner, Mr. and Mrs. Duke had almost resignedly agreed to present the following literary treasures to the soldiers of these United States for their edification and entertainment:

One sixth-grade geography. One *Wild Flowers of Northern Wisconsin*. Two duplicate copies of *Little Women*. The *Congressional Record* for part of 1902. One black, depressed, religious volume entitled *The Dragon's Fight With the Woman for 1260 Prophetic Days*, from which the last seven hundred days were missing, leaving the issue of the combat in serious doubt. Four novels, all by women, severally called *Griselda of the Red Hand*, *Bramleigh of British Columbia*, *Lady Tip-Tippet*, and *Billikins' Lonely Christmas*.

Theo looked at them. She laughed. Then she was sitting by the table, her head down, sobbing. Her parents glanced at each other in hurt amazement.

"I can't understand the girl. After all the pains we took to try to help her!" sighed Mrs. Duke later, when they were undressing.

"O-o-o-oh," yawned Mr. Duke as he removed his collar from the back button—with the slight, invariable twinge in his rheumatic shoulder blades. "Oh, she's nervous and tired from her work down at that Red Cross place. I'm in favor of her having a little experience, but at the same time there's no need of overdoing. Plenty of other people to help out."

He intended to state this paternal wisdom to Theo at breakfast, but Theo at breakfast was not one to whom to state things paternally. Her normally broad shining lips were sucked in. She merely nodded to her parents, then attended with strictness to her oatmeal and departed—

after privily instructing Lizzie to give the smaller pile of books in the dining room to the junk collector.

Three novels from the pile she did take to the public library for the A. L. A. To these she added twenty books, mostly trigonometries, bought with her own pocket money. Consequently she had no lunch save a glass of milk for twenty days. But as the Dukes didn't know that, everybody was happy.

The battle of the books led to other sanguinary skirmishes.

VI

There was the fireless cooker.

It was an early, homemade fireless cooker, constructed in the days when anything in the shape of one box inside another, with any spare scraps of sawdust between, was regarded as a valuable domestic machine. Aside from the fact that it didn't cook, the Dukes' cooker took up room in the kitchen, gathered a film of grease which caught a swamp of dust, and regularly banged Lizzie's shins. For six years the Dukes had talked about having it repaired. They had run through the historical, scientific, and financial aspects of cookers at least once a season.

"I've wondered sometimes if we couldn't just have the furnace man take out the sawdust and put in something else or—— Theo, wouldn't you like to run into Whaley & Baumgarten's one of these days, and price all of the new fireless cookers?" beamed Mrs. Duke.

"Too busy."

In a grieved, spacious manner Mrs. Duke reproved: "Well, my dear, I certainly am too busy, what with the party for the new rector and his bride——"

"Call up the store. Tell 'em to send up a good cooker on trial," said Theo.

"But these things have to be done with care and thought——"

Theo was stalking away as she retorted: "Not by me they don't!"

She was sorry for her rudeness afterward, and that evening she was gay and young as she played ballads for her father and did her mother's hair. After that, when she was going to bed, and very tired, and horribly confused in her thinking, she was sorry because she had been sorry because she had been rude.

The furnace went wrong, and its dissipations were discussed by Mr. Duke, Mrs. Duke, Mrs. Harry McPherson *née* Duke, Lizzie, the furnace man, and the plumber, till Theo ran up to her room and bit the pillow to keep from screaming. She begged her father to install a new furnace: "The old one will set the house afire—it's a terrible old animal."

"Nonsense. Take a chance on fire," said he. "House and everything well insured anyway. If the house did burn down there'd be one good thing—wouldn't have to worry any more about getting that twelve tons of coal we're still shy."

When Mr. Duke was summoned to Duluth by the iron-mining company Mrs. Duke sobbingly called Theo home from the midst of tearing work.

Theo arrived in terror. "What is it? What's happened to Papa?"

"Happened? Why, nothing. But he didn't have a chance to take a single thing to Duluth, and he simply won't know what to do without his traveling bag—the one he got in London—all the fittings and everything that he's used to, so he could put his hand on a toothbrush right in the dark——"

"But, Mother dear, I'm sure bathrooms in Duluth have

electric lights, so he won't need to put his hand on tooth-brushes in the dark. And he can get nice new lovely brushes at almost any drug store and not have to fuss——"

"Fuss? Fuss? It's you who are doing the fussing. He just won't know what to do without his traveling bag."

While she helped her mother and Lizzie drag the ponderous bag down from the attic; while her mother, merely thinking aloud, discussed whether "your father" would want the madras pajamas or the flannelette; while, upon almost tearful maternal request, Theo hunted all through the house for the missing cut-glass soap case, she was holding herself in. She disliked herself for being so unsympathetic. She remembered how touched she had been by exactly the same domestic comedy two years before. But unsympathetic she was, even two days later, when her mother triumphantly showed Mr. Duke's note: "I can't tell you how glad I was to see good old bag showing up here at hotel; felt lost without it."

"Just the same, my absence that afternoon cost the Red Cross at least fifty dollars, and for a lot less than that he could have gone out and bought twice as good a bag—lighter, more convenient. Things! Poor Dad is the servant of that cursed pig-iron bag," she meditated.

She believed that she was being very subtle about her rebellion, but it must have been obvious, for after Mr. Duke's return her mother suddenly attacked her at dinner.

"So far as I can make out from the way you're pouting and sulking and carrying on, you must have some sort of a socialistic idea that possessions are unimportant. Now you ought——"

"Anarchist, do you mean, Mother dear?"

"Kindly do not interrupt me! As I was saying: It's things that have made the world advance from barbarism. Motor cars, clothes you can wash, razors that enable a man to look neat, canned foods, printing presses, steamers, bathrooms—those are what have gotten men beyond living in skins in horrid damp caves."

"Of course. And that's why I object to people fussing so about certain things, and keeping themselves from getting full use of bigger things. If you're always so busy arranging the flowers in the vase in a limousine that you never have time to go riding, then the vase has spoiled the motor for——"

"I don't get your logic at all. I certainly pay very little attention to the flowers in our car. Lizzie arranges them for me!" triumphed Mrs. Duke.

Theo was charging on. She was trying to get her own ideas straight. "And if a man spends valuable time in tinkering with a worn-out razor when he could buy a new one, then he's keeping himself in the damp cave and the bearskin undies. That isn't thrift. It's waste."

"I fancy that people in caves, in prehistoric times, did not use razors at all, did they, Lyman?" her mother majestically corrected.

"Now you always worry about Papa's bag. It was nice once, and worth caring for, but it's just a bother now. On your principle a factory would stop running for half the year to patch up or lace up the belting, or whatever it is they do, instead of getting new belting and thus—— Oh, can't you see? Buy things. Use 'em. But throw them away if they're more bother than good. If a bag keeps you from enjoying traveling—chuck it in the river! If a man makes a tennis court and finds he really doesn't like tennis, let the court get weedy rather than spend glorious free October afternoons in mowing and raking——"

"Well, I suppose you mean rolling it," said her mother domestically. "And I don't know what tennis has to do with the subject. I'm sure I haven't mentioned tennis.

And I trust you'll admit that your knowledge of factories and belting is not authoritative. No. The trouble is, this Red Cross work is getting you so you can't think straight. Of course with this war and all, it may be permissible to waste a lot of good time and money making dressings and things for a lot of green nurses to waste, but you girls must learn the great principle of thrift."

"We have! I'm practicing it. It means—oh, so much, now. Thrift is doing without things you don't need, and taking care of things as long as they're useful. It distinctly isn't wasting time and spiritual devotion over things you can't use—just because you happen to be so unfortunate as to own 'em. Like our eternal fussing over that clock in the upper hall that no one ever looks at——"

Not listening, her mother was placidly rolling on: "You seem to think this house needs too much attention. You'd like it, wouldn't you, if we moved to a couple of rooms in the Dakota Lodging House!"

Theo gave it up.

Two days later she forgot it.

Creeping into her snug life, wailing for her help, came a yellow-faced apparition whose eyes were not for seeing but mere gashes to show the suffering within. It was—it had been—one Stacy Lindstrom, a sergeant of the A. E. F.

Stacy had lain with a shattered shoulder in a shell pit for three days. He had had pneumonia. Four distinct times all of him had died, quite definitely died—all but the desire to see Theo.

His little, timid, vehemently respectable mother sent for Theo on the night when he was brought home, and despite Mrs. Duke's panicky protest Theo went to him at eleven in the evening.

"Not going to die for little while. Terribly weak, but all here. Pull through—if you want me to. Not asking you to

like me. All I want—want you to want me to live. Made
'em send me home. Was all right on the sea. But weak.
Got touch of typhoid in New York. Didn't show up till
on the train. But all right and cheerful—— Oh! I hurt so.
Just hurt, hurt, hurt, every inch of me. Never mind. Well,
seen you again. Can die now. Guess I will."

Thus in panting words he muttered, while she knelt by
him and could not tell whether she loved him or hated
him; whether she shrank from this skinny claw out-
stretched from the grave or was drawn to him by a longing
to nurse his soul back to a desire for life. But this she knew:
Even Red Cross efficiency was nothing in the presence of
her first contact with raw living life—most rawly living
when crawling out from the slime of death.

She overruled Mrs. Lindstrom; got a nurse and Doctor
Rollin—Rollin, the interior medicine specialist.

"Boy's all right. Hasn't got strength enough to fight
very hard. Better cheer him up," said Doctor Rollin.
"Bill? My bill? He's a soldier, isn't he? Don't you suppose
I wanted to go into the army too? Chance to see beautiful
cases for once. Yes. Admit it. Like to have fool salutes too.
Got to stay home, nurse lot of dam-fool women. Charge a
soldier? Don't bother me," he grumbled, while he was
folding up his stethoscope, and closing his bag, and trying
to find his hat, which Mrs. Lindstrom had politely concealed.

Every day after her work Theo trudged to the Lindstrom house—a scrubbed and tidied cottage in whose living room was a bureau with a lace cover, a gilded shell, and
two photographs of stiff relatives in Norway. She watched
Stacy grow back into life. His hands, which had been yellow and drawn as the talons of a starved Chinaman, became pink and solid. The big knuckles, which had been
lumpy under the crackly skin, were padded again.

She had been surprised into hot pity for him. She was saved equally by his amusement over his own weakness, and by his irritableness. Though he had called for her, during the first week he seemed to dislike her and all other human beings save his nurse. In the depths of lead-colored pain nothing mattered to him save his own comfort. The coolness of his glass of water was more to him than the war. Even when he became human again, and eager at her coming, there was nothing very personal in their talk. When he was able to do more than gasp out a few words she encouraged in him the ambition to pile up money which she detested.

Uncomfortably she looked at him, thin against a plump pillow, and her voice was artificially cheery as she declared: "You'll be back in the bank soon. I'm sure they'll raise you. No reason why you shouldn't be president of it some day."

He had closed his pale eyelids. She thought he was discouraged. Noisily she reassured, "Honestly! I'm sure you'll make money—lots of it."

His eyes were open, blazing. "Money! Yes! Wonderful thing!"

"Ye-es."

"Buys tanks and shells, and food for homeless babies. But for me—I just want a living. There isn't any Stacy Lindstrom any more." He was absorbed in that bigger thing over there, in that Nirvana—a fighting Nirvana! "I've got ambitions, big 'uns, but not to see myself in a morning coat and new gloves on Sunday!"

He said nothing more. A week after, he was sitting up in bed, reading, in a Lindstromy nightgown of white cotton edged with red. She wondered at the book. It was *Colloquial French.*

"You aren't planning to go back?" she asked casually.

"Yes. I've got it straight now." He leaned back, pulled the bedclothes carefully up about his neck and said quietly, "I'm going back to fight. But not just for the duration of the war. Now I know what I was meant for. I can do things with my hands, and I get along with plain folks. I'm going back on reconstruction work. We're going to rebuild France. I'm studying—French, cottage architecture, cabbages. I'm a pretty good farmer—'member how I used to work on the farm, vacations?"

She saw that all self-consciousness was gone from him. He was again the Stacy Lindstrom who had been lord of the Red River carts. Her haunted years of nervousness about life disappeared, and suddenly she was again too fond of her boy companion to waste time considering whether she was fond of him. They were making plans, laughing the quick curt laughs of intimates.

A week later Mrs. Lindstrom took her aside.

Mrs. Lindstrom had always, after admitting Theo and nodding without the slightest expression in her anæmic face, vanished through the kitchen doorway. Tonight, as Theo was sailing out, Mrs. Lindstrom hastened after her through the living room.

"Miss! Miss Duke! Yoost a minute. Could you speak wit' me?"

"Why, yes."

"Dis—ay—da boy get along pretty gude, eh? He seem werry gude, today. Ay vish you should——" The little woman's face was hard. "Ay don't know how to say it elegant, but if you ever—— I know he ain't your fella, but he always got that picture of you, and maybe now he ban pretty brave soldier, maybe you could like him better, but—I know I yoost ban Old Country woman. If you and him marry—I keep away, not bother you. Your folks is rich and—— Oh, I gif, I gif him to you—if you vant him."

Mrs. Lindstrom's sulky eyes seemed to expand, grow misty. Her Puritanical chest was terribly heaving. She sobbed: "He always talk about you ever since he ban little fella. Please excuse me I spoke, if you don't vant him, but I vanted you should know, I do anyt'ing for him. And you."

She fled, and Theo could hear the scouring of a pot in the kitchen. Theo fled the other way.

It was that same evening, at dinner, that Mrs. Duke delicately attempted social homicide.

"My dear, aren't you going to see this Lindstrom boy rather oftener than you need to? From what you say he must be convalescing. I hope that your pity for him won't lead you into any foolish notions and sentiment about him."

Theo laughed. "No time to be sentimental about anything these days. I've canned the word——"

"'Canned'! Oh, Theo!"

"——'sentiment' entirely. But if I hadn't, Stace wouldn't be a bad one to write little poems about. He used to be my buddy when——"

"Please—do—not—be—so—vulgar! And Theo, however you may regard Stacy, kindly do stop and think how Mrs. Lindstrom would look in this house!"

The cheerful, gustatory manner died in Theo. She rose. She said with an intense, a religious solemnity: "This house! Damn this house!"

The Lindstroms were not mentioned again. There was no need. Mrs. Duke's eyebrows adequately repeated her opinions when Theo came racing in at night, buoyant with work and walking and fighting over Stacy's plans.

Theo fancied that her father looked at her more sympathetically. She ceased to take Mr. Duke as a matter of course, as one more fixed than the radiators. She realized

that he spent these autumn evenings in staring at the fire.
When he looked up he smiled, but his eyes were scary.
Theo noticed that he had given up making wistful suggestions to Mrs. Duke that he be permitted to go back to real
work, or that they get a farm, or go traveling. Once they
had a week's excursion to New York, but Mrs. Duke had
to hasten back for her committees. She was ever firmer
with her husband; more ready with reminders that it was
hard to get away from a big house like this; that men
oughtn't to be so selfish and just expect Lizzie and her——

Mr. Duke no longer argued. He rarely went to his office.
He was becoming a slippered old man.

VII

Eddie Barnes was back in Vernon on the sixth of his
positively last, final, ultimate farewells.

Theo yelled in joy when he called. She was positively
blowzy with healthy vulgarity. She had won an argument
with Stacy about teaching the French to plant corn, and
had walked home almost at a trot.

"Fine to see you! Saying an eternal farewell again?"
she brutally asked Eddie.

For one of the young samurai Eddie was rather sheepish.
He stalked about the largest drawing room. His puttees
shone. Eddie really had very nice legs, the modern young
woman reflected.

"Gosh, I'm an awful fareweller. Nope, I'm not going tc
do a single weep. Because this time—I've got my orders.
I'll be in France in three weeks. So I just thought—I just
thought—maybe—I'd ask you if you could conveniently
—— Ouch, that tooth still aches; have to get this bridge
finished tomorrow sure. Could you marry me?"

"Ungh!" Theo flopped into a chair.

"You've queered all my poetic tactics by your rude merry mirth. So just got to talk naturally."

"Glad you did. Now let me think. Do I want to marry you?"

"We get along bully. Listen—wait till I get back from France, and we'll have some celebration. Oh, boy! I'll stand for the cooties and the mud till the job's done, but when I get back and put the Croix de Guerre into the safe-deposit I'm going to have a drink of champagne four quarts deep! And you and I—we'll have one time! Guess you'll be pretty sick of Red Cross by——"

"No. And I know a man who thinks that when the war is over then the real work begins."

Eddie was grave, steady, more mature than he had ever seemed. "Yes. Stacy Lindstrom. See here, honey, he has big advantages over me. I'm not picturesque. I never had to work for my bread and butter, and I was brought up to try to be amusing, not noble. Nothing more touching than high ideals and poverty. But if I try to be touching, you laugh at me. I'm—— I may get killed, and I'll be just as dead in my expensible first lieut's pants as any self-sacrific-ing private."

"I hadn't thought of that. Of course. You have disad-vantages. Comfort isn't dramatic. But still—— It's the champagne and the big time. I've——"

"See here, honey, you'd be dreadfully bored by poverty. You do like nice things."

"That's it. Things! That's what I'm afraid of. I'm in-terested in tractors for France, but not in the exact shade of hock glasses. And beauty—— It's the soul of things, but it's got to be inherent, not just painted on. Nice things! Ugh! And—— If I married you what would be your plans for me? How would I get through twenty-four hours a day?"

"Why—uh—why, how does anybody get through 'em? You'd have a good time—dances, and playin' round and maybe children, and we'd run down to Palm Beach——"

"Yes. You'd permit me to go on doing what I always did till the war came. Nope. It isn't good enough. I want to work. You wouldn't let me, even in the house. There'd be maids, nurses. It's not that I want a career. I don't want to be an actress or a congresswoman. Perfectly willing to be assistant to some man. Providing he can really use me in useful work. No. You pre-war boys are going to have a frightful time with us post-war women."

"But you'll get tired——"

"Oh, I know, I know! You and Father and Mother will wear me out. You-all may win. You and this house, this horrible sleek warm house that Mrs.—— that she isn't fit to come into! She that gave him——"

Her voice was rising, hysterical. She was bent in the big chair, curiously twisted, as though she had been wounded.

Eddie stroked her hair, then abruptly stalked out.

Theo sat marveling: "Did I really send Eddie away? Poor Eddie. Oh, I'll write him. He's right. Nice to think of brave maiden defiantly marrying poor hero. But they never do. Not in this house."

VIII

The deep courthouse bell awakening Theo to bewildered staring at the speckled darkness—a factory whistle fantastically tooting, then beating against her ears in long, steady waves of sound—the triumphant yelping of a small boy and the quacking of a toy horn—a motor starting next door, a cold motor that bucked and snorted before it began to sing, but at last roared away with the horn blaring—finally the distant "Extra! Extra!"

Her sleepy body protestingly curled tighter in a downy ball in her bed on the upper porch, but her mind was frantically awake as the clamor thickened. "Is it really peace this time? The armistice really signed?" she exulted.

In pleasant reasonable phrases the warm body objected to the cold outside the silk comforter. "Remember how you were fooled on Thursday. Oo-oo! Bed feels so luxurious!" it insisted.

She was a practical heroine. She threw off the covers. The indolent body had to awaken, in self-defense. She merely squeaked "Ouch!" as her feet groped for their slippers on the cold floor. She flung downstairs, into rubbers and a fur coat, and she was out on the walk in time to stop a bellowing newsboy.

Yes. It was true. Official report from Washington. War over.

"Hurray!" said the ragged newsboy, proud of being out adventuring by night; and "Hurray!" she answered him. She felt that she was one with awakening crowds all over the country, from the T Wharf to the Embarcadero. She wanted to make great noises.

The news had reached the almost-Western city of Vernon at three. It was only four, but as she stood on the porch a crush of motor cars swept by, headed for downtown. Bumping behind them they dragged lard cans, saucepans, frying pans. One man standing on a running board played Mr. Zip on a cornet. Another dashing for a trolley had on his chest a board with an insistent electric bell. He saw her on the porch and shouted, "Come on, sister! Downtown! All celebrate! Some carnival!"

She waved to him. She wanted to get out the electric and drive down. There would be noise—singing.

Four strange girls ran by and shrieked to her, "Come on and dance!"

Suddenly she was asking herself: "But do they know what it means? It isn't just a carnival. It's sacred." Sharply: "But do I know all it means, either? World-wide. History, here, now!" Leaning against the door, cold but not conscious that she was cold, she found herself praying.

As she marched back upstairs she was startled. She fancied she saw a gray figure fleeing down the upper hall. She stopped. No sound.

"Heavens, I'm so wrought up! All jumpy. Shall I give Papa the paper? Oh, I'm too trembly to talk to anyone."

While the city went noise-mad it was a very solemn white small figure that crawled into bed. The emotion that for four years had been gathering burst into sobbing. She snuggled close, but she did not sleep. Presently: "My Red Cross work will be over soon. What can I do then? Come back to packing Papa's bag?"

She noticed a glow on the windows of the room beside the sleeping porch. "They're lighting up the whole city. Wonder if I oughtn't to go down and see the fun? Wonder if Papa would like to go down? No, Mother wouldn't let him! I want the little old brown shack. Where Stacy could come and play. Mother used to give him cookies then.

"I wish I had the nerve to set the place afire. If I were a big fighting soul I would. But I'm a worm. Am I being bad to think this way? Guess so—committed mental arson, but hadn't the nerve—— My God, the house *is* afire!"

She was too frightened to move. She could smell smoke, hear a noise like the folding of stiff wrapping paper. Instantly, apparently without ever having got out of bed, she was running by a bedroom into which flames were licking from the clothes chute that led to the basement. "That dratted old furnace!" She was bursting into her parents' room, hysterically shaking her mother.

"Get up! Get up!"

With a drowsy dignity her mother was saying, "Yes—I know—peace—get paper morning—let me sleep."

"It's fire! Fire! The house is afire!"

Her mother sat up, a thick gray lock bobbing in front of one eye, and said indignantly, "How perfectly preposterous!"

Already Mr. Duke was out of bed, in smoke-prickly darkness, flapping his hands in the air. "Never could find that globe. Ought to have bedside light. Come, Mother, jump up! Theo, have you got on a warm bathrobe?" He was cool. His voice trembled, but only with nervousness.

He charged down the back hall, Theo just behind. Mrs. Duke remained at the head of the front stairs, lamenting, "Don't leave me!"

The flames were darting hissing heads into the hall. As Theo looked they caught a box couch and ran over an old chest of drawers. The heat seemed to slap her face.

"Can't do anything. Get out of this. Wake the servants. You take your mother down," grumbled Mr. Duke.

Theo had her mother into a loose gown, shoes, and a huge fleecy couch cover, and down on the front porch by the time Mr. Duke appeared driving the maids—Lizzie a gorgon in curl papers.

"Huh! Back stairs all afire," he grunted, rubbing his chin. His fingers, rubbing then stopping, showed that for a split second he was thinking, "I need a shave."

"Theo! Run down to the corner. Turn in alarm. I'll try to phone. Then save things," he commanded.

Moved by his coolness to a new passion of love Theo flung her arm, bare as the sleeve of her bathrobe fell from it, about his seamed neck, beseeching: "Don't save anything but the cloisonné. Let 'em burn. Won't have to go in there, risk your life for things. Here—let me phone!"

Unreasoning she slammed the front door, bolted him
out. She shouted their address and "Fire—hustle alarm!"
at the telephone operator. In the largest drawing room she
snatched bit after bit of cloisonné from the cabinet and
dumped them into a wastebasket. Now the lower hall, at
her back, was boiling with flame-tortured smoke. The noise
expanded from crackling to a roar.

The window on the porch was smashed. Her father's arm
was reaching up to the catch, unlocking the window. He
was crawling in. As the smoke encircled him he puffed like
a man blowing out water after a dive.

Theo ran to him. "I didn't want you here! I have the
cloisonné——"

As calmly as though he were arguing a point at cards
he mumbled, "Yes, yes, yes! Don't bother me. You forgot
the two big *saras* in the wall safe."

While the paint on the balusters in the hall bubbled and
charred, and the heat was a pang in her lungs, he twirled
the knob of the safe behind the big picture and drew out
two cloisonné plates. Flames curled round the door jamb
of the room like fingers closing on a stick.

"We're shut off!" Theo cried.

"Yep. Better get out. Here. Drop that basket!"

Mr. Duke snatched the cloisonné from her, dropped it,
hurled away his two plates, shoved her to the window he
had opened, helped her out on the porch. He himself was
still in the burning room. She gripped his arm when he
tried to dart back. The cloisonné was already hidden from
them by puffs of smoke.

Mr. Duke glanced back. He eluded her; pulled his arm
free; disappeared in the smoke. He came back with a cheap
china vase that for a thing so small was monumentally
ugly. As he swung out of the window he said, "Your

mother always thought a lot of that vase." Theo saw through eyes stinging with smoke that his hair had been scorched.

Fire engines were importantly unloading at the corner, firemen running up. A neighbor came to herd the Dukes into her house, and into more clothes.

Alone, from the room given to her by the neighbor, Theo watched her home burn. The flames were leering out of all the windows on the ground floor. Her father would never read the three-volume history that was too valuable for soldiers. Now the attic was glaring. Gone the elephant of a London traveling bag. Woolly smoke curled out of the kitchen windows as a fireman smashed them. Gone the fireless cooker that would not cook. She laughed. "It's nicely cooked itself! Oh, I'm beastly. Poor Mother. All her beautiful marked linen——"

But she did not lose a sensation of running ungirdled, of breathing Maytime air.

Her father came in, dressed in the neighbor-host's corduroy hunting coat, a pair of black dress trousers and red slippers. His hair was conscientiously combed, but his fingers still querulously examined the state of his unshaven chin.

She begged: "Daddy dear, it's pretty bad, but don't worry. We have plenty of money. We'll make arrangements——"

He took her arms from about his neck, walked to the window. The broken skeleton of their home was tombed in darkness as the firemen controlled the flames. He looked at Theo in a puzzled way.

He said hesitatingly: "No, I won't worry. I guess it's all right. You see—I set the house afire."

She was silent, but her trembling fingers sought her lips as he went on: "Shoveled hot coals from the furnace into

kindling bin in the basement. Huh! Yes. Used to be good
furnace tender when I was a real man. Peace bells had
woke me up. Wanted to be free. Hate destruction, but—no
other way. Your mother wouldn't let me sell the house. I
was going mad, sticking there, waiting—waiting for death.
Now your mother will be willing to come. Get a farm.
Travel. And I been watching you. You couldn't have had
Stacy Lindstrom, long as that house bossed us. You almost
caught me, in the hall, coming back from the basement. It
was kind of hard, with house afire, to lie there in bed, quiet,
so's your mother wouldn't ever know—waiting for you to
come wake us up. You almost didn't, in time. Would have
had to confess. Uh, let's go comfort your mother. She's
crying."

Theo had moved away from him. "But it's criminal!
We're stealing—robbing the insurance company."

The wrinkles beside his eyes opened with laughter.

"No. Watched out for that. I was careful to be careless,
and let all the insurance run out last month. Huh! Maybe
I won't catch it from your mother for that, though! Girl!
Look! It's dawn!"

YOUNG MAN AXELBROD

YOUNG MAN AXELBROD

THE cottonwood is a tree of a slovenly and plebeian habit. Its woolly wisps turn gray the lawns and engender neighborhood hostilities about our town. Yet it is a mighty tree, a refuge and an inspiration; the sun flickers in its towering foliage, whence the tattoo of locusts enlivens our dusty summer afternoons. From the wheat country out to the sagebrush plains between the buttes and the Yellowstone it is the cottonwood that keeps a little grateful shade for sweating homesteaders.

In Joralemon we call Knute Axelbrod "Old Cottonwood." As a matter of fact, the name was derived not so much from the quality of the man as from the wide grove about his gaunt white house and red barn. He made a comely row of trees on each side of the country road, so that a humble, daily sort of a man, driving beneath them in his lumber wagon, might fancy himself lord of a private avenue.

And at sixty-five Knute was like one of his own cottonwoods, his roots deep in the soil, his trunk weathered by rain and blizzard and baking August noons, his crown spread to the wide horizon of day and the enormous sky of a prairie night.

This immigrant was an American even in speech. Save for a weakness about his j's and w's, he spoke the twangy Yankee English of the land. He was the more American because in his native Scandinavia he had dreamed of America as a land of light. Always through disillusion and weariness he beheld America as the world's nursery for justice, for broad, fair towns, and eager talk; and always he kept a young soul that dared to desire beauty.

As a lad Knute Axelbrod had wished to be a famous scholar, to learn the ease of foreign tongues, the romance of history, to unfold in the graciousness of wise books. When he first came to America he worked in a sawmill all day and studied all evening. He mastered enough book-learning to teach district school for two terms; then, when he was only eighteen, a great-hearted pity for faded little Lena Wesselius moved him to marry her. Gay enough, doubtless, was their hike by prairie schooner to new farmlands, but Knute was promptly caught in a net of poverty and family. From eighteen to fifty-eight he was always snatching children away from death or the farm away from mortgages.

He had to be content—and generously content he was —with the second-hand glory of his children's success and, for himself, with pilfered hours of reading—that reading of big, thick, dismal volumes of history and economics which the lone mature learner chooses. Without ever losing his desire for strange cities and the dignity of towers he stuck to his farm. He acquired a half-section, free from debt, fertile, well-stocked, adorned with a cement silo, a chicken-run, a new windmill. He became comfortable, secure, and then he was ready, it seemed, to die; for at sixty-three his work was done, and he was unneeded and alone.

His wife was dead. His sons had scattered afar, one a dentist in Fargo, another a farmer in the Golden Valley. He had turned over his farm to his daughter and son-in-law. They had begged him to live with them, but Knute refused.

"No," he said, "you must learn to stand on your own feet. I vill not give you the farm. You pay me four hundred dollars a year rent, and I live on that and vatch you from my hill."

On a rise beside the lone cottonwood which he loved best of all his trees Knute built a tar-paper shack, and here he "bached it"; cooked his meals, made his bed, sometimes sat in the sun, read many books from the Joralemon library, and began to feel that he was free of the yoke of citizenship which he had borne all his life.

For hours at a time he sat on a backless kitchen chair before the shack, a wide-shouldered man, white-bearded, motionless; a seer despite his grotesquely baggy trousers, his collarless shirt. He looked across the miles of stubble to the steeple of the Jackrabbit Forks church and meditated upon the uses of life. At first he could not break the rigidity of habit. He rose at five, found work in cleaning his cabin and cultivating his garden, had dinner exactly at twelve, and went to bed by afterglow. But little by little he discovered that he could be irregular without being arrested. He stayed abed till seven or even eight. He got a large, deliberate, tortoise-shell cat, and played games with it; let it lap milk upon the table, called it the Princess, and confided to it that he had a "sneaking idee" that men were fools to work so hard. Around this coatless old man, his stained waistcoat flapping about a huge torso, in a shanty of rumpled bed and pine table covered with sheets of food-daubed newspaper, hovered all the passionate aspiration of youth and the dreams of ancient beauty.

He began to take long walks by night. In his necessitous life night had ever been a period of heavy slumber in close rooms. Now he discovered the mystery of the dark; saw the prairies wide-flung and misty beneath the moon, heard the voices of grass and cottonwoods and drowsy birds. He tramped for miles. His boots were dew-soaked, but he did not heed. He stopped upon hillocks, shyly threw wide his arms, and stood worshiping the naked, slumbering land.

These excursions he tried to keep secret, but they were bruited abroad. Neighbors, good, decent fellows with no sense about walking in the dew at night, when they were returning late from town, drunk, lashing their horses and flinging whisky bottles from racing democrat wagons, saw him, and they spread the tidings that Old Cottonwood was "getting nutty since he give up his farm to that son-in-law of his and retired. Seen the old codger wandering around at midnight. Wish I had his chance to sleep. Wouldn't catch me out in the night air."

Any rural community from Todd Center to Seringapatam is resentful of any person who varies from its standard, and is morbidly fascinated by any hint of madness. The countryside began to spy on Knute Axelbrod, to ask him questions, and to stare from the road at his shack. He was sensitively aware of it, and inclined to be surly to inquisitive acquaintances. Doubtless that was the beginning of his great pilgrimage.

As a part of the general wild license of his new life— really, he once roared at that startled cat, the Princess: "By gollies! I ain't going to brush my teeth tonight. All my life I've brushed 'em, and alvays wanted to skip a time vunce"—Knute took considerable pleasure in degenerating in his taste in scholarship. He wilfully declined to finish *The Conquest of Mexico*, and began to read light novels borrowed from the Joralemon library. So he rediscovered the lands of dancing and light wines, which all his life he had desired. Some economics and history he did read, but every evening he would stretch out in his buffalo-horn chair, his feet on the cot and the Princess in his lap, and invade Zenda or fall in love with Trilby.

Among the novels he chanced upon a highly optimistic story of Yale in which a worthy young man "earned his way through" college, stroked the crew, won Phi Beta Kappa, and had the most entertaining, yet moral, conversations on or adjacent to "the dear old fence."

As a result of this chronicle, at about three o'clock one morning, when Knute Axelbrod was sixty-four years of age, he decided that he would go to college. All his life he had wanted to. Why not do it?

When he awoke he was not so sure about it as when he had gone to sleep. He saw himself as ridiculous, a ponderous, oldish man among clean-limbed youths, like a dusty cottonwood among silver birches. But for months he wrestled and played with that idea of a great pilgrimage to the Mount of Muses; for he really supposed college to be that sort of place. He believed that all college students, except for the wealthy idlers, burned to acquire learning. He pictured Harvard and Yale and Princeton as ancient groves set with marble temples, before which large groups of Grecian youths talked gently about astronomy and good government. In his picture they never cut classes or ate.

With a longing for music and books and graciousness such as the most ambitious boy could never comprehend, this thick-faced farmer dedicated himself to beauty, and defied the unconquerable power of approaching old age. He sent for college catalogues and school books, and diligently began to prepare himself for college.

He found Latin irregular verbs and the whimsicalities of algebra fiendish. They had nothing to do with actual life as he had lived it. But he mastered them; he studied twelve hours a day, as once he had plodded through eighteen hours a day in the hayfield. With history and English literature he had comparatively little trouble; already he knew much of them from his recreative reading. From German neighbors he had picked up enough Plattdeutsch to make German easy. The trick of study began to come back to him from his small school teaching of forty-five years before. He began to believe that he could really put it through. He kept assuring himself that in college, with rare and sympathetic instructors to help him, there would not be this baffling search, this nervous strain.

But the unreality of the things he studied did disillusion him, and he tired of his new game. He kept it up chiefly because all his life he had kept up onerous labor without any taste for it. Toward the autumn of the second year of his eccentric life he no longer believed that he would ever go to college.

Then a busy little grocer stopped him on the street in Joralemon and quizzed him about his studies, to the delight of the informal club which always loafs at the corner of the hotel.

Knute was silent, but dangerously angry. He remembered just in time how he had once laid wrathful hands upon a hired man, and somehow the man's collar bone had been broken. He turned away and walked home, seven miles, still boiling. He picked up the Princess, and, with her mewing on his shoulder, tramped out again to enjoy the sunset.

He stopped at a reedy slough. He gazed at a hopping plover without seeing it. Suddenly he cried:

"I am going to college. It opens next veek. I t'ink that I can pass the examinations."

Two days later he had moved the Princess and his sticks of furniture to his son-in-law's house, had bought a new slouch hat, a celluloid collar and a solemn suit of black, had wrestled with God in prayer through all of a star-clad night, and had taken the train for Minneapolis, on the way to New Haven.

While he stared out of the car window Knute was warning himself that the millionaires' sons would make fun of him. Perhaps they would haze him. He bade himself avoid all these sons of Belial and cleave to his own people, those who "earned their way through."

At Chicago he was afraid with a great fear of the lightning flashes that the swift crowds made on his retina, the batteries of ranked motor cars that charged at him. He prayed, and ran for his train to New York. He came at last to New Haven.

Not with gibing rudeness, but with politely quizzical eyebrows, Yale received him, led him through entrance examinations, which, after sweaty plowing with the pen, he barely passed, and found for him a roommate. The roommate was a large-browed soft white grub named Ray Gribble, who had been teaching school in New England and seemed chiefly to desire college training so that he might make more money as a teacher. Ray Gribble was a hustler; he instantly got work tutoring the awkward son of a steel man, and for board he waited on table.

He was Knute's chief acquaintance. Knute tried to fool himself into thinking he liked the grub, but Ray couldn't keep his damp hands off the old man's soul. He had the skill of a professional exhorter of young men in finding out Knute's motives, and when he discovered that Knute

had a hidden desire to sip at gay, polite literature, Ray said
in a shocked way:

"Strikes me a man like you, that's getting old, ought
to be thinking more about saving your soul than about
all these frills. You leave this poetry and stuff to these
foreigners and artists, and you stick to Latin and math.
and the Bible. I tell you, I've taught school, and I've
learned by experience."

With Ray Gribble, Knute lived grubbily, an existence
of torn comforters and smelly lamp, of lexicons and loga-
rithm tables. No leisurely loafing by fireplaces was theirs.
They roomed in West Divinity, where gather the theo-
logues, the lesser sort of law students, a whimsical genius
or two, and a horde of unplaced freshmen and "scrub
seniors."

Knute was shockingly disappointed, but he stuck to his
room because outside of it he was afraid. He was a gro-
tesque figure, and he knew it, a white-polled giant squeezed
into a small seat in a classroom, listening to instructors
younger than his own sons. Once he tried to sit on the
fence. No one but "ringers" sat on the fence any more,
and at the sight of him trying to look athletic and young,
two upper-class men snickered, and he sneaked away.

He came to hate Ray Gribble and his voluble companions of the submerged tenth of the class, the hewers of
tutorial wood. It is doubtless safer to mock the flag than
to question that best-established tradition of our democracy—that those who "earn their way through" college are necessarily stronger, braver, and more assured of
success than the weaklings who talk by the fire. Every
college story presents such a moral. But tremblingly the
historian submits that Knute discovered that waiting on
table did not make lads more heroic than did football
or happy loafing. Fine fellows, cheerful and fearless, were

many of the boys who "earned their way," and able to
talk to richer classmates without fawning; but just as
many of them assumed an abject respectability as the
most convenient pose. They were pickers up of unconsid-
ered trifles; they toadied to the classmates whom they
tutored; they wriggled before the faculty committee on
scholarships; they looked pious at Dwight Hall prayer-
meetings to make an impression on the serious minded;
and they drank one glass of beer at Jake's to show the
light minded that they meant nothing offensive by their
piety. In revenge for cringing to the insolent athletes
whom they tutored, they would, when safe among their
own kind, yammer about the "lack of democracy of college today." Not that they were so indiscreet as to do anything about it. They lacked the stuff of really rebellious
souls. Knute listened to them and marveled. They sounded
like young hired men talking behind his barn at harvest
time.

This submerged tenth hated the dilettantes of the class
even more than they hated the bloods. Against one Gilbert
Washburn, a rich esthete with more manner than any
freshman ought to have, they raged righteously. They
spoke of seriousness and industry till Knute, who might
once have desired to know lads like Washburn, felt
ashamed of himself as a wicked, wasteful old man.

Humbly though he sought, he found no inspiration
and no comradeship. He was the freak of the class, and
aside from the submerged tenth, his classmates were afraid
of being "queered" by being seen with him.

As he was still powerful, one who could take up a barrel
of pork on his knees, he tried to find friendship among the
athletes. He sat at Yale Field, watching the football try-
outs, and tried to get acquainted with the candidates.
They stared at him and answered his questions grudgingly

—beefy youths who in their simple-hearted way showed that they considered him plain crazy.

The place itself began to lose the haze of magic through which he had first seen it. Earth is earth, whether one sees it in Camelot or Joralemon or on the Yale campus—or possibly even in the Harvard yard! The buildings ceased to be temples to Knute; they became structures of brick or stone, filled with young men who lounged at windows and watched him amusedly as he tried to slip by.

The Gargantuan hall of Commons became a tri-daily horror because at the table where he dined were two youths who, having uncommonly penetrating minds, discerned that Knute had a beard, and courageously told the world about it. One of them, named Atchison, was a superior person, very industrious and scholarly, glib in mathematics and manners. He despised Knute's lack of definite purpose in coming to college. The other was a play-boy, a wit and a stealer of street signs, who had a wonderful sense for a subtle jest; and his references to Knute's beard shook the table with jocund mirth three times a day. So these youths of gentle birth drove the shambling, wistful old man away from Commons, and thereafter he ate at the lunch counter at the Black Cat.

Lacking the stimulus of friendship, it was the harder for Knute to keep up the strain of studying the long assignments. What had been a week's pleasant reading in his shack was now thrown at him as a day's task. But he would not have minded the toil if he could have found one as young as himself. They were all so dreadfully old, the money-earners, the serious laborers at athletics, the instructors who worried over their life work of putting marks in class-record books.

Then, on a sore, bruised day, Knute did meet one who was young.

Knute had heard that the professor who was the idol of the college had berated the too-earnest lads in his Browning class, and insisted that they read *Alice in Wonderland*. Knute floundered dustily about in a second-hand bookshop till he found an "Alice," and he brought it home to read over his lunch of a hot-dog sandwich. Something in the grave absurdity of the book appealed to him, and he was chuckling over it when Ray Gribble came into the room and glanced at the reader.

"Huh!" said Mr. Gribble.

"That's a fine, funny book," said Knute.

"Huh! *Alice in Wonderland!* I've heard of it. Silly nonsense. Why don't you read something really fine, like Shakespeare or *Paradise Lost?*"

"Vell——" said Knute, all he could find to say.

With Ray Gribble's glassy eye on him, he could no longer roll and roar with the book. He wondered if indeed he ought not to be reading Milton's pompous anthropological misconceptions. He went unhappily out to an early history class, ably conducted by Blevins, Ph.D.

Knute admired Blevins, Ph.D. He was so tubbed and eyeglassed and terribly right. But most of Blevins' lambs did not like Blevins. They said he was a "crank." They read newspapers in his class and covertly kicked one another.

In the smug, plastered classroom, his arm leaning heavily on the broad tablet-arm of his chair, Knute tried not to miss one of Blevins' sardonic proofs that the correct date of the second marriage of Themistocles was two years and seven days later than the date assigned by that illiterate ass, Frutari of Padua. Knute admired young Blevins' performance, and he felt virtuous in application to these hard, unnonsensical facts.

He became aware that certain lewd fellows of the lesser

sort were playing poker just behind him. His prairie-
trained ear caught whispers of "Two to dole," and "Raise
you two beans." Knute revolved, and frowned upon these
mockers of sound learning. As he turned back he was
aware that the offenders were chuckling, and continuing
their game. He saw that Blevins, Ph.D., perceived that
something was wrong; he frowned, but he said nothing.
Knute sat in meditation. He saw Blevins as merely a boy.
He was sorry for him. He would do the boy a good turn.

When class was over he hung about Blevins' desk till
the other students had clattered out. He rumbled:

"Say, Professor, you're a fine fellow. I do something for
you. If any of the boys make themselves a nuisance, you
yust call on me, and I spank the son of a guns."

Blevins, Ph.D., spake in a manner of culture and nasti-
ness:

"Thanks so much, Axelbrod, but I don't fancy that will
ever be necessary. I am supposed to be a reasonably good
disciplinarian. Good day. Oh, one moment. There's something I've been wishing to speak to you about. I do wish
you wouldn't try quite so hard to show off whenever I call
on you during quizzes. You answer at such needless length,
and you smile as though there were something highly
amusing about me. I'm quite willing to have you regard
me as a humorous figure, privately, but there are certain
classroom conventions, you know, certain little conventions."

"Why, Professor!" wailed Knute, "I never make fun of
you! I didn't know I smile. If I do, I guess it's yust because I am so glad when my stupid old head gets the lesson
good."

"Well, well, that's very gratifying, I'm sure. And if
you will be a little more careful——"

Blevins, Ph.D., smiled a toothy, frozen smile, and

trotted off to the Graduates' Club, to be witty about old
Knute and his way of saying "yust," while in the deserted
classroom Knute sat chill, an old man and doomed.
Through the windows came the light of Indian summer;
clean, boyish cries rose from the campus. But the lover of
autumn smoothed his baggy sleeve, stared at the black-
board, and there saw only the gray of October stubble
about his distant shack. As he pictured the college watching him, secretly making fun of him and his smile, he was
now faint and ashamed, now bull-angry. He was lonely
for his cat, his fine chair of buffalo horns, the sunny doorstep of his shack, and the understanding land. He had
been in college for about one month.

Before he left the classroom he stepped behind the instructor's desk and looked at an imaginary class.

"I might have stood there as a prof if I could have come
earlier," he said softly to himself.

Calmed by the liquid autumn gold that flowed through
the streets, he walked out Whitney Avenue toward the
butte-like hill of East Rock. He observed the caress of
the light upon the scarped rock, heard the delicate music
of leaves, breathed in air pregnant with tales of old New
England. He exulted: "'Could write poetry now if I yust
—if I yust could write poetry!"

He climbed to the top of East Rock, whence he could
see the Yale buildings like the towers of Oxford, and see
Long Island Sound, and the white glare of Long Island
beyond the water. He marveled that Axelbrod of the
cottonwood country was looking across an arm of the
Atlantic to New York state. He noticed a freshman on a
bench at the edge of the rock, and he became irritated.
The freshman was Gilbert Washburn, the snob, the dilet-
tante, of whom Ray Gribble had once said: "That guy
is the disgrace of the class. He doesn't go out for anything,

high stand or Dwight Hall or anything else. Thinks he's
so doggone much better than the rest of the fellows that
he doesn't associate with anybody. Thinks he's literary,
they say, and yet he doesn't even heel the 'Lit,' like the
regular literary fellows! Got no time for a loafing, mooning
snob like that."

As Knute stared at the unaware Gil, whose profile was
fine in outline against the sky, he was terrifically public-
spirited and disapproving and that sort of moral thing.
Though Gil was much too well dressed, he seemed moodily
discontented.

"What he needs is to vork in a threshing crew and sleep
in the hay," grumbled Knute almost in the virtuous manner of Gribble. "Then he vould know when he vas vell
off, and not look like he had the earache. Pff!" Gil Washburn rose, trailed toward Knute, glanced at him, sat down
on Knute's bench.

"Great view!" he said. His smile was eager.

That smile symbolized to Knute all the art of life he
had come to college to find. He tumbled out of his moral
attitude with ludicrous haste, and every wrinkle of his
weathered face creased deep as he answered:

"Yes: I t'ink the Acropolis must be like this here."

"Say, look here, Axelbrod; I've been thinking about
you."

"Yas?"

"We ought to know each other. We two are the class
scandal. We came here to dream, and these busy little
goats like Atchison and Giblets, or whatever your roommate's name is, think we're fools not to go out for marks.
You may not agree with me, but I've decided that you
and I are precisely alike."

"What makes you t'ink I come here to dream?"
bristled Knute.

"Oh, I used to sit near you at Commons and hear you try to quell old Atchison whenever he got busy discussing the reasons for coming to college. That old, moth-eaten topic! I wonder if Cain and Abel didn't discuss it at the Eden Agricultural College. You know, Abel the mark-grabber, very pious and high stand, and Cain wanting to read poetry."

"Yes," said Knute, "and I guess Prof. Adam say, 'Cain, don't you read this poetry; it von't help you in algebry.'"

"Of course. Say, wonder if you'd like to look at this volume of Musset I was sentimental enough to lug up here today. Picked it up when I was abroad last year."

From his pocket Gil drew such a book as Knute had never seen before, a slender volume, in a strange language, bound in hand-tooled crushed levant, an effeminate bibe-lot over which the prairie farmer gasped with luxurious pleasure. The book almost vanished in his big hands. With a timid forefinger he stroked the levant, ran through the leaves.

"I can't read it, but that's the kind of book I alvays t'ought there must be some like it," he sighed.

"Listen!" cried Gil. "Ysaye is playing up at Hartford tonight. Let's go hear him. We'll trolley up. Tried to get some of the fellows to come, but they thought I was a nut."

What an Ysaye was, Knute Axelbrod had no notion; but "Sure!" he boomed.

When they got to Hartford they found that between them they had just enough money to get dinner, hear Ysaye from gallery seats, and return only as far as Meriden. At Meriden Gil suggested:

"Let's walk back to New Haven, then. Can you make it?"

Knute had no knowledge as to whether it was four miles

or forty back to the campus, but "Sure!" he said. For the
last few months he had been noticing that, despite his
bulk, he had to be careful, but tonight he could have
flown.

In the music of Ysaye, the first real musician he had
ever heard, Knute had found all the incredible things of
which he had slowly been reading in William Morris and
"Idylls of the King." Tall knights he had beheld, and
slim princesses in white samite, the misty gates of forlorn
towns, and the glory of the chivalry that never was.

They did walk, roaring down the road beneath the
October moon, stopping to steal apples and to exclaim
over silvered hills, taking a puerile and very natural joy
in chasing a profane dog. It was Gil who talked, and Knute
who listened, for the most part; but Knute was lured
into tales of the pioneer days, of blizzards, of harvesting,
and of the first flame of the green wheat. Regarding the
Atchisons and Gribbles of the class both of them were
youthfully bitter and supercilious. But they were not
bitter long, for they were atavisms tonight. They were
wandering minstrels, Gilbert the troubadour with his
man-at-arms.

They reached the campus at about five in the morning.
Fumbling for words that would express his feeling, Knute
stammered:

"Vell, it vas fine. I go to bed now and I dream about
——"

"Bed? Rats! Never believe in winding up a party when
it's going strong. Too few good parties. Besides, it's only
the shank of the evening. Besides, we're hungry. Besides
—oh, besides! Wait here a second. I'm going up to my
room to get some money, and we'll have some eats. Wait!
Please do!"

Knute would have waited all night. He had lived almost

seventy years and traveled fifteen hundred miles and endured Ray Gribble to find Gil Washburn.

Policemen wondered to see the celluloid-collared old man and the expensive-looking boy rolling arm in arm down Chapel Street in search of a restaurant suitable to poets. They were all closed.

"The Ghetto will be awake by now," said Gil. "We'll go buy some eats and take 'em up to my room. I've got some tea there."

Knute shouldered through dark streets beside him as naturally as though he had always been a nighthawk, with an aversion to anything as rustic as beds. Down on Oak Street, a place of low shops, smoky lights and alley mouths, they found the slum already astir. Gil contrived to purchase boxed biscuits, cream cheese, chicken-loaf, a bottle of cream. While Gil was chaffering, Knute stared out into the street milkily lighted by wavering gas and the first feebleness of coming day; he gazed upon Kosher signs and advertisements in Russian letters, shawled women and bearded rabbis; and as he looked he gathered contentment which he could never lose. He had traveled abroad tonight.

The room of Gil Washburn was all the useless, pleasant things Knute wanted it to be. There was more of Gil's Paris days in it than of his freshmanhood: Persian rugs, a silver tea service, etchings, and books. Knute Axelbrod of the tar-paper shack and piggy farmyards gazed in satisfaction. Vast bearded, sunk in an easy chair, he clucked amiably while Gil lighted a fire.

Over supper they spoke of great men and heroic ideals. It was good talk, and not unspiced with lively references to Gribble and Atchison and Blevins, all asleep now in their correct beds. Gil read snatches of Stevenson and

Anatole France; then at last he read his own poetry.

It does not matter whether that poetry was good or bad. To Knute it was a miracle to find one who actually wrote it.

The talk grew slow, and they began to yawn. Knute was sensitive to the lowered key of their Indian-summer madness, and he hastily rose. As he said good-by he felt as though he had but to sleep a little while and return to this unending night of romance.

But he came out of the dormitory upon day. It was six-thirty of the morning, with a still, hard light upon red-brick walls.

"I can go to his room plenty times now; I find my friend," Knute said. He held tight the volume of Musset, which Gil had begged him to take.

As he started to walk the few steps to West Divinity Knute felt very tired. By daylight the adventure seemed more and more incredible.

As he entered the dormitory he sighed heavily:

"Age and youth, I guess they can't team together long." As he mounted the stairs he said: "If I saw the boy again, he vould get tired of me. I tell him all I got to say." And as he opened his door, he added: "This is what I come to college for—this one night. I go avay before I spoil it."

He wrote a note to Gil, and began to pack his telescope. He did not even wake Ray Gribble, sonorously sleeping in the stale air.

At five that afternoon, on the day coach of a westbound train, an old man sat smiling. A lasting content was in his eyes, and in his hands a small book in French.

SPEED

SPEED

A̶t two in the morning, on Main Street of a Nebraska prairie town that ought to have been asleep since ten, a crowd was packed under a lone arc-light, chattering, laughing, and every moment peering down the dim street to westward.

Out in the road were two new automobile tires, and cans of gasoline, oil, water. The hose of a pressure air-pump stretched across the cement sidewalk, and beside it was an air-gauge in a new chamois case. Across the street a restaurant was glaring with unshaded electric lights; and a fluffy-haired, pert-nose girl alternately ran to the window and returned to look after the food she was keeping warm. The president of the local motor club, who was also owner of the chief garage, kept stuttering to a young man in brown union overalls, "Now be all ready—for land's sake, be ready. Remember, gotta change those casings in three minutes." They were awaiting a romantic event—the smashing of the cross-continent road-record by a Mallard car driven by J. T. Buffum.

Everyone there had seen pictures of Buffum in the sporting and automobile pages of the Lincoln and Kansas City papers; everyone knew that face, square, impassive, heavy-cheeked, kindly, with the unsmoked cigar between firm teeth, and the almost boyish bang over a fine forehead. Two days ago he had been in San Francisco, between the smeared gold of Chink dens and the tumult of the Pacific. Two days from now he would be in distant New York.

Miles away on the level prairie road a piercing jab of light grew swiftly into two lights, while a distant drumroll turned into the burring roar of a huge unmuffled engine. The devouring thing burst into town, came fulminating down on them, stopped with a clashing jerk. The crowd saw the leather-hooded man at the mighty steering wheel nod to them, grinning, human, companionable—the great Buffum.

"Hurray! Hurray!" came the cries, and the silence changed to weaving gossip.

Already the garage youngster, with his boss and three men from another garage, was yanking off two worn casings, filling the gas tank, the oil well, the radiator. Buffum stiffly crawled from the car, stretched his shoulders, his mighty arms and legs, in a leonine yawn. "Jump out, Roy. Eats here," he muttered to the man in the passenger seat. This man the spectators did not heed. He was merely Buffum's mechanic and relay driver, a poor thing who had never in his life driven faster than ninety miles an hour.

The garage owner hustled Buffum across to the lunchroom. The moment the car had stormed into town the pretty waitress, jumping up and down with impatience, had snatched the chicken from the warming oven, poured out the real coffee, proudly added real cream. The lunch and the changing of casings took three and a quarter minutes.

The clatter of the motor smote the quiet houses and was gone. The town became drab and dull. The crowd yawned and fumbled its way home.

Buffum planned to get in two hours of sleep after leaving this Nebraska town. Roy Bender, the relay driver, took the wheel. Buffum sat with his relaxed body swaying to the leaping motion, while he drowsily commented in a hoarse, slow shout that pushed through the enveloping roar: "Look out for that hill, Roy. Going to be slippery."

"How can you tell?"

"I don't know. Maybe I smell it. But watch out, anyway. Good night, little playmate. Wake me up at four-fifteen."

That was all of the conversation for seventy-two miles.

It was dawn when Buffum drove again. He was silent; he was concentrated on keeping the speedometer just two miles higher than seemed safe. But for a mile or so, on straight stretches, he glanced with weary happiness at the morning meadows, at shimmering tapestry of grass and young wheat, and caught half a note of the song of a meadowlark. His mouth, so grimly tight in dangerous places, rose at the corners.

Toward noon, as Buffum was approaching the village of Apogee, Iowa, the smooth blaring of the motor was interrupted by a noise as though the engine was flying to pieces.

He yanked at the switch; before the car had quite halted, Roy and he had tumbled out at opposite sides, were running forward to lift the hood. The fan-guard, a heavy wire soldered on the radiator, had worked loose and bent a fan-blade, which had ripped out a handful of honeycomb. The inside of the radiator looked as though it had been hacked with a dull knife. The water was cascading out.

Buffum speculated: "Apogee next town. Can't get radiator there. None nearer 'n Clinton. Get this soldered. Here! You!"

The "Here! You!" was directed at the driver of an ancient roadster. "Got to hustle this boat into next town. Want you to haul me in."

Roy Bender had already snatched a tow-rope from the back of the racing car, was fastening it to the front axle of the Mallard, the rear of the roadster.

Buffum gave no time for disputes. "I'm J. T. Buffum. Racin' 'cross continent. Here's ten dollars. Want your machine ten minutes. I'll drive." He had crowded into the seat. Already, with Roy steering the Mallard, they were headed for Apogee.

A shouting crowd ran out from house and store. Buffum slowly looked them over. Of a man in corduroy trousers and khaki shirt, who had plumped out of a garage, he demanded: "Who's the best solderer in town?"

"I am. Good as anybody in Iowa."

"Now, wait! Know who I am?"

"Sure! You're Buffum."

"My radiator is shot to thunder. Got to be soldered. I want six hours' work done in one hour, or less. How about the hardware store? Isn't there a solderer there that's even better than you?"

"Yes, I guess maybe old Frank Dieters is."

"Get him, and get the other good man, and get busy. One of you work on each side. Roy Bender here will boss you." Already Roy was taking down the radiator. "One hour, remember. Hurry! Plenty of money in it——"

"Oh, we don't care anything about the money!"

"Thanks, old man. Well, I might as well grab a little sleep. Where'll I get a long-distance connection?" he yawned.

"Across the street at Mrs. Rivers'. Be less noise than in the garage, I guess."

Over the way was a house that was a large square box with an octagonal cupola on the mansard roof. It was set back in a yard of rough grass and old crabapple trees. At the gate were a smallish, severe woman, in spectacles and apron, and a girl of twenty-five or -six. Buffum looked at the girl twice, and tried to make out what it was that distinguished her from all the other women in the crowd that had come pushing and giggling to see the famous car.

She was sharply individualized. It was not that she was tall and blazing. She was slight—and delicate as a drypoint etching. Her chin was precise though soft; she had a Roman nose, a feminized charming version of the Roman nose. The thing that made her distinctive, Buffum reflected, was her poise. The girl by the gate was as quietly aloof as the small cold moon of winter.

He plodded across the road. He hesitated before speaking.

"I hope there hasn't been an accident," she murmured to him.

"No, just a small repair."

"But, why does everyone seem so much concerned?"

"Why, it's—it's—I'm J. T. Buffum."

"Mr.—uh—Buffum?"

"I reckon you never heard of me."

"Why, uh—should I have?" Her eyes were serious, regretful at discourtesy.

"No. You shouldn't. I just mean—— Motor-fans usually have. I'm a racer. I'm driving from San Francisco to New York."

"Really? It will take you—ten days?"

"Four to five days."

"In two days you will be in the East? See the—the ocean? Oh!"

In her voice was wistfulness. Her eyes saw far-off things. But they came back to Apogee, Iowa, and to the big, dusty man in leather, with a penitent: "I'm ashamed not to have heard of you, but I—we haven't a car. I hope they will make your repair quickly. May Mother and I give you a glass of milk or something?"

"I'd be glad if you'd let me use your telephone. So noisy at——"

"Of course! Mother, this is Mr. Buffum, who is driving across the country. Oh—my name is Aurilla Rivers."

Buffum awkwardly tried to bow in two directions at once. Then he followed Aurilla Rivers' slender back. He noticed how smooth were her shoulder-blades. They were neither jagged nor wadded. It seemed to him that the blue silk of her waist took life from the warm and eager flesh beneath. In her studied serenity she had not lost her youth.

As he drew away from the prying crowd and the sound of hasty hammers and wrenches, he was conscious of clinging peace. The brick of the walk was worn to a soft rose, shaded by gently moving branches of lilac bushes. At the end was a wild-grape arbor and an ancient bench. The arbor was shadowy, and full of the feeling of long and tranquil years. In this land of new houses and new red barns and blazing miles of wheat, it seemed mysterious with antiquity.

And on the doorstep was the bleached vertebra of a whale. Buffum was confused. He traveled so much and so swiftly that he always had to stop to think whether he was East or West, and now—— Yes, this was Iowa. Of course. But that vertebra belonged to New England.

And to New England belonged the conch shell and the

mahogany table in the wide hall with its strip of rag-carpet down which Miss Rivers led him to the telephone —an old-fashioned wall instrument. Buffum noticed that Miss Rivers conscientiously disappeared through the wide door at the end of the hall into a garden of pinks and pansies and sweet William.

"Please get me long distance."

"I'm long distance and short distance and——"

"All right. This is Buffum, the transcontinental racer. I want to talk to Detroit, Michigan—Mallard Motor Company—office of the president."

He waited ten minutes. He sat on the edge of a William and Mary chair, and felt obese, clumsy, extremely dirty. He ventured off his chair—disapproving of the thunder of his footsteps—and stood at the door of the parlor. The corner by the bow window seemed to be a shrine. Above a genuine antediluvian haircloth sofa were three pictures. In the center was a rather good painting of a man who was the very spirit of 1850 in New England—burnsides, grim white forehead, Roman nose, prim triangle of shirt-front. On the right was a watercolor of a house, white doored, narrow eaved, small windowed, standing out against gray sand and blue water, with a moored motor-dory beyond. On the woodshed ell of the pictured house was nailed up the name-board of a ship—*Penninah Sparrow.*

On the left of the portrait was a fairly recent enlarged photograph of a man somewhat like the granther of 1850, so far as Romanness of nose went, but weaker and more pompous, a handsome old buck, with a pretentious broad eyeglass ribbon and hair that must have been silvery over a face that must have been deep-flushed.

By the sofa was a marble-topped stand on which were fresh sweet peas.

Then central called, and Buffum was talking to the
president of the Mallard Motor Company, who for two
days and nights had sat by the ticker, watching his flashing progress.

"Hello, chief. Buffum speaking. Held up for about an
hour. Apogee, Iowa. Think I can make it up. But better
move the schedule up through Illinois and Indiana. Huh?
Radiator leak. 'By!"

He inquired the amount of toll, and rambled out to the
garden. He had to hurry away, of course, and get some
sleep, but it would be good for him to see Aurilla Rivers
again, to take with him the memory of her cool resoluteness. She was coming toward him. He meekly followed her
back through the hall, to the front steps. There he halted
her. He would see quite enough of Roy Bender and the
car before he reached New York.

"Please sit down here a moment, and tell me——"

"Yes?"

"Oh, about the country around here, and uh—— Oh!
I owe you for the telephone call."

"Please! It's nothing."

"But it's something. It's two dollars and ninety-five
cents."

"For a telephone call?"

He caught her hand and pressed the money into it.
She plumped down on the steps, and he discreetly lowered
his bulk beside her. She turned on him, blazing;

"You infuriate me! You do things I've always wanted
to—sweep across big distances, command men, have
power. I suppose it's the old Yankee shipmasters coming
out in me."

"Miss Rivers, I noticed a portrait in there. It seemed to
me that the picture and the old sofa make a kind of shrine.

And the fresh flowers." She stared a little before she said:
"Yes. It's a shrine. But you're the first one that ever
guessed. How did you———"

"I don't know. I suppose it's because I went through
some California missions a few days ago. Tell me about
the people in the pictures."

"You wouldn't—— Oh, some day, perhaps."

"Some day! Now, you see here, child! Do you realize
that in about forty minutes I'll be kiting out of here at
seventy miles an hour? Imagine that I've met you a
couple of times in the bank or the post office, and finally
after about six months I've called here, and told your
mother I like pansies. All right. All that is over. Now, who
are you, Aurilla Rivers? Who and what and why and how
and when?

She smiled. She nodded. She told.

She was a school teacher now, but before her father
had died—well, the enlarged photograph in there was her
father, Bradley Rivers, pioneer lawyer of Apogee. He had
come out from Cape Cod, as a boy. The side-whiskered
man of the central portrait was her grandfather, Captain
Zenas Rivers, of West Harlepool, on the Cape. The house
in the picture was the Rivers' mansion, birthplace of her
father.

"Have you been on the Cape yourself?" Buffum queried. "I remember driving through Harlepool, but I don't
recall anything but white houses and a meeting-house
with a whale of a big steeple."

"The dream of my life has been to go to Harlepool.
Once when Father had to go to Boston he did run down
there by himself. That's when he brought back the portrait
of Grandfather, and the painting of the old house, and
the furniture and all. He said it made him so melancholy to

see the changes in the town, and he never would go again. Then—he died. I'm saving up money for a trip back East. I do believe in democracy, but at the same time I feel that families like the Riverses owe it to the world to set an example, and I want to find my own people again. My own people!"

"Maybe you're right. I'm from the soil. Di-rect! But somehow I can see it in you, same as I do in the portrait of your grandfather. I wish I—— Well, never mind."

"But you are an aristocrat. You do things that other people don't dare to. While you were telephoning, I saw our school principal, and he said you were a Vi-king and all kinds of——"

"Here! Now! You! Quit! Stop! Wait! A lot of people, especially on newspapers, give me a lot of taffy just because I can drive fast. What I need is someone like you to make me realize what a roughneck I am."

She looked at him clear-eyed, and pondered: "I'm afraid most of the Apogee boys think I'm rather prim."

"They would! That's why they're stuck in Apogee." Buffum searched her eyes and speculated: "I wonder if we aren't alike in this way: Neither of us content to plod. Most people never think of why they're living. They reckon and guess and s'pose that maybe some day they'll do better, and then—bing!—they're dead. But you and I —I seem—I've known you a long time. Will you remember me?"

"Oh, yes. There aren't so many seventy-an-hour people in Apogee!"

From the gate Roy Bender was bellowing: "Ready in two minutes, boss!"

Buffum was on his feet, drawing on his gauntlets and leather coat. She looked at him gravely, while he urged:

"Going on. Day from now, the strain will begin to kind

of get me. Will you think about me then? Will you wireless
me some good thoughts?"

"Yes!"—very quietly. He yanked off his big gauntlet.
He felt her hand fragile in his. Then he was gone, march-
ing down the walk, climbing into the car, demanding of
Roy: "Look over oil and battery and ev'thing?"

"You bet. We did everything," said the garage man.
"Get a little rest?"

"Yes. Had a chance to sit in the shade and loaf."

"Saw you talking to Aurilla Rivers——"

Roy interrupted: "All right, all right, boss. Shoot!"

Buffum heard the garage man out:

"Fine girl, Aurilla is. Smart's a whip. She's a real swell.
Born and brought up here, too."

"Who's this that Miss Rivers is engaged to?" Buffum
risked.

"Well, I guess probably she'll marry Reverend Dawson. He's a dried-up old stick but he comes from the East.
Some day she'll get tired of school teaching, and he'll grab
her. Marry in haste and repent at Reno, like the fellow
says."

"That's right. Fix up the bill, Roy? G'by."

Buffum was off. Five minutes later he was six and three-
quarters miles away. In his mind was but one thought—
to make up the lost time; in his eyes was no vision save
speedometer and the road that rushed toward him.

A little after dark he rumbled at Roy: "Here. Take her.
Going to get some sleep." He did sleep, for an hour, then
struggling into full wakefulness he dug his knuckles into
his eyes like a sleepy boy, glanced at the speedometer, laid
a hand on the steering wheel and snapped at Roy: "All
right. Move over."

At dawn nothing existed in the world save the compul-
sion to keep her at top speed. The earth was shut off from

him by a wall of roar and speed. He did not rouse to human
feeling even when he boomed into Columbus Circle, the
breaker of the record.

He went instantly to bed: slept twenty-six and one-
quarter hours, then attended a dinner given to himself,
and made a speech that was unusually incoherent, because all through he remembered that he was due in San
Francisco in eight days. He was to sail for Japan, and a
road race round the shore of Hondo. Before he returned,
Aurilla Rivers would undoubtedly have married the Reverend Mr. Dawson, have gone to Cape Cod on her wedding
trip. She would think only with disgust of large men with
grease on their faces.

He could take one day for the trip up and back. He
could get to Cape Cod more quickly by motor than by
train. He was going to have one more hour with Aurilla,
on his way to San Francisco. He would be more interesting
to her if he could gossip of her ancestral background. He
could take pictures of the place to her, and perhaps an old
chair from the mansion. As he drove down Front Street,
in West Harlepool, he saw the house quite as it had appeared in Aurilla's picture with the name-board of a
wrecked ship over the woodshed, the *Penninah Sparrow*.

Down the road was a one-room shop with the sign
"Gaius Bearse, Gen'l Merchandise. Clam Forks, Wind-
mills, and Souvenirs." Out on the porch poked a smallish
man. Buffum ambled toward him and saw that the man
was very old.

"Good morning. This Cap'n Bearse?" inquired Buffum.

"I be."

"Uh, uh! Say—uh, Cap'n, can you tell me who's living
in the Rivers mansion now?"

"The which mansion?"

"Rivers. The house across there."

"Huh! That's the Kendrick house."

"But it was built by a Rivers."

"No, 'twa'n't. That house was built by Cap'n Cephas. Kendricks living in it ever since. Owned now by William Dean Kendrick. He's in the wool business, in Boston, but his folks comes down every summer. I ought to know. The Kendricks are kin of mine."

"B-but where did the Riverses live?"

"The Riverses? Oh, them! Come from the West, don't ye? Spend the summer here?"

"No. What makes you think I come from the West?"

"Rivers went out there. Bradley Rivers. He the one you're thinking of?"

"Yes."

"Friend of yours——"

"No. Just happened to hear about him."

"Well, I'll tell you. There never was any Rivers family."

"What?"

"The father of this here Bradley Rivers called himself Zenas Rivers. But land, Zenas' right name was Fernao Ribeiro. He was nothing but a Portygee deckhand. Fernao, or Zenas, became a wrecker. He was a good hand in a dory, but when he was drinking, he was a caution for snakes. He come straight from the Cape Verde Islands."

"I understand Bradley Rivers' ancestors were howling aristocrats, and came over on the *Mayflower*."

"Maybe so, maybe so. Aristocrats at drinking Jamaica rum, I guess. But they didn't come on no *Mayflower*. Zenas Rivers came over on the brig *Jennie B. Smith!*"

"I understand Zenas owned this—this Kendrick House?"

"Him? Why, boy, if Zenas or Brad either ever set foot across the threshold of that house, it was to fill the wood box, or maybe sell lobsters!"

"B-but—what kind of looking man was Zenas?"

"Thick-set, dark-complected fellow—reaɪ Portygee."

"Didn't he have a Roman nose?"

"Him? Huh! Had a nose like a herring."

"But Bradley had a Roman nose. Where'd he get it?"

"From his maw. She was a Yankee, but her folks wa'n't much account. So she married Zenas. Brad Rivers always was an awful liar. He came back here about seven-eight years ago, and he boasted he was the richest man in Kansas or maybe 'twas Milwaukee."

"Did he buy a picture of the Kendrick mansion while he was here?"

"Believe he did. He got one of these artists to paint a picture of the Kendrick house. And he bought a couple of things of me—a horsehair sofy, and a picture of old Cap'n Gould that May Gould left here."

"Did—did this Captain Gould in the portrait have a Roman nose? And side whiskers? Stern looking?"

"That's him. What's Brad been telling you, boy?'"

"Nothing!" sighed Buffum. "Then Rivers was just a plain dub? Like me?"

"Plain? Brad Rivers? Well, Zenas sent Brad to school to Taunton for a year or so, but just the same, we always allowed he was so ordinary that there wa'n't a dog belonging to a Kendrick or a Bearse or a Doane that would bite him. Ask any of the old codgers in town."

"I will, but—thanks."

He came down from the Apogee street, inconspicuously creeping through the dust, a large, amiable man in a derby.

He had only fifty-one minutes before the return of the Apogee branch train to the junction to connect with the next express westward.

He rang; he pounded at the front door; he went round to the back; and there he discovered Aurilla's mother, washing napkins. She looked at him over her spectacles, and she sniffed: "Yes?"

"Do you remember I came through here recently? Racing car? I wanted to see Miss Rivers for a moment."

"You can't. She's at school, teaching."

"When will she be back? It's four now."

"Maybe right away, maybe not till six."

His train left at four-forty-nine. He waited on the front steps. It was four-twenty-one when Aurilla Rivers came along the walk. He rushed to her, his watch in his hand, and before she could speak, he was pouring out:

"'Member me? Darn glad! Got less 'n twenty-eight minutes before have to catch train San Francisco steamer Japan possibly India afterwards glad to see me please oh please don't be a Rivers be Aurilla just got twenty-seven 'n' half minutes glad?"

"Why—why—ye-es——"

"Thought about me?"

"Of course."

"Ever wish I might come shooting through again?"

"You're so egotistical!"

"No, just in a hurry. Only got twenty-seven minutes more! Ever wish I'd come back? Oh—please! Can't you hear the Japan steamer whistling—calling us?"

"Japan!"

"Like to see it?"

"Terribly."

"Will you come with me? I'll have a preacher meet us on the train. If you'll phone to Detroit, find out all about me. Come! Quick! Marry me! Just twenty-six and a half more."

She could only whisper in answer: "No. I mustn't think of it. It tempts me. But Mother would never consent."

"What has your mother to do——"

"Everything! With our people, the individual is nothing, the family's sacred. I must think of Bradley Rivers, and old Zenas, and hundreds of fine old Yankees, building up something so much bigger than just one individual happiness. It's, oh, noblesse oblige!" How could he, in face of her ancestor worship, tell the truth? He burst out:

"But you'd like to? Aurilla! Just twenty-five minutes now! He chucked his watch into his pocket. "See here. I want to kiss you. I'm going seven thousand miles away, and I can't stand it, unless—— I'm going to kiss you, there under the grape arbor!" His fingers slipped under her elbow.

She came reluctantly, appealing, "No, no, please, no!" till he swept the words away with a kiss, and in the kiss she forgot all that she had said, and clung to him, begging: "Oh, don't go away. Don't leave me here in this dead village. Stay here—catch the next steamer! Persuade Mother——"

"I must catch this one. I'm due there—big race. Come!"

"With—without clothes?"

"Buy 'em on way—San Francisco!"

"No, I mustn't. And there are others to consider besides Mother."

"Mr. Dawson? Really care for him?"

"He's very gentle and considerate and really such a good scholar. Mother wants Mr. Dawson to get a pastorate on Cape Cod, and she thought that way I might pick up with the old threads, and be a real Rivers again. As Mrs. Dawson, I could find the old house and all——" She was interrupted by his two hands behind her shoulders, by his eyes searching hers with a bitter honesty.

"Don't you ever get tired of ancestors?" he cried.

"I do not! Whatever I may be—they were splendid.

Once in a mutiny on the clipper that he was commanding, Zenas Rivers——"

"Dear, there wasn't any Zenas Rivers. He was a Portuguese immigrant named Ribeiro, Fernao Ribeiro. The picture there in the house is a Captain Gould."

She had slipped from his embrace. But he went steadily on, trying with eyes and voice to make her understand his tenderness:

"Old Zenas was a squat, dark chap, a wrecker, and not very nice. The first real aristocrat in your family is you."

"Wait! You mean that—that it wasn't any of it true? But the Rivers' mansion?"

"There isn't any. The house in the picture has always belonged to the Kendricks. I've just been on Cape Cod, and I found——"

"It isn't true? Not any of it, about the Rivers——"

"None of it. I didn't mean to tell you. If you don't believe me, you can write."

"Oh, don't! Wait!" She turned, looked to the right. He remembered that down the street to the right was a rise of ground with a straggly village cemetery. She murmured:

"Poor Dad! I loved him, oh, so much, but—I know Dad told fibs. But never to harm people. Just because he wanted us to be proud of him. Mr.—what is your name?"

"Buffum."

"Come."

He followed her swift steps into the house, into the room of the shrined portraits. She looked from "Zenas Rivers" to the sketch of the "Rivers' Mansion." She patted the glass over her father's photograph. She blew the dust from her fingers. She sighed: "It smells musty in here, so musty!" She ran to the mahogany chest of drawers and took out a sheet of parchment. On it, he saw, was a coat of arms. She picked up a pencil, turned over the parchment, and drew a flying motor car.

She turned and thrust the sketch at him, crying: "There's the coat of arms of the family to come, the crest of a new aristocracy that knows how to work!" With a solemnity that wasn't solemn at all, he intoned: "Miss Rivers, would you mind marrying me, somewhere between here and California?"

"Yes," he kissed her—"if you can make"—she kissed him—"Mother understand. She has friends and a little money. She can get along without me. But she believes the aristocracy fable."

"May I lie to her?"

"Why, once might be desirable."

"I'll tell her my mother was a Kendrick of Harlepool, and I'll be terribly top-lofty, but in a hurry—especially the hurry! Just got thirteen minutes now!"

From the hall sounded Mrs. Rivers' petulant voice: "Aurilly!"

"Y-yes, Mother?"

"If you and that man are going to catch the train, you better be starting."

"W-w-why," Aurilla gasped; then, to Buffum: "I'll run right up and pack my bag."

"It's all 'tended to, Aurilly. Minute I saw that dratted man coming again, I knew he'd be in a hurry. But I do think you might let me know my son-in-law's name before you go. You only got eleven minutes. You better hurry—hurry—hurry!"

THE KIDNAPED MEMORIAL

THE KIDNAPED MEMORIAL

Wakamin is a town with a soul. It used to have a sentimental soul which got thrills out of neighborliness and "The Star-Spangled Banner," but now it wavers between two generations, with none of the strong, silly ambition of either. The pioneering generation has died out, and of the young men, a hundred have gone to that new pioneering in France. Along the way they will behold the world, see the goodness and eagerness of it, and not greatly desire to come back to the straggly ungenerous streets of Wakamin.

Those who are left, lords of the dead soul of Wakamin, go to the movies and play tight little games of bridge and aspire only to own an automobile, because a car is the sign of respectability.

Mr. Gale felt the savorlessness of the town within ten minutes after he had arrived. He had come north to wind up the estate of his cousin, the late proprietor of the Wakamin Creamery. Mr. Gale was from the pine belt of Alabama but he did not resemble the stage Southerner. There was a look of resoluteness and industry about his broad

321

red jaw. He spoke English very much like a man from New York or San Francisco. He did not say "Yessuh," nor "Ah declah"; he had neither a large white hat nor a small white imperial; he was neither a Colonel nor a Judge. He was Mr. Gale, and he practiced law, and he preferred lemonade to mint juleps. But he had fought clear through the War for the Southern Confederacy; and once, on a gray wrinkled morning before a cavalry battle, he had spoken to Jeb Stuart.

While he was settling up the estate, Mr. Gale tried out the conversational qualities of the editor and the justice of the peace, and gave up his attempt to get acquainted with the Wakamites—except for Mrs. Tiffany, at whose house he went to board. Mrs. Captain Tiffany was daughter and widow of Territorial Pioneers. She herself had teamed-it from St. Paul, with her young husband, after the War. The late Captain Tiffany had been the last commander of the Wakamin G. A. R. Post, and Mrs. Tiffany had for years been president of the Women's Relief Corps. After the barniness of the Wakamin Hotel Mr. Gale was at home in her cottage, which was as precise and nearly as small as the whitewashed conch shell at the gate. He recovered from the forlorn loneliness that had obsessed him during walks on these long, cold, blue twilights of spring. Nightly he sat on the porch with Mrs. Tiffany, and agreed with her about politics, corn-raising, religion, and recipes for hot biscuits.

When he was standing at the gate one evening of April, a small boy sidled across the street, made believe that he was not making-believe soldiers, rubbed one shin with the other foot, looked into the matter of an electric-light bug that was sprawling on its foolish back, violently chased nothing at all, walked backward a few paces, and came up to Mr. Gale with an explosive, "Hello!"

"Evening, sir."

"You staying with Mrs. Tiffany?"

"Yes, for a while."

"Where do you come from?"

"I'm from Alabama."

"Alabama? Why, gee, then you're a Southerner!"

"I reckon I am, old man."

The small boy looked him all over, dug his toe into the leaf-mold at the edge of the curb, whistled, and burst out, "Aw, gee, you aren't either! You don't wear gray, and you haven't got any darky body servant. I seen lots of Confederuts in the movies, and they always wear gray, and most always they got a body servant, and a big sword with a tossel on it. Have you got a sword with a tossel?"

"No, but I've got a suit of butternuts back home."

"Gee, have you? Say, were you ever a raider?"

"No, but I know lots about raiders, and once I had dinner with Colonel Mosby."

"Gee, did you? Say, what's your name? Say, are you a gen'rul?"

"No, I was a high private. My name is Gale. What is your name, if I may ask you, as one man to another?"

"I'm Jimmy Martin. I live across the street. My dad's got a great big phonograph and seventy records. Were you a high private? How high? Gee, tell me about the raiders!"

"But James, why should a loyal Northerner like you desire to know anything about the rebel horde?"

"Well, you see, I'm the leader of the Boy Scouts, and we haven't any Scout Master, at least we did have, but he moved away, and I have to think up games for the Scouts, and gee, we're awfully tired of discovering the North Pole, and being Red Cross in Belgium, and I always have to be the Eskimos when we discover the North Pole, or they won't play, and I thought maybe we could be raiders and capture a Yankee train."

"Well, you come sit on the porch, James. It occurs to me that you are a new audience for my stories. Let us proceed to defend Richmond, and do a quick dash into Illinois, to our common benefit. Is it a bargain?"

It was, and Jimmy listened, and Mrs. Tiffany came out and listened also and the three lovers of the Heroic Age sat glowing at one another till from across the village street, long and thin and drowsy, came the call, "Jim-m-m-ee Mar-r-r-tin!"

Later, Jimmy's mother was surprised to discover her heir leading a Confederate raid, and she was satisfied only when she was assured that the raid was perfectly proper, because it was led by General Grant, and because all the raiders had voluntarily set free their slaves.

It was Jimmy Martin who enticed Mr. Gale to go spearing pickerel, and they two, the big slow-moving man and the boy who took two skips to his one solid pace, plowed through the willow thickets along the creek all one Saturday afternoon.

At the end of the trip, Jimmy cheerfully announced that he would probably get a whale of a licking, because he ought to have been chopping stovewood. Mr. Gale suggested strategic measures; he sneaked after Jimmy, through a stable door to the Martins' woodshed, and cut wood for an hour, while Jimmy scrabbled to pile it.

In the confidences of Jimmy and in Mrs. Tiffany's stories of her Vermont girlhood and pioneer days in Minnesota, Mr. Gale found those green memories of youth which he had hoped to discover, on coming North, in comradely talks with veterans of the Wakamin G. A. R.

But now there was no G. A. R. at all in Wakamin.

During the past year the local post had been wiped out. Of the four veterans remaining on Decoration Day a year before, three had died and one had gone West to live with his son, as is the Mid-Western way. Of the sturdy old men who had marched fifty strong to Woodlawn Cemetery a decade before, not one old man was left to leaven the land.

But they did live on in Mrs. Tiffany's gossip, as she begged Mr. Gale to assure her that there would be a decorating of the graves, though the comrades were gone. This assurance Mr. Gale always gave, though upon sedulous inquiry at the barber shop he discovered that there was very little chance for a celebration of the Day. The town band had broken up when the barber, who was also the bandleader, had bought a car. The school principal had decided that this year it was not worth while to train the girls to wear red-white-and-blue cheesecloth, and sing "Columbia, the Gem of the Ocean" from a decked-over hay wagon.

Mr. Gale endeavored to approve this passing of Decoration Day. He told himself that he was glad to hear that all of his old enemies had gone. But no matter how often he said it, he couldn't make it stick. He felt that he, too, was a derelict, as he listened to Mrs. Tiffany's timid hopes for a celebration. To her, the Day was the climax of the year, the time when all her comrades, living and dead, drew closer together. She had a dazed faith that there would be some sort of ceremony.

She went on retrimming the blue bonnet which she had always worn in the parade, at the head of the W. R. C. Not till the day before the holiday did she learn the truth. That evening she did not come down to supper. She called in a neighbor's daughter to serve Mr. Gale. The young woman giggled, and asked idiotic questions about Society Folks in the South, till Mr. Gale made his iron-

gray eyebrows a line of defense. He tramped out the road
eastward from town, after supper, growling to himself between periods of vacuous unhappiness:

"Feel's if it's me and the boys I fought with, not them
I fought against, they're going to neglect tomorrow. Those
Yanks were lively youngsters. Made me do some tall
jumping. Hate to think of 'em lying there in the cemetery,
lonely and waiting, trusting that we—that the Dam-
yanks—will remember them. Look here, J. Gale, Esq., you
sentimental old has-been, what do you mean, whimpering
about them? You know good and well you never did like
Yanks—killed your daddy and brother. But—poor old
codgers, waiting out there——"

His walk had brought him to a fenced field. He peered
across. It was set with upright and ghostly stones. He had
come to the cemetery. He stopped, prickly. He heard
creepy murmurs in the dusk. He saw each white stone as
the reproachful spirit of an old soldier robbed of his pension of honor. He turned away with a measured calmness
that was more panicky than a stumbling retreat.

The morning of the empty Decoration Day was radiant
as sunshine upon a beech trunk. But nowhere was the
old-time bustle of schoolgirls in bunting, of mothers preparing lunch baskets, of shabby and halting old civilians
magically transformed into soldiers. A few families mechanically hung out flags. Mrs. Tiffany did not. When Mr.
Gale came down to breakfast he found her caressing an
ancient silken flag. She thrust it into a closet, locked the
door, hastened out to the kitchen. She was slow in the
serving of breakfast, looked dizzy, often pressed her hand
against her side. Mr. Gale begged her to let him help. She
forbade him sternly. She seemed to have a calm and em-
bittered control of herself.

He hastened out of the house. There was no business

to which he could attend on this holiday. He made shameless overtures for the company of Jimmy Martin, who was boisterous over the fact that summer vacation had begun, and his dear, dear teachers gone away. The Martin family was not going to any of the three or four picnics planned for the day, and Jimmy and Mr. Gale considered gravely the possibility of a fishing trip. They sat in canvas chairs on the tiny lawn, and forgot a certain difference in age.

The door of the Tiffany house slammed. They stopped, listened. Nervous footsteps were crossing the porch, coming along the gravel walk. They looked back. Running toward them was Mrs. Tiffany. She wore no hat. Her hair was like a shell-torn flag, thin gray over the yellowed skin of her brow. Her hands dabbled feebly in the air before her glaring eyes. She moaned:

"Oh, Mr. Gale, I can't stand it! Don't they know what they're doing? My boy lies there, my husband, and he's crying for me to come to him and show I remember him. I tell you I can hear him, and his voice sounds like a rainy wind. I told him I'd go to Woodlawn all by myself, I said I'd fill my little basket with flowers, and crabapple blossoms, but he said he wanted the others to come too, he wanted a Decoration Day parade that would honor all the graves. Oh, I heard him——"

Mr. Gale had sprung up. He put his arm about her shoulder. He cried, "There will be a parade, ma'am! We'll remember the boys, every one of them, every grave. You go in the house, honey, and you put on your bonnet, and pack a little sack for you and me to eat after the ceremony, maybe you'll have time to bake a batch of biscuits, but anyway, in an hour or so, maybe hour and a half, you'll hear the parade coming, and you be all ready." Mr. Gale's voice had something of the ponderous integrity of distant cannon. He smoothed her disordered hair. He patted her, like the soft pawing of a fond old dog, and led her to the paint-blistered door of the house.

He went back to his canvas chair, scratching his scalp, shaking his head. Jimmy, who had edged away, returned and sighed, "Gee, I wisht I could do something."

"I bet you would, if you were a little older, James, but —better run away. This old Rebel has got to stir up his sleepy brain and conjure up a Federal parade, with a band and at least twenty flags, out of the sparrows in the street. Good-by."

After five minutes, or it may have been ten, of clawing at his chin, Mr. Gale looked happy. He hastened down the street. He entered the drug store, and from the telephone booth he talked to hotel clerks in three different towns within ten miles of Wakamin.

He hurried to the livery stable which operated the two cars in town that were for hire. One of the cars was out. The second was preparing to leave, as he lumbered up to the door.

"I want that car," he said to the stableman-chauffeur.

"Well, you can't have it." The stableman bent over, to crank up.

"Why not?"

"Because I'm going to take a skirt out for a spin, see?"

"Look here. I'm Mr. Gale who——"

"Aw, I know all about you. Seen you go by. You out-of-town guys think we have to drop everything else just to accommodate you——"

Mr. Gale puffed across the floor like a steam-roller. He said gently, "Son, I've been up all night, and I reckon I've had a lee-tle mite too much liquor. I've taken a fancy to going riding. Son, I've got the peacefulest heart that a grown-up human ever had; I'm like a little playing pussy-cat, I am; but I've got a gun in my back pocket that carries the meanest .44-40 bullet in the South. Maybe you've heard about us Southern fire-eaters, heh? Son, I only want that car for maybe two hours. Understand?"

He bellowed. He was making vast, vague, loosely swinging gestures, his perspiring hands very red. He caught the stableman by the shoulder. The man's Adam's apple worked grotesquely up and down. He whimpered:

"All right. I'll take you."

Mr. Gale pacifically climbed into the car. "Joralemon, son, and fast, son, particular fast," he murmured.

In the speeding car he meditated: "Let's see. Must be forty years since I've toted any kind of a gun—and twenty years since I've called anybody 'son.' Oh, well."

Again, "Let's see. I'll be a Major. No, a Colonel; Colonel Gale of the Tenth New York. Private Gale, I congratulate you. I reckon the best you ever got from a darky was 'Cap'n' or 'boss.' You're rising in the world, my boy. Poor woman! Poor, faithful woman——"

When they reached the town of Joralemon, Mr. Gale leaned out from the car and inquired of a corner loafer, "Where's the Decoration Day parade? The G. A. R.?"

"At the exercises in Greenwood Cemetery."

"Greenwood, son," he blared, and the stableman made haste.

At the entrance to the cemetery Mr. Gale insinuated, "Now wait till I come back, son. I'm getting over that liquor, and I'm ugly, son, powerful ugly."

"All right," growled the stableman. "Say, do I get paid——?"

"Here's five dollars. When I come back with my friends, there'll be another five. I'm going to steal a whole Decoration Day parade."

"How?"

"I'm going to surround them."

"My—Gawd!" whispered the stableman.

The Southerner bristled at the sight of the Northern regimental flag among the trees of the cemetery. But he shrugged his shoulders and waddled into the crowd. The morning's radiance brought out in hot primary colors the red and yellow of flowers in muddy glass vases upon the graves. Light flashed from the mirrory brown surfaces of polished granite headstones, with inscriptions cut in painfully white letters. The air was thick with the scent of dust and maple leaves and packed people. Round a clergyman in canonicals were the eight veterans now left in Joralemon; men to whose scrawny faces a dignity was given by their symbolic garb. From their eyes was purged all the meanness of daily grinding. The hand of a sparse-bearded Yankee, who wore an English flag pinned beside his G. A. R. button, was resting on the shoulder of a Teutonic-faced man with the emblem of the Sigel Corps.

Round the G. A. R. were ringed the Sons of Veterans, the Hose and Truck Company, the Women's Relief Corps, and the Joralemon Band; beyond them a great press of townspeople. The road beside the cemetery was packed with cars and buggies, and the stamp of horses' feet as they restlessly swished at flies gave a rustic rhythm to the pause in the clergyman's voice.

Here in a quiet town, unconscious of the stir of the world beyond, was renewed the passion of their faith in the Union.

Mr. Gale shoved forward into the front row. Everyone glared at the pushing stranger. The voice of the gray, sunken-templed clergyman sharpened with indignation for a second. Mr. Gale tried to look unconcerned. But he felt hot about the spine. The dust got into his throat. The people about him were elbowing and sticky. He was not happy. But he vowed, "By thunder, I'll pull this off if I have to kidnap the whole crowd."

As the clergyman finished his oration, Mr. Gale pushed among the G. A. R. He began loudly, cheerfully, "Gentlemen——"

The clergyman stared down from his box rostrum. "What do you mean, interrupting this ceremony?"

The crowd was squeezing in, like a street mob about a man found murdered. Their voices united in a swelling whisper. Their gaping mouths were ugly. Mr. Gale was rigid with the anger that wipes out all fear of a crowd, and leaves a man facing them as though they were one contemptible opponent.

"Look here," he bawled, "I had proposed to join you in certain memorial plans. It may interest you to know that I am Colonel John Gale, and that I led the Tenth New York through most of the war!"

"Ah," purred the clergyman, "you are Colonel—Gale, is it?"

"I am." The clergyman licked his lips. With fictitious jocularity Mr. Gale said, "I see you do not salute your superior officer. But I reckon a dominie isn't like us old soldiers. Now, boys, listen to me. There's a little woman——"

The clergyman's voice cut in on this lumbering amiability as a knife cuts butter: "My dear sir, I don't quite understand the reason for this farce. I am a 'dominie,' as you are pleased to call it, but also I am an old soldier, the present commander of this post, and it may 'interest you to know' that I fought clear through the war in the Tenth New York! And if my memory is still good, you were not my commanding officer for any considerable period!"

"No!" bellowed Mr. Gale, "I wa'n't! I'm a Southerner.

From Alabama. And after today I'm not even sure I'm reconstructed! I'm powerful glad I never was a blue-bellied Yank, when I think of that poor little woman dying of a broken heart up in Wakamin!"

With banal phrases and sentimental touches, with simple words and no further effort to be friendly, he told the story of Mrs. Captain Tiffany, though he did not satisfy the beggar ears of the crowd with her name.

His voice was at times almost hostile. "So," he wound up, "I want you-all to come to Wakamin and decorate the graves there, too. You, my dear sir, I don't care a damaged Continental whether you ever salute me or not. If you boys do come to Wakamin, then I'll know there's still some *men*, as there were in the '60's. But if you eight or nine great big husky young Yanks are afraid of one poor old lone Johnny Reb, then by God, sir, I win another scrimmage for the Confederate States of America!"

Silence. Big and red, Mr. Gale stood among them like a sandstone boulder. His eyes were steady and hard as his clenched fist. But his upper lip was trembling and covered with a triple row of sweat drops.

Slowly, as in the fumbling stupor of a trance, the clergyman drew off his canonicals and handed them to a boy. He was formal and thin and rather dry of aspect in his black frock coat. His voice was that of a tired, polite old gentleman, as he demanded of Mr. Gale, "Have you a car to take us to Wakamin?"

"Room for five."

To a man beside him the clergyman said, "Will you have another car ready for us?" Abruptly his voice snapped: "'Tention. Fall in. Form twos. B' th' right flank. For'ard. March!"

As he spoke he leaped down into the ranks, and the veterans tramped toward the gate of the cemetery, through the parting crowd. Their faces were blurred with weariness and dust and age, but they stared straight ahead, they marched stolidly, as though they had been ordered to occupy a dangerous position and were too fagged to be afraid.

The two rear-line men struck up with fife and drum. The fifer was a corpulent banker, but he tootled with the agility of a boy. The drummer was a wisp of humanity. Though his clay-hued hands kept up with the capering of "When Johnny Comes Marching Home Again," his yellowish eyes were opening in an agonized stare, and his chin trembled.

"Halt!" the clergyman ordered. "Boys, seems to me the commander of this expedition ought to be Colonel Gale. Colonel, will you please take command of the post?"

"W—why, I wouldn't hardly call it regular."

"You old Rebel, I wouldn't call any of this regular!"

"Yes," said Mr. Gale. "'Tention!"

The old drummer, his eyes opening wider and wider, sank forward from the knees, and held himself up only by trembling bent arms. Two men in the crowd caught him. "Go on!" he groaned. His drumsticks clattered on the ground.

Uneasily exchanging glances, the other old men waited. Each face said, "Risky business. Hot day. We might collapse, too."

The clergyman slipped the drum belt over his own head, picked up the sticks. "Play, confound you, Lanse!" he snapped at the pompous banker-fifer, and together they rolled into a rude version of "Marching Through Georgia."

The squad straightened its lines and marched on without even an order from Mr. Gale, who, at the head of the procession, was marveling, "I never did expect to march to that tune!"

The two motor cars shot from Joralemon to Wakamin, with steering wheels wrenching and bucking on the sandy road, and old men clinging to seat-edge and robe-rack. They stopped before the Tiffany cottage.

Mrs. Tiffany sat on the porch, her blue bonnet lashed to her faded hair, with a brown veil, a basket of flowers and a shoe-box of lunch on her knees. As the cars drew up, she rushed out, with flustered greetings. The old men greeted her elaborately. One, who had known Captain Tiffany, became the noisy spokesman. But he had little of which to speak. And the whole affair suddenly became a vacuous absurdity. Now that Mr. Gale had them here, what was he going to do with them?

The quiet of the village street flowed over them. This was no parade; it was merely nine old men and an old woman talking in the dust. There was no music, no crowd of spectators, none of the incitements of display which turn the ordinary daily sort of men into one marching thrill. They were old, and tired, and somewhat hungry, and no one saw them as heroes. A small automobile passed; the occupants scarce looked at them.

The unparading parade looked awkward, tried to keep up brisk talk, and became dull in the attempt.

They were engulfed in the indifferent calm of the day. After the passing of the one automobile, there was no one to be seen. The box-elder trees nodded slowly. Far off a rooster crowed, once. In a vacant lot near by a cud-chewing cow stared at them dumb and bored. Little sounds of insects in the grass underlaid the silence with a creeping sleepiness. The village street, stretching out toward the wheat fields beyond, grew hotter and more hazy to their old eyes. They all stood about the cars, plucking at hinges and door-edges, wondering how they could give up this childish attempt and admit that they

were grannies. A sparrow hopped among them uncon-
cernedly.

"Well?" said the clergyman.

"Wel-l——" said Mr. Gale.

Then Jimmy Martin strolled out in front of his house.
He saw them. He stopped short. He made three jubilant
skips, and charged on them.

"Are you going to parade?" he shrilled at Mr. Gale.

"Afraid not, Jimmy. Reckon we haven't quite got the
makings. The young people don't appear to care. Reckon
we'll give up."

"No, no, no!" Jimmy wailed. "The Scouts want to
come!"

He dashed into his house, while the collapsed parade
stared after him with mild elderly wonder. He came back
to the gate. He wore a Boy Scout uniform and a red
neckerchief, and he carried a cheap bugle.

He stood at the gate, his eyes a glory, and he blew the
one bugle call he knew—the Reveille. Wavering at first,
harsh and timorous, the notes crept among the slumber-
ous trees, then swelled, loud, madly imploring, shaking
with a boy's worship of the heroes.

Another boy ran out from a gate down the street, looked,
came running, stumbling, panting. He was bare headed,
in corduroy knickers unbuckled at the knees, but in his
face was the same ageless devotion that had made a splendor of the mere boys who marched out in '64 and '65. He
saluted Jimmy. Jimmy spoke, and the two of them, curiously dignified, very earnest, marched out before the scat-
ter of old people and stood at attention, their serious faces
toward Woodlawn and the undecked graves.

From a box-elder down the street climbed another boy;
one popped out of a crabapple orchard; a dozen others from
drowsy distances. They scurried like suddenly disturbed

ants. They could be heard calling, clattering into houses. They came out again in Scout uniforms; they raced down the street and fell into line.

They stood with clean backs rigid, eyes forward, waiting to obey orders. As he looked at them, Mr. Gale knew that some day Wakamin would again have a soul.

Jimmy Martin came marching up to Mr. Gale. His voice was plaintive and reedy, but it was electric as he reported: "The Boy Scouts are ready, sir."

"'Tention!" shouted Mr. Gale.

The old men's backs had been straightening, the rheumy redness of disappointment had gone from their eyes. They lined out behind the boys. Even the Wakamin stableman seemed to feel inspiration. He sprang from his car, helped Mrs. Tiffany in, and wheeled the car to join the procession. From nowhere, from everywhere, a crowd had come, and stood on the sidewalk, rustling with faint cheering. Two women hastened to add flowers to those in Mrs. Tiffany's basket. The benumbed town had awakened to energy and eagerness and hope.

To the clergyman Mr. Gale suggested, "Do you suppose that just for once this Yankee fife-and-drum corps could play 'Dixie'?" Instantly the clergyman-drummer and the banker-fifer flashed into "Way Down South in the Land of Cotton." The color-bearer raised the flag.

Mr. Gale roared, "Forward! M——"

There was a high wail from Mrs. Tiffany: "Wait! Land o' goodness! What's Decoration Day without one single sword, and you menfolks never thinking——"

She ran into her house. She came out bearing in her two hands, as though it were an altar vessel, the saber of Captain Tiffany.

"Mr. Gale, will you carry a Northerner's sword?" she asked.

"No, ma'am, I won't!"

She gasped.

He buckled on the sword belt, and cried, "This isn't a Northerner's sword any more, nor a Southerner's, ma'am. It's an American's! Forward! March!"

MOTHS IN THE ARC LIGHT

MOTHS IN THE ARC LIGHT

Bates lay staring at the green-shaded light on his desk and disgustedly he realized that he must have been sleeping there for hours on the leather couch in his office. His eyes were peppery, his mouth dry. He rose, staggering with the burden of drowsiness, and glanced at his watch. It was three in the morning.

"Idiot!" he said.

He wreathed to the window, twelve stories above the New York pavements. The stupidity that lay over his senses like uncombed wool was blown away as he exulted in the beauty of the city night. It was as nearly quiet now as Manhattan ever becomes. Stilled were the trolleys and the whang of steel beams in the new building a block away. One taxicab bumbled on the dark pavement beneath. Bates looked across a swamp of roofs to East River, to a line of topaz lights arching over a bridge. The sky was not dark but of a luminous blue—a splendid, aspiring, naked blue, in which the stars hung golden.

"But why shouldn't I fall asleep here? I'll finish the night on the couch, and get after the New Bedford specifications before breakfast. I've never spent twenty-four hours in the office before. I'll do it!"

He said it with the pride of a successful man. But he ended, as he rambled back to the couch and removed his coat and shoes: "Still, I do wish there were somebody who cared a hang whether I came home or stayed away for a week!"

When the earliest stenographer arrived she found Bates at work. But often he was first at the office. No one knew of his discovery that before dawn the huckstering city is enchanted to blue and crocus yellow above shadowy roofs. He had no one who would ever encourage him to tell about it.

To Bates at thirty-five the world was composed of re-enforced concrete; continents and striding seas were office partitions and inkwells, the latter for signing letters beginning "In reply to your valued query of seventh inst." Not for five years had he seen storm clouds across the hills or moths that flutter white over dusky meadows. To him the arc light was the dancing place for moths, and flowers grew not in pastures but in vases on restaurant tables. He was a city man and an office man. Papers, telephone calls, eight-thirty to six on the twelfth floor, were the natural features of life, and the glory and triumph of civilization was getting another traction company to introduce the Carstop Indicator.

But he belonged to the new generation of business men. He was not one of the race who boast that they have had "mighty little book learning," and who cannot be pictured without their derby hats, whether they are working, motoring, or in bed. Bates was slender, immaculate, polite as a well-bred woman, his mustache like a penciled eyebrow; yet in decision he was firm as a chunk of flint.

When he had come to New York from college Bates had

believed that he was going to lead an existence of polite
society and the opera. He had in fourteen years been to
the opera six times. He dined regularly with acquaintances
at the Yale Club, he knew two men in his bachelor
apartment building by their first names, and he attended
subscription dances and was agreeable to young women
who had been out for three years. But New York is a thief
of friends. Because in one night at a restaurant you may
meet twenty new people therefore in one day shall you also
lose twenty older friends. You know a man and like him;
he marries and moves to Great Neck; you see him once in
two years. After thirty Bates was increasingly absorbed
in the one thing that always wanted him, that appreciated
his attention—the office.

He had gone from a motor company to the Carstop
Indicator Company. He had spent a year in the Long
Island City factory which manufactures the indicators
for the Eastern trade. He had worked out an improvement
in the automatic tripping device. At thirty-five he was a
success. Yet he never failed when he was dining alone to
wish that he was to call on a girl who was worth calling
on.

After fourteen years of the candy-gobbling, cabaret-
curious, nice-man-hunting daughters of New York, Bates
had become unholily cautious. His attitude to the average
débutante was that of an aviator to an anti-aircraft shell.
And he was equally uncomfortable with older, more earnest women. They talked about economics. Bates had read
a book all about economics shortly after graduation, but
as he could never quite remember the title it didn't help
him much in earnest conversations. He preferred to talk
to his stenographer. He mentioned neither wine suppers
nor her large black eyes. "Has the draftsman sent over the
blue prints for Camden?" he said. Or: "Might hurry up

the McGulden correspondence." That was real conversation. It got somewhere.

Then he began to talk to the girl in the building across the street.

That building was his scenery. He watched it as an old maid behind a lace curtain gapes at every passer-by on her village street. It had the charm of efficiency that is beginning to make American cities beautiful with a beauty that borrows nothing from French châteaux or English inns. The architect had supposed that he was planning neither a hotel nor a sparrow's paradise, but a place for offices. He had left off the limestone supporting caps that don't support anything, and the marble plaques which are touchingly believed to imitate armorial shields but which actually resemble enlarged shaving mugs. He had created a building as clean and straight and honest as the blade of a sword. It made Bates glad that he was a business man.

So much of the building opposite was of glass that the offices were as open to observation as the coops at a dog show. Bates knew by sight every man and woman in twenty rooms. From his desk he could not see the building, but when he was tired it was his habit to loaf by the window for a moment. He saw the men coming in at eight-thirty or nine, smoking and chatting before they got to work, settling at desks, getting up stiffly at lunch-time, and at closing hour, dulled to silence, snapping out the lights before they went home. When he worked late at night Bates was saved from loneliness by the consciousness of the one or two men who were sure to be centered under desk lights in offices across the way.

He sympathized with the office boy at whom the red-mustached boss was always snarling in the eleventh-floor office on the right, and was indignant at the boy he saw

stealing stamps on the thirteenth. He laughed over a clerk
on the eleventh changing into evening clothes at six—
hopping on one leg to keep his trousers off the floor, and
solemnly taking dress tie and collar from the top drawer
of his desk. And it was a personal sorrow when tragedy
came to his village; when the pretty, eager secretary of the
manager in the twelfth-floor office exactly opposite was
missing for several days, and one morning a funeral wreath
was laid on her desk by the window.

The successor of the dead girl must have come immediately, but Bates did not notice her for a week. It was
one of those weeks when he was snatched from Task A to
Task B, and from B to hustle out C, when the salesman out
on the road couldn't sell milk to a baby, when the telephone rang or a telegram came just as Bates thought he
had a clear moment, when he copied again every night the
list of things he ought to have done day before yesterday,
and his idea of heaven was a steel vault without telephone
connection. But at the end of the storm he had nothing to
do except to try to look edifyingly busy, and to amble
round and watch the stenographers stenograph and the
office boy be officious.

He sat primly lounging in the big chair by the window,
smoking a panetela and unconsciously gazing at the building across the street. He half observed that the manager
in the office just opposite was dictating to a new secretary,
a slim girl in blue taffeta with crisp white collar and cuffs.
She did not slop over the desk tablet, yet she did not sit
grimly, like the oldish stenographer in the office just above
her. She seemed at the distance to be unusually businesslike. In all the hive that was laid open to Bates' observation she was distinguished by her erect, charming
shoulders, her decisive step, as she was to be seen leaving

the manager's desk, going through the partition—which to Bates' eye was an absurdly thin sheet of oak and glass— hastening to her typewriter, getting to work.

Bates forgot her; but at dusk, spring dusk, when he stood by his window, late at the office yet with nothing to do, enervated with soft melancholy because there was no place he wanted to go that evening, he noticed her again. Her chief and she were also staying late. Bates saw them talking; saw the chief sign a pile of correspondence, give it to her, nod, take his derby, yawn and plunge out into the general office, heading for the elevator. The secretary briskly carried away the correspondence. But she stopped at her desk beside a window. She pressed her eyes with her hand, passed it across them with the jerky motion of a medium coming out of a trance.

"Poor tired eyes!" Bates heard himself muttering.

No scent of blossoms nor any sound of eager birds reached the cement streets from the spring-flushed country, but there was restlessness in the eternal clatter, and as the darkening silhouette of the building opposite cut the reflected glow in the eastern sky his melancholy became a pain of emptiness. He yearned across to the keen-edged girl and imagined himself talking to her. In five minutes she was gone, but he remained at the window, then drooped slowly up to the Yale Club for dinner.

Doubtless Bates' life was making him selfish, but that evening while he was being incredibly bored at a musical comedy he did think of her, and for a second hoped that her eyes were rested.

He looked for her next morning as soon as he reached the office, and was displeased with the entire arrangement of the heavenly bodies because the light wasn't so good across there in the morning as in the afternoon.

Not till three o'clock was he certain that she was wearing what appeared to be a waist of corn-colored rough silk, and that for all her slight nervousness her throat was full and smooth. Last night he had believed her twenty-eight. He promoted her to twenty-three.

He sighed: "Capable-looking young woman. Wish my secretary were as interested in her work. She walks with—well, graceful. Now who can I get hold of for dinner to-night?"

II

He saw her coming in at nine o'clock; saw her unpin her hat and swiftly arrange her hair before her reflection in the ground glass of the partition. He saw her take morning dictation; bring customers in to the boss. He saw her slipping out to lunch, alone, at noon. He saw her quick, sure movements slacken as the afternoon became long and weary. He saw her preparing to go home at night, or staying late, even her straight shoulders hunched as she heavily picked out the last words on her typewriter. All through the day he followed her, and though he knew neither her name nor her origin, though he had never heard her voice, yet he understood this girl better than at marriage most men understand the women they marry.

The other people in her office treated her with respect. They bowed to her at morning, at night. They never teased her, as the fluffy telephone girl was teased. That interested Bates, but for many weeks she was no part of his life.

On an afternoon in early summer, when his hands were twitching and his eyeballs were hot coals from too-constant study of specifications, when everybody in the world seemed to be picking at his raw nerves and he longed for someone who would care for him, who would bathe his eyes and divert his mind from the rows of figures that danced blood-red against darkness as he closed his stinging lids, then he caught himself deliberately seeking the window, passionately needing a last glimpse of her as the one human being whom he really knew.

"Confound her, if she isn't over there I'll—well, I won't go home till she is!"

She was by the window, reading a letter. She looked up, caught him staring at her. It was a very dignified Mr. Bates who plumped on his hat and stalked away. Obviously he would never do anything so low as to spy on offices across the street! The word stuck in his mind, and scratched it. Certainly he had never spied, he declared in a high manner as he fumbled at a steak minute that was exactly like all the ten thousand steaks minute he had endured at restaurants. Well, he'd take care that no one ever came in and misunderstood his reflective resting by the window. He would never glance at that building again!

And so at nine o'clock next morning, with three telegrams and an overdue letter from Birmingham Power and Traction unopened on his desk, he was peering across the street and admiring a new hat, a Frenchy cornucopia with fold above fold of pale-blue straw, which the girl was removing from her sleek hair.

There are several ways of stopping smoking. You can hide your tobacco in a drawer in the next room, and lock the drawer, and hide the key. You can keep a schedule of the number of times you smoke. You can refuse to buy cigarettes, and smoke only those you can cadge from friends. These methods are all approved by the authorities, and there is only one trouble with them—not one of them makes you stop smoking.

There are also numerous ways of keeping from studying the architecture of buildings across the street. You can be scornful, or explain to yourself that you don't know anything about employees of other offices, and don't want to know anything. You can relax by sitting on the couch instead of standing by the window. The only trouble with these mental exercises is that you continue to find yourself gaping at the girl across and——

And you feel like a spy when you catch her in self-betrayals that pinch your heart. She marches out of the manager's office, cool, competent, strong, then droops by her desk and for a strained moment sits with thin fingers pressed to her pounding temples.

Every time she did that Bates forgot his coy games. His spirit sped across the cañon and hovered about her, roused from the nagging worries about business and steaks minute and musical comedies which had come to be his most precious concerns. With agitating clearness he could feel his finger tips caressing her forehead, feel the sudden cold of evaporation on his hand as he bathed the tired, cramped back of her neck with alcohol.

He gave up his highly gentlemanly effort not to spy. He wondered if perhaps there wasn't something to all these metaphysical theories, if he wasn't sending currents of friendship across to cheer her frail, brave spirit in its fight to be businesslike. He forgot that he was as visible at his window as she at hers. So it happened that one evening when he was frankly staring at the girl she caught him, and turned her head away with a vexed jerk.

Bates was hurt because he had hurt her. He who had regarded life only from the standpoint of Bates, bachelor, found himself thinking through her, as though his mind had been absorbed in hers. With a shock of pain he could feel her lamenting that it was bad enough to be under the business strain all day, without being exposed to ogling in her house of glass. He wanted to protect her—from himself.

For a week he didn't once stand by the window, even to

look down at the street, twelve stories below, which he had watched as from his mountain shack a quizzical hermit might con the life of the distant valley. He missed the view, and he was glad to miss it. He was actually giving up something for somebody. He felt human again.

Though he did not stand by the window it was surprising how many times a day he had to pass it, and how innocently he caught glimpses of the life across the way. More than once he saw her looking at him. Whenever she glanced up from work her eyes seemed drawn to his. But not flirtatiously, he believed. In the distance she seemed aloof as the small cold winter moon.

There was another day that was a whirl of craziness. Everybody wanted him at once. Telegrams crossed each other. The factory couldn't get materials. Two stenographers quarreled, and both of them quit, and the typewriter agency from which he got his girls had no one to send him just then save extremely alien enemies who confounded typewriters with washing machines. When the office was quiet and there was only about seven more hours of work on his desk, he collapsed. His lax arms fell beside him. He panted slowly. His spinning head drooped and his eyes were blurred.

"Oh, buck up!" he growled.

He lifted himself to his feet, slapped his arms, found himself at the window. Across there she was going home. Involuntarily—looking for a greeting from his one companion in work—he threw up his arm in a wave of farewell.

She saw it. She stood considering him, her two hands up to her head as she pinned her hat. But she left the window without a sign. Suddenly he was snapping: "I'll make you notice me! I'm not a noon-hour window flirt! I won't stand your thinking I am!"

With a new energy of irritation he went back. Resting

his eyes every quarter of an hour he sat studying a legal claim, making notes. It was eight—nine—ten. He was faint, yet not hungry. He rose. He was surprised to find himself happy. He hunted for the source of the glow, and found it. He was going to draw that frosty moon of a girl down to him.

In the morning when he came in he hastened to the window and waited till she raised her head. He waved—a quick, modest, amiable gesture. Every morning and evening after that he sent across his pleading signal. She never answered but she observed him and—well, she never pulled down the window shade.

His vacation was in July. Without quite knowing why, he did not want to go to the formal seaside hotel at which he usually spent three weeks in being polite to aunts in their nieces' frocks, and in discovering that as a golfer he was a good small-boat sailor. He found himself heading for the Lebanon Valley, which is the valley of peace; and he discovered that yellow cream and wild blackberries and cowslips and the art of walking without panting still exist. He wore soft shirts and became tanned; he stopped worrying about the insolvency of the Downstate Interurban Company, and was even heard to laugh at the landlord's stories.

At least a tenth of his thoughts were devoted to planning a vacation for the girl across. She should lie with nervous fingers relaxed among the long-starred grasses, and in the cornflower blue of the sky and comic plump white clouds find healing. After arranging everything perfectly he always reminded himself that she probably hadn't been with her firm long enough to have earned more than a five-day vacation, and with etched scorn he pointed out that he was a fool to think about a girl of whom he knew only that:

She seemed to take dictation quickly.

She walked gracefully.

She appeared at a distance to have delicate oval cheeks.

She was between sixteen and forty.

She was not a man.

About Article Five, he was sure.

He was so strong-minded and practical with himself that by the end of his holidays the girl was cloudy in his mind. He was cured of sentimentalizing. He regarded with amusement his reënforced-concrete romance, his moth dance under the arc light's sterile glare. He would—oh, he'd call on Christine Parrish when he got back. Christine was the sister of a classmate of his; she danced well and said the right things about Park Avenue and the Washington Square Players.

He got back to town on Monday evening, just at closing time. He ran up to his office, to announce his return. He dashed into his private room—less dashingly to the window. The girl across was thumbing a book, probably finding a telephone number. She glanced up, raising a finger toward her lips. Then his hat was off, and he was bowing, waving. She sat with her half-raised hand suspended. Suddenly she threw it up in a flickering gesture of welcome.

Bates sat at his desk. The members of his staff as they came in to report—or just to be tactful and remind the chief of their valuable existence—had never seen him so cheerful. When they were gone he tried to remember what it was he had planned to do. Oh, yes; call up Christine Parrish. Let it go. He'd do it some other night. He went to the window. The girl was gone, but the pale ghost of her gesture seemed to glimmer in the darkening window.

He dined at the new Yale Club, and sat out on the roof after dinner with a couple of temporary widowers and Bunk Selby's kid brother, who had graduated in the spring. The city beneath them flared like burning grass.

Broadway was a streak of tawny fire; across the East
River a blast furnace stuttered flames; the Biltmore and
Ritz and Manhattan, the Belmont and Grand Central
Station were palaces more mysterious in their flashing
first stories, their masses of shadow, their splashes of
white uplifted wall, than Venice on carnival night. Bates
loved the hot beauty of his city; he was glad to be back;
he didn't exactly know why, but the coming fall and
winter gave promise of endless conquest and happiness.
Not since he had first come to the city had he looked forward so exultantly. Now, as then, the future was not all
neatly listed, but chaotic and trembling with adventure.

All he said to the men smoking with him was "Good
vacation—fine loaf." Or, "Got any money on copper?"

But they looked at him curiously.

"You sound as though you'd had a corking time. What
you been doing? Licking McLoughlin at tennis or something?"

Bunk Selby's kid brother, not having been out of college long enough to have become reliable and stupid, ventured: "Say, Bunk, I bet your young friend Mr. Bates is
in love!"

"Huh!" said Bunk with married fatness. "Batesy?
Never! He's the buds' best bunker."

III

At two minutes of nine the next morning Bates was at
the window. To him entered his stenographer, bearing
mail.

"Oh, leave it on the desk," he complained.

At one minute past nine the girl across could be seen in
the general office, coming out of the dimness to her window. He waved his arm. She sent back the greeting. Then

she turned her back on him. But he went at his mail
humming.

She always answered after that, and sometimes during
the day she swiftly peered at him. It was only a curt, quick
recognition, but when he awoke he looked forward to it.
His rusty imagination creaking, he began to make up
stories about her. He was convinced that whatever she
might be she was different from the good-natured, commonplace women in his own office. She was a mystery.
She had a family. He presented her with a father of lean
distinction, hawk nose, classical learning—and the most
alarming inability to stick to the job, being in various
versions a bishop, a college president, and a millionaire who
had lost his money.

He decided that she was named Emily, because Emily
meant all the things that typewriters and filing systems
failed to mean. Emily connoted lavender-scented chests,
old brocade, and twilit gardens brimmed with dewy,
damask roses, spacious halls of white paneling, and books
by the fire. Always it was Bates who restored her to the
spacious halls, the brocade, and the arms of her bishop-
professor-millionaire father.

There was one trouble with his fantasy: He didn't dare
see her closer than across the street, didn't dare hear her
voice, for fear the first sacred words of the lady of the
damask roses might be: "Say, listen! Are you the fella
that's been handing me the double O? Say, you got your
nerve!"

Once when he was sailing out of the street entrance,
breezy and prosperous, he realized that she was emerging
across the way, and he ducked back into the hall. It was
not hard to avoid her. The two buildings were great towns.
There were two thousand people in Bates' building, per-

haps three thousand in hers; and in the streams that tumbled through the doorways at night the individual people were as unrecognizable as in the mad passing of a retreating brigade.

It was late October when he first definitely made out her expression, first caught her smile across the chill and empty air that divided them. In these shortening days the electric lights were on before closing time, and in their radiance he could see her more clearly than by daylight.

In the last mail came a letter from the home office, informing him with generous praise that his salary was increased a thousand a year. All the world knows that vice presidents are not like office boys; they do not act ignorantly when they get a raise. But it is a fact that, after galloping to the door to see whether anybody was coming in, Bates did a foxtrot three times about his desk. He rushed to the window. Four times he had to visit it before she glanced up. He caught her attention by waving the letter. Her face was only half toward him, but he could make out her profile, gilded by the light over her desk. He held out the letter and with his forefinger traced each line, as though he were reading it to her. When he had finished he clapped his hands and whooped.

The delicate still lines of her face wrinkled; her lips parted; she was smiling, nodding, clapping her hands.

"She—she—she understands things!" crowed Bates.

He had noted that often instead of going out she ate a box lunch at her desk, meditatively looking down to the street as she munched a cake; that on Friday—either the office busy day or the day when her week's salary had almost run out—she always stayed in, and that she lunched at twelve. One Friday in early winter he had the housekeeper at his bachelor apartments prepare sandwiches, with coffee in a vacuum bottle. He knew that his subordinates, with their inevitable glad interest in any eccentricities of the chief, would wonder at his lunching in.

"None of their business, anyway!" he said feebly. But he observed to his stenographer: "What a rush! Guess I won't go out for lunch." He strolled past the desk of young Crackins, the bookkeeper, whom he suspected of being the office wit and of collecting breaks on the part of the boss as material for delicious scandal.

"Pretty busy, Crackins? Well, so am I. Fact, I don't think I'll go out to lunch. Just have a bite here."

Having provided dimmers for the fierce light that beats about a glass-topped desk he drew a straight chair to the window and spread his feast on the broad sill at a few minutes after twelve. Emily was gnawing a doughnut and drinking a glass of milk. He bowed, but he inoffensively nibbled half a sandwich before he got over his embarrassment and ventured to offer her a bite. She was motionless, the doughnut gravely suspended in air. She sprang up—left the window.

"Curse it, double curse it! Fool! Beast! Couldn't even let her eat lunch in peace! Intruding on her—spoiling her leisure."

Emily had returned to the window. She showed him a small water glass. She half filled it with milk from her own glass, and diffidently held it out. He rose and extended his hand for it. Across the windy space he took her gift and her greeting.

He laughed; he fancied that she was laughing back, though he could see her face only as a golden blur in the thin fall sunshine. They settled down, sharing lunches. He was insisting on her having another cup of coffee when he was conscious that the door to his private room had opened, that someone was entering.

Frantically he examined a number of imaginary specks on his cup. He didn't dare turn to see who the intruder was. He held up the cup, ran a finger round the edge and muttered "Dirty!" The intruder pattered beside him. Bates looked up at him innocently. It was Crackins, the office tease. And Crackins was grinning.

"Hair in the soup, Mr. Bates?"

"In the—— Oh! Oh, yes. Hair in the soup. Yes. Dirty —dirty cup—have speak—speak housekeeper," Bates burbled.

"Do you mind my interrupting you? I wanted to ask you about the Farmers' Rail-line credit. They're three weeks behind in payment——"

Did Bates fancy it or was Crackins squinting through the window at Emily? With an effusiveness that was as appropriate to him as a mandolin to an Irish contractor, Bates bobbed up and led Crackin back to the main office. He couldn't get away for ten minutes. When he returned Emily was leaning against the window jamb and he saw her by a leaded casement in the bishop's mansion, dreaming on hollyhocks and sundial below.

She pantomimed the end of her picnic; turned her small black lunch box upside down and spread her hands with a plaintive gesture of "All gone!" He offered her coffee, sandwiches, a bar of chocolate; but she refused each with a shy, quick shake of her head. She pointed at her typewriter, waved once, and was back at work.

As Christmas approached, as New York grew so friendly that men nodded to people who hadn't had the flat next door for more than seven years, Bates wondered if Emily's Christmas would be solitary. He tried to think of a way to send her a remembrance. He couldn't. But on the day before he brought an enormous wreath to the office, and waited till he caught her eye. Not till four-thirty, when the lights were on, did he succeed. He hung the wreath at the window and bowed to her, one hand on his heart, the other out in salutation.

Snow flew through the cold void between them and among cliffs of concrete and steel ran the icy river of December air, but they stood together as a smile transfigured her face—face of a gold-wreathed miniature on warm old ivory, tired and a little sad, but tender with her Christmas smile.

IV

She was gone, and he needed her. She had been absent a week now, this evening of treacherous melancholy. Winter had grown old and tedious and hard to bear; the snow that had been jolly in December was a filthy smear in February. Had there ever been such a thing as summer— ever been a time when the corners had not been foul with slush and vexatious with pouncing wind? He was tired of shows and sick of dances, and with a warm personal hatred he hated all the people from out of town who had come to New York for the winter and crowded the New Yorkers out of their favorite dens in tea rooms and grills.

And Emily had disappeared. He didn't know whether she had a new job or was lying sick in some worn-carpeted room, unattended, desperate. And he couldn't find out. He didn't know her name.

Partly because he dreaded what might happen to her, partly because he needed her, he was nervously somber as he looked across to her empty window tonight. The street below was a crazy tumult, a dance of madmen on a wet pavement purple from arc lights—frenzied bells of surface cars, impatient motors, ripping taxis, home-hungry people tumbling through the traffic or standing bewildered in the midst of it, expecting to be killed, shivering and stamping wet feet. A late-working pneumatic riveter punctured his nerves with its unresting r-r-r-r—the grinding machine of a gigantic dentist. The sky was wild, the jagged clouds rushing in panic, smeared with the dull red of afterglow. Only her light, across, was calm—and she was not there.

"I can't stand it! I've come to depend on her. I didn't know I could miss anybody like this. I wasn't living—then. Something has happened to me. I don't understand! I don't understand!" he said.

She was back next morning. He couldn't believe it. He kept returning to make sure, and she always waved, and he was surprised to see how humbly grateful he was for that recognition. She pantomimed coughing for him, and with a hand on her brow indicated that she had had fever. He inquiringly laid his cheek on his hand in the universal sign for going to bed. She nodded—yes, she had been abed with a cold.

As he left the window he knew that sooner or later he must meet her, even if she should prove to be the sort who would say "Listen, kiddo!" He couldn't risk losing her again. Only—well, there was no hurry. He wanted to be sure he wasn't ridiculous. Among the people he knew the greatest rule of life was never to be ridiculous.

He had retired from the window in absurd envy because the men and girls in the office across were shaking Emily's hand, welcoming her back. He began to think about them and about her office. He hadn't an idea what the business of the office was—whether they sold oil stock or carrier pigeons or did blackmail. It was too modern to have lettering on the windows. There were blue prints to be seen on the walls, but they might indicate architecture, machinery—anything.

He began to watch her office mates more closely, and took the most querulous likes and dislikes. Her boss—he was a decent chap; but that filing girl, whom he had caught giggling at Emily's aloof way, she was a back-alley cat, and Bates had a back-alley desire to slap her.

He was becoming a clumsy sort of mystic in his aching care for her. When he waved good-night he was sending her his deepest self to stand as an invisible power beside her all the dark night. When he watched the others in her office he was not a peering gossip; he was winning them over to affection for her.

But not too affectionate!

He disapproved of the new young man who went to work in the office opposite a week or two after Emily's return. The new young man went about in his shirt sleeves, but the shirt seemed to be of silk, and he wore large intelligentsia tortoise-shell spectacles, and smoked a college sort of pipe in a dear-old-dormitory way. He had trained his molasses-colored locks till each frightened hair knew its little place and meekly kept it all day long. He was a self-confident, airy new young man, and apparently he was at least assistant manager. He was to be beheld talking easily to Emily's chief, one foot up on a chair, puffing much gray smoke.

The new young man appeared to like Emily. He had his own stenographer in his coop 'way over at the left, but he was always hanging about Emily's desk, and she looked up at him brightly. He chatted with her at closing hour, and at such times her back was to the window; and across the street Bates discreditably neglected his work and stood muttering things about drowning puppies.

She still waved good-night to Bates, but he fancied that she was careless about it.

"Oh, I'm just the faithful old dog. Young chap comes along—I'm invited to the wedding! I bet I've been best man at more weddings than any other man in New York.

I know the Wedding March better than the organist of St. Thomas', and I can smell lost rings across the vestry. Of course. That's all they want me for," said Bates.

And he dictated a violent letter to the company which made the cards for the indicator, and bitterly asked the office boy if he could spare time from the movies to fill the inkwells during the next few months.

Once Emily and the new young man left the office together at closing time, and peering twelve stories down Bates saw them emerging, walking together down the street. The young man was bending over her, and as they were submerged in the crowd Emily glanced at him with a gay upward toss of her head.

The lonely man at the window above sighed. "Well—well, I wanted her to be happy. But that young pup—— Rats! He's probably very decent. Heavens and earth, I'm becoming a moral Peeping Tom! I hate myself! But—I'm going to meet her. I won't let him take her away! I won't!"

Easy to say, but like paralysis was Bates' training in doing what other nice people do—in never being ridiculous. He despised queer people, socialists and poets and chaps who let others know they were in love.

Still thinking about it a week later he noticed no one about him as he entered a near-by tea room for lunch, and sat at a tiny, white, fussy table, with a paranoiac carmine rabbit painted in one corner of the bare top. He vaguely stared at a menu of walnut sandwiches, cream-cheese sandwiches, and chicken hash.

He realized that over the top of the menu he was looking directly at Emily, alone, at another dinky white table across the room.

Suppose she should think that he had followed her? That he was a masher? Horrible!

He made himself small in his chair, and to the impatient

waitress modestly murmured: "Chicken hash, please; cuppa coffee."

His fear melted as he made sure that Emily had not seen him. She was facing in the same direction as he, and farther down the room, so that her back was toward him, and her profile. She was reading a book while she neglectfully nibbled at a soft white roll, a nice-minded tea-room roll. He studied her hungrily.

She was older than he had thought, from her quick movements. She was twenty-seven, perhaps. Her smooth, pale cheeks, free of all padding or fat, all lax muscles of laziness, were silken. In everything she was fine; the product of breeding. She was, veritably, Emily!

He had never much noticed how women were dressed, but now he found himself valuing every detail: The good lines and simplicity of her blue frock with chiffon sleeves, her trim brown shoes, her unornamented small blue toque, cockily aside her head with military smartness. But somehow—— It was her overcoat, on the back of her chair, that got him—her plain brown overcoat with bands of imitation fur; rather a cheap coat, not very warm. The inside was turned back, so that he saw the tiny wrinkles in the lining where it lay over her shoulders—wrinkles as feminine as the faint scent of powder—and discovered that she had patched the armhole. He clenched his fists with a pity for her poverty that was not pity alone but a longing to do things for her.

Emily was stirring, closing her book, absently pawing for her check as she snatched the last sentences of the story before going back to work. He had, so far, only picked juicy little white pieces out of the chicken hash, and had ignobly put off the task of attacking the damp, decomposed toast. And he was hungry. But he didn't know what to do if in passing she recognized him.

He snatched his coat and hat and check, and galloped out, not looking back.

He went to a hotel and had a real lunch, alternately glowing because she really was the fine, fresh, shining girl he had fancied and cursing himself because he had not gone over and spoken to her. Wittily. Audaciously. Hadn't he been witty and audacious to the Binghamton traction directors?

And—now that he knew her he wasn't going to relinquish her to the windy young man with the owl spectacles!

At three-thirty-seven that afternoon without visible cause he leaped out of his chair, seized his hat, and hustled out through the office. He sedately entered the elevator. The elevator runner was a heavy, black-skirted amiable Irishwoman who remembered people. He wondered if he couldn't say to her, "I am about to go across the street and fall in love."

As for the first time in all his study of it he entered the building opposite, he was panting as though he had been smoking too much. His voice sounded thick as he said "Twelve out," in the elevator.

Usually, revolving business plans, he walked through buildings unseeing, but he was as aware of the twelfth-floor hall, of the marble footboards, the floor like fruit cake turned to stone, wire-glass lights, alabaster bowls of the indirect lighting, as though he were a country boy new to this strange indoor world where the roads were tunnels. He was afraid, and none too clear why he should be afraid, of one slim girl.

He had gone fifty feet from the elevator before it occurred to him that he hadn't the slightest idea where he was going.

He had lost his directions. There were two batteries of elevators, so that he could not get his bearings from them.

He didn't know on which side her office was. Trying to look as though he really had business here he rambled till he found a window at the end of a corridor. He saw the *Times* tower, and was straight again. Her office would be on the right. But—where?

He had just realized that from the corridor he couldn't tell how many outside windows each office had. He had carefully counted from across the street and found that her window was the sixth from the right. But that might be in either the Floral Heights Development Company or the Alaska Belle Mining Corporation, S. Smith—it was not explained whether S. Smith was the Belle or the Corporation.

Bates stood still. A large, red, furry man exploded out of the Floral Heights office and stared at him. Bates haughtily retired to the window at the end of the corridor and glowered out. Another crushing thought had fallen on him. Suppose he did pick the right office? He would find himself in an enclosed waiting room. He couldn't very well say to an office boy: "Will you tell the young lady in the blue dress that the man across the street is here?"

That would be ridiculous.

But he didn't care a hang if he was ridiculous!

He bolted down the corridor, entered the door of the Alaska Belle Mining Corporation. He was in a mahogany and crushed-morocco boudoir of business. A girl with a black frock and a scarlet smile fawned, "Ye-es?" He wasn't sure, but he thought she was a flirtatious person whom he had noted as belonging in an office next to Emily's. He blundered: "C-could I see some of your literature?"

It was twenty minutes later when he escaped from a friendly young man—now gorgeous in a new checked suit, but positively known by Bates to have cleaned the lapels of his other suit with stuff out of a bottle two evenings before—who had tried to sell him stock in two gold mines and a ground-floor miracle in the copper line. Bates was made to feel as though he was betraying an old friend before he was permitted to go. He had to accept a library of choice views of lodes, smelters, river barges, and Alaskan scenery.

He decorously deposited the booklets one by one in the mail chute, and returned to his favorite corridor.

This time he entered the cream-and-blue waiting room of the Floral Heights Development Company. He had a wild, unformed plan of announcing himself as a building inspector and being taken through the office, unto the uttermost parts, which meant to Emily's desk. It was a romantic plan and adventurous—and he instantly abandoned it at the sight of the realistic office boy, who had red hair and knickers and the oldest, coldest eye in the world.

"You people deal in suburban realty, don't you?"

"Yep!"

"I'd like to see the manager." It would be Emily who would take him in!

"Whadyuhwannaseeimbout?"

"I may consider the purchase of a lot."

"Oh, I thought you was that collector from the towel company."

"Do I look it, my young friend?"

"You can't tell, these days—the way you fellows spend your money on clothes. Well, say, boss, the old man is out, but I'll chase Mr. Simmons out here."

Mr. Simmons was, it proved, the man whom Bates disliked more than any other person living. He was that tortoise-spectacled, honey-haired, airy young man who dared to lift his eyes to Emily. He entered with his cut-out open; he assumed that he was Bates' physician and confessor; he chanted that at Beautiful Floral Heights by the Hackensack, the hydrants gave champagne, all babies weighed fifteen pounds at birth, values doubled overnight, and cement garages grew on trees.

Bates escaped with another de-luxe library, which included a glossy postcard showing the remarkable greenness of Floral Heights grass and the redness and yellowness of "Bungalow erected for J. J. Keane." He took the postcard back to his office and addressed it to the one man in his class whom he detested.

V

For four days he ignored Emily. Oh, he waved goodnight; there was no reason for hurting her feelings by rudeness. But he did not watch her through the creeping office hours. And he called on Christine Parrish. He told himself that in Christine's atmosphere of leisure and the scent of white roses, in her chatter about the singles championship and Piping Rock and various men referred to as Bunk and Poodle and Georgie, he had come home to his own people. But when Christine on the davenport beside him looked demurely at him through the smoke of her cigarette he seemed to hear the frightful drum fire of the Wedding March, and he rushed to the protecting fireplace.

The next night when Emily, knife-clean Emily, waved good-by and exhaustedly snapped off her light Bates darted to the elevator and reached the street entrance before she appeared across the way. But he was still stiff with years of training in propriety. He stood watching her go down the street, turn the corner.

Crackins, the bookkeeper, blandly whistling as he left the building, was shocked to see Bates running out of the doorway, his arms revolving grotesquely, his unexercised legs stumbling as he dashed down a block and round the corner.

Bates reached her just as she entered the Subway kiosk and was absorbed in the swirl of pushing people. He put out his hand to touch her unconscious shoulder, then withdrew it shiveringly, like a cat whose paw has touched cold water.

She had gone two steps down. She did not know he was there.

"Emily!" he cried.

A dozen Subway hurriers glanced at him as they shoved past. Emily turned, half seeing. She hesitated, looked away from him again.

"Emily!"

He dashed down, stood beside her.

"Two lovers been quarreling," reflected an oldish woman as she plumped by them.

"I beg your pardon!" remonstrated Emily.

Her voice was clear, her tone sharp. These were the first words from his princess of the tower.

"I beg yours, but—I tried to catch your attention. I've been frightfully clumsy, but—— You see, hang it, I don't know your name, and when I—I happened to see you, I—I'd thought of you as 'Emily.'"

Her face was still, her eyes level. She was not indignant, but she waited, left it all to him.

He desperately lied: "Emily was my mother's name."

"Oh! Then I can't very well be angry, but——"

"You know who I am, don't you? The man across the street from——"

"Yes. Though I didn't know you at first. The man across is always so self-possessed!"

"I know. Don't rub it in. I'd always planned to be very

superior and amusing and that sort of stuff when I met you, and make a tremendous impression."

Standing on the gritty steel-plated steps that led to the cavern of the Subway, jostled by hurtling people, he faltered on: "Things seem to have slipped, though. You see, I felt beastly lonely tonight. Aren't you, sometimes?"

"Always!"

"We'd become such good friends—you know, our lunches together, and all."

Her lips twitched, and she took pity on him with: "I know. Are you going up in the Subway? We can ride together, at least as far as Seventy-second."

This was before the days of shuttles and H's, when dozens of people knew their way about in the Subway, and one spoke confidently of arriving at a given station.

"No, I wasn't going. I wanted you to come to dinner with me! Do, please! If you haven't a date. I'm—I'm not really a masher. I've never asked a girl I didn't know, like this. I'm really—— Oh, hang it, I'm a solid citizen. Disgustingly so. My name is Bates. I'm g.m. of my office. If this weren't New York we'd have met months ago. Please! I'll take you right home after——"

Young women of the Upper West Side whose fathers were in Broad Street or in wholesale silk, young women with marquetry tables, with pictures in shadow boxes in their drawing rooms, and too many servants belowstairs, had been complimented when Bates took them to dinner. But this woman who worked, who had the tension wrinkle between her brows, listened and let him struggle.

"We can't talk here. Please walk up a block with me," he begged.

She came but she continued to inspect him. Once they were out of the hysteria of the Subway crowd, the ache of his embarrassment was relieved, and on a block of dead old brownstone houses embalmed among loft buildings he stopped and laughed aloud.

"I've been talking like an idiot. The crowd flustered me. And it was so different from the greeting I'd always planned. May I come and call on you sometimes, and present myself as a correct old bachelor, and ask you properly to go to dinner? Will you forgive me for having been so clumsy?"

She answered gravely: "No, you weren't. You were nice. You spoke as though you meant it. I was glad. No one in New York ever speaks to me as though he meant anything—except giving dictation."

He came close to saying: "What does the chump with the foolish spectacles mean?"

He saved himself by a flying mental leap as she went on: "And I like your laugh. I will go to dinner with you to-night if you wish."

"Thank you a lot. Where would you like to go? And shall we go to a movie or something to kill time before dinner?"

"You won't—— I'm not doing wrong, am I? I really feel as if I knew you. Do you despise me for tagging obediently along when I'm told to?"

"Oh! Despise—— You're saving a solitary man's life! Where——"

"Any place that isn't too much like a tea room. I go to tea rooms twice a day. I am ashamed every time I see a boiled egg, and I've estimated that if the strips of Japanese toweling I've dined over were placed end to end they would reach from Elkhart to Rajputana."

"I know. I wish we could go to a family dinner—not a smart one but an old-fashioned one, with mashed turnips, and Mother saying: 'Now eat your nice parsnips; little girls that can't eat parsnips can't eat mince pie.'"

"Oh, there aren't any families any more. You are nice!"

She was smiling directly at him, and he wanted to tuck her hand under his arm, but he didn't, and they went to a movie till seven. They did not talk during it. She was relaxed, her small tired hands curled together in her lap. He chose the balcony of the Firenze Room in the Grand Royal Hotel for dinner, because from its quiet leisure you can watch gay people and hear distant music. He ordered a dinner composed of such unnecessary things as hors d'œuvres, which she wouldn't have in tea rooms. He did not order wine.

When the waiter was gone and they faced each other, with no walking, no movies, no stir of the streets to occupy them, they were silent. He was struggling enormously to find something to say, and finding nothing beyond the sound observation that winters are cold. She glanced over the balcony rail at a bouncing pink-and-silver girl dining below with three elephantishly skittish men in evening clothes. She seemed far easier than he. He couldn't get himself to be masterful. He examined the crest on a fork and carefully scratched three triangles on the cloth, and ran his watch chain between his fingers, and told himself not to fidget, and arranged two forks and a spoon in an unfeasible fortification of his water glass, and delicately scratched his ear and made a knot in his watch chain, and dropped a fork with an alarming clang, and burst out:

"Er-r-r—— Hang it, let's be conversational! I find myself lots dumber than an oyster. Or a fried scallop."

She laid her elbows on the table, smiled inquiringly, suggested: "Very well. But tell me who you are. And what does your office do? I've decided you dealt in Christmas mottoes. You have cardboard things round the walls."

He was eloquent about the Carstop Indicator. The device was, it seemed, everything from a city guide to a

preventive of influenza. All traction magnates who failed
to introduce it were——

"Now I shall sell you a lot at Floral Heights," she interrupted.

"Oh, you're right. I'm office mad. But it really is a good
thing. I handle the Eastern territory. I'm a graduate—now
I shall be autobiographical and intimate and get your
sympathy for my past—I come from Shef.—Sheffield
Scientific School of Yale University. My father was a
chemical engineer, and I wrote one poem, at the age of
eleven, and I have an uncle in Sing Sing for forgery. Now
you know all about me. And I want to know if you really
are Emily?"

"Meaning?"

"I didn't—er—exactly call you Emily because of my
mother, but because the name means old gardens and a
charming family. I have decided that your father was
either a bishop or a Hartford banker."

She was exploring hors d'œuvres. She laid down her fork
and said evenly: "No. My father was a mill superintendent
in Fall River. He was no good. He drank and gambled and
died. My mother was quite nice. But there is nothing
romantic about me. I did have three years in college, but
I work because I have to. I have no future beyond possibly
being manager of the girls in some big office. I am very
competent but not very pleasant. I am horribly lonely in
New York, but that may be my fault. One man likes me—
a man in my office. But he laughs at my business ambitions. I am not happy, and I don't know what's ahead
of me, and some day I may kill myself—and I definitely
do not want sympathy. I've never been so frank as this
to anyone, and I oughtn't to have been with you."

She stopped dead, looked at the trivial crowd below, and
Bates felt as though he had pawed her soul.

Awkwardly kind he ventured: "You live alone?"

"Yes."

"Can't you find some jolly girls to live with?"

"I've tried it. They got on my nerves. They were as hopeless as I was."

"Haven't you some livelier girl you can play with?"

"Only one. And she's pretty busy. She's a social worker. And where can we go? Concerts sometimes, and walks. Once we tried to go to a restaurant. You know—one of these Bohemian places. Three different drunken men tried to pick us up. This isn't a very gentle city."

"Emily—Emily—— I say, what is your name?"

"It's as unromantic as the rest of me: Sarah Pardee."

"Look here, Miss Pardee, I'm in touch with a good many different sorts of people in the city. Lived here a good while, and classmates. Will you let me do something for you? Introduce you to people I know; families and——"

She laid down her fork, carefully placed her hands flat on the table, side by side, palms down, examined them, fitted her thumbs closer together, and declared: "There is something you can do for me."

"Yes?" he thrilled.

"Get me a better job!"

He couldn't keep from grunting ɪs though he had quite unexpectedly been hit by something.

"The Floral Heights people are nice to work for, but there's no future. Mr. Ransom can't see a woman as anything but a stenographer. I want to work up to office manager of some big concern or something."

He pleaded:

"B-but—— Of course I'll be glad to do that, but don't you want—— How about the human side? Don't you want to meet real New Yorkers?"

"No."

"Houses where you could drop in for tea on Sunday?"

"No."

"Girls of your own age, and dances, and——"

"No. I'm a business woman, nothing else. Shan't be anything else, I'm afraid. Not strong enough. I have to get to bed at ten. Spartan. It isn't much fun but it—oh, it keeps me going."

"Very well. I shall do as you wish. I'll telephone you by tomorrow noon."

He tried to make it sound politely disagreeable, but it is to be suspected that he was rather plaintive, for a glimmer of a smile touched her face as she said: "Thank you. If I could just find an opening. I don't know many employers here. I was in a Boston office for several years."

This ending, so like a lecture on auditing and costs, concluded Bates' quest for high romance.

He was horribly piqued and dignified, and he talked in an elevated manner of authors whom he felt he must have read, seeing that he had always intended to read them when he got time. Inside he felt rather sick. He informed himself that he had been a fool; that Emily—no, Miss Sarah Pardee!—was merely an enameled machine; and that he never wanted to see her again.

It was all of six minutes before he begged: "Did you like my waving good-night to you every evening?"

Dubiously: "Oh—yes."

"Did you make up foolish stories about me as I did about you?"

"No. I'll tell you." She spoke with faint, measured emphasis. "I have learned that I can get through a not very appealing life only by being heartless and unimaginative—except about my work. I was wildly imaginative as a girl; read Keats, and Kipling of course, and pretended that every man with a fine straight back was Strickland Sahib. Most stenographers keep up making believe. Poor tired things, they want to marry and have children, and file numbers and vocabularies merely bewilder them. But I—well, I want to succeed. So—work. And keep clear-brained, and exact. Know facts. I never allow fancies to bother me in office hours. I can tell you precisely the number of feet and inches of sewer pipe at Floral Heights, and I do not let myself gurgle over the pigeons that come up and coo on my window sill. I don't believe I shall ever be sentimental about anything again. Perhaps I've made a mistake. But—I'm not so sure. My father was full of the choicest sentiment, especially when he was drunk. Anyway, there I am. Not a woman, but a business woman."

"I'm sorry!"

He took her home. At her suggestion they walked up, through the late-winter clamminess. They passed a crying child on a doorstep beside a discouraged delicatessen. He noted that she looked at the child with an instant of mothering excitement, then hastened on.

"I'm not angry at her now. But even if I did want to see her again, I never would. She isn't human," he explained to himself.

At her door—door of a smug semiprivate rooming house on West Seventy-fourth Street—as he tried to think of a distinguished way of saying good-by he blurted: "Don't get too interested in the young man with spectacles. Make him wait till you study the genus New Yorker a little more. Your Mr. Simmons is amiable but shallow."

"How did you know I knew Mr. Simmons?" she marveled. "How did you know his name?"

It was the first time she had been off her guard, and he was able to retreat with a most satisfactory "One notices! Good-night. You shall have your big job."

He peeped back from two houses away. She must have gone in without one glance toward him.

He told himself that he was glad their evening was over. But he swooped down on the Yale Club and asked five several men what they knew about jobs for a young woman, who, he asserted entirely without authorization, was a perfect typist, speedy at taking dictation, scientific at filing carbons—and able to find the carbons after she had scientifically filed them!—and so charming to clients that before they even saw one of the selling force they were longing to hand over their money.

He telephoned about it to a friend in a suburb, which necessitated his sitting in a smothering booth and shouting: "No, no, no! I want Pelham, not Chatham!" After he had gone to bed he had a thought so exciting and sleep-dispelling that he got up, closed the windows, shivered, hulked into his bathrobe and sat smoking a cigarette, with his feet inelegantly up on the radiator. Why not make a place for Emily in his own office?

He gave it up reluctantly. The office wasn't big enough to afford her a chance. And Emily—Miss Pardee—probably would refuse. He bitterly crushed out the light of the cigarette on the radiator, yanked the windows open and climbed back into bed. He furiously discovered that during his meditation the bed had become cold again. There were pockets of arctic iciness down in the lower corners.

"Urg!" snarled Bates.

He waved good morning to Emily next day, but brusquely, and she was casual in her answer. At eleven-seventeen, after the sixth telephone call, he had found the place. He telephoned to her.

"This is Mr. Bates, across the street."

He leaped up and by pulling the telephone out to the

end of its green tether he could just reach the window and see her at the telephone by her window.

He smiled, but he went on sternly: "If you will go to the Technical and Home Syndicate—the new consolidation of trade publications—and ask for Mr. Hyden— H-y-d-e-n—in the advertising department, he will see that you get a chance. Really big office. Opportunities. Chance to manage a lot of stenographers, big commercial-research department, maybe a shot at advertising soliciting. Please refer to me. Er-r-r."

She looked across, saw him at the telephone, startled. Tenderness came over him in a hot wave.

But colorless was her voice as she answered "That's very good of you."

He cut her off with a decisive "Good luck!" He stalked back to his desk. He was curiously gentle and hesitating with his subordinates all that day.

"Wonder if the old man had a pal die on him?" suggested Crackins, the bookkeeper, to the filing girl. "He looks peaked. Pretty good scout, Batesy is, at that."

A week later Emily was gone from the office across. She had not telephoned good-by. In a month Bates encountered Hyden, of the Technical Syndicate office, who informed him: "That Miss Pardee you sent me is a crackajack. Right on the job, and intelligent. I've got her answering correspondence—dictating. She'll go quite a ways."

That was all. Bates was alone. Never from his twelfth-floor tower did he see her face or have the twilight benediction of farewell.

VI

He told himself that she was supercilious, that she was uninteresting, that he did not like her. He admitted that his office had lost its exciting daily promise of romance—

that he was tired of all offices. But he insisted that she had nothing to do with that. He had surrounded her with a charm not her own.

However neatly he explained things to himself, it was still true that an empty pain like homesickness persisted whenever he looked out of his window—or didn't look out but sat at his desk and wanted to. When he worked late he often raised his head with a confused sense of missing something. The building across had become just a building across. All he could see in it was ordinary office drudges doing commonplace things. Even Mr. Simmons of the esthetic spectacles no longer roused interesting rage. As for Emily's successor, Bates hated her. She smirked, and her hair was a hurrah's nest.

March had come in; the streets were gritty with dust. Bates languidly got himself to call on Christine Parrish again. Amid the welcome narcissus bowls and vellum-backed seats and hand-tooled leather desk fittings of the Parrish library he was roused from the listlessness that like a black fog had been closing in on him. He reflected that Christine was sympathetic, and Emily merely a selfish imitation of a man. But Christine made him impatient. She was vague. She murmured: "Oh, it must be thrilling to see the street railways in all these funny towns." Funny towns! Huh! They made New York hustle. Christine's mind was flabby. Yes, and her soft shining arms would become flabby too. He wanted—oh, a girl that was compact, cold-bathed.

As he plodded home the shivering fog that lay over him hid the future. What had he ahead? Lonely bachelorhood —begging mere boys at the club to endure a game of poker with him?

He became irritable in the office. He tried to avoid it. He was neither surprised nor indignant when he overheard

Crackins confide to his own stenographer: "The old man has an ingrowing grouch. We'll get him operated on. How much do you contribute, Countess? Ah, we thank you."

He was especially irritable on a watery, bleary April day when every idiot in New York and the outlying districts telephoned him. He thought ill of Alexander Graham Bell. The factory wanted to know whether they should rush the Bangor order. He hadn't explained that more than six times before. A purchasing agent from out of town called him up and wanted information about theater-ticket agencies and a tailor. The girl in the outside office let a wrong-number call get through to him, and a greasy voice bullied: "Is dis de Triumph Bottling Vorks? Vod? Get off de line! I don't vant you! Hang up!"

"Well, I most certainly don't want you!" snapped Bates. But it didn't relieve him at all.

"Tr-r-r-r!" snickered the telephone bell.

Bates ignored it.

"Tr-r-r-r-. R-r-r-r! Tr-r-r-r!"

"Yeah!" snarled Bates.

"Mr. Bates?"

"Yep!"

"Sarah Pardee speaking."

"Who?"

"Why—why, Emily! You sound busy, though. I won't——"

"Wait! W-w-wait! For heaven's sake! Is it really you? How are you? How are you? Terribly glad to hear your voice! How are you? We miss you——"

"We?"

"Well, I do! Nobody to say good-night. Heard from Hyden; doing fine. Awfully glad. What—er—what——"

"Mr. Bates, will you take me out to dinner some time this week; or next?"

"Will you come tonight?"

"You have no engagement?"

"No, no! Expected to dine alone. Please come. Will you meet me—— Shall we go up to the Belle Chic?"

"Please may we go to the Grand Royal again, and early, about six-thirty?"

"Of course. I'll meet you in the lobby. Six-thirty. Good-by."

He drew the words out lingeringly, but she cut him off with a crisp telephonic "G'-by."

Afterward he called up an acquaintance and broke the dinner engagement he had had for four days. He lied badly, and the man told him about it.

In his idiotic, beatific glow it wasn't for half an hour that the ugly thought crept grinning into his mind, but it persisted, squatting there, leering at him: "I wonder if she just wants me to get her another job?"

It served to quiet the intolerable excitement. In the Grand Royal lobby he greeted her with only a nod. . . . She was on time. Christine Parrish had a record minimum of twenty minutes late.

They descended the twisting stairs to the Firenze Room.

"Would you prefer the balcony or downstairs?" he said easily.

She turned.

She had seemed unchanged. Above the same brown fur-trimmed coat, which he knew better than any other garment in the world, was the same self-contained inspection of the world. Standing on the stairs she caught the lapel of her coat with a nervous hand, twisted it, dropped her eyes, looked up pleadingly.

"Would I be silly if I asked for the same table we had before? We—oh, it's good luck."

"Of course we'll have it."

"That's why I suggested dining early, so it wouldn't be taken. I have something rather serious to ask your advice about."

"Serious?"

"Oh, not—not tragic. But it puzzles me."

He was anxious as he followed her. Their table was untaken. He fussily took her coat, held her chair.

Her eyes became shrewdly clear again while he ordered dinner, and she said: "Will you please examine the crest on one of the forks?"

"Why?"

"Because you did last time. You were adorably absurd, and very nice, trying not to alarm the strange girl."

He had obediently picked up a fork, but he flung it down and commanded: "Look here, what is this that puzzles you?"

Her hand drooping over the balcony rail by their table was visibly trembling. She murmured: "I have discovered that I am a woman."

"I don't quite——"

"I've tried to keep from telling you, but I can't. I do —I do miss our good-nights and our lunches. I have done quite well at the Technical Syndicate, but I don't seem to care. I thought I had killed all sentimentality in me. I haven't. I'm sloppy-minded. No! I'm not! I don't care! I'm glad." A flush on her cheek like the rosy shadow of a wine glass on linen, she flung out: "I find I cared more for our silly games than I do for success. There's no one across the way now to smile at me. There's just a blank brick wall, with a horrible big garage sign, and I look at it before I go home nights. Oh, I'm a failure. I can't go on—fighting— alone—always alone!"

He had caught both her hands. He was unconscious of waiters and other guests. But she freed herself.

"No! Please! Just let me babble. I don't know whether I'm glad or sorry to find I haven't any brains. None! No courage! But all I want—— Will you dine with me once a month or so? Let me go Dutch——"

"Oh, my dear!"

"—and sometimes take me to the theater? Then I won't feel solitary. I can go on working, and make good, and perhaps get over—— Please! Don't think I'm a Bernard Shaw superwoman pursuing a man. It's just that—— You were the first person to make me welcome in New York. Will you forgive——"

"Emily, please don't be humble! I'd rather have you make me beg, as you used to." He stopped, gasped and added quietly: "Emily, will you marry me?"

"No."

"But you said——"

"I know. I miss you. But you're merely sorry for me. Honestly I'm not a clinger. I can stand alone—almost alone. It's sweet of you, and generous, but I didn't ask that. Just play with me sometimes."

"But I mean it. Dreadfully. I've thought of you every hour. Will you marry me? Now!"

"No."

"Some time?"

"How can I tell? A month ago I would have cut a girl who was so sloppy-minded that she would beg a man for friendship. I didn't know! I didn't know anything! But—— No! No!"

"See here, Emily. Are you free? Can I depend on you? Are you still interested in young Simmons?"

"He calls on me."

"Often?"

"Yes."

"You refused?"

"Yes. That was when I discovered I was a woman. But not—not his woman!"

"Mine, then! Mine! Think, dear- -it's incredible, but the city didn't quite get us. We're still a man and a woman! What day is this? Oh, Wednesday. Listen. Thursday you go to the theater with me."

"Yes."

"Friday you find an excuse and have to see someone at the Floral Heights Company, and you wave to me from across the street, so that my office will be blessed again; and we meet afterward and go to supper with my friends the Parrishes."

"Yes-es."

"Saturday we lunch together, and walk clear through Van Cortlandt Park, and I become a masterful brute, and propose to you, and you accept me."

"Oh, yes, I suppose so. But that leaves Sunday. What do we do Sunday?"

THE HACK DRIVER

THE HACK DRIVER

I DARE say there's no man of large affairs, whether he is bank president or senator or dramatist, who hasn't a sneaking love for some old rum-hound in a frightful hat, living back in a shanty and making his living by ways you wouldn't care to examine too closely. (It was the Supreme Court Justice speaking. I do not pretend to guarantee his theories or his story.) He may be a Maine guide, or the old garageman who used to keep the livery stable, or a perfectly useless innkeeper who sneaks off to shoot ducks when he ought to be sweeping the floors, but your pompous big-city man will contrive to get back and see him every year, and loaf with him, and secretly prefer him to all the highfalutin leaders of the city.

There's that much truth, at least, to this Open Spaces stuff you read in advertisements of wild and woolly Western novels. I don't know the philosophy of it; perhaps it means that we retain a decent simplicity, no matter how much we are tied to Things, to houses and motors and expensive wives. Or again it may give away the whole game of civilization; may mean that the apparently civilized man is at heart nothing but a hobo who prefers flannel shirts and bristly cheeks and cussing and dirty tin plates to all the trim, hygienic, forward-looking life our women-folks make us put on for them.

When I graduated from law school I suppose I was about as artificial and idiotic and ambitious as most youngsters. I wanted to climb, socially and financially. I wanted to be famous and dine at large houses with men who shuddered at the Common People who don't dress for dinner. You see, I hadn't learned that the only thing duller than a polite dinner is the conversation afterward, when the victims are digesting the dinner and accumulating enough strength to be able to play bridge. Oh, I was a fine young calf! I even planned a rich marriage. Imagine then how I felt when, after taking honors and becoming fifteenth assistant clerk in the magnificent law firm of Hodgins, Hodgins, Berkman and Taupe, I was set not at preparing briefs but at serving summonses! Like a cheap private detective! Like a mangy sheriff's officer! They told me I had to begin that way and, holding my nose, I feebly went to work. I was kicked out of actresses' dressing rooms, and from time to time I was righteously beaten by large and indignant litigants. I came to know, and still more to hate, every dirty and shadowy corner of the city. I thought of fleeing to my home town, where I could at once become a full-fledged attorney-at-law. I rejoiced one day when they sent me out forty miles or so to a town called New Mullion, to serve a summons on one Oliver Lutkins. This Lutkins had worked in the Northern Woods, and he knew the facts about a certain timberland boundary agreement. We needed him as a witness, and he had dodged service.

When I got off the train at New Mullion, my sudden affection for sweet and simple villages was dashed by the look of the place, with its mud-gushing streets and its rows of shops either paintless or daubed with a sour brown. Though it must have numbered eight or nine thousand inhabitants, New Mullion was as littered as a mining camp. There was one agreeable-looking man at the station—the expressman. He was a person of perhaps forty, red-faced, cheerful, thick; he wore his overalls and denim jumper as though they belonged to him, he was quite dirty and very friendly and you knew at once he liked people and slapped them on the back out of pure easy affection.

"I want," I told him, "to find a fellow named Oliver Lutkins."

"Him? I saw him 'round here 'twan't an hour ago. Hard fellow to catch, though—always chasing around on some phony business or other. Probably trying to get up a poker game in the back of Fritz Beinke's harness shop. I'll tell you, boy—— Any hurry about locating Lutkins?"

"Yes. I want to catch the afternoon train back." I was as impressively secret as a stage detective.

"I'll tell you. I've got a hack. I'll get out the bone-shaker and we can drive around together and find Lutkins. I know most of the places he hangs out."

He was so frankly friendly, he so immediately took me into the circle of his affection, that I glowed with the warmth of it. I knew, of course, that he was drumming up business, but his kindness was real, and if I had to pay hack fare in order to find my man, I was glad that the money would go to this good fellow. I got him down to two dollars an hour; he brought from his cottage, a block away, an object like a black piano-box on wheels.

He didn't hold the door open, certainly he didn't say "Ready, sir." I think he would have died before calling anybody "sir." When he gets to Heaven's gate he'll call St. Peter "Pete," and I imagine the good saint will like it.

He remarked, "Well, young fellow, here's the handsome equipage," and his grin—well, it made me feel that I had always been his neighbor. They're so ready to help a stranger, those villagers. He had already made it his own task to find Oliver Lutkins for me.

He said, and almost shyly: "I don't want to butt in on your private business, young fellow, but my guess is that you want to collect some money from Lutkins—he never pays anybody a cent; he still owes me six bits on a poker game I was fool enough to get into. He ain't a bad sort of a Yahoo but he just naturally hates to loosen up on a coin of the realm. So if you're trying to collect any money off him, we better kind of you might say creep up on him and surround him. If you go asking for him—anybody can tell you come from the city, with that trick Fedora of yours—he'll suspect something and take a sneak. If you want me to, I'll go into Fritz Beinke's and ask for him, and you can keep out of sight behind me."

I loved him for it. By myself I might never have found Lutkins. Now, I was an army with reserves. In a burst I told the hack driver that I wanted to serve a summons on Lutkins; that the fellow had viciously refused to testify in a suit where his knowledge of a certain conversation would clear up everything. The driver listened earnestly —and I was still young enough to be grateful at being taken seriously by any man of forty. At the end he pounded my shoulder (very painfully) and chuckled: "Well, we'll spring a little surprise on Brer Lutkins."

"Let's start, driver."

"Most folks around here call me Bill. Or Magnuson. William Magnuson, fancy carting and hauling."

"All right, Bill. Shall we tackle this harness shop—Beinke's?"

"Yes, jus' likely to be there as anywheres. Plays a lot

of poker and a great hand at bluffing—damn him!" Bill
seemed to admire Mr. Lutkins's ability as a scoundrel; I
fancied that if he had been sheriff he would have caught
Lutkins with fervor and hanged him with affection.

At the somewhat gloomy harness shop we descended and
went in. The room was odorous with the smell of dressed
leather. A scanty sort of a man, presumably Mr. Beinke,
was selling a horse collar to a farmer.

"Seen Nolly Lutkins around today? Friend of his looking for him," said Bill, with treacherous heartliness.

Beinke looked past him at my shrinking alien self; he
hesitated and owned: "Yuh, he was in here a little while
ago. Guess he's gone over to the Swede's to get a shave."

"Well, if he comes in, tell him I'm looking for him.
Might get up a little game of poker. I've heard tell that
Lutkins plays these here immoral games of chance."

"Yuh, I believe he's known to sit in on Authors,"
Beinke growled.

We sought the barber shop of "the Swede." Bill was
again good enough to take the lead, while I lurked at the
door. He asked not only the Swede but two customers if
they had seen Lutkins. The Swede decidedly had not; he
raged:"I ain't seen him, and I don't want to, but if you find
him you can just collect the dollar thirty-five he owes me."
One of the customers thought he had seen Lutkins "hiking
down Main Street, this side of the hotel."

"Well, then," Bill concluded, as we labored up into the
hack, "his credit at the Swede's being ausgewent, he's
probably getting a scrape at Heinie Gray's. He's too darn
lazy to shave himself."

At Gray's barber shop we missed Lutkins by only five
minutes. He had just left—presumably for the poolroom.
At the poolroom it appeared that he had merely bought a
pack of cigarettes and gone on. Thus we pursued him,

just behind him but never catching him, for an hour, till it was past one and I was hungry. Village born as I was, and in the city often lonely for good coarse country wit, I was so delighted by Bill's cynical opinions on the barbers and clergymen and doctors and draymen of New Mullion that I scarcely cared whether I found Lutkins or not.

"How about something to eat?" I suggested. "Let's go to a restaurant and I'll buy you a lunch."

"Well, ought to go home to the old woman. And I don't care much for these restaurants—ain't but four of 'em and they're all rotten. Tell you what we'll do. Like nice scenery? There's an elegant view from Wade's Hill. We'll get the old woman to put us up a lunch—she won't charge you but a half dollar, and it'd cost you that for a greasy feed at the caef—and we'll go up there and have a Sunday-school picnic."

I knew that my friend Bill was not free from guile; I knew that his hospitality to the Young Fellow from the City was not altogether a matter of brotherly love. I was paying him for his time; in all I paid him for six hours (including the lunch hour) at what was then a terrific price. But he was no more dishonest than I, who charged the whole thing up to the Firm, and it would have been worth paying him myself to have his presence. His country serenity, his natural wisdom, was a refreshing bath to the city-twitching youngster. As we sat on the hilltop, looking across orchards and a creek which slipped among the willows, he talked of New Mullion, gave a whole gallery of portraits. He was cynical yet tender. Nothing had escaped him, yet there was nothing, no matter how ironically he laughed at it, which was beyond his understanding and forgiveness. In ruddy color he painted the rector's wife who when she was most in debt most loudly gave the

responses at which he called the "Episcopalopian church."
He commented on the boys who came home from college
in "ice-cream pants," and on the lawyer who, after
years of torrential argument with his wife, would put on
either a linen collar or a necktie, but never both. He made
them live. In that day I came to know New Mullion better
than I did the city, and to love it better.

If Bill was ignorant of universities and of urban ways,
yet much had he traveled in the realm of jobs. He had
worked on railroad section gangs, in harvest fields and
contractors' camps, and from his adventures he had
brought back a philosophy of simplicity and laughter. He
strengthened me. Nowadays, thinking of Bill, I know what
people mean (though I abominate the simpering phrase)
when they yearn over "real he-men."

We left that placid place of orchards and resumed the
search for Oliver Lutkins. We could not find him. At last
Bill cornered a friend of Lutkins and made him admit
that "he guessed Oliver'd gone out to his ma's farm, three
miles north."

We drove out there, mighty with strategy.

"I know Oliver's ma. She's a terror. She's a cyclone,"
Bill sighed. "I took a trunk out for her once, and she
pretty near took my hide off because I didn't treat it like
it was a crate of eggs. She's somewheres about nine feet
tall and four feet thick and quick's a cat, and she sure
manhandles the Queen's English. I'll bet Oliver has heard
that somebody's on his trail and he's sneaked out there
to hide behind his ma's skirts. Well, we'll try bawling her
out. But you better let me do it, boy. You may be great at
Latin and geography, but you ain't educated in cussing."

We drove into a poor farmyard; we were faced by an
enormous and cheerful old woman. My guardian stockily
stood before her and snarled, "Remember me? I'm Bill

Magnuson, the expressman. I want to find your son Oliver. Friend of mine here from the city's got a present for him."

"I don't know anything about Oliver and I don't want to," she bellowed.

"Now you look here. We've stood for just about enough plenty nonsense. This young man is the attorney general's provost, and we got legal right to search any and all premises for the person of one Oliver Lutkins."

Bill made it seem terrific, and the Amazon seemed impressed. She retired into the kitchen and we followed. From the low old range, turned by years of heat into a dark silvery gray, she snatched a sadiron, and she marched on us, clamoring, "You just search all you want to—providin' you don't mind getting burnt to a cinder!" She bellowed, she swelled, she laughed at our nervous retreat.

"Let's get out of this. She'll murder us," Bill groaned and, outside: "Did you see her grin? She was making fun of us. Can you beat that for nerve?"

I agreed that it was lese majesty.

We did, however, make adequate search. The cottage had but one story. Bill went round it, peeking in at all the windows. We explored the barn and the stable; we were reasonably certain that Lutkins was not there. It was nearly time for me to catch the afternoon train, and Bill drove me to the station. On the way to the city I worried very little over my failure to find Lutkins. I was too absorbed in the thought of Bill Magnuson. Really, I considered returning to New Mullion to practice law. If I had found Bill so deeply and richly human might I not come to love the yet uncharted Fritz Beinke and the Swede barber and a hundred other slow-spoken, simple, wise neighbors? I saw a candid and happy life beyond the neat learnings of universities' law firms. I was excited, as one who has found a treasure.

But if I did not think much about Lutkins, the office did. I found them in a state next morning; the suit was ready to come to trial; they had to have Lutkins; I was a disgrace and a fool. That morning my eminent career almost came to an end. The Chief did everything but commit mayhem; he somewhat more than hinted that I would do well at ditch-digging. I was ordered back to New Mullion, and with me they sent an ex-lumber-camp clerk who knew Lutkins. I was rather sorry, because it would prevent my loafing again in the gorgeous indolence of Bill Magnuson.

When the train drew in at New Mullion, Bill was on the station platform, near his dray. What was curious was that the old dragon, Lutkins's mother, was there talking to him, and they were not quarreling but laughing.

From the car steps I pointed them out to the lumber-camp clerk, and in young hero-worship I murmured: "There's a fine fellow, a real man."

"Meet him here yesterday?" asked the clerk.

"I spent the day with him."

"He help you hunt for Oliver Lutkins?"

"Yes, he helped me a lot."

"He must have! He's Lutkins himself!"

But what really hurt was that when I served the summons Lutkins and his mother laughed at me as though I were a bright boy of seven, and with loving solicitude they begged me to go to a neighbor's house and take a cup of coffee.

"I told 'em about you, and they're dying to have a look at you," said Lutkins joyfully. "They're about the only folks in town that missed seeing you yesterday."

GO EAST, YOUNG MAN

GO EAST, YOUNG MAN

THE grandfather was Zebulun Dibble. He had a mustache like a horse's mane; he wore a boiled shirt with no collar, and he manufactured oatmeal, very wholesome and tasteless. He moved from New Hampshire out to the city of Zenith in 1875, and in 1880 became the proud but irritated father of T. Jefferson Dibble.

T. Jefferson turned the dusty oatmeal factory into a lyric steel-and-glass establishment for the manufacture of Oatees, Barlenated Rice and Puffy Wuffles, whereby he garnered a million dollars and became cultured, along about 1905. This was the beginning of the American fashion in culture which has expanded now into lectures by poetic Grand Dukes and Symphonies on the radio.

T. Jefferson belonged to the Opera Festival Committee and the Batik Exposition Conference, and he was the chairman of the Lecture Committee of the Phoenix Club. Not that all this enervating culture kept him from burning up the sales manager from nine-thirty A.M. to five P.M. He felt that he had been betrayed; he felt that his staff, Congress, and the labor unions had bitten the hand that fed them, if the sale of Rye Yeasties (Vitaminized) did not annually increase four per cent.

But away from the office, he announced at every club and committee where he could wriggle into the chairman's seat that America was the best country in the world, by heavens, and Zenith the best city in America, and how were we going to prove it? Not by any vulgar boasting and boosting! No, sir! By showing more culture than any other burg of equal size in the world! Give him ten years! He'd see that Zenith had more square feet of old masters, more fiddles in the symphony orchestra, and more marble statues per square mile than Munich!

T. Jefferson's only son, Whitney, appeared in 1906. T. Jefferson winced every time the boys called him "Whit." He winced pretty regularly. Whit showed more vocation for swimming, ringing the doorbells of timorous spinsters, and driving a flivver than for the life of culture. But T. Jefferson was determined.

Just as he bellowed, "By golly, you'll sell Barley Gems to the wholesalers or get out!" in the daytime, so when he arrived at his neat slate-roofed English Manor Style residence in Floral Heights, he bellowed at Whit, "By golly, you'll learn to play the piano or I'll lam the everlasting daylights out of you! Ain't you *ashamed!* Wanting to go skating! The idea!"

Whitney was taught—at least theoretically he was taught—the several arts of piano-playing, singing, drawing, water-color painting, fencing, and French. And through it all Whit remained ruddy, grinning, and irretrievably given to money-making. For years, without T. Jefferson's ever discovering it, he conducted a lucrative trade in transporting empty gin bottles in his father's spare sedan from the Zenith Athletic Club to the emporia of the bootleggers.

But he could draw. He sang like a crow, he fenced like a sculptor, but he could draw, and when he was sent to Yale he became the chief caricaturist of the *Yale Record*.

For the first time his father was delighted. He had Whit's original drawings framed in heavy gold, and showed all of them to his friends and his committees before they could escape. When Whit sold a small sketch to *Life*, T. Jefferson sent him an autographed check for a hundred dollars, so that Whit, otherwise a decent youth, became a little vain about the world's need of his art. At Christmas, senior year, T. Jefferson (with the solemn expression of a Father about to Give Good Advice to his Son) lured him into the library, and flowered in language:

"Now, Whitney, the time has come, my boy, when you must take thought and decide what rôle in this world's— what rôle in the world—in fact, to what rôle you feel your talents are urging you, if you get what I mean."

"You mean what job I'll get after graduation?"

"No, no, no! The Dibbleses have had enough of jobs! I have money enough for all of us. I have had to toil and moil. But the Dibbleses are essentially an artistic family. Your grandfather loved to paint. It is true that circumstances were such that he was never able to paint anything but the barn, but he had a fine eye for color—he painted it blue and salmon-pink instead of red; and he was responsible for designing the old family mansion on Clay Street—I should never have given it up except that the bathrooms were antiquated—not a single colored tile in them.

"It was he who had the Moorish turret with the copper roof put on the mansion, when the architect wanted a square tower with a pagoda roof. And I myself, if I may say so, while I have not had the opportunity to develop my creative gifts, I was responsible for raising the fund of

$267,800 to buy the Rembrandt for the Zenith Art Institute, and the fact that the Rembrandt later proved to be a fake, painted by a scoundrel named John J. Jones, was no fault of mine. So—in fact—if you understand me—how would you like to go to Paris, after graduation, and study art?"

"Paris!"

Whit had never been abroad. He pictured Paris as a series of bars, interspersed with sloe-eyed girls (he wasn't quite sure what sloe eyes were, but he was certain that the eyes of all Parisian cuties were sloe), palms blooming in January, and Bohemian studios where jolly artists and lively models lived on spaghetti, red wine, and a continuous singing of "*Auprès de Ma Blonde.*"

"Paris!" he said; and, "That would be elegant, sir!"

"My boy!" T. Jefferson put his puffy palm on Whit's shoulder in a marvelous impersonation of a Father about to Send His Son Forth into the Maelstrom of Life, "I am proud of you.

"I hope I shall live to see you one of the world's great pictorial artists, exhibiting in London, Rome, Zenith, and elsewhere, and whose pictures will carry a message of high ideals to all those who are dusty with striving, lifting their souls from the sordid struggle to the farther green places.

"That's what I often tell my sales manager, Mr. Mountgins—he ought to get away from mere thoughts of commerce and refresh himself at the Art Institute—and the stubborn jackass, he simply won't increase the sale of Korn Krumbles in southern Michigan! But as I was saying, I don't want you to approach Paris in any spirit of frivolity, but earnestly, as an opportunity of making a bigger and better—no, no, I mean a bigger and—a bigger —I mean a better world! I give you my blessings."

"Great! Watch me, Dad!"

When, after Christmas, Whit's classmates reveled in the great Senior Year pastime of wondering what they would do after graduation, Whit was offensively smug.

"I got an idea," said his classmate, Stuyvesant Wescott, who also came from Zenith. "Of course it's swell to go into law or bond selling—good for a hundred thou. a year—and a fellow oughtn't to waste his education and opportunities by going out for lower ideals. Think of that poor fish Ted Page, planning to teach in a prep school—associate with a lot of dirty kids and never make more'n five thou. a year! But the bond game is pretty well jammed. What do you think of getting in early on television? Millions in it!"

Mr. Whitney Dibble languidly rose, drew a six-inch scarlet cigarette holder from his pocket, lighted a cigarette and flicked the ash off it with a disdainful forefinger. The cigarette holder, the languor, the disdain, and the flicking habit were all strictly new to him, and they were extremely disapproved of by his kind.

"I am not," he breathed, "at all interested in your low-brow plans. I am going to Paris to study art. In five years from now I shall be exhibiting in—in all those galleries you exhibit in. I hope you have success with your money-grubbing and your golf. Drop in to see me at my *petit château* when you're abroad. I must dot out now and do a bit of sketching."

Whitney Dibble, riding a Pullman to greatness, arrived in Paris on an October day of pearl and amber. When he had dropped his baggage at his hotel, Whit walked out exultantly. The Place de la Concorde seemed to him a royal courtyard; Gabriel's twin buildings of the Marine Ministry were the residences of emperors themselves. They seemed taller than the most pushing skyscraper of New York, taller and nobler and more wise.

All Paris spoke to him of a life at once more vivid and more demanding, less hospitable to intrusive strangers, than any he had known. He felt young and provincial, yet hotly ambitious.

Quivering with quiet exultation, he sat on a balcony that evening, watching the lights fret the ancient Seine, and next morning he scampered to the atelier of Monsieur Cyprien Schoelkopf, where he was immediately to be recognized as a genius.

He was not disappointed. Monsieur Schoelkopf (he was of the celebrated Breton family of Schoelkopf, he explained) had a studio right out of fiction; very long, very filthy, with a naked model on the throne. The girls wore smocks baggy at the throat, and the men wore corduroy jackets.

Monsieur Schoelkopf was delighted to accept Whit, also his ten thousand francs in advance.

Whit longed to be seated at an easel, whanging immortal paint onto a taut canvas. He'd catch the model's very soul, make it speak through her eyes, with her mere body just indicated. . . . Great if his very first picture should be a salon piece!

But before leaping into grandeur he had to have a Bohemian background, and he went uneasily over the Left Bank looking for an apartment. (To live in comfort on the Right Bank would be bourgeois and even American.)

He rented an apartment 'way out on the Avenue Félix-Faure. It was quiet and light—and Whit was tired.

That evening he went to the famous Café Fanfaron, on the Boulevard Raspail, of which he had heard as the international (i. e., American) headquarters for everything that was newest and most shocking in painting, poetry, and devastating criticism in little magazines.

In front of the café the sidewalk was jammed with

tables at which sat hundreds of young people, most of them laughing, most of them noticeable—girls in slinksy dresses, very low, young men with jaunty tweed jackets, curly hair and keen eyes; large men (and they seemed the most youthful of all) with huge beards that looked false.

Whit was waved to a table with a group of Americans. In half an hour he had made a date to go walking in the Bois de Boulogne with a large-eyed young lady named Isadora, he had been reassured that Paris was the one place in the world for a person with Creative Hormones, and he had been invited to a studio party by a lively man who was twenty-four as far up as the pouches beneath his eyes, and sixty-four above.

It was a good party.

They sat on the floor and drank cognac and shouted. The host, with no great urging, showed a few score of his paintings. In them, the houses staggered and the hills looked like garbage heaps, so Whit knew they were the genuine advanced things, and he was proud and happy.

From that night on, Whit was in a joyous turmoil of artistic adventure. He was the real thing—except, perhaps, during the hours at Monsieur Schoelkopf's, when he tried to paint.

Like most active young Americans, he discovered the extreme difficulty of going slow. During a fifty-minute class in Yale he had been able to draw twenty caricatures, all amusing, all vivid. That was the trouble with him! It was infinitely harder to spend fifty minutes on a square inch of painting.

Whit was reasonably honest. He snarled at himself that his pictures had about as much depth and significance as a *croquis* for a dressmakers' magazine.

And Monsieur Schoelkopf told him all about it. He stood tickling the back of Whit's neck with his beard, and observed "Huh!" And when Monsieur Schoelkopf said "Huh!" Whit wanted to go off and dig sewers.

So Whit fled from that morgue to the Café Fanfaron, and to Isadora, whom he had met his first night in Paris.

Isadora was not a painter. She wrote. She carried a brief case, of course. Once it snapped open, and in it Whit saw a bottle of vermouth, some blank paper, lovely pencils all red and blue and green and purple, a handkerchief and a pair of silk stockings. Yet he was not shocked when, later in the evening, Isadora announced that she was carrying in that brief case the manuscript of her novel.

Isadora came from Omaha, Nebraska, and she liked to be kissed.

They picnicked in the Forest of Fontainebleau, Isadora and he. Whit was certain that all his life he had longed for just this; to lunch on bread and cheese and cherries and Burgundy, then to lie under the fretwork of oak boughs, stripped by October, holding the hand of a girl who knew everything and who would certainly, in a year or two, drive Edith Wharton and Willa Cather off the map; to have with her a relationship as innocent as children, and, withal, romantic as the steeple-hatted princesses who had once hallooed to the hunt in this same royal forest.

"I think your water-color sketch of Notre Dame is wonderful!" said Isadora.

"I'm glad you like it," said Whitney.

"So original in concept!"

"Well, I tried to give it a new concept."

"That's the thing! The new! We must get away from the old-fashioned Cubists and Expressionists. It's so old-fashioned now to be crazy! We must have restraint."

"That's so. Austerity. That's the stuff. . . . Gee, dog-gone it, I wish there was some more of that wine left," said Whit.

"You're a darling!"

She leaned on her elbow to kiss him, she sprang up and fled through the woodland aisle. And he gamboled after her in a rapture which endured even through a bus ride back to the Fontainebleau station with a mess of tourists who admired all the wrong things.

The Fanfaron school of wisdom had a magnificent show window but not much on the shelves. It was a high-class evening's entertainment to listen to Miles O'Sullivan, the celebrated Irish critic from South Brooklyn, on the beauties of Proust. But when, for the fifth time, Whit had heard O'Sullivan gasp in a drowning voice, "I remember dear old Marcel saying to me, 'Miles, *mon petit*, you alone understand that exteriority can be expressed only by interiority,'" then Whit was stirred to taxi defiantly over to the Anglo-American Pharmacy and do the most American thing a man can do—buy a package of chewing gum.

Chewing gum was not the only American vice which was in low repute at the Fanfaron. In fact, the exiles agreed that with the possible exceptions of Poland, Guatemala, and mid-Victorian England, the United States was the dumbest country that had ever existed. They were equally strong about the inferiority of American skyscrapers, pork and beans, Chicago, hired girls, jazz, Reno, evening-jacket lapels, Tom Thumb golf courses, aviation records, tooth paste, bungalows, kitchenettes, dinettes, diswashettes, eating tobacco, cafeterias, Booth Tarkington, corn flakes, flivvers, incinerators, corn on the cob, Coney Island, Rotarians, cement roads, trial marriages, Fundamentalism, preachers who talk on the radio, drugstore sandwiches, letters dictated but not read, noisy streets, noiseless typewriters, Mutt and Jeff, eye shades, mauve-and-crocus-yellow golf stockings, chile con carne, the Chrysler

Building, Jimmy Walker, Hollywood, all the Ruths in Congress, Boy Scouts, Tourists-Welcome camps, hot dogs, Admiral Byrd, flagpole sitters, safety razors, the Chautauqua, and President Hoover.

The exiles unanimously declared that they were waiting to join the Foreign Legion of whatever country should first wipe out the United States in war.

For three months Whit was able to agree with all of this indictment, but a week after his picnic with Isadora he went suddenly democratic. Miles O'Sullivan had denounced the puerility of American fried chicken.

Now it was before dinner, and Miles was an excellent reporter. The more Whit listened, the more he longed for the crisp, crunching taste of fried chicken, with corn fritters and maple sirup, candied sweet potatoes, and all the other vulgarities loathed by the artistic American exiles who were brought up on them.

Whit sprang up, muttering "Urghhg," which Miles took as a tribute to his wit.

It wasn't.

Whit fled down the Boulevard Raspail. He had often noted, with low cultured sneers, a horribly American restaurant called "Cabin Mammy's Grill." He plunged into it now. In a voice of restrained hysteria he ordered fried chicken, candied sweets and corn fritters with sirup.

Now, to be fair on all sides—which is an impossibility—the chicken was dry, the corn fritters were soggy, the fried sweets were poisonous and the sirup had never seen Vermont. Yet Whit enjoyed that meal more than any of the superior food he had discovered in Paris.

The taste of it brought back everything that was native in him. . . . Return home for Christmas vacation in his freshman year; the good smell of the midwestern snow; the girls whom he had loved as a brat; the boys with whom he had played. A dinner down at Momauguin in senior year, and the kindly tragedy of parting.

They had been good days; cool and realistic and decent.

So Whit came out of Cabin Mammy's Grill thinking of snow on Chapel Street and the New Haven Green—and he was buffeted by the first snow of the Paris winter, and that wasn't so good.

Although he was a college graduate, Whitney had learned a little about geography, and he shouldn't have expected Paris to be tropical. Yet he had confusedly felt that this capital of the world could never conceivably be cold and grim. He turned up the collar of his light topcoat and started for—oh, for Nowhere.

After ten blocks, he was exhilarated by the snow and the blasty cold which had first dismayed him. From time to time he muttered something like a sketch for future thoughts:

"I can't paint! I'd be all right drawing machinery for a catalogue. That's about all! Paris! More beautiful than any town in America. But I'm not part of it. Have nothing to do with it. I've never met a real Frenchman, except my landlady, and that hired girl at the apartment and a few waiters and a few cops and the French literary gents that hang around the Fanfaron because we give 'em more of a hand than their own people would.

"Poor old T. Jefferson! He wants me to be a Genius! I guess you have to have a little genius to be a Genius. Gosh, I'd like to see Stuyvy Wescott tonight. With him, it would be fun to have a drink!"

Without being quite conscious of it, Whit drifted from the sacred Left Bank to the bourgeois Right. Instead of returning to the Fanfaron and Isadora, he took refuge at the Café de la Paix.

Just inside the door was a round-faced, spectacled

American, perhaps fifty years old, looking wistfully about
for company.

Whit could never have told by what long and involved
process of thought he decided to pick up this Babbitt. He
flopped down at the stranger's table, and muttered, "Mind
'f I sit here?"

"No, son, tickled to death! American?"

"You bet."

"Well, say, it certainly is good to talk to a white man
again! Living here?"

"I'm studying art."

"Well, well, is that a fact!"

"Sometimes I wonder if it is! I'm pretty bad."

"Well, what the deuce! You'll have a swell time here
while you're a kid, and I guess prob'ly you'll learn a lot,
and then you can go back to the States and start something. Easterner, ain't you?"

"No; I was born in Zenith."

"Well, is that a fact! Folks live there?"

"Yes. My father is T. Jefferson Dibble of the Small
Grain Products Company."

"Well, I'm a son-of-a-gun! Why, say, I know your dad.
My name's Titus—Buffalo Grain Forwarding Corp.—
why, I've had a lot of dealings with your dad. Golly!
Think of meeting somebody you know in *this* town! I'm
leaving tomorrow, and this is the first time I've had a shot
at any home-grown conversation. Say, son, I'd be honored
if you'd come out and bust the town loose with me this
evening."

They went to the Exhibit of the Two Hemispheres,
which Miles O'Sullivan had recommended as the dirtiest
show in Europe. Whit was shocked. He tried to enjoy it.
He told himself that otherwise he would prove himself a

provincial, a lowbrow—in fact, an American. But he was increasingly uncomfortable at the antics of the ladies at the Exhibit. He peeped at Mr. Titus, and discovered that he was nervously twirling a glass and clearing his throat.

"I don't care so much for this," muttered Whit.

"Neither do I, son! Let's beat it!"

They drove to the New Orleans bar and had a whisky-soda. They drove to the Kansas City bar and had a high-ball. They drove to the El Paso bar and had a rock and rye. They drove to the Virginia bar, and by now Mr. Titus was full of friendliness and manly joy.

Leaning against the bar, discoursing to a gentleman from South Dakota, Mr. Titus observed:

"I come from Buffalo. Name's Titus."

"I come from Yankton. Smith is my name."

"Well, well, so you're this fellow Smith I've heard so much about!"

"Ha, ha, ha, that's right."

"Know Buffalo?"

"Just passing through on the train."

"Well, now, I want to make you a bet that Buffalo will increase in pop'lation not less than twenty-seven per cent this decade."

"Have 'nother?"

"Have one on me."

"Well, let's toss for it."

"That's the idea. We'll toss for it. . . . Hey, Billy, got any galloping dominoes?"

When they had gambled for the drink, Mr. Titus bellowed, "Say, you haven't met my young friend Whinney Dibble."

"Glad meet you."

"He's an artist!"

"Zatta fact!"

"Yessir, great artist. Sells pictures everywhere. London and Fort Worth and Cop'nagen and everywhere. Thousands and thousands dollars. His dad's pal of mine. Wish I could see good old Dibble! Wish he were here tonight!"

And Mr. Titus wept, quietly, and Whit took him home.

Next morning, at a time when he should have been in the atelier of Monsieur Schoelkopf, Whit saw Mr. Titus off at the Gare St.-Lazare, and he was melancholy. There were so many pretty American girls taking the boat train; girls with whom he would have liked to play deck tennis.

So it chanced that Whit fell into the lowest vice any American can show in Paris. He constantly picked up beefy and lonesome Americans and took them to precisely those places in Paris, like the Eiffel Tower, which were most taboo to the brave lads of the Fanfaron.

He tried frenziedly to paint one good picture at Monsieur Schoelkopf's; tried to rid himself of facility. He produced a decoration in purple and stony reds which he felt to be far from his neat photography.

And looking upon it, for once Monsieur Schoelkopf spoke: "You will be, some time, a good banker."

The day before Whit sailed for summer in Zenith, he took Isadora to the little glassed-in restaurant that from the shoulder of Montmartre looks over all Paris. She dropped her flowery airs. With both hands she held his, and besought him:

"Whit! Lover! You are going back to your poisonous Middle West. Your people will try to alienate you from Paris and all the freedom, all the impetus to creation, all the strange and lovely things that will exist here long after machines have been scrapped. Darling, don't let them get you, with their efficiency and their promise of millions!"

"Silly! Of course! I hate business. And next year I'll be back here with you!"

He had told the Fanfaron initiates not to see him off at the train. Feeling a little bleak, a little disregarded by this humming city of Paris, he went alone to the station, and he looked for no one as he wretchedly followed the porter to a seat in the boat train.

Suddenly he was overwhelmed by the shouts of a dozen familiars from the Fanfaron. It wasn't so important—though improbable—that they should have paid fifty centimes each for a *billet de quai*, for that they should have arisen before nine o'clock to see him off was astounding.

Isadora's kind arms were around him, and she was wailing, "You won't forget us; darling, you won't forget me!"

Miles O'Sullivan was wringing his hand and crying, "Whit, lad, don't let the dollars get you!"

All the rest were clamoring that they would feverishly await his return.

As the train banged out, he leaned out waving to them, and he was conscious that whatever affectations and egotism they had shown in their drool at the Fanfaron, all pretentiousness was wiped now from their faces, and that he loved them.

He would come back to them.

All the way to Cherbourg he fretted over the things he had not seen in Paris. He had been in the Louvre only three times. He had never gone to Moret or to the battlemented walls of Provins.

Whit ran into the living room at Floral Heights, patted T. Jefferson on the shoulder, kissed his mother and muttered:

"Gee, it certainly is grand to be back!"

"Oh, you can speak to us in French, if you want to,"

said T. Jefferson Dibble, "we've been studying it so we can return to Paris with you some time. *Avez vous oo un temps charmant cette*—uh—year?"

"Oh, sure, *oui*. Say, you've redecorated the breakfast room. That red-and-yellow tiling certainly is swell."

"Now *écoutez—écoute, moh fis*. It's not necessary for you, Whitney, now that you have become a man of the world, to spare our feelings. I know, and you know, that that red-and-yellow tiling is vulgar. But to return to pleasanter topics, I long for your impressions of Paris. How many times did you go to the Louvre?"

"Oh. Oh, the Louvre! Well, a lot."

"I'm sure of it. By the way, a funny thing happened, Whitney. A vulgarian by the name of Titus, from Buffalo, if I remember, wrote to me that he met you in Paris. A shame that such a man, under pretense of friendship with me, should have disturbed you."

"I thought he was a fine old coot, Dad."

"*Mon père!* No, my boy, you are again being conciliatory and trying to spare my feelings. This Titus is a man for whom I have neither esteem nor—in fact, we have nothing in common. Besides, the old hellion, he did me out of eleven hundred and seventy dollars on a grain deal sixteen years ago! But as I say, your impressions of Paris! It must seem like a dream wreathed with the vapors of golden memory.

"Now, I believe, you intend to stay here for two months. I have been making plans. Even in this wretched midwestern town, I think that, with my aid, you will be able to avoid the banalities of the young men with whom you were reared. There is a splendid new Little Theater under process of organization, and perhaps you will wish to paint the scenery and act and even design the costumes.

"Then we are planning to raise a fund to get the E.

Heez Flemming Finnish Grand Opera Company here for a week. That will help to occupy you. You'll be able to give these hicks your trained European view of Finnish Grand Opera. So, to start with this evening, I thought we might drop in on the lecture by Professor Gilfillan at the Walter Peter Club on 'Traces of Mechanistic Culture in the Coptic.'"

"That would be splendid, sir, but unfortunately—— On the way I received a wire from Stuyv Wescott asking me to the dance at the country club this evening. I thought I'd dine with you and Mother, and then skip out there. Hate like the dickens to hurt their feelings."

"Of course, of course, my boy. A gentleman, especially when he is also a man of culture, must always think of *noblesse oblige*. I mean, you understand, of the duties of a gentleman. But don't let these vulgarians like Wescott impose on you. You see, my idea of it is like this. . ."

As he drove his father's smaller six to the country club, Whit was angry. He was thinking of what his friends—ex-friends—at the club would do in the way of boisterous "kidding." He could hear them—Stuyv Wescott, his roommate in Yale, Gilbert Scott, Tim Clark (Princeton '28) and all the rest—mocking:

"Why, it's our little Alphonse Gauguin!"

"Where's the corduroy pants?"

"I don't suppose you'd condescend to take a drink with a poor dumb Babbitt that's been selling hardware while you've been associating with the counts and jukes and highbrows and highbrowesses!"

And, sniggering shamefacedly, "Say, how's the little midinettes and the *je ne sais quoi's* in Paris?"

He determined to tell them all to go to hell, to speak with quiet affection of Isadora and Miles O'Sullivan, and to hustle back to Paris as soon as possible. Stick in this provincial town, when there on Boulevard Raspail were inspiration and his friends?

Stay here? What an idea!

He came sulkily into the lounge of the country club, cleared now for dancing. Stuyvy Wescott, tangoing with a girl who glittered like a Christmas tree, saw him glowering at the door, chucked the girl into the ragbag, dashed over and grunted, "Whit, you old hound, I'm glad to see you! Let's duck the bunch and sneak down to the locker room. The trusty gin awaits!"

On the way, Stuyv nipped Gil Scott and Tim Clark out of the group.

Whit croaked—Youth, so self-conscious, so conservative, so little "flaming," so afraid of what it most desires and admires!—he croaked, "Well, let's get the razzing over! I s'pose you babies are ready to pan me good for being a loafer while you've been saving the country by discounting notes!"

The other three looked at him with mild, fond wonder.

Stuyv said meekly, "Why, what a low idea! Listen, Whit, we're tickled to death you've had a chance to do something besides keep the pot boiling. Must have been swell to have a chance at the real Europe and art. We've all done pretty well, but I guess any one of us would give his left leg to be able to sit down on the Champs Élysées and take time to figure out what it's all about."

Then Whit knew that these were his own people. He blurted, "Honestly, Stuyv, you mean to say you've envied me? Well, it's a grand town, Paris. And some great eggs there. And even some guys that can paint. But me, I'm no good!"

"Nonsense! Look, Whit, you have no idea what this money-grubbing is. Boy, you're lucky! And don't stay

here! Don't let the dollars get you! Don't let all these
babies with their promises of millions catch you! Beat it
back to Paris. Culture, that's the new note!"

"Urghhg!" observed Whit.

"You bet," said Tim Clark.

Tim Clark had a sister, and the name of that sister was
Betty.

Whit Dibble remembered her as a sub-flapper, always
going off to be "finished" somewhere in the East. She was
a Young Lady of twenty-odd now, and even to Whit's
professionally artistic eye it seemed that her hair, sleek
as a new-polished range, was interesting. They danced together, and looked at each other with a fury of traditional
dislike.

Midmost of that dance Whit observed, "Betty.
Darlingest!"

"Yeah?"

"Let's go out and sit on the lawn."

"Why?"

"I want to find out why you hate me."

"Hm. The lawn. I imagine it takes a training in Yale
athletics and Paris artisticking to be so frank. Usually
the kits start out with a suggestion of the club porch and the
handsome modernist reed chairs and *then* they suggest
the lawn and 'Oh, Greta, so charmé to meet you' afterwards!"

But during these intolerabilities Betty had swayed with
him to the long high-pillared veranda, where they crouched
together on a chintz-covered glider.

Whit tried to throw himself into what he conceived,
largely from novels, to be Betty's youthful era. He murmured: "Kiddo, where have you been all my life?"

From Betty's end of the glider, a coolness like the long

wet stretches of the golf course; a silence; then a very little
voice:

"Whit, my child, you have been away too long! It's a
year now, at least, since anyone—I mean anyone you could
know—has said 'Where have you been all my life?' Listen,
dear! The worst thing about anybody's going artistic, like
you, is that they're always so ashamed of it. Jiminy! Your
revered father and the Onward and Upward Bookshop
have grabbed off Culture for keeps in this town. And
yet——

"Dear, I think that somewhere there must be people
who do all these darn' arts without either being ashamed
of 'em—like you, you poor fish!—or thinking they make
the nice gilded cornice on the skyscraper, like your dad.
Dear, let's us be *us*. Cultured or hoboes, or both. G'night!"

She had fled before he could spring up and be wise in the
manner of Isadora and Miles O'Sullivan, or the more
portentous manner of T. Jefferson Dibble.

Yet, irritably longing all the while for Betty Clark, he
had a tremendous time that night at the country club, on
the land where his grandfather had once grown corn.

What did they know, there in Paris? What did either
Isadora or Miles O'Sullivan know of those deep provincial-
isms, smelling always of the cornfields, which were in him?
For the first time since he had left Paris, Whit felt that in
himself might be some greatness.

He danced that night with many girls.

He saw Betty Clark only now and then, and from afar.
And the less he saw of her, the more important it seemed to
him that she should take him seriously.

There had been a time when Whit had each morning
heard the good, noisy, indignant call of T. Jefferson demanding, "Are you going to get up or ain't you going to

get up? Hey! Whit! If you don't wanna come down for breakfast, you ain't gonna have any breakfast!"

Indeed it slightly disturbed him, when he awoke at eleven of the morning, to find there had been no such splendid, infuriating, decent uproar from T. Jefferson.

He crawled out of bed and descended the stairs. In the lower hall he found his mother.

(It is unfortunate that in this earnest report of the turning of males in the United States of America toward culture, it is not possible to give any great attention to Mrs. T. Jefferson Dibble. Aside from the fact that she was a woman, kindly and rather beautiful, she has no existence here except as the wife of T. Jefferson and the mother of Whitney.)

"Oh, Whit! Dear! I do hope your father won't be angry! He waited such a long while for you. But I am so glad, dearie, that he understands, at last, that possibly you may have just as much to do with all this Painting and Art and so on as he has! . . . But I mean to say: Your father is expecting you to join him at three this afternoon for the meeting of the Finnish Opera Furtherance Association. Oh, I guess it will be awfully interesting—it will be at the Thornleigh. Oh, Whit, dear, it's lovely to have you back!"

The meeting of the Finnish Opera Furtherance Association at the Hotel Thornleigh was interesting.

It was more than interesting.

Mrs. Montgomery Zeiss said that the Finns put it all over the Germans and Italians at giving a real modernistic version of opera.

Mr. T. Jefferson Dibble said that as his son, Whitney, had been so fortunate as to obtain a rather authoritative knowledge of European music, he (Whitney) would now explain everything to them.

After a lot of explanation about how artistic opera was,

and how unquestionably artistic Zenith was, Whit muttered that he had to beat it. And while T. Jefferson stared
at him with a sorrowful face, Whit fled the room.

At five o'clock Whit was sitting on the dock of Stuyv
Wescott's bungalow on Lake Kennepoose, muttering,
"Look, Stuyv, have you got a real job?"

"Yeah, I guess you'd call it a job."

"D'you mind telling me what you are making a year
now?"

"About three thou. I guess I'll make six in a coupla
years."

"Hm! I'd like to make some money. By the way—it just
occurs to me, and I hope that I am not being too rude in
asking—what *are* you doing?"

"I am an insurance agent," remarked Stuyv with a
melancholy dignity.

"And you're already making three thousand dollars a
year?"

"Yeah, something like that."

"I think I ought to be making some money. It's funny.
In Europe it's the smart thing to live on money that somebody else made for you. I don't know whether it's good or
bad, but fact is, somehow, most Americans feel lazy, feel
useless, if they don't make their own money.

"Prob'ly the Europeans are right. Prob'ly it's because
we're restless. But anyway, I'll be hanged if I'm going to
live on the Old Man the rest of my life and pretend I'm a
painter! The which I ain't! Listen, Stuyv! D'yuh think
I'd make a good insurance man?"

"Terrible!"

"You're helpful. Everybody is helpful. Say! What's this
new idea that it's disgraceful to make your own living?"

"Don't be a fool, Whit. Nobody thinks it's disgraceful, but you don't get this new current of thought in the Middle West that we gotta have art."

"Get it! Good heavens, I've got nothing else! I will say this for Paris—you can get away from people who believe in art just by going to the next café. Maybe I'll have to live there in order to be allowed to be an insurance agent!"

Stuyv Wescott was called to the telephone, and for three minutes Whit sat alone on the dock, looking across that clear, that candid, that sun-iced lake, round which hung silver birches and delicate willows and solid spruce. Here, Whit felt, was a place in which an American might find again, even in these days of eighty-story buildings and one-story manners, the courage of his forefathers.

A hell-diver, forever at his old game of pretending to be a duck, bobbed out of the mirror of the lake, and Whitney Dibble at last knew that he was at home.

And not so unlike the hell-diver in her quickness and imperturbable complexity, Betty Clark ran down from the road behind the Wescott bungalow and profoundly remarked, "Oh! Hello!"

"I'm going to be an insurance man," remarked Whit.

"You're going to be an artist!"

"Sure I am. As an insurance man!"

"You make me sick."

"Betty, my child, you have been away too long! It's a year now, at least, since anyone—I mean anyone you could know—has said, 'You make me sick!'"

"Oh—oh! You make me sick!"

T. Jefferson was extremely angry when Whit appeared for dinner. He said that Whit had no idea how he had offended the Opera Committee that afternoon. Consequently, Whit had to go through the gruesome ordeal of accompanying his father to an artistic reception in the evening. It was not until eleven that he could escape for a poker game in an obscure suite of the Hotel Thornleigh.

There were present here not only such raw collegians as Stuyv Wescott, Gil Scott, and Tim Clark, but also a couple of older and more hardened vulgarians, whereof one was a Mr. Seidel, who had made a million dollars by developing the new University Heights district of Zenith.

When they had played for two hours, they stopped for hot dogs; and Room Service was again drastically ordered to "hustle up with the White Rock and ice."

Mr. Seidel, glass in hand, grumbled: "So you're an artist, Dibble? In Paris?"

"Yeah."

"And to think that a fella that could bluff me out of seven dollars on a pair of deuces should live over there, when he'd be an A-1 real-estate salesman."

"Are you offering me a job?"

"Well, I hadn't thought about it. . . . Sure I am!"

"How much?"

"Twenty-five a week and commissions."

"It's done."

And the revolution was effected, save for the voice of Stuyv Wescott, wailing, "Don't do it, Whit! Don't let these babies get you with their promise of millions!"

Whit had never altogether lost his awe of T. Jefferson and he was unable to dig up the courage to tell his father of his treachery in becoming American again until eleven of the morning, when he called upon him at his office.

"Well, well, my boy, it's nice to see you!" said T. Jefferson. "I'm sorry that there is nothing really interesting for us to do today. But tomorrow noon we are going to a luncheon of the Bibliophile Club."

"That's what I came to see you about, Dad. I'm sorry, but I shan't be able to go tomorrow. I'll be working."

"Working?"

"Yes, sir. I've taken a job with the Seidel Development Company."

"Well, that may be interesting for this summer. When you return to Paris——"

"I'm not going back to Paris. I can't paint. I'm going to sell real estate."

The sound that T. Jefferson now made was rather like a carload of steers arriving at the Chicago stockyards. In this restricted space it is possible to give only a hundredth of his observations on Life and Culture, but among many other things he said:

"I might have known! I might have known it! I've always suspected that you were your mother's boy as much as mine. How sharper than a serpent's tooth! Serpent in a fella's own bosom!

"Here I've given up my life to manufacturing Puffy Wuffles, when all the time my longing was to be artistic, and now when I give you the chance—— Serpent's tooth! The old bard said it perfectly! Whit, my boy, I hope it isn't that you feel I can't afford it! In just a few days now, I'm going to start my schemes for extending the plant; going to get options on the five acres to the eastward. The production of Ritzy Rice will be doubled in the next year. And so, my boy . . . You'll either stick to your art or I'll disown you, sir! I mean, cut you off with a shilling! Yes, sir, a shilling! I'll by thunder make you artistic, if it's the last thing I do!"

On the same afternoon when he had, and very properly, been thrown out into the snowstorm with a shawl over his head, Whit borrowed five thousand from Stuyv Wescott's father, with it obtained options on the five acres upon which his father planned to build, with them reported to Mr. Seidel, from that low realtor received the five thousand dollars to repay Mr. Wescott, plus a five-thousand-dollar commission for himself and spent twenty-five dollars in flowers, and with them appeared at the house of Betty Clark at six-fifteen.

Betty came down, so lovely, so cool, so refreshing in skirts that clipped her ankles; and so coolly and refreshingly she said: "Hey, Whit, my dear! What can I do for you?"

"I don't think you can do anything besides help me spend the five thousand and twenty-five dollars I've made today. I spent the twenty-five for these flowers. They're very nice, aren't they?"

"They certainly are."

"But do you think they're worth twenty-five dollars?"

"Sure they are. Listen, darling! I'm so sorry that you wasted your time making five thousand dollars when you might have been painting. But of course an artist has to be an adventurer. I'm glad that you've tried it and that it's all over. We'll go back to Paris as soon as we're married, and have a jolly li'l' Bohemian flat there, and I'll try so hard to make all of your artistic friends welcome."

"Betty! Is your brother still here?"

"How should I know?"

"Would you mind finding out?"

"Why no? But why?"

"Dear Betty, you will understand what a scoundrel I am in a few minutes. Funny! I never meant to be a scoundrel. I never even meant to be a bad son. . . . Will you yell for Timmy, please?"

"Of course I will." She yelled, very competently.

Tim came downstairs, beaming. "I hope it's all over."

"That's the point," said Whit. "I am trying to persuade

T. Jefferson that I don't want to be an artist. I'm trying—
Lord knows what I'm trying!" With which childish statement Whit fled from the house.

He found a taxi and gave the driver the address of his
boss, Mr. Seidel, at the Zenith Athletic Club.

In his room, sitting on the edge of his bed, Mr. Seidel
was eating dinner. "Hello, boy, what's the trouble?" he
said.

"Will you let me pay for a telephone call if I make it
here?"

"Sure I will."

Whit remarked to the Athletic Club telephone girl, "I'd
like to speak to Isadora at the Café Fanfaron, Paris."

The voice of that unknown beauty answered, "Which
state, please?"

"France."

"France?"

"Yes, France."

"France, *Europe?*"

"Yes."

"And what was the name, please?"

"Isadora."

"What is the lady's last name?"

"I don't know. . . . Hey, get me Miles O'Sullivan, same
address."

"Just a moment, please. I will get the supervisor."

A cool voice said, "To whom do you wish to speak,
please?"

"I wish to speak, if I may, to Miles O'Sullivan at the
Café Fanfaron. In Paris. . . . Right. Thank you very much.
Will you call me as soon as you can?

"All right, thank you. . . . I am speaking from the
Zenith Athletic Club and the bill is to be charged to Mr.
Tiberius Seidel."

When the telephone rang, it was the voice of the head waiter of the Fanfaron, a Russian, that answered.

He said, "*Allo—allo!*"

"May I speak to Miles O'Sullivan?" demanded Whit.

"*Je ne comprends pas.*"

"*C'est Monsieur Dibble que parle—d'Amérique.*"

"*D'Amérique?*"

"*Oui, et je desire* to talk to Monsieur Miles O'Sullivan, right away, *tout suite.*"

"*Mais oui; je comprends. Vous desirez parler avec Monsieur Miles O'Sullivang?*"

"That's the idea. Make it snappy."

"*Oui*, right away."

Then O'Sullivan's voice on the phone.

While Mr. Seidel smiled and watched the second hand of his watch, Whit bellowed into the telephone, "Miles! Listen! I want to speak to Isadora."

That voice, coming across four thousand miles of rolling waves and laboring ships and darkness, mumbled, "Isadora *who?* Jones or Pater or Elgantine?"

"For heaven's sake, Miles, this is Whitney Dibble speaking from America! I want to speak to Isadora. *My* Isadora."

"Oh, you want to speak to Isadora? Well, I think she's out in front. Listen, laddie, I'll try to find her."

"Miles, this has already cost me more than a hundred dollars."

"And you have been caught by the people who think about dollars?"

"You're darned right I have! Will you please get Isadora quick?"

"You mean quickly, don't you?"

"Yeah, quick or quickly, but please get Isadora."

"Right you are, my lad."

It was after only $16.75 more worth of conversation that Isadora was saying to him, "Hello, Whit darling, what is it?"

"Would you marry a real-estate man in Zenith, in the Middle West? Would you stand for my making ten thousand dollars a year?"

From four thousand miles away Isadora crowed, "Sure I will!"

"You may have to interrupt your creative work."

"Oh, my darling, my darling, I'll be so glad to quit four-flushing!"

Mr. Whitney Dibble looked at his chief and observed, "After I find out how much this long-distance call has cost, do you mind if I make a local call?"

Mr. Seidel observed, "Go as far as you like, but please give me a pension when you fire me out of the firm."

"Sure!"

Whit telephoned to the mansion of T. Jefferson Dibble.

T. Jefferson answered the telephone with a roar: "Yes, yes, yes, what do you want?"

"Dad, this is Whit. I tried to tell you this morning that I am engaged to a lovely intellectual author in Paris—Isadora."

"Isadora *what?*"

"Do you mean to tell me you don't know who Isadora is?"

"Oh, *Isadora!* The writer? Congratulations, my boy. I'm sorry I misunderstood you before."

"Yes. Just talked to her, long-distance, and she's promised to join me here."

"That's fine, boy! We'll certainly have an artistic center here in Zenith."

"Yeah, we certainly will."

Mr. Seidel remarked, "That local call will cost you just five cents besides the eighty-seven fifty."

"Fine, boss," said Whitney Dibble. "Say, can I interest you in a bungalow on Lake Kennepoose? It has two baths, a lovely living room, and—— Why do you waste your life in this stuffy club room, when you might have a real home?"